TOM CLANCY

TERMINAL VELOCITY

ALSO BY TOM CLANCY

TOM CLANCY

TERMINAL VELOCITY

M. P. WOODWARD

SPHERE

SPHERE

First published in the United States in 2025 by G. P. Putnam's Sons
(an imprint of Penguin Random House LLC)
First published in Great Britain in 2025 by Sphere

5 7 9 10 8 6

Copyright © Clancy Media LLC 2025

The moral right of the author has been asserted.

A CIP catalogue record for this book
is available from the British Library.

HARDBACK ISBN
978-1-4087-3281-6

TRADE PAPERBACK ISBN
978-1-4087-3280-9

Printed and bound in Great Britain by
Clays Ltd, Elcograf S.p.A.

Papers used by Sphere are from well-managed forests
and other responsible sources.

FSC
MIX
Paper | Supporting
responsible forestry
www.fsc.org
FSC® C104740

Sphere
An imprint of
Little, Brown Book Group
Carmelite House
50 Victoria Embankment
London EC4Y 0DZ

The authorised representative
in the EEA is
Hachette Ireland
8 Castlecourt Centre
Dublin 15, D15 XTP3, Ireland
(email: info@hbgi.ie).

An Hachette UK Company
www.hachette.co.uk

www.littlebrown.co.uk

PRINCIPAL CHARACTERS

UNITED STATES GOVERNMENT

JACK RYAN, SR.—President of the United States
MARY PAT FOLEY—Director of national intelligence
DAN MURRAY—United States attorney general

AMERICAN OPERATORS

JOHN CLARK—Director of operations for The Campus (black side) and chief security officer for Hendley Associates, a private equity firm (white side)
DOMINGO "DING" CHAVEZ—Former CIA officer; Campus operator
JACK RYAN, JR.—Lead Campus operator; Hendley venture capitalist
KENDRICK MOORE—former SEAL, Campus operator
AMANDA "MANDY" COBB—former FBI special agent, Campus operator
LISANNE ROBERTSON—Logistics and intelligence director (black side) for the Campus; Hendley project manager
GAVIN BIERY—Hendley information technology director, Campus cybersecurity director
CARY MARKS—active-duty Green Beret, Campus operator

JAD MUSTAFA—active-duty Green Beret, Campus operator

TOM BUCK—active-duty Marine Raider, Campus operator

MITCH WHITCOMB—sheriff, Asotin County, eastern Washington State

IRV DUPREE—active-duty senior master sergeant, U.S. Air Force, C-17 loadmaster

THEODORE BOLTON ("T-BOLT")—Department of Energy security team leader

THE INDIANS AND PAKISTANIS

RAFA BIN YASIN—son of the Emir, Saif Rahman Yasin, a terrorist who died in U.S. captivity

FAHIM BAJWA—Rafa's half brother and the chief operating officer of Assurance Global Industries, a major global construction company

IMRAN KHAN—brigadier general, Pakistani Inter-Services Intelligence (ISI) directorate

RUSTAM RAJABOV—Tajik mujahideen fighter

DAVAL RAI—CEO, Assurance Global Industries, Srini Rai's father

SRINI RAI—professor of orthopedics at the University of Texas Dell Medical School

SANJAY BODAS—husband of Srini Rai, AGI's chief business development officer

DREN SHALA—security specialist for AGI

AGON IVANAJ—security specialist for AGI

PROLOGUE

SOUTHERN FRANCE
TWENTY YEARS AGO

FAHIM BAJWA STOOD IN THE DOORWAY AND TOOK ONE FINAL LOOK AT HIS DORmitory room at Avignon's elite international prep school, École Internationale D'Avignon. He had stripped his bed down to the mattress ticking, emptied his desk, and shipped his belongings to Paris.

"What will you do here all by yourself?" he asked his roommate, Riccardo, an Italian student a year his junior, lazing on the other twin bed.

The Italian propped himself on an elbow and responded in English, as was customary at École. "I suppose I'll be at the top of the class," he replied. "For once."

Pleased with that remark—because it was probably true—Fahim grinned. "My parting gift to you, my friend."

Fahim appeared older than he was, handsome for a seventeen-year-old boy, with long black eyelashes and olive skin. His mother was the daughter of Turkish immigrants—she was also an addict and a prostitute, something Fahim hid from his fellow students.

As cover, he told anyone who asked that his father was a Saudi

1

oil tycoon—an unverifiable story, since Fahim had never met the man and genuinely didn't know. He deepened the lie by saying his mother was a devout Muslim and refused to leave the Arab kingdom.

While neither of those things was true, his biological parents had bestowed upon him his good looks and penetrating intelligence. The father he'd never met—whom he assumed to be a rich Gulf Arab who'd frequented his mother while in Marseille on business—covered Fahim's tuition and room and board through a blind trust in a Swiss bank account.

"Don't forget," Riccardo added, swiveling to sit on the bed's edge, his red-striped Gucci luggage nearby, since he, too, would leave in a few days. "You promised two weekends in Paris."

"Did I?"

"*Mes oui, mon ami!* I expect you to dazzle the ladies up there at the Sorbonne. Paris women should be easy prey for a rich Arab like you. And think of the American tourist girls."

Growing up in a tenement in Marseille, Fahim had honed his natural charisma to get what he wanted. That often included the seduction of older women. Having secured a spot at Sorbonne University's College of Engineering, his friends had high expectations for his upcoming romantic adventures.

Fahim extended his hand. "Give me six months to get established. By then, I plan to be dating an heiress."

"In six months, I expect you to be halfway to your baccalaureate."

The graduate's grin faded. "As do I."

"*Au revoir, mon ami. Bonne chance.*"

Fahim hurried through the corridors, saying goodbye to faculty and students. Once outside, he rushed down the stone steps to the parking lot, where he kept his secondhand Honda motorcycle.

His financial trust had its limits. His father, whoever he was, had set it up to pay for education-related expenses only, a rule administered anonymously by a faceless functionary at a Zurich bank. But being a clever boy, when Fahim was thirteen, he set up a basic e-commerce spoof of École's bookstore. The banker who doled out his trust fund never realized that École's tuition included the textbooks. Money for books Fahim already owned went straight into his bank account, allowing him to amass enough for the bike.

He fired up the engine with a kick and turned south, pleased to feel the hot wind on his arms. The Mullah Fawwah had demanded Fahim come to the Marseille mosque to say goodbye to his half brother, Rafa. The mullah also said he needed to speak urgently with Fahim.

Though Fahim suspected it had something to do with a graduation gift, he didn't want to go. He'd never been comfortable with the stern conventions of Islam and studiously avoided the mullah's mosque. But the mullah had insisted.

His route took him along the Rhône River, following it to the northeast before he would turn on the highway. As he roared by Avignon's stately castles, he spotted the sign for the bridge. On impulse, he leaned the bike into a turn.

Although Fahim considered himself an orphan, one of his earliest memories was of his mother, Claudette, singing to him and Rafa, who was three years younger. Claudette's only song was the nursery rhyme "On the Bridge of Avignon," which she sang when they were alone, a rare occurrence. Fahim had learned to care for his brother, as their mother often left them alone for hours in a tenement high-rise in Marseille's crime-ridden 3rd arrondissement.

The French child welfare department took the boys away from Claudette when Fahim was nine and Rafa was six. Despite her failings, Claudette's voice remained buried in Fahim's mind, to the extent that he often found himself at the Saint-Bénézet Bridge throughout his years at the boarding school.

Better known as the Bridge of Avignon, it was completed in 1185. In the thirteenth century, it served as a link for Catholic pilgrimage and a stronghold of the Avignon papacy, playing a significant role in the history of Western civilization. Although only four of its original twenty-two stone arches remained anchored in the Rhône, it was designated a World Heritage Site, one of the most popular tourist attractions in Provence.

Parking was easy with the motorcycle. Fahim removed his helmet, leaned the bike on its kickstand, and purchased a ticket to walk to the end of the bridge in the middle of the river. With Claudette's voice haunting him, he wandered among the tourists, passed the Philippe Bell Tower, and strolled to the broken edge of the remaining span. He disregarded the foreigners, concentrating on the rush of water as the Rhône flowed against the stone piers.

Thus, with the sun beating down on his back and his place assured in the Sorbonne's civil engineering academy, the seventeen-year-old marveled at the ancient engineers who could build something that had lasted more than a thousand years. A river cruise boat passed by, its tourists manning the rails and snapping pictures of the bridge. Fahim stood up straight and inhaled the fresh air.

On the bridge of Avignon, we're all dancing, we're all dancing . . .

Filled with the generosity of spirit that arises when a young man contemplates the transition from one phase of life to the next, Fahim felt ready to head south to Marseille, where he would say goodbye to his half brother—and put up with the Mullah Fawwah for the last time.

BECAUSE FAHIM APPRECIATED ARCHITECTURE AND WAS FEELING NOSTALGIC, HIS first stop in Marseille was the Basilique Notre-Dame de la Garde.

Perched on a high observation post above the port, the Guardian of Marseille was a masterpiece of Byzantine and Romanesque architecture. Fahim remembered his Catholic mother dragging him to the church, hiking up the hill to catch a glimpse of the sea, filling his head with images of exotic lands. He could recall asking her whether his father was in one of those lands.

"He came from there," she replied, pointing. "Far across the sea. He is very smart."

"And Rafa?" young Fahim asked of his three-year-old brother, whose hand he held.

"Rafa's father is a very special holy man," she replied gravely.

When he was done with his visit to the Guardian, he climbed a nearby hill. Fahim rapped three times on the mosque's heavy oaken door. "I have come to see Mullah Fawwah and Rafa," he said to the bearded twentysomething man who opened it. The sun hung low in the west, casting long shadows from the mosque's minarets and domes. "They're here?"

"Who asks?"

Because he rarely visited, Fahim wasn't recognized. He gave his name and explained his family connection.

"Wait," the man said, closing the door to the Marseille Muslim academy for boys, the madrassa attached to the mosque.

As Fahim waited, he stepped back onto the tiled portico to admire the Eastern architecture. The neighborhood was home to many North African Muslims and boasted fifty mosques. This one was constructed by Turkish pilgrims in the sixteenth century and inspired thoughts of Central Asia with its soaring arches and golden domes.

The heavy door swung open again. Mullah Fawwah, mid-fifties with a shaggy beard and growing paunch, scrutinized Fahim closely.

"You're late," he said harshly, his eyes darting over Fahim's head. "Why?"

"My train was delayed," Fahim lied. He felt uneasy sharing details about the motorbike with the mullah.

The mullah looked at the street corners, then ushered Fahim inside. "It's just as well. Come in and shut the door. Hurry." Fahim did as asked. "Now remove your shirt."

"My shirt? Why?"

"Something has happened," the mullah said brusquely. "Just do it, Fahim. And then wash yourself in preparation for prayer. Hurry up."

Fahim was used to the rituals of entering the mosque—removing his shoes, performing the ablutions. It struck him as odd, however, that the mullah asked him to remove his shirt. The religious scholar looked Fahim over and handed him a damp rag before letting him dress again. "Wait over here," he said, leading Fahim to a windowless anteroom. The door clicked heavily behind the mullah as he rushed away. Fahim felt as if he'd been locked inside.

Confused by how he'd been received, he waited silently. With his father's blind trust paying his way at the Sorbonne, he consoled himself that he would never come here again, and studied the vibrant tile mosaic that dominated the space to pass the time. It depicted a colorful rendering of a palm tree grove with two men on horseback picking dates.

Midway up the door was a hinged wooden flap with a brass handle. When the interval grew longer than it should, Fahim opened the flap. Like the confessional booths his mother had dragged him to at the Garde du Notre Dame Church, the opening was covered by a tightly woven straw screen.

Through the screen, Fahim witnessed a hive of activity. A dozen young men were stretched out on prayer rugs, chanting incessantly, *"There is one true caliph. He is the king of the believers, the rightful heir of Muhammad . . ."*

Beyond the men in prayer, Fahim observed others rushing by with luggage, creating a large pile along the wall. They hurried between the buttresses supporting the coved ceiling with noticeable urgency. Amid that crowd, Fahim spotted Mullah Fawwah leading Rafa. Concerned that he might be violating a religious rule, Fahim quickly closed the flap.

Rafa and the mullah entered a few seconds later. Fahim reached for his brother's hand, which he accepted with a distant expression.

The Mullah Fawwah sat them on a bench and addressed Fahim, saying, "We are at war. The world as we know it has changed forever. That is why you are here today."

Fahim, who'd spent much of the day placidly admiring the sunny Provençal landscape, was taken aback. "What?" he asked. He found that all religious people tended to overdramatize.

"The devil Americans have invaded our homeland," the mullah continued. "They have brought an army to Saudi Arabia, the birthplace of the Prophet. On an evil raid in Baghdad, the devils arrested one of our brothers. They will come here next. For us."

Fahim nodded tenuously. In his Western civilization courses, the instructors had forced debate on the clash of civilizations and the American armed response. To the student, ensconced in the thick walls of Avignon, it had seemed an inconsequential, remote problem.

"Fahim!" the mullah barked, jerking him by the shoulder. "You know your half brother's father is a holy man who commands our respect."

"Yes," Fahim said. He glanced at Rafa, who continued to stare at the wall. "So I've long been told."

"He is not *just* a holy man," the mullah shot. "He is the Prophet, Allah's messenger on earth, the true heir of Muhammad. The devil Americans will seek to capture him and kill Rafa, his heir.

That is why we leave at midnight on a ship from the Port of Marseille."

"Going where?"

"Pakistan. And then north, to Kashmir, our ancestral home, the Garden of Eternity as described by the Prophet." The mullah gestured to the tile motif. "The capital of Umayyad, the scene depicted on these walls, a paradise on earth. I must protect your holy brother and take him there—and that is why you are here. *Inshallah*, you will be there soon, too. But first, there is something you must do."

Fahim swallowed. "I . . . don't understand."

Rafa glanced at Fahim before lowering his eyes. "With this attack on one of our brothers, my father, the Prophet, has declared jihad. At-Takwir is at hand."

"What is At-Takwir?"

Rafa inhaled sharply. "You don't know?"

The mullah squeezed Rafa's arm, then turned to Fahim. "It's not your fault. I allowed you to be raised as a nonbeliever for a reason. That reason has arrived, and like us, you are now a soldier. We have very little time. The devils will come."

"Can you tell me what At-Takwir is?" Fahim asked again.

Rafa canted his head toward the ceiling and closed his eyes. "It is the end of days."

Fahim turned to the Mullah Fawwah, his voice quavering. "Mullah, I must go to Paris. I have to leave now. My train," he lied.

Three knocks on the door preceded the mullah's response. The religious scholar opened it to reveal a fierce-looking man in black trousers and shirt carrying a hard gray case. He wore a belt with a pistol on his hip and said nothing as he stood beside the tile mosaic wall.

"Fahim, listen to me," the mullah said. "The devil Americans are coming for us. And that includes you. You can't leave—until you finish something."

"But I am not a . . ." Fahim let his point drift, fearing he might offend them. He wanted to express that he was not a Muslim—certainly not a holy warrior. He was a young man who sought to build bridges, charm women, and earn his place in the world. He revised his response. "Why are the Americans coming for us?"

"Because they hate us and want to see our faith expunged from the earth. Trust me, Fahim, they will arrest you, torture you, imprison you for the rest of your life, if they don't kill you first. They will do it because of your brother. We cannot allow that."

Fahim glanced at Rafa, who gazed blankly at the wall, much like the man with the pistol.

"I have to go to Paris," the student protested.

The mullah's eyes hardened. "You have been designated by the Prophet for a special mission, for which we have long been preparing you. I had not planned to tell you this until the Prophet, the Emir of Umayyad, struck the devils a fatal blow. But the Americans will come here. Tonight. Which is why we must act. *You* must act."

Terrified by their apocalyptic talk and the crazy notion that Rafa's father was the true heir of Muhammad, Fahim stood up. The man with the pistol moved before the door.

"I am not a part of this," he beseeched the mullah. "Rafa and I don't share the same father, only the same mother. Mine is a wealthy Gulf Arab who placed conditions on my education. I promise never to speak of my association with you, if that is your wish, and I can conceal myself from the Americans. They'll never know about me. How could they? You took Rafa to be a student here to follow his father's path. But I went away to school."

"Fahim, follow me," the mullah said, motioning him through the door.

Again, Fahim observed the rushing men in black, the piles of luggage, the hushed voices of prayer echoing across the alcove. The mullah's long dishdasha swept over the tiled floor, swishing over his bare feet. Fahim followed him into a side room with a computer, Eastern art on the walls, and a desk cluttered with papers.

"Sit," the mullah ordered. Fahim took the hard-backed wooden chair, while the mullah hunched forward on one with clicking springs. "You think your father is a Gulf Arab, do you?"

"How else can I have a blind trust? I know what my mother is. My father visited her for pleasure. I understand that. But he looks after me from afar, even if she isn't able."

The holy man perched rimless glasses on the end of his nose and clicked the computer mouse, opening a web page. Fahim recognized it as belonging to the Swiss bank that sent him money every month. "Rafa's father, the Emir of the Umayyad Revolutionary Council, the Prophet, oversees your development, Fahim."

A brilliant student, always quick with an answer, Fahim suddenly found himself adrift. "I don't understand. Are you saying that the Emir is also my father?"

"Of course not. I am saying that *I* am your benefactor—through the Prophet. We have been preparing you for the great struggle, our future engineer, builder of bridges—and you have exceeded our expectations."

"My father—"

"Fahim, open your eyes! Your father is not a Gulf Arab. He was an Indian on the faculty of L'Université d'Aix-Marseille, a filthy Hindu who died years ago. But none of this matters, as it was all part of Allah's design. You are a half brother to the bloodline of Allah's messengers on earth, blessed by Him to bring about His will. The Emir has always protected you."

Sensing the boy's shock, the mullah offered a reprieve. He

leaned forward and grasped Fahim's narrow wrists. "Boy, you have always been part of this. Rather than fear it, embrace it. You will go to Paris, attend the Sorbonne, and walk among the infidels. You will be exactly what we've prepared you to be. The Emir will pay your way and clear your path into commercial construction, where you will serve us. *Inshallah*."

Fahim swallowed. "So . . . I can leave?"

"Yes, you can go to Paris," the mullah said. "But only if you commit your soul to the prophets, the Emir and Rafa. You must perform your *islah* to ensure allegiance to the faith."

"What is *islah*?"

"An act of jihad to wed your soul to the Prophet's. Once completed, you can leave. If you do not . . . Well, you're a smart boy. You understand we can have no loose ends."

Bewildered yet relieved by the prospect of his life continuing as before, Fahim nodded grimly. "I just want to go to Paris. Tell me what I need to do."

The mullah's eyes sparkled. "Yes? Good. Come." He led Fahim through the arcade to the anteroom. Upon entering, Fahim noticed Rafa conferring with the other man in low tones. The gray case was open between them.

"Fahim will commit to the jihad," the holy man announced. "He is ready to perform his *islah*."

On hearing this, Rafa turned to him. "Then we should all recite the *Shahada*."

The mullah murmured his agreement and motioned for them to kneel.

Perhaps this is all they desire from me, Fahim thought as he bent over his knees in prayer. The mullah led them through the chant, pausing so Fahim could repeat the words. It was the same recitation he had heard in the prayer room. "*There is one true caliph . . .*"

When the anteroom fell silent, Rafa extended a black semiautomatic pistol to Fahim. "You will commit your *islah* tonight, brother. We will do it together, purifying our shared blood."

Fahim was reluctant to touch the weapon. "Why do I need this?"

"To kill them. Before we burn them."

"Kill who?"

"Our disgusting mother and her infidel."

Fahim recoiled, unwilling to touch the gun.

"What," Rafa said, "you think she loved us? She's a whore, a liar, an addict. She sold herself. She will sell us, too. She must die."

"Rafa, I . . ."

Disappointed, Rafa shoved the gun in his belt and turned away. "Mullah," he grumbled. "I told you. He is weak. Corrupt. Western."

"Rafa!" Fahim shot with wide eyes, his voice hoarse. "You want me to kill Claudette, our mother, like it's nothing!"

"Do not say her name!" the mullah snapped. He gestured at the man with the pistol belt. "Abdul is our best field commander. After you perform your *islah*, he will go to Paris and remain nearby as your contact." The mullah turned to the warrior. "Tell us, Abdul, the apostate is still there, yes, with her infidel customer? We can take them now?"

"If we hurry," Abdul replied. "The whore is in Le Panier, fifth floor. We have a brother tailing her pimp, ready to strike and steal the keys."

"Very well." The mullah turned to Fahim. "This is it, boy. You will release your mother's soul into Jahannam to cleanse your own. That is your *islah*. If you do not perform it, *you* will enter hell."

The lyrics drifted through Fahim's head once more. *On the bridge of Avignon . . .*

He swallowed hard, banishing the song, reflecting on the Sorbonne, the life he had earned, and the mullah's vow of continued support. They would execute her anyway, he reasoned, his pulse pounding. And if their black hearts could murder Claudette, they wouldn't hesitate to kill him.

"There is only one true caliph," he replied morosely. "Give me the gun."

PART ONE

PRIMER

1

CLARKSTON, WASHINGTON
EARLY JUNE, PRESENT DAY

MITCH WHITCOMB CLOSED THE SCREEN DOOR CAREFULLY AND GROPED HIS WAY across his front porch in the dark, his Resistol wide-brim hat perched on his head and his Justin Ropers pinched in his hand. He would have liked to have thrown the porch light on, but that would probably wake Molly, who insisted on sleeping with the curtains pulled back to let the cool night air stream through the windows.

That didn't make much sense to Mitch, the Asotin County sheriff. First of all, even though it was barely four a.m., the temperature was stuck in the mid-seventies. The whole week had been a scorcher, baking the Palouse, a long stretch of high desert plains that dominated the farmlands where Washington, Idaho, and Oregon come together.

For another thing, Mitch had paid good money for a pair of Mitsubishi mini-splits to air-condition their sprawling farmhouse. Having reached his mid-sixties, it was hard enough to get a good night's sleep, and the whole point of the Mitsubishis was to cool the house down to make it feel like October year-round, his favorite month. But Molly had her ways—and thirty-five years of marriage told him the argument wasn't worth it, so here he was, tiptoeing across his porch in the dark like some kid trying not to wake his girlfriend's father.

At the bottom step, he pulled on his boots, then crunched across the gravel to the pole barn, where he parked his John Deere, his '57 T-Bird—tarped to keep the barn swallows from destroying it—and his official Ram police truck.

He fished through his pocket for the key to unlock the tiny office built into the front of the barn, then punched in the numbers to his gun safe. It took him a few minutes to get his police belt on with his Glock 22, and lodge his pump-action 12-gauge into the socket that straddled the Ram's transmission hump.

He settled behind the truck's wheel, angling his elbow to avoid touching the computer rig. Once he stabbed the ignition button, the noisy diesel would sound off, and, again, because Molly had the windows open, probably wake her. But what could he do? Old Tyler Ross, the fire chief, hit him on the emergency pager Mitch slept with, and when he called the chief back from the powder room down the hall, Ross said he was looking at a homicide. That was a mighty rare thing out here in Asotin County.

The Ram bumped along the dirt road that Mitch was always after the county to oil, then turned onto Evans, which passed through town and eventually led to a highway beside the Snake River. "Hey, Dot, are you in the office?" he asked over the truck's Motorola, rolling south.

"*Where else would I be?*"

Mitch grinned. Dot tended to get a little cranky at the end of her night shift. "I put that address in the GPS. It drew a blank. Help me out, will you?"

"*I just relayed the address Chief Ross gave me.*"

"Well, you can locate his pumpers on the radio grid, can't you? Check in on them and just tell me where they are."

"Roger that, Sheriff. Wait one."

Mitch watched the highway dashes flash in his headlights while he awaited a response. With his windows down, he listened to the night insects buzzing in the wheat fields. Cruising along the Snake at a relaxed thirty-five, he enjoyed the cool air settling along the banks. He had always liked waking up before everyone else, even as a boy. It made him feel like he was getting a head start on the day, and that invigorating feeling surged through him as he caught the scent of the sagebrush. But then he reprimanded himself; it was a homicide that had dragged him out of bed.

"Okay, I got a twenty," Dot said when she returned. *"Stay on 129 until you're a mile or so south of Hostetler. Must be an unmarked road or something. The pumpers are near Asotin Creek down there. There's no road registered with the county, so it's gotta be private."*

Mitch thought that through. He knew Clarkston like the tops of his scuffed Justins. He tried to picture where a couple of big pumper trucks might access Asotin Creek. South of Hostetler, there was nothing but rolling ranchland, baked yellow after a spring drought.

"Thanks, Dot," he concluded. "I'll find it."

As it turned out, the fire wasn't that hard to locate. Five miles south of town, he saw the two county engines and the fire chief's red pickup with lights blazing across a broad field. Dawn was still an hour off, but stars were winking out, signaling its approach. The sheriff soon spotted the narrow gravel road to access the ranch and roared the Ram across it with his patrol lights flashing.

Now that he was here, facing the hills beyond Asotin Creek, he recognized the property. It had belonged to Doc Sutton, who eventually got tired of playing gentleman farmer in the blowing cold winters and pulled stakes for Sarasota.

If Mitch recalled correctly, a young guy who'd come up from California bought the place. And because he was a young guy from California, Mitch hadn't paid much attention to the goings on down here. It seemed like two or three fellas like that were moving to this part of the country every week.

The sheriff wasn't sure what the Californian planned to do with this three-hundred-acre property. He didn't see any cattle in his headlights—only the big red pumpers, a gaggle of exhausted firemen, and the charred remains of a barn, its embers still glowing. Smoke drifted over the field as if Mitch were standing on the wrong side of a bonfire.

The sheriff parked the Ram, swiveled out, and hitched up his Wranglers. Tyler Ross, the chief, looked like hell in his yellow Nomex turnout gear. His face was streaked with soot, and the men standing around him gazed at the ground with hangdog expressions.

"What the hell happened here?" the sheriff asked.

Ross rubbed his face with a handkerchief, smearing the soot, then blew his nose. "Ugly. Four deceased. We all went in right before the roof caved. Dog led us to them. Thought someone might still be alive."

"Aw, shit. Any of your people hurt?"

"No," Ross replied. "We're okay. The victims, though . . . Another story."

"You said four people—you mean in the barn? Not in the house?"

"Yeah. They're in the barn. We went for the house first and found it empty."

"And they burned in the barn? Like they got trapped in there?"

"They were shot, Mitch. As soon as we knew it was a crime scene, we put out the fire and did what we could to preserve it."

Whitcomb removed his hat and placed it over his heart as if in prayer. His eyes roamed over the property. A pretty simple scene. The house, fields, and driveway looked fine, except for the pumpers, which would likely ruin the chance of finding a perpetrator's tire print. The barn was partially collapsed, glowing like a heap of hot coals.

"You mentioned a dog, Ty. What dog?"

"That one, over there."

Mitch yanked his Maglite off his belt and aimed it at the home. The two-story farmhouse with a wraparound porch stood to the right of the barn, slightly uphill. An American flag hung at an angle over the steps. The house was dark, but the front door stood open. A black Labrador retriever lay on the porch with its chin on its paws, watching them.

"How's that, Chief?" Mitch asked. "You're saying the dog was in the barn?"

"No. She was trying to get into the barn, scratching like hell at the wood where it hadn't caught fire yet. The roof was burning by then."

The chief clenched his jaw, swallowed, and inclined his head at the ruins. "Whole family in there, Mitch. Looks like two kids and two parents. We never had a chance to save 'em. I think they were probably already dead. Look to me like they were bound first, then shot."

Mitch paled. "Bound . . ." he repeated.

"Yeah. I didn't see any brass casings on the floorboards—that's your department. But they each have signs of bullet wounds to the head. You'll see what I mean."

The sheriff tugged his hat onto his head and swept his flashlight over the smoldering beams. What remained of the charred roof lay at an angle, dripping and steaming from the fire hose water. He shifted the beam to the two-story farmhouse, allowing it to rest on the open front door. "Was the house like that when you arrived?"

"The door? No. We went in the house on arrival to evacuate the family, just in case. Door was unlocked. Place was empty. The dog burst out of the rear laundry room and ran for the barn."

"No sign of struggle in the house?"

"Not that I saw, but I'm no expert. Come on, Mitch, I'll take you into the barn. Put these on. I warn you, it's not for the faint of heart."

After donning a Nomex coat and swapping his hat for a helmet, Mitch ducked under one smoldering beam after another, following the chief. The wood hissed and popped about his ears. Sweat beaded on his forehead and his throat rasped.

"We didn't move 'em," the fireman said. "There you go."

The sheriff raised a handkerchief to his nose when the smell of burnt people reached him. He could see four corpses sitting upright in folding metal chairs that hadn't caught fire. As corpses go, they were oddly preserved, dried and desiccated by the fire, which added to the barn's hideous hell.

"God help us," Mitch muttered. He looked away, closed his eyes, and breathed through his handkerchief. It was a struggle to get back to examining the crime scene—but such was the job.

Their arms had been pulled back and bound to the chairs. The sheriff squatted and inspected their wrists with the flashlight. Their flesh had puffed out, biting into copper wire used as binding. He wanted to vomit. His breath caught. Despite his professional duty, he needed a few seconds. He stood and looked away.

"I know," the chief sympathized with a thick-gloved hand on the sheriff's shoulder. "Killer wanted to bind them with something that wouldn't melt or burn."

Mitch steeled himself and took a knee to examine the smoking remains of the male, presumably the father. His face was stained in dark blood that had oozed from a hole near his right temple. Some vile, hateful bastard had shot the man where he sat. The wife and kids had suffered the same fate. As a detective, Mitch had seen all kinds of twisted, grisly mayhem—nothing as bad as this.

"How'd the fire report come in?" Mitch asked, standing, his voice low.

"The neighbor up the creek, George Butters, called it in. He was up caring for a colicky horse when he smelled the smoke. He drove out and saw the fire."

"I'll talk to George," Mitch remarked. "You know anything else about these people?"

"I pulled records while waiting for you. Property's owned by a fella named Cole Hunt. He bought it off Doc Sutton last year. According to George, the wife is Marla. Kids are Maddie and Robbie, fourteen and twelve. Sadly, I think that's who we're lookin' at here."

"My dear Lord."

BY THE TIME THE SUN CRESTED THE ROLLING BROWN HILLS, MITCH HAD THREE OF HIS five deputies roping off the house and the barn remnants with yellow crime scene tape. The sheriff had never handled one that ran across a whole property, but that's what he was looking at. There were no signs of forcible entry into the house and, sadly, much of the usable evidence was likely consumed by fire in the barn.

Disgusted by what transpired here, the first responders refused to leave. While the chief looked for the primer the arsonist used for ignition, the rest of his crew assisted the sheriff and surveyed the property. Mitch asked them to inspect the dirt driveway's perimeter for tire treads that differed from the relatively new F-250 Super Duty they discovered in the garage. It wasn't much, but it was a start.

The Asotin County Sheriff's Office wasn't large. However, Mitch's experience as a detective in Spokane, two hours to the north, had made him the primary investigator for three municipal departments and two counties. Whether he liked it or not, he'd be the lead detective on this murder case. He and his deputies would gather the bodies and evidence for transport to the crime lab in Spokane, operated by the Washington State Patrol. That's when the main forensic work would begin.

But first, he needed to secure the scene. The dog sniffed at his boots and nudged his knees. The sheriff lifted her into the Ram's back seat and stroked her ears, wondering what living nightmare the poor creature had witnessed.

Perhaps there was one good thing that could emerge from this. He and Molly hadn't had a dog since the last of the kids moved out five years ago. Molly said it was so they could travel, but they never did, really, except to visit her good friend in Seattle, six hours to the west. If no one claimed this handsome Lab after the notice went out, then Mitch intended to keep her. The name on her collar read LUNA.

Intending to begin the investigation from his truck's computer, he suddenly recalled some beef jerky in the seat console and offered it to her. "Hey there, Luna. Chew on this."

She sniffed it, but showed no interest in eating, choosing instead to rest her chin on her paws as though she'd been in the back of this truck a thousand times.

Under Luna's watchful amber eyes, Mitch got to work on the keyboard of his dash-mounted computer. He quickly confirmed what the fire chief had said. According to the Asotin County Assessor's Office, the property owner was Cole Hunt. A previous mailing address indicated that the family had moved from Coronado, near San Diego. Maddie and Robbie were students at the local public schools.

As Mitch waited for his deputies to report in, he rubbed Luna's ears and sipped the coffee that Dot had brought from the station. Next, he double-clicked on Mr. Cole Hunt, the property owner.

A credit report showed Hunt paid his bills on time. The property tax records said the same. The man had no criminal history, no file of any kind. Mitch thumbed through the mail his deputy had pulled from the box along the road. The usual stuff—junk credit card offers and an insurance bill.

He performed a plain-old Google search and waded through a dozen links for other people named Cole, Marla, Maddie, and Robbie, but came up with nothing useful, not even on Facebook.

Mitch thought that was odd. Then again, Hunt was from Southern California. For all the sheriff knew, the man might be a retired tech whiz who understood enough about the internet to want to disconnect from it entirely. There were plenty of those types out in these hills these days, although most seemed to settle across the river in Lewiston, Idaho.

When a deputy interviewed George Butters, who owned the nearby ranch and had reported the fire, he mentioned that Hunt kept a herd of cattle on the southern part of the property, beyond the creek. Hunt didn't ride horses; instead, he used his ATV to tend to the herd. He had sought out George for advice on ranching.

That got Mitch's antennae twitching. While stroking the dog's head, he tried to remember if he'd heard anything about Hunt down at the Washington Cattlemen's Club, where he played poker every Thursday. The Cattlemen were instrumental in supporting Mitch's campaigns, and for that reason, he never missed a game.

"Hey, Hal." Harold Wagner ran the Cattlemen's Club and answered on the third ring.

"Morning, Mitch. Kind of an early one."

"Yeah. I got something goin'. Wish I didn't."

"Crime?" Wagner asked.

"Probable homicide. The victim is a fella named Cole Hunt." The sheriff felt he needed to omit the family's gory details. Such a shock had to be handled carefully in a small town like Clarkston. "Hunt's place is out here by the creek. According to George Butters, he's been running a few head up those hills. You know him?"

"I know Hunt. He's dead?"

"Yeah."

Wagner remained silent for a moment, then offered, "I hate to hear that. Though I didn't know him well. He's got about two hundred head of Angus in the hills over the creek."

"Was he doing all right with them? Any problems?"

"Lots of problems. Some of the boys around here have a bettin' pool goin' on when he'd go into foreclosure. Plenty of people anxious to buy that land. The creek's a good water source, hot as it's been. Nobody would have wanted to come by it this way. Jesus."

As Mitch saw it, Wagner had given him his first lead. Hunt's land was valuable. Someone wanted it. But murdering a whole family? That didn't add up.

Luna raised her head and licked her lips. Mitch retrieved the jerky from the seat console. This time, she ate it.

The sheriff returned to his thoughts, rubbing his nose as he struggled to shake off the memory of the stench.

Based on the execution-style killing, whatever the Hunts had got up to had pissed off some mighty mean hombres. In Mitch's view, that was usually about money, and, at least according to Hal Wagner, Cole was losing it. Then again, he was from California. Maybe he was sitting on a pile, tucked away in a bank somewhere, in which case this might be a robbery.

Luna nudged his shoulder, causing Mitch to spill out the rest of the jerky bag. While she ate, he searched his computer for evidence of Cole Hunt's employment. Since the man was relatively new to the state, the Washington databases weren't helpful. He scraped Hunt's Social Security number from the Asotin County Assessor's Office and used it to check Hunt's W-9 history with the IRS.

That's when the sheriff hit a brick wall. According to the IRS, there was no such Social Security number. How the hell was that possible?

He was tapping his fingers, sipping his coffee, and pondering the vagaries of bureaucracy when Luna nudged him again. This time, she growled and barked insistently at something she saw through the windshield. And just as humans have been behaving since the Paleolithic period, Mitch Whitcomb heeded his canine companion's warning and warily studied the road.

Three black Suburbans were speeding down the highway. The lead SUV had a flashing blue light on the dash as it turned onto the gravel drive.

The sheriff groaned and shook his head. That convoy could mean only one thing.

Feds.

2

DAN MURRAY, THE UNITED STATES ATTORNEY GENERAL, GRASPED THE PODIUM WITH both hands, leaned forward into the microphone, and surveyed Class 2516 with satisfaction. Forty fresh faces stared back at him, each clear-eyed, intelligent, and, best of all, curious.

Serving in the government post that previous attorneys general had bluntly characterized as "one damn thing after another," Murray relished afternoons like this. He had plenty to do at his office in Main Justice on Pennsylvania Avenue, where the work was indeed, well, one damn thing after another.

In that Department of Justice building, a steady flow of alleged misdeeds flew over his desk like the prairie wind in his native Oklahoma. Visits like this to see the shinier side of the DOJ were a matter of mental hygiene, and nothing cleared his head quite like commissioning a new class of agents here at the FBI Academy in Quantico.

Murray had already shaken their hands and posed for pictures when they walked one by one across the stage. With that done, he wanted to speak plainly to them, a rare opportunity, for he sensed it would be the last time he'd share a room with most of them.

"Congratulations, special agents," he began. "We get to officially call you *special agents* now. Sounds pretty cool, doesn't it? Enjoy the title. You've earned it. And, though most of you have advanced law or accounting degrees, you've worked your asses off to ensure you'll be making government pay, same as me. But at least you can call yourselves *special agents*."

At the back of the room, up the center steps, Murray noticed a door opening. Armbruster, his chief of staff, slipped through shoulder-first and shot him a cautious glance.

Murray avoided it, deliberately focusing on the fresh faces rising in the tiered rows at the Academy's executive briefing center. The class was about half men and half women. They were Asian, Black, Caucasian, and Hispanic. Clean-cut and youthful, the men wore white shirts, dark jackets, and solid ties. The women were in pantsuits with open-collared shirts. They were as lean and fit as greyhounds.

"But you're not here for the money," Murray continued into the microphone. "There isn't a single person in my Justice Department who couldn't make a fortune in the private sector. Yet they trade all that for government pay because they're in this job for something more. And that something is clipped to your belts. If you would, ladies and gentlemen, please do me the honor of placing your shiny new shields on the tables before you."

Murray considered himself lucky to be here. His FBI director was currently in London at a Five Eyes security conference hosted by MI5 at Thames House, the expansive headquarters of Britain's internal security service. With the planets aligning for him to address these graduates, Murray studiously avoided Armbruster's hand gestures at the back of the room.

"All right, good work. Now, please take the shields out of their wallets," the attorney general instructed. "Go on. Pull them free— I want to see naked metal on the tables. Miss Ramirez, I understand you're the class leader. Take down the names of anyone who doesn't comply."

They chuckled as they removed the gold shields.

"For the rest of your careers," Murray said seriously, "you'll carry those shields in their wallets, nudged up against your identification cards and your Glock 19s. You'll probably never take that metal out of its holder again. Don't forget, I was an agent once upon a time, sitting right where you are, though we didn't have a fancy briefing center back then."

He paused for a moment, reminiscing. What, forty years ago? Something like that. After the Academy, he worked his way up from special agent to special agent in charge, then to legal attaché in London, and eventually to FBI director. He was appointed to the top position at Justice, attorney general, by his longtime friend President Jack Ryan.

But leading the FBI had been the best job of his career. During moments like this, Murray missed it dearly. He could almost curse the President for promoting him to a cabinet-level position with all its challenges and sleepless nights. Days like this kept him on the straight and narrow.

"All right," he continued to the class. "Can anyone tell me the name of that lady with the scales in her hand at the center of your badges?"

Eleven hands shot up instantly. Murray cracked a smile at the eagerness and picked a graduate at random. "You. What's your name?"

"Anthony LaPaglia," the new lawman answered.

"Special Agent LaPaglia. Okay. Who is that gal on your shield?"

"She's Justitia, goddess of justice."

"*Roman* goddess of justice, Special Agent LaPaglia. With a name like yours, you should take a little Italian credit."

The agent grinned sheepishly.

Desperately trying to get Murray's attention, Armbruster twitched at the back of the room like a third-base coach signaling a runner. The attorney general raised two fingers at him. The one-damn-thing-after-another job could wait two more minutes for him, couldn't it?

"Well, my special agents, as the head of the United States Justice Department, I want you to know something important. You do *not* work for your director. Nor do you work for me . . . or for President Ryan, for that matter. You work for that woman on your shield there, Justitia, Lady Justice, because she represents the special faith and confidence your fellow citizens have placed in you. Go on, take a long look at her sword, her scales, her, *ah*, blindfold."

He vocally tripped over that last word, *blindfold*. Though he'd told himself he shouldn't, it involuntarily forced him to think of his wife, Liz.

While he stood here at this podium in Quantico, Liz Murray was at Bethesda for a surgical consultant with the world's most renowned ophthalmologist, First Lady Cathy Ryan.

Murray's wife had lost her vision in her left eye due to advanced wet macular degeneration. Her right eye was at a stage where she was only a year or two away from losing her ability to read or drive.

Cathy Ryan had called a week earlier to inform Liz about an exciting new experimental laser surgery designed to cauterize the damaged blood vessels beneath the macula that caused the disease. If the laser treatment was successful, it could completely restore Liz's vision in her right eye. However, Cathy warned, if it didn't work, she would likely be left blind.

The Belgian eye surgeon, in D.C. for a conference, had only done the surgery twice on humans, but was willing to do his best for the attorney general's wife. Cathy ran the idea by Liz, who was more than ready to take the chance. Dan was all for trusting Cathy

Ryan—but he didn't like the idea of a Belgian surgeon playing guinea pig with his wife's one decent eye.

He set it aside for now, contemplating the new agents observing Justitia and her blindfold. He took a deep breath, disregarded Armbruster, and cleared his throat.

"Listen up, special agents. Could you do me a favor? Henceforth, when you're out there in your field offices, working with your confidential informants and building up your cases, I want you to pause—once a week—and take your shield from your wallet. Find a quiet moment to study it . . . maybe a lunch break or a little downtime at home or even sitting at your desk. Whatever it is, I want you to reserve a moment to pull your badge out of its wallet and stare at Lady Justitia once a week. And when you do, I want you to remind yourselves that *she* is your boss. Can you do that for me?

"Because here's the thing. There may come a point when you follow your leads to a place that no one will like—your special agent in charge, the assistant district attorney, the local police chief . . . whoever. One day, you might find yourselves as the last, immovable barrier between doing what is easy or popular and, instead, doing what is *just*, not thinking about it, but acting on it. You, my special agents, stand on the ramparts between good and evil. You are the guardians of your nation.

"Remaining vigilant will take courage, skill, and sacrifice. All of you have those attributes in spades or you would never have sought this work. So I ask you always to remember to do what is *just*. Not for me, understand—but for *her*, and the people of the United States of America. That's what we're all trusting you to do. That's why we give you that cool title, *special agent*—because it is truly special."

He wanted to say a few other things, but Armbruster was waving him into home plate. Maybe that was just as well. Murray was anxious to hear what Mrs. Ryan thought about Liz's prospects and he'd made his point. Having garnered the newly commissioned agents' rapt attention, he wished them well and trotted up the tiered floor to the drumbeat of their applause.

The exit door barely latched when Armbruster leaned close to his ear.

"Another POSEIDON SPEAR incident," his chief of staff whispered.

Murray froze. "Damnit. Please tell me it wasn't here, in the States."

"Afraid so, sir. Eastern Washington, near the Idaho border. Whole family."

"When?"

"This morning."

"Same MO?"

"Yes. The alert came in through the Seattle district."

The attorney general sighed. *One damn thing after another.* "Has anyone told the President's national security team yet?"

"That's why I've been signaling you, boss. You're requested in the Oval Office in forty-one minutes."

3

THE WHITE HOUSE

GARY MONTGOMERY, THE HEAD OF THE PRESIDENT'S SECRET SERVICE DETAIL, LED Murray to the private study off the Oval Office.

The drive from Quantico had taken an hour, even with the grille lights flashing in his armored SUV, much to the attorney general's chagrin. Feeling like a truant for keeping the President waiting, Murray sat at the shining table and absently watched CNN, thinking about the Belgian surgeon.

The TV commanded his full attention as the news network reported the seizure of a drug boat south of Miami with six hundred pounds of cocaine, some of which was cut with fentanyl, according to the initial field lab kits.

Well. That was good news—interdicting a haul from the Tiburonista cartel in Venezuela. CNN reported that federal agents had twenty-five narco-traffickers in custody, cooling their heels in a Miami-Dade jail.

Murray smiled. Roland Maxwell, his DEA chief, deserved an *attaboy* for coordinating matters with the Coast Guard to act on the shipment. He opened his leather folio to jot a note to call Maxwell. He was clicking his ballpoint when Montgomery opened the door.

"Oh, good," Mary Pat Foley said as she entered with a deep breath and her locked metal briefcase. She set it down on the table. "At least I'm not the only one who's late."

"Well," Murray replied to the director of national intelligence with a tap on his smartwatch, "you're later than me."

"If you tell on me, Dan, I swear to God I'll never forgive you."

She bent over to rummage through the small refrigerator next to the TV and emerged with a Diet Coke. "Hey," she said, cracking open the can, her ears tuning in to the news broadcast, "did the DEA move on that Venezuelan drug ship?"

"Yeah. Maxwell took the lead."

"That's the tip that came in from that prime minister you prosecuted from Guyana, right?"

"*Former* prime minister," Murray replied. "That *a-hole* is busy doing life in Leavenworth for killing an American citizen and staging a coup. I thought we were going tomorrow, but it looks like Max went early."

"Probably to protect his sources."

"Probably."

The broadcast broke for commercials. Murray found the remote and hit the mute button. "Speaking of sources, MP, if you're in touch with Ding, please thank him for me. That roll-up of the Tiburonista network is still paying dividends."

"I'll pass it on to Clark," she said, sipping her soda. "Ding's still recovering from that nightmare. I don't want to give him PTSD."

The curved door on the opposite side of the room swung open. Alma Winters, the President's personal secretary, addressed them with her trademark soft, southern charm. "Good afternoon, Madam Director, Mr. Attorney General. We had to rearrange a few things with the boss's schedule—but he's ready for you now."

"How much time do we have?" Murray asked, rising.

"Not much, I'm afraid. The Senate majority leader is coming by later to discuss budgets. You know how that goes. Please, follow me."

Mary Pat set the soda down on the table and pointed at Murray. "I mean it, Dan. Don't you dare tell him I was later than you."

The two cabinet officers found President Jack Ryan rounding the Resolute desk in shirtsleeves, his suit jacket draped over a side chair.

"Sofas," the President commanded. "Alma may have told you— I only have seven minutes. Heard you were late, Mary Pat."

Murray grinned at her as they took opposite positions on the butter-cream damask couches.

President Jack Ryan, Sr., sat in the chair between them, facing the fireplace adorned with portraits of previous chief executives. With his guidance, the White House Office of the Curator rotated the presidential portraits seasonally. This month, the hearth displayed the visages of Ulysses S. Grant, Abraham Lincoln, and Dwight Eisenhower.

Jack touched a buzzer to summon the Navy steward. "Iced tea," he requested when the petty officer arrived. "And three Tylenols. What about you two? Want anything?"

Knowing how short their visit would be, they both shook their heads.

Ryan crossed his legs, waggled his foot, and raised an eye at Murray while he waited for the tea and pain reliever. "Cathy said it looks good for Liz, Dan. Sounds like she wants to do that surgery."

"Oh, sir?"

"The First Lady called a minute ago. I don't pretend to understand half of what she said—other than she liked the Belgian doc."

Murray filed the comment away.

The steward returned with a silver tray and handed the President his iced tea—lemon only, no sweetener—and a dish with three capsules.

While the President gulped down the pills, Murray explained his wife's medical situation to Mary Pat. He was about to express his concerns regarding the risk when the Navy man retreated behind the service door, shutting it firmly. The attorney general cut himself short. They could discuss Liz later.

He opened his folio and passed papers to the President and Mary Pat.

"Here's the Seattle SAC's sitrep," he began, referencing the FBI special agent in charge who'd written the situation report. "I'm happy to summarize, sir, given our limited window."

"Please," the President replied, massaging his temples.

"This morning, at three a.m. Pacific in Clarkston, Washington, the local fire department responded to a barn fire on a remote ranch."

"Where's Clarkston?" Mary Pat asked.

"Southeast corner of Washington State."

"Across the Snake River from Lewiston," the President clarified. "Where Lewis and Clark camped with the Nez Perce tribe before descending the Columbia. Hence the town names. Go on, Dan."

The entire cabinet understood that the President turned to history as a coping mechanism whenever he had a rough day. "Anyway, Mr. President, the firemen found a family of four in a burned barn. They were likely dead before the fire started—gunshots to the head. When the local sheriff logged the homicide in the NCIC database, it triggered a flag with Justice. Seattle sent agents to take control of the crime scene."

"And that's when you called the White House, Mary Pat?" Ryan asked.

"Yes, sir. Because of the POSEIDON SPEAR association," she said. "Sadly."

Ryan shook his head. "What was the operative's name?"

"Cole Hunt," Mary Pat and Dan replied in unison.

Murray tilted his head to her, yielding the floor.

"Mr. President, Cole Hunt was with DEVGRU, SEAL Team Six. He retired as a special operations senior chief, an E-8, two years ago. He led the Cairo raid that took out a key engineer for the Umayyad Revolutionary Council a few years back."

"URC. You mean LOTUS," the President recalled.

"Yes, sir," she replied. "Our code name for the URC was LOTUS. That's right."

Ryan folded his hands over his stomach. "Give me a little more on the Cairo op and how it relates to the bigger picture, POSEIDON SPEAR."

Mary Pat unlocked her hard case, removed a red folder, and perched tortoiseshell glasses on her nose. "POSEIDON SPEAR was a joint operational mission to root out active elements of LOTUS after we eliminated the group's leader, Saif Rahman Yasin—nom de guerre, the Emir."

Ryan uncrossed his legs. "*That* SOB."

"Yes."

"Was POSEIDON SPEAR only in Cairo?" the President asked. "Or did it cover other locations?"

"Several locations, sir. There were multiple ops around the world with various cells. The Cairo op used DEVGRU to eliminate the Emir's lead scientist, who we assessed at the time as the technical mastermind behind the plot to poison Lake Mead with nuclear waste from Nevada's Yucca Mountain site." She glanced over her glasses at the commander in chief.

"I don't recall anything about a Cairo op," the President said. "Or POSEIDON SPEAR, for that matter. Care to refresh my memory?"

"You *do* recall the fate of the Emir, Mr. President?"

"I have a mental gift for remembering people who tried to kill me," the President replied sardonically. "I know Clark took him into custody and *persuaded* the Emir to give up his network."

"Yes, sir." She dropped the page she had been reading and lifted another. "Cairo was a kill order run by the POSEIDON SPEAR task force. Cole Hunt was a sniper temporarily assigned to a CIA Special Activities Division officer. Egyptian intelligence assisted with ingress and egress. The cover we used—weapons, rifle, all of that—made it look like an Egyptian job, a rival faction from the Muslim Brotherhood."

"Okay," Ryan said. "And Hunt's *not* the only one who's turned up dead from the Cairo op?"

"Regrettably, sir, the others have also been hit," Murray answered. "Local police found the Special Activities man, Mike Rogers, with his family in California. He's a chiseled star in the lobby at Langley now. Identical MO. Bullet through the temple, then burned to conceal evidence."

Ryan stared into his iced tea. "How many SPEAR participants have we lost in all?"

"Cole Hunt makes three, sir," Mary Pat answered. "The second was a Delta operator named Ted McCune, hit six weeks ago—shot and burned along with his wife in Billings, Montana. What's notable about McCune is that he wasn't in on the Cairo hit. But he took down another Umayyad terrorist in Karachi, also under the POSEIDON SPEAR rubric."

"Two operators might be a coincidence," Murray explained. "Three across two SPEAR ops makes this a likely URC-related operation."

The President put his glass on a coaster and swore. "Was SPEAR run through NCTC?"

"Yes, sir," Mary Pat responded. "But to be honest, we didn't bother briefing you on it. At the time, it was business as usual for NCTC, mopping up. The global war on terror was in its final phase."

"That's how I saw it, too," Murray confessed. "Guess we were wrong. We underestimated them, I'm sad to admit."

"Meaning?"

"Meaning we failed three SPEAR vets whose identities had our best covert protection," Mary Pat said sadly. "We believe someone—or some *thing*—is in our systems."

"Have we started an internal investigation?" Ryan asked.

As the ultimate head of the FBI's Counterintelligence Division, Murray fielded the question. "Yes, but Mary Pat and I agreed we should keep it limited, closely held, in case this is a data compromise. Now that we've seen a third victim, we may have to get more proactive with a new specialized task force to root out this . . . mole."

The President winced at the wretched word and glanced at the mantel clock. Alma would enter any minute to tell him that Senator Rex Jorgenson was outside. The most senior member of the opposition party was sensitive to extended waiting periods.

Mary Pat read the tension in Jack's mouth. "I know you have a meeting, sir, but there's something else. I neglected to give this to you earlier because I haven't fully vetted it yet. And, like Dan mentioned, we're worried about a mole, so I didn't want to bring it up through the usual channels."

"And what's that?"

"A motive. We thought we took care of the URC, LOTUS, with SPEAR. Now, this is all a bit raw, but I've directed the CIA Southwest Asia desk to scrub contacts for anything related to Umayyad. Our best cohesive analysis suggests that the Emir may have had a son. Various HUMINT reports speak of a man named Rafa bin Yasin operating a separatist cell in the disputed regions of Kashmir, crossing the border between India and Pakistan. Disparate voice intercepts refer to him as either a prophet or a caliph or the son of the Emir."

"Rafa bin Yasin," Ryan repeated. "Did that name come up under Clark's interrogation of the Emir?"

"Not in the transcripts, sir. Or we would have added it to the SPEAR assignments."

"You mentioned human intelligence reporting. So—the CIA is out there working assets and agents for hearsay. Aren't we getting anything from the NSA directly?"

"No, sir. While we assess that there is a nascent terror band called the Umayyad Caliphate, we've concluded that it communicates by messenger. HUMINT reporting suggests that this leader, Rafa, the possible son of the Emir, is in constant motion, hard to pin down."

"In motion where?"

She referenced her notes. "Primarily northern Pakistan, above Peshawar, foothills of the Hindu Kush and Karakoram mountains. Reporting suggests the rural populace in that area is ripe for radicalization and recruitment. ISIS has been active there. They see it as beyond the reach of our resources."

Ryan tented his fingers, pondering the point. "Out of reach. You mean because they're holed up in a disputed region where Pakistanis, Indians, and Chinese often skirmish over borders."

"Yes, sir. They're likely aware that we would be cautious about military pursuit in that area."

"I hate when terrorists are smart," Ryan replied. "Should we ask the Pakistanis to move on him?"

"I've relayed our interest over to the head of Pakistan's Inter-Services Intelligence, ISI. I've also spoken with the head of India's Intelligence Bureau, the IB. They both said essentially the same thing, but from opposite points of view. The ISI believes this Rafa is a scourge who the Indians protect to poke Pakistani Kashmir. The IB thinks Rafa is a Pakistani whose goal is to upset Indian Kashmir. Both countries claim the region as its own, as you know."

The President frowned. "And Kashmir is split down the middle—Muslim and Hindu. A microcosm of India-Pakistan itself."

"Or a flash point. The only thing the two countries' intel services can agree on is that Rafa's a separatist with links to Daesh, ISIS. Otherwise, the Indians say he's funded by the Pakistanis. The Pakistanis say he's funded by the Indians."

The President stared at the portraits over the mantel, his exhausted eyes resting on Dwight Eisenhower, the first sitting American president to visit India. "The last time the Indians went after a suspected terrorist in Pakistan, they launched an air raid that damn near started a nuclear war. A billion people could have died if it wasn't for Scott's shuttle diplomacy."

"As you said, sir, it's an ideal place for a terrorist to hide from us."

Right on cue, Alma Winters poked her head through the door. "Majority Leader Jorgenson is here, sir. Mr. Van Damm told me to make sure you were on time."

"Thanks, Alma," Jack muttered. "Put Arnie and Jorgy in the Cabinet Room. Have the stewards bring them coffee, maybe one of your sweet biscuits. And, Alma, please swear to Jorgy up and down that I'm dealing with a critical national security issue."

"Yes, sir. I will."

"Look," the President said after Alma left. "I think all we can do for now is protect our POSEIDON SPEAR people. That's at least in our control. Keep pressing your folks for better intelligence on Umayyad . . . Rafa . . . whomever. I can't kick the India-Pakistan hornet's nest without incontrovertible proof of a threat to the U.S. homeland. It's just too touchy an area for direct action from us. If we get proof, we can lean on the Pakistanis or Indians to move on this group. And you need to find this mole—quickly."

Mary Pat shut her briefcase.

"Understood," Murray said. "My team will work up WITSEC packages for them, maybe even offer up whole new identities. We're looking at about eight additional SPEAR participants, along with their families. And we'll activate a counterintelligence op with the FBI to root out the mole."

"Very well," the President finished. But something didn't sit right with him. His director of national intelligence was unusually quiet. "I know you want me to tell you to take him out," he told her. "But you understand—I can't order direct action in Kashmir without incontrovertible proof. It's too diplomatically sensitive— and it's not like we have control of the airspace with drones there. We would have to ask for Pakistan's or India's permission."

"Yes, sir. Understood," she replied flatly.

Still dissatisfied, Ryan stood and headed for the door. Mary Pat and Murray followed, veering to leave through the secret entrance that went back through the private study. That was the usual way they accessed the Oval Office to discuss national security matters.

"Oh no," the President admonished. "You're going out the main door. Senator Jorgenson needs to see we were hard at work in here. I'm serious."

AFTER MAKING SMALL TALK WITH ARNIE VAN DAMM AND SENATE MAJORITY LEADER Rex Jorgenson outside the Cabinet Room, the DNI and attorney general exited through a side security door and walked to West Executive Avenue, the closed boulevard where senior West Wing staff parked.

A light spring rain dappled the pavement. Murray saw his black Suburban and security driver waiting behind the wheel. It roared to life and batted the raindrops with its wipers. "Where's your vehicle?" he asked when he didn't see Mary Pat's SUV standing by.

"I sent them to pick up Ed. He's giving an alumni talk at Langley, so I thought it would be nice for him to arrive with a bit of pomp and circumstance. I'm hoping you can give me a ride."

"Of course." After a few more steps, Murray added, "You know, MP, I think all we did was make our boss busier today. Not proud of that."

"I disagree," she replied, heels clicking on the sidewalk, briefcase swinging in her hand. "We just have to spin up a team to root out these URC bastards before they hit another one of our people. Simple."

Murray paused beside his idling Suburban. The rain on the lush green landscape smelled good, a welcome harbinger of balmy summer days. A bus stopped beyond the security fence, disgorging a hundred middle schoolers on a spring trip. The eighteen-acre enclave of the White House often felt oddly peaceful to Murray, a stark contrast to the actual discussion in the Oval Office.

"How is *that* simple?" he asked incredulously. "Anything we do through normal channels could leak."

The DNI lifted her briefcase over her head as shelter from the rain. "Who said anything about normal channels?"

"How else do we assemble an op?"

She grinned. "Have your driver take us down to Leesburg."

"Why? What's in Leesburg?"

"John Clark's farm."

4

LEESBURG, VIRGINIA

AS THE RAIN INTENSIFIED, JOHN CLARK PULLED HIS WORN VIETNAM-ERA TIGER-striped jungle hat from the back pocket of his Levi's and snugly fit it on his head.

He quickened his pace to a run, dodged muddy puddles, and sprinted to the chicken coop for cover. After struggling with the intricate door latch designed to keep foxes out of the henhouse—quite literally—he squeezed in among the stacked rows of clucking Bovan Browns, Leghorns, and Rhode Island Reds.

The drumming rain on the roof shingles lent the cramped, musty coop a cozy atmosphere. However, Clark's presence unsettled a few birds, who protested with high-pitched squawks.

"Come on now," he murmured as he removed his hat and reached in for an egg. "It's just me."

The Red didn't buy it and pecked his hand with a lightning-fast jerk of her head. Clark cursed as he sprang backward, checking to see if the hen had drawn blood, but noticed nothing more than a pink welt. He then shifted to the Leghorn's nesting box on the lower shelf to try again with a friendlier bird.

He quickly gathered four eggs in his hat. His wife, Sandy, needed at least three for the cake she was baking with their daughter, Patricia. When Clark pointed out that there were three perfectly good store-bought eggs in the refrigerator, Sandy shot him a look that sent a chill down his spine.

As if that weren't enough, his daughter had added, "It's Ding's birthday, Dad. He deserves the farm-fresh eggs, don't you think?"

Clark couldn't fathom a world where Ding Chavez, who was currently sixty yards away in Clark's den watching a Nationals game, would care one way or the other about the eggs used in his birthday cake. Rubbing the spot where the Rhode Island Red had tagged him, Clark tried in vain to banish the word that was rattling around his head: *henpecked*.

If for nothing more than that word alone, he welcomed the distraction of the black Suburban with its headlights on, speeding down his driveway. He didn't know who it was, but it wasn't hard to figure out it had come from D.C., probably in a hurry, which meant—God willing—he might have something more interesting to do. Clutching the eggs in his hat, he waved the vehicle over to him.

The rear window lowered when the SUV drew close. "Hey, Farmer John. What you doing there?" Mary Pat Foley asked with a grin from the back seat.

"Farming," Clark responded mirthlessly. "And standing in the rain."

"Didn't anyone tell you not to keep all your eggs in one basket?"

"Are you done?"

"Almost. Dan Murray's with me."

The attorney general leaned forward in the back seat for a greeting.

"Is there somewhere private the three of us can talk?" she asked. "Preferably dry?"

"Over there." Clark gestured with the hat. "Stables. See you there in five mikes."

After leaving the eggs with Patricia, Clark found the attorney general and director of national intelligence standing between the long, overhanging heads of Sophie, his quarter horse mare, and Rusty, his retired racing thoroughbred. Mary Pat was leaning on the shiplap wall, inspecting her high heels with a frown. That the expensive shoes had sustained mud damage seemed like rough justice to Clark after her smart-ass Farmer John crack.

"Damn," Clark said, removing his dripping oilskin coat and hanging it on a peg. "Cats and dogs out there."

Mary Pat looked up from her feet. "Yeah. How's vacation treating you so far? Get much riding in?"

"A little yesterday," Clark answered. "But this storm is going to muddy things up for a while. Just as well. I'd rather be in the office."

"Then why did you take time off?" Murray asked, hands on his hips.

Clark withdrew a carrot from his hanging coat and offered it to the mare, who crunched it noisily. "Gerry Hendley, Howard Brennan, and the other white-side bankers closed a big deal in Zurich and declared a two-week company holiday in celebration. I thought it only fair that my black-side Campus people get rest, too."

Mary Pat Foley and Dan Murray were both aware that there were two sides to the Hendley business. The legitimate one, the white side, was a boutique private equity firm that sought out undervalued companies to acquire and resell for a profit. It also happened that the firm's founder, Gerry Hendley, was a former senator and loyal friend of the President of the United States. Some of Hendley's private equity returns were funneled into a black-side operation called The Campus, which employed several former operators directly and maintained relationships with a few select active-duty military members.

With operations run by John Clark—a retired SEAL with a long history of executing sensitive matters for the President—The Campus conducted targeted, covert operations that required absolute discretion.

As Mary Pat Foley saw their current predicament, few things required greater discretion than hitting a reemerging terrorist network that had somehow penetrated the U.S. government's most sensitive personnel records.

"That's generous of you," she remarked. "Is Jack Junior over in Europe with the white side? Or is he taking time off with the Campus people?"

"Neither. He and Lisanne are in Texas. She's getting a high-tech prosthetic arm fitted by a doctor friend of hers. It's going to give her an articulated hand, movable fingers, the whole deal. Then, there's a wedding."

Mary Pat canted a leg forward and opened her mouth in shock. "Jack and Lisanne are *eloping*?"

"No, not them." Clark chuckled. "You think the First Lady would let that happen? The doc who's performing her prosthetic surgery in Austin is getting married this week. Lisanne's in the wedding party. Something like that." He rubbed the mare's nose.

"How about Ding?" she inquired. "How's he doing?"

"He's recovering on my sofa, watching a Nationals game as we speak. Away game—Marlins."

"How about his surgery? His knee, wasn't it?"

"Yeah, the knee. That beating in Venezuela aggravated an old jump wound to his left leg, tearing the patella. He should be all right in a month or so." Clark grabbed a pitchfork and tossed some hay into Rusty's stable. The stallion flapped his lips in blubbering approval.

"Well, you should let him know that we seized a drug ship with fentanyl-laced cocaine fresh from Venezuela," Murray offered. "Ding's op saved a few lives."

"I saw that on CNN," Clark said. He stuffed his hands into his jeans pockets. "But I can't imagine the attorney general and the director of national intelligence traveled sixty miles over country roads to discuss the news."

"No," Mary Pat confessed. "John, I presume we're secure here?"

Clark looked around at his horses and folded his arms over his chest. "Both Rusty and Sophie have top secret clearances. The rain ought to squelch out any outdoor listening devices."

Mary Pat raised her hand. "All right, all right. It's a habit."

"So they tell me. Now, why are you two standing around in my Leesburg stable?"

"POSEIDON SPEAR," Murray responded. "An operative by the name of Cole Hunt was found dead this morning. Did you know him?"

Clark bowed his head and stared at the concrete floor. "Yeah. Hunt was with DEVGRU. Found dead where?"

"His home."

"Pacific Northwest somewhere, wasn't it?"

"Yes. And it gets worse. His family was killed, too."

Clark sighed. "Burned?"

"Yes."

"So this is a pattern now."

Murray nodded gravely. "Three crimes, same MO. Mike Rogers from CIA SAD, Ted McCune from Delta, and now Hunt from DEVGRU."

Clark dug the toe of his boot into a floor crack. "All POSEIDON SPEAR—but crossing separate ops."

"Which is the reason we drove down," said Mary Pat. "You led the team that apprehended the Emir . . . interrogated him right here in this barn. That led to SPEAR. Our assessment is that the Umayyad Revolutionary Council still has a cell operating in the United States."

"And a mole with targeting information," Clark finished.

"Something like that."

"Okay. I get it. Campus can pick up where we left off, operate in the shadows, and avoid a tip-off to go find these scumbags. We'll need a few leads to get started. Do we have any?"

Mary Pat crossed her arms. "One. I have the NSA scrambling to get anything we can related to the Emir's old group. On our way down here, the watch officer at the NSA called to tell me about a voice intercept in northern Pakistan. I'll give you the full report, but suffice to say, they were celebrating the death of a quote-unquote American infidel devil."

"That's pretty thin," Clark grumbled.

"There's more. Our Southwest Asia desk believes the Emir has an heir, perhaps a son. Reporting suggests he goes by the name Rafa bin Yasin. We assess that he's operating in eastern Pakistan, getting help from Daesh, probably ISIS-Khorasan."

Clark stared at the stable floor.

"What?" she asked.

"When I was interrogating the Emir, he bragged that he would never really die—talked about a legacy."

"You think he meant a son? It wasn't in your transcripts."

He shook his head. "A lot of things weren't in my transcript. The Emir referred to women a lot. One of them was French. We know he liked prostitutes. He killed one they picked up in Vegas. Maybe look into France for a bastard son."

"You don't have more detailed notes that you maybe kept from us?"

Clark cracked his knuckles. "That was a long time ago. Whatever I had I gave to the NCTC. I don't recall us pushing hard on the French angle, though. Didn't seem relevant—and we thought we got everyone else, didn't we?"

"Yes," she acknowledged. "As soon as we're done, the NCTC will get the French intel agency, DGSE, spun up for any associations with Rafa. In the meantime, we'd like The Campus to get to work on protecting our people in the U.S. and rooting out whoever is passing around POSEIDON SPEAR operative names."

"Wait," Clark protested. "If this Rafa is in eastern Pakistan or Western India, let's just track him down there, paste him with a drone strike."

"Off-limits," she responded.

"Send in SAD, then. Kill the guy now before this gets worse."

"Can't. The President's orders. Kashmir is a powder keg right now. He told us specifically not to get kinetic until we can get better intel. I'm working that from the top down. We want you to work from the bottom up. We need you to root out the mole."

Clark turned his attention back to Rusty. He stroked the stallion's forelock. "Midas was an adviser to SPEAR. I'd like to warn him ASAP."

The attorney general raised an eyebrow. "Midas?"

"Bartosz Jankowski. He was a light colonel in Delta. Back in the day, he was in on some hits on an Umayyad gunrunner who smuggled material from Russia through Tajikistan. If there's a SPEAR operator kill list leaked to the Emir's old network, Midas is sure to be on it."

"I'm working on WITSEC packages for everyone involved in SPEAR," the attorney general offered. "I'll make sure to add Bartosz. Just get me his info."

Clark grimaced. "Ordering tier-one operators to live in hiding is a pretty tough sell."

"Well, we have to—" Murray cut himself off when Ding Chavez appeared on crutches under the barn light wearing a windbreaker and his game day Nationals hat.

"Hey, Ding," Clark greeted him. "Did the Nats win?"

"Negative. We got killed."

"Well, get in here out of the rain."

Chavez swiped the water from his shoulders. "I saw the Beltway Suburban. Good afternoon, Attorney General Murray, Director Foley."

They asked about his knee and thanked him for his contribution to the drug ship seizure. After the polite chitchat was exhausted, the two visitors glanced at Clark. The interval under the drumming rain grew awkward.

"Ding has to be part of this," Clark said. "If you're asking for Campus help, then he'll be my operations deputy—even if he can't get into the action for the time being. But that's what you said anyway—that we can't get kinetic."

"I'll approve Ding as part of this op," Mary Pat granted. "All right with you, Dan?"

After the attorney general assented, the DNI recapped the terrorist threat to Ding.

"Okay," Ding summarized. "So you want us to pull together a team to root this American Umayyad cell out?"

"Indeed," Clark said. "And there's a mole, so we need to stay below the radar."

"Who are you thinking for this, boss?" Ding asked.

"Mandy Cobb can run the mole hunt, given her ex-FBI background. Gavin can help her with the computer forensics. Since they're not on the FBI payroll, that lessens the risk of a leak."

"That could work," Mary Pat agreed.

Dan Murray looked doubtful. "What's Mandy Cobb's FBI record?"

Ding answered. "She was on a fly team that went after terror cells. She was with us in Venezuela. Quiet and effective. Good fit for this."

"Something else, Dan," Clark said. "Mandy and Gavin will need real FBI creds if they're going to sniff around local police departments."

"I'll take care of it. We can create personnel records for them and issue them ID badges."

"Plus a shield and a gun. They need to be *actual* agents in the system."

The attorney general nodded. "They will be."

"All right, then." Clark offered his hand to the two cabinet officers.

"The President wants this done fast, unofficially," Murray said, releasing Clark's grip.

"Of course he does. We'll get to it ASAP."

A minute later, Ding and Clark stood leaning on the rough beams of the stable, watching the Suburban's taillights fade at the end of the driveway. The rain had picked up, hammering on the stable's metal roof.

"Let's go call Midas," Clark said, his voice raised over the patter.

"To warn him?"

"Yeah. But also to brief him up. He operated in those tribal areas in northern Pakistan—he still has mujahideen contacts out there."

"Brief him up so he can get us better intel on a mole here in the States?"

"Negative. So he can haul ass to Pakistan and kill this little bastard Rafa before this gets any worse."

5

"THIS WAY, THIS WAY!" THE SMALL, LEATHERY MAN URGED, LEADING JACK RYAN, JR.,
and his fiancée, Lisanne Robertson, through the bustling crowd
outside the Indira Gandhi International Airport in Delhi, India.

Struggling with jet lag and burdened by an overstuffed backpack, a shoulder bag, and a large roller, Jack found himself falling
behind. "Hold up!" he shouted hoarsely, his voice lost amid the
honking cars and chattering travelers.

It wasn't just the luggage that slowed him. He was bleary-eyed
from the twenty-hour Lufthansa flight from Austin to Frankfurt
to Delhi. The heat and crowds provided a harsh awakening after
the business-class cabin, where he'd watched movies, read books,
and dined like a king. In harsh contrast, his head now throbbed,
his throat rasped, and his jeans clung uncomfortably to his legs.

Not so for Lisanne. As bright-eyed and beautiful as when they
left the U.S., she glided behind their escort, a corporate driver
dressed in a black suit and tie.

Carrying only a purse because she was still recovering from
prosthetic arm surgery, she stopped and waited for Jack. "You
have to hurry. We'll lose him."

"The bags are slowing me down."

"This way! This way!" the driver shouted from among forty people clad in drapey Indian dhotis, saris, and kurta pajamas under a merciless sun. "The car is just over here!"

Lisanne, ex–Texas state trooper, ex-Marine, and current Campus director of logistics, turned away from Jack to keep up with their guide. The crowd closed around Jack, jostling him with such force that he stopped to readjust his backpack straps.

He couldn't blame Lisanne for the unfair distribution of luggage. Years ago, she'd lost her left arm below the elbow in a fight with a terrorist. However, as of five days ago, she was surgically equipped with a fully articulated prosthetic that used electromyography sensors to interpret nerve signals from the muscles in her upper arm. While the surgery was still recent enough that she had to avoid lifting anything, the advanced mechanical appendage showed tremendous promise.

In fact, Lisanne was so thrilled with the working fingers, rotatable wrist, and sensitive grip that she barely slept during the flights. As she practiced her exercises, she often jabbed Jack to demonstrate how she could delicately hold a bag of peanuts, crush a paper coffee cup, or grasp the edge of a tiny meal tray.

Which was all well and good, Jack thought as he fought through the airport horde. But while his fiancée was officially a bionic woman, he was left to handle the more mundane aspects of international travel—like hauling a hundred and twenty pounds of luggage across a congested boulevard in hundred-degree heat.

"Jack, hurry!" she called over her shoulder, fifty feet ahead of him, two high-pitched English words drifting across a polyglot sea. A honking yellow bus festooned with a fringe of dangling balls nearly ran Jack over, forcing him to stop in the middle of the road. When the bus lurched forward, the guide and Lisanne had vanished.

"Jack!"

Standing at least six inches taller than the crowd, Jack spotted Lisanne by a silver minivan with its rear hatch open amid a jumble of cars.

"Did you have to pack this much?" he asked, panting, dark circles under his armpits.

"It's an Indian wedding. There are at least five outfits in there."

He thought better of complaining and stacked the bags at the edge of the minivan's narrow cargo area, only to see them tumble onto the scorching pavement while he struggled to remove his backpack. Exiting another brightly colored bus, a swarm of sandal-clad Indian pedestrians trampled over the bags and hemmed Jack in.

"We could have planned this better," he said, crouching.

Lisanne, who'd leaned down to help him, rolled her eyes and abandoned the effort. She walked to the side of the vehicle and forcefully opened its door.

As Jack sweated and labored, he remembered the last time he'd irritated her on this trip.

Somewhere over the Arabian Sea in an Air India 787, he absently mentioned to Lisanne that he wished he were in Zurich with the rest of the white-side Hendley team, arguing that it was a career mistake to miss out on the deal the white-siders were pursuing.

The eye roll he'd just experienced was identical in shape, duration, and sentiment to the one in midair.

He stacked the bags and vowed to keep his mouth shut. But he couldn't shake the image of the white-side team at a luxurious Swiss hotel, reviewing reports and proposals. Gerry Hendley and his entourage had traveled to Zurich to acquire a European satellite company, LodeStar, which they aimed to transform into a rocket-launch firm for hire, planning to resell it for a big return.

Jack had very much wanted to lead that project. Instead, Hendley's chief investment officer, Howard Brennan—Jack's whiteside superior—assigned the deal to Thad Vandermullen, a newly arrived banker from Wall Street who spoke fluent German and had experience in the satellite industry. Howard advised Jack to forget about mergers and acquisitions, head to Texas, and support his fiancée during her surgical recovery.

Jack understood and agreed with the advice for the most part. But his third vodka tonic over the Arabian Sea had diluted that clarity, causing him to voice his concerns. Lisanne's first reaction had been the eye roll; her second was to demonstrate her new hand's dexterity by carefully raising its mechanical middle finger.

"I'm sorry," he muttered now as he climbed into the minivan beside her, his back drenched in sweat. The driver threw the vehicle into gear and steered haltingly, honking at the mob as though piloting a ship through fog. Jack touched his fiancée's knee.

She returned the touch with her natural hand. "It's fine."

The driver lowered his window and hollered at a man who was stopped in the road for no apparent reason, forcing a detour on the shoulder. Jack adjusted the air-conditioning vents and wiped his dripping forehead with his elbow.

"You know," he tried to explain. "Forty-eight hours ago, I didn't even know we were going to India. We both thought Srini meant we'd stay in Austin when she asked you to be in her wedding—not flying to the other side of the world."

Srini Rai, a professor of orthopedics at the University of Texas Dell Medical School and Lisanne's best friend from college, performed the advanced prosthetic surgery. While preparing for the procedure, the women rekindled their relationship to the extent that Srini insisted Lisanne join her bridal party at her upcoming wedding ceremony, set to take place in Amritsar, India, the following week—much to the dismay of Jack Ryan, Jr.

"This trip was intended as a gift," Lisanne countered. "A beautiful and wonderful surprise vacation, which—if I may remind you—her family is paying for. And you know how long I've wanted to see India."

"I'm just saying. I didn't have a lot of time to prepare. It's all a bit . . . disorienting."

"Honestly, Jack. I've seen you jump between white-side and black-side operations with two seconds' notice."

The vehicle jerked forward. It stopped a hundred yards later at another jam. "I know. But this is . . . different."

She peered at him with a mixture of confusion and sorrow. "Gerry Hendley declared two weeks off now that LodeStar is closed."

"LodeStar," he repeated wistfully, eyes aimed at the hazy sky.

"Let it go, Jack."

He continued staring through the window for two silent minutes.

"Have you considered the business aspects of *this* trip?" she asked when the car sped up again.

"Yes."

"Well, maybe you can strike up a rapport with him."

By *him*, she meant Srini's father, Daval Rai, and the sprawling company he ran. One of India's wealthiest men, Daval was the founder, CEO, and chairman of Assurance Global Industries, AGI, a worldwide construction behemoth with projects on every continent, some of which might present investment opportunities for Hendley Associates.

Jack wasn't sure where he might insert Hendley capital into Daval Rai's vast business empire, but he held a faint hope of using the trip to keep up with the likes of Thad Vandermullen. However, thinking of the Fifth Amendment, he wisely remained silent.

"It's only a week," she threw into the void. "We had the time off scheduled for my recovery anyway. Even Mr. Clark is on vacation this week."

The seasoned corporate driver was well acquainted with the relationship dynamics of a traveling American couple. After advancing two miles down a road that had now come to a standstill, he leaned over the front seat to interject with a gentle voice, "Hello, ma'am and sir. I apologize for the interruption. It might take us some time to reach the train station."

"Is there a problem?" Jack asked.

"The bridge over the Yamuna River is out, making rush hour very, very bad. Probably three hours delay. So sorry, sir."

Thinking of the first-class train tickets that were now worthless, Jack stared vacantly at the vehicular chaos, contrasting it to Switzerland's neat, orderly streets.

"Thank you, Devanshu," Lisanne said. "Perhaps take us to the AGI office in New Delhi, then?"

"Yes, ma'am. That is also three hours."

Exasperated, Jack swiveled rearward on his knee to rummage through the cargo bay to find the small bag with their phones. Though he didn't expect any work emails, he thought he could at least read up on the news back home.

"Hey!" Lisanne exclaimed when he jostled her new arm.

"Excuse me," he grunted while unsnapping flaps and opening zippers.

"What's the matter?"

"Lis, you're not going to believe this." His face was white and damp.

"Believe what?"

"The bag with our passports and phones is gone."

6

ARLINGTON, VIRGINIA

GAVIN BIERY TYPED HIS CODE INTO THE CIPHER LOCK, PLACED THE BAG OF DUNKIN' Donuts on the table, and turned on the lights in the Hendley black-side basement conference room.

While theoretically still on vacation, Gavin—Hendley's info-tech director—had been so relieved when John Clark called to tell him there would be an emergency meeting at zero seven hundred this morning that he'd volunteered to bring the pastries. Finding the room empty, he occupied a chair, took a bite of his donut, and swiveled eagerly.

For the past week, Gavin had been at home feeling bored. Like Jack, he divided his responsibilities between the Hendley Associates private equity white side and the Campus black side. Gavin's white-side job was as an IT specialist, while his mission at The Campus was information warfare. Juggling these two roles, he worked long hours and thought he would enjoy the unexpected vacation.

However, after spending so much time in his condo, the melancholy patter of May raindrops and his cat Princess's plaintive meowing reminded him of a truth he had been conveniently avoiding through obsessive office hours: he wanted a girlfriend.

He had certainly made an effort. A year earlier, he AI-enhanced his picture and posted his profile on all the popular dating apps, calling his profession "hacker for hire," which sounded attractive—to him. Through texts, he charmed each prospective date with the intricacies of the "art of the hack," as he referred to it, and dispatched what he considered pithy witticisms. So far, he had only discovered that his sense of humor was, perhaps, unique. He had yet to go on an actual date.

"Have you hooked up the laptop to the projector yet?" Clark asked, entering with a Starbucks paper coffee decanter and a stack of cups.

"On it," Gavin replied, abandoning his half-eaten jelly donut and wiping powdered sugar from his beard. "What feed do you want to show, Mr. C.?"

"Bring up the NGA."

The NGA was the National Geospatial-Intelligence Agency, one of eighteen analytical organizations reporting to Mary Pat Foley.

The Campus could be seen as Mrs. Foley's nineteenth spy agency were it officially recognized. However, since it wasn't, the covert organization relied on the raw data feeds from major national collection services, including the NSA for communications intelligence (COMINT), the CIA for human intelligence (HUMINT), and the NGA for satellite imagery intelligence (IMINT). Gavin Biery, as the director of black-side cyber programs, oversaw the feeds.

"Anything in particular from the NGA?" Gavin asked.

Perched on a credenza, Clark sipped his coffee. "Yeah. I want the latest imagery for Khairi, Pakistan. And after that, get into the

NSA servers and look for all communications on the name Rafa bin Yasin." Clark wrote the town and the name on the whiteboard behind him.

"I'll see what I can find."

While Gavin typed queries into the NGA and NSA databases, Mandy Cobb arrived and tossed her backpack on the table. Before joining The Campus, she'd been an FBI special agent working with the DEA on Latin American drug cases out of Miami. Before that, she'd been in the Bureau's counterterrorism group.

"Sorry for the casual attire," she said as she slid into the seat next to Gavin. "Hitting the gym after this. Did you say Pakistan, Mr. C.? And that's our guy, Rafa bin Yasin, Rafa son of Yasin?"

"Yeah," Clark replied.

"Who is he?"

"Let's wait on Midas and Master Chief Moore."

Gavin found Mandy's faintly feminine scent, dirty-blond ponytail, and snug gym attire acutely distracting. While he pulled up satellite-image files of Pakistan's northeastern Punjab region, he wondered why he couldn't find a woman like Ms. Cobb on the dating apps.

Clark addressed two broad-shouldered men who arrived next. "Mornin', Midas, Chief. Shut the door and grab a seat. Coffee and donuts over there."

Kendrick Moore, a retired SEAL master chief, had a smoothly shaved scalp and face. By contrast, former Delta lieutenant colonel Bartosz Jankowski, Midas, sported a thick grizzled beard and a mane of dark hair. Both men wore jeans and untucked short-sleeve button-downs—standard operator off-duty attire. Below the jeans, Midas's hairy toes protruded from Birkenstocks. The master chief's were hidden by green Crocs.

"Okay, let's kick this off," Clark announced.

"We're it?" Moore asked, looking around the room.

"Yeah. We're keeping this op small."

The assembled team engaged in lighthearted small talk about vacation activities. The good times abruptly halted when Clark pressed a button on his laptop. A photo of the burned Hunt family illuminated the screen.

"Sorry to ruin your breakfasts," Clark said. "But I needed to get your attention."

Mandy studied the image intently, while Gavin averted his gaze. Veterans who had witnessed much death, Midas and Moore shook their heads and sighed. It was clear that two of the deceased were children.

Clark touched the screen with a wooden pointer stick. "This was a family of four, the Hunts. That was Cole Hunt, a former DEVGRU operator. He moved to Washington State two years ago from Coronado after retiring from the Naval Special Warfare."

"Oh, shit," Moore muttered, paling.

"You knew him?"

"Yeah. Not well. I was LANT fleet; he was PAC. But we crossed paths on DEVGRU a few years ago."

DEVGRU, an amalgam of the words *Development* and *Group*, was the intentionally bland name for the elite commandos of what was formerly known as SEAL Team Six.

"I knew him, too," Clark said. "These other victims are his wife, Marla, and their kids, Maddie and Robbie. They were fourteen and twelve."

"When did this happen?" Mandy asked, her eyes narrowed.

"About twenty-four hours ago. The Bureau's Seattle district has sent evidence technicians to the scene. I doubt they'll find much. Because, unfortunately, we've seen this before." He advanced the slide.

"Jesus," Midas muttered in response to another grisly photo of charred bodies.

"Former Delta operator Ted McCune didn't have kids," Clark continued wearily. "But that's him with his wife. This happened three weeks ago in Montana." Another click. "And that's Mike Rogers from the CIA's Special Activities Division. His wife and daughter are the charred bodies next to him. She was five years old. This crime scene was one month back, also out west, near San Luis Obispo, California."

Midas crushed his coffee cup. "Rogers, McCune, and Hunt. I think I see where this is going."

"Why do you say that?" Mandy asked.

Clark advanced the slide to reveal a photo of a man in a checkered keffiyeh with thick dark eyebrows and a long gray beard. The photo was stamped with classification markings.

"A few years back," Clark explained, "Ding and I led a Campus op to take down this guy, Saif Yasin, aka the Emir. He ran an organization called the Umayyad Revolutionary Council. The NCTC code-named the group LOTUS."

"Jihadists?" Mandy asked.

"Yeah. The Emir tried to blow up the Yucca Mountain nuclear waste site in Nevada—an attempt to contaminate the U.S. water supply across the West. We stopped him before he could do it and spent a few years going after the remnants of LOTUS in a counterterror op called POSEIDON SPEAR. All three of the dead operators you just saw were part of SPEAR."

"And so was I," said Midas. "I was the ops liaison between the NCTC and the in-country teams."

"So this is a kill list," Mandy said. "Revenge murders. This group, the URC or LOTUS—it's still around?"

"We didn't think so," Clark replied. "Until Mary Pat Foley and Dan Murray visited Ding and me at my farm yesterday."

He flipped to another slide that revealed a youth with dark features. The identification photo was smeared with French immigration markings. "This guy, here, is our only photo of a man we suspect to be the Emir's illegitimate son, Rafa bin Yasin."

"He looks like he's ten years old in that picture," observed Moore.

"He was. This was the ID card from his housing project in Marseille, where his mother lived."

"Have we tracked her down?" Mandy asked.

"French intel, DGSE, sent us a report a few hours ago. The kid's mom died in a fire not long after we nabbed the Emir. Nobody ever found this kid's body, and he went off-grid. Emir-related terrorists that the DGSE rounded up over the years reported that the Emir made many covert visits to the housing project where the kid lived."

Midas cursed. "That son of a bitch had a son."

"Yeah. We didn't put all the dots together until the past twenty-four hours. NSA intercepts in India are coming in with little fragments that suggest this kid, now all grown up, is responsible for these hits on our people. We have intercepts referring to an Umayyad caliph in India, another one in Pakistan mentioned a name." Clark tapped the ID photo with his pointer. "Rafa bin Yasin."

"So he's in India-Pak."

"Yes. Pakistani ISI and Indian IB both say he's a threat to stability in Kashmir. They blame each other for him, which makes Rafa a slippery character."

"Do we know much about his operation?" Moore asked.

Clark cleared his throat and read aloud from a CIA document, quoting the analyst who'd written it in response to the emergency request for intelligence put out by Mary Pat Foley. "The Islamabad station reports a person of interest, possibly Rafa bin Yasin, is recruiting ISIS-K veterans from Afghanistan in a movement called the Umayyad Caliphate, UC, a reference to the second great caliphate after Muhammad's passing. By the year eight hundred, the

Umayyad Caliphate encompassed Afghanistan, Pakistan, northern India, and Tajikistan, among other modern-day countries across Eurasia. We assess that this person of interest looks to reestablish the caliphate in disputed Kashmir, most likely on the Pakistani side of the border. He has built a mobile army of fifty to eighty fighters that moves between India and Pakistan in the ungoverned areas near Kashmir."

"Do we have any actual linkage between the CIA's analysis of Rafa active in Pakistan and these killings here?" Mandy asked.

"Some," said Clark. "In addition to the chatter about another infidel dying in the U.S., an NSA search algorithm coupled Pakistan with a trigger word. It led to a data snatch through a messaging app we broke a while ago." Clark looked at the transcript and wrote on the whiteboard. "Here's the trigger word: *qisas*."

Mandy responded instantly. "I worked with the counterterror teams at the Bureau. *Qisas* is a form of retaliation in the Quran. It's the classic verse about an eye for an eye, nose for a nose, tooth for a tooth."

"Correct," Moore said. "And the burnings, while sick, fit with the jihadis' version of retribution. Cremation is a major sin in Islam. Sort of the ultimate FU. ISIS regularly burned victims."

"The NCTC's read is that there's a kill list of people who took out the old Umayyad Revolutionary Council," Clark continued. "Rafa is our guy leading the hits."

"How could he have a kill list with operator names and addresses?" Mandy asked. "Sounds like POSEIDON SPEAR was a closely held operation."

"It was," Midas confirmed. "Mary Pat Foley was running the NCTC then. SPEAR was highly compartmentalized, eyes-only, code-word classified. It consisted of operators from SEAL, Delta, and CIA Special Activities working on assignment to the NCTC."

"Exactly," said Clark. "Which is why you're all here. We don't know how Rafa bin Yasin is getting this information. It could be that he captured and tortured an operator in Afghanistan, maybe, but we have no evidence of that. Our core concern is that there's a mole, someone giving him information that he's passing on to a U.S.-based sleeper cell that's going on to do these killings—justified, in their minds, as a matter of law."

"And Director Foley wants an off-the-books team to root them out," Mandy finished.

"Yes. Us."

Clark rummaged through his briefcase to find a padded envelope. He withdrew two wallets and slid them across the table to Mandy and Gavin. "Attorney General Murray has cleared you two as special agents. Get out to the Hunt murder scene and find our perp. ASAP."

Gavin opened one of the wallets to find his face on an FBI ID next to a gold badge with the Bureau's shield. "Really?" he asked. "You want me out in the field?"

"Yes. We don't know if this mole is human or a remote hack. Mandy knows her way around the Bureau. You'll help her in running down any cyber leads. The Hunt crime scene is a good place to start."

"What about us?" Moore asked, waggling his finger between Midas and himself. "We're backing up the FBI in the U.S. on potential counterterror hits?"

"Midas, you still have your Tajik contact in that neck of the woods? The guy who tracked down that gunrunner?"

"Might take me a minute to find him, Mr. C., but yeah, he retired to the southern side of the Karakoram Range. He used to spend winters in Jhelum, India. I think he's still out there."

"He hates jihadis, right?"

"He hates *firangi*, foreigners who mess with those tribal areas. Rode all the way to Bagram just to volunteer in the fight against foreign ISIS fighters. And he has a special bone to pick with Russians. They killed his wife."

"Roger that. Your job will be to slip into Pakistan undetected, use him as a guide, and link up with our main attacking force."

"Link up," Moore repeated dubiously. "With what attacking force?"

Clark and Ding traded a glance. "An airborne element consisting of you and our two Green Berets. You will seek and destroy Rafa and his band of Umayyad Caliphate warriors, then exfil on the ground, through India, traveling out under civilian cover."

"Okay," Moore replied. "So we have military support for this one?"

"Negative. Zero footprint. Fully deniable op. Completely off-book."

"Then how do we drop into Pakistani Kashmir with enough weapons to take on a well-organized jihadi militia?"

"That's what I need you to figure out, Master Chief."

7

SIRSA, INDIA

JACK FELT A SENSE OF RELIEF UPON NOTICING THAT LISANNE HAD DRIFTED INTO A deep sleep, even though he wasn't entirely accustomed to how her mechanical fingers twitched as she dreamed.

She occupied the window seat in the fourth row of the train's first-class car. Exhausted after their long journey to the U.S. embassy in New Delhi for new passports, followed by a visit to the AGI headquarters in the central business district for replacement tickets, Lisanne had earned some shut-eye. Jack had, too, but he remained wide-awake.

The Italian leather seat was comfortably reclined with an extended footrest and his stomach felt pleasantly settled after lunch in the dining car. The rapid, muffled *ka-thunk* of the train's steel wheels and the vibrating hum of the locomotive somewhere ahead was a dulling drone, and it had been many hours since he'd slept. Despite all that, Jack couldn't relax. He suspected they'd picked up a tail.

He hadn't mentioned it to Lisanne yet. For starters, she needed the healing sleep. Worse, perhaps, he found it illogical that someone would surveil them. The Campus didn't officially exist; they were traveling as legitimate tourists, and India was not a DOA—denied operating area. If he and Lisanne were winding their way through, say, Yemen or Belarus, then maybe he should be more cautious. But this was India, an ally.

And yet—he maintained the sneaking suspicion that the man in the khaki Nehru jacket was following them.

Careful not to wake Lisanne, Jack lowered his electric footrest. He shifted on his hip and slid his new prepaid Android burner phone from his pocket. He'd acquired two devices at a pop-up shop for the local Indian wireless carrier in New Delhi to replace the ones they'd lost.

He opened the Android camera app and aimed the lens at the curved glass above the luggage rails. The darkly tinted sky-view windows reflected the cabin's interior. He tilted the lens until the reflection of a man in an ill-fitting Nehru jacket appeared on his screen.

The suspected surveillant sat three rows back. From this obtuse angle, Jack could only distinguish the top of his head, swathed in dark hair. Nevertheless, Jack was one hundred percent positive it was the same man he'd seen smoking a cigarette at a coffee shop near the embassy gates and, again, standing by a magazine rack in the train station's convenience store. The watcher had never looked at Jack or Lisanne, not once. Yet here he was in the same car, a discreet three rows away. To Jack, that could only mean one thing: tradecraft.

He studied the reflected image on his phone screen, noting the man's finer details. The hair was longish, shoulder-length, not a touch of gray. Though he was undoubtedly a military-aged male, he didn't display the telltale stiffness of military bearing. Based on the tradecraft, Jack was about seventy percent sure the man was an intelligence officer.

He held the remainder in doubt due to the error with the

Nehru jacket, which was out of place in the heat. It seemed improbable that the experienced, murderous bloodhounds of the former KGB, now known dually as the *Federalnaya Sluzhba Bezopasnosti*, or the Federal Security Service (FSB), and the *Sluzhba Vneshney Razvedki*, or the Foreign Intelligence Service (SVR), would make such a mistake. Nor could Jack imagine that the careful officers of the *Guóānbù*, the Chinese Communist Party's Ministry of State Security, would miss that detail.

The Russian and Chinese spies would know better. Then again, he supposed the Indian Intelligence Bureau might be surveilling him. India had its fair share of struggles with jihadi terrorists, whose most infamous act was the chilling, tragic massacre at the Taj Mahal Palace hotel in Mumbai, which claimed the lives of one hundred sixty-six citizens. The world's most populous country would suffer embarrassment if John Patrick Ryan, Jr., became the jihadis' next victim. Under that pretext, it was *possible* that the man three rows back was a guardian angel.

But Jack quickly dismissed that theory as well. Earlier that day, he had read transcripts of IB surveillance reports at the American embassy. While Lisanne processed their new passports in the diplomatic section, Jack slipped out the back for a brief tête-à-tête with the CIA's New Delhi station chief, Suhas Chauhan.

Suhas had a dark complexion, a Saddam Hussein mustache, and fluency in five languages, including Spanish, which made him a Swiss Army knife for the Agency, allowing him to post at stations from Dushanbe to Santiago. He knew nothing about The Campus. However, records indicated that the First Son was cleared to the top. Suhas had also seen Jack and Clark in action in Panama a year before.

Based on that interaction—and a few other rumors—Officer Suhas understood Jack to work directly for Mary Pat Foley as a sometime adviser. Only hours before Jack's arrival in Delhi, the chief of station had received a cable from the Office of the Director of National Intelligence, ODNI, that commanded all officers in Southwest Asia to press on assets for information related to a terrorist suspect named Rafa bin Yasin.

Suhas assumed Jack had something to do with that cable, but being a professional, he was not prepared to bring it up unless Jack did himself. Per Jack's only request, Suhas allowed him to review the CIA's intercepts of IB reporting. He also furnished Jack with a field weapon.

While Lisanne completed diplomatic paperwork in the consular office, Jack found no mention of himself or Lisanne visiting the country. This made sense to him, as the Rai family had arranged the travel on their behalf. Jack could only conclude that the man was likely *not* from the IB. He was determined to learn more.

He tapped the phone's video app and quietly got up from his seat to leave his fiancée undisturbed. With the phone in his left hand, he walked down the swaying aisle toward the dining car, watching brown hills blur by through the panoramic windows.

As expected, the watcher kept his head down as Jack approached. The reading lamp in the man's headrest illuminated a well-worn, soft-covered leather book in his hands. While Jack walked by, he kept the Android's video app rolling.

The dining car was filled with the aromas of cumin and cardamom. Jack overlooked the steaming chafing dishes filled with samosas, tikka masala, and paneer. Instead, he chose a sealed bag of salted plantain chips and returned to his seat.

He didn't bother with a second video surveillance pass. The man in the buttoned-up Nehru was still reading his book, his thick arms resting on a built-in tray. The train's horn sounded off somewhere ahead. The watcher didn't move a muscle. Again, Jack thought, *Tradecraft.*

Jack slid back into his seat, leaving the plantains on his lap. He opened the phone's video album to check out the short film he'd produced, pausing on the frame that showed the surveillant's hands, the book, and the contours of the Nehru coat.

The book was written in a language with squiggly characters that Jack suspected was Hindi. He zoomed in closely on the suit jacket, searching for a bulge that might indicate a weapon. He was unable to detect any incriminating wrinkles.

He tried to open the bag of plantains quietly to avoid disturbing Lisanne, but the stiff Mylar wrapper made a racket. She lifted her head and moved her mechanical fingers. "Hey," she whispered blearily. "You're hungry? Again?"

"Yes. Sorry. I tried to keep it quiet."

"Try harder."

She shifted to the other side of her seat and leaned against the window. Jack ate a few plantains guiltily. After Lisanne closed her eyes again, he fired up the phone for another look at the video. This time, he saw something.

He zoomed in on the freeze-frame of the man's right hand as it held a dirt-smeared page of the dog-eared book. Among the wrinkled, dark-complexioned soft tissue where the suspect's thumb joined the back of his hand, Jack spotted a raised, pink stripe. When he maxed the video app's zoom, he recognized the stripe as a scar from an old wound.

And he knew exactly what had caused that wound. At some point during his training, the man had gripped a semiautomatic pistol too high, letting the slide eject backward and crease his skin.

Jack swallowed a mouthful of chips and leaned close to Lisanne. "Wake up."

She sat rapidly upright. Her mechanical hand balled into a plastic fist. "Just because—"

He put his finger to his mouth and lightly shook his head, projecting a hard stare.

"What?" she whispered, recognizing the look.

"There's a stop in ten minutes," he said softly. "We're getting off."

"Why?"

"We have a tail."

"Who?"

"Three rows behind us. Khaki Nehru jacket. We picked him up in Delhi. I've been worried about him for a while. And then I saw this." Jack showed her the enlarged image of the man's hand.

Like Jack, Lisanne immediately recognized the scar. "Why didn't you say something?"

"I wasn't sure. Until now."

"He might be police—a shadow to keep us safe. Maybe he's private security—working for Daval Rai." She then corrected herself. "But, of course, why wouldn't he just tell us?"

Jack leaned closer to her and told her about his conference with Suhas Chauhan, discounting the notion that he might be with the Indian security service. "I don't know who he works for," Jack concluded. "Let's lose him."

She nodded and checked the digital display that hung from the train's ceiling. "So we get off at the next stop. Ten minutes."

"Yes. If he follows and presents himself as a threat, I'm going to take him."

"What do you mean *take him*? You're not armed."

Jack slowly crossed his leg and raised the cuff of his Levi's. Just above the top of his Blundstone boot was an ankle holster exposing the grip of a snout-nosed Glock 43 pistol.

"Where'd you get that?"

"From Suhas," he replied.

"For the love of God, Jack. We're supposed to be on vacation."

8

TO PUSH HIS FOLLOWER INTO A DECISION, JACK STROLLED TO THE REAR BAGGAGE compartment, while Lisanne moved forward when the train started to brake. Muscling his fiancée's roller bag and backpack free, Jack shot random glances at the watcher, who remained focused on his book.

The doors parted with a whoosh and Jack stepped onto the platform. Humid, smoky air forced him to cough.

While a few passengers stood on the splintered wood platform fifty yards behind him, a crowd huddled against a chain-link fence, clutching a scattered assortment of ragged luggage. Resting on the tracks beyond the sleek, top-of-the-line AGI Express, a dozen rusting trains squealed and clanked in slow motion.

Lisanne strode toward him, her loose blouse fluttering behind her in the hot wind. Jack imagined the watcher's eyes on them and quickly descended the ramp to the station building.

"What on earth is this town?" she asked as they passed beneath a wide mason arch pocked in gray where the stucco had flaked off. Young children perched on the walls to either side chattered and leaped among the branches of a sprawling jujube tree.

"Just keep going," Jack urged.

The station lobby was roughly the size of Jack's gymnasium at

St. Joseph's Middle School, where he had been a star point guard on his eighth-grade team. The station was packed with people, produce carts, and, wherever Jack could find an empty patch of tiled floor, sleeping gray dogs.

He waved at a fly that landed on his nose and angled his shoulder through the crowd, trying to keep his bag from colliding with a dog or a child. Behind him, through the arch, the silver and blue AGI express train shot forward in ghostly silence. A long line of teetering brown boxcars trundled into its place.

"Do you have a plan?" Lisanne asked.

"Working on it."

They faced a sudden gauntlet of Indian vendors. It took mere seconds for the hawkers to spot the two tall Americans, one of whom was a statuesque woman with a black-and-white mechanical arm and striking green eyes. The sellers thrust bunches of cauliflower, carrots, and beetroot before Lisanne like offerings to a queen.

"We're not exactly incognito here," she remarked, waving them away.

"Use your new phone to take a selfie. See if he's back there."

Lisanne paused, dug her phone from her purse, and smiled into it while merchants tugged at her sleeves. "I don't see him."

"Let's keep walking."

Her discouraged entourage fell away as she slipped farther into the bazaar. She stopped at a wobbly cart piled with colorful saris. A woman in her late twenties with bright hazel eyes, high cheekbones, and quick hands draped a flowing garment across Lisanne's shoulders. "I like this," Lisanne said to Jack, trading smiles with the Indian beauty. "I think I should buy it."

Jack shrugged the heavy backpack on his shoulders. "You brought plenty of clothes. That scarf might be the final straw on this camel."

"You really don't understand women," she muttered.

The Indian woman and Lisanne formed a feminine connection, rapidly comparing silks and handily bridging the language with gestures. The merchant offered Lisanne a compact mirror to inspect the scarf on her shoulders.

"I see the watcher," Lisanne said, holding the mirror before her face. "He just passed through the arch by the tree."

"Shit. What's he doing?"

"Scanning the crowd. He just spotted us."

"Should we lose him in the streets?"

Lisanne grinned widely at the Indian woman and opened the translation app on her phone, typing, *Thank you. It's beautiful. I'll take it. How much?* The phone relayed her words in Hindi, and the beauty held up ten graceful fingers.

"Pay her, Jack."

"How much?"

"Whatever her hand signal means. Looks like ten."

"Rupees? That's like . . . twelve cents."

"Well, give her about, I don't know, the equivalent of twenty dollars. I can use the sari to blend in. You need something, too." She noticed a stack of soft fore-and-aft Indian hats called *topis* resting on the cart. Lifting one, she asked the woman how much it cost through her phone. The reply was seven fingers.

"Give her twenty-five bucks. No, forty. I like her. Put the hat on. We should buy you a shirt, too."

Jack handed over a roll of pink rupees without bothering to count them, gauging the value by its thickness. Her hazel eyes sparkling, the woman pocketed the money and examined Lisanne's arm. Lisanne opened and closed the mechanical fingers, causing the young woman to cover her mouth in amazement. After yelping involuntarily, a group of children rushed forward for a closer look.

"Great disguise," Jack said as he extracted her. He forced them through the children with his new hat pulled low. Lisanne covered her hair with the scarf.

Jack found the surveillant leaning against the far wall. He had flanked them, stationing himself with a view of the door. The only good thing about their relative positions was that the watcher remained focused on the arches. "Lis—he's covering the street exit. I don't know if we can catch a cab or a bus. Maybe we take another train?"

"Next express train isn't for hours."

"We could jump on one of those crappy-looking boxcar rigs. They never stop rolling through."

"He'll keep following us."

Jack's face flushed. A thick swarm of flies buzzed near his eyes, his jeans clung to his legs like wet plaster, and this unknown observer had the upper hand. As thoughts of the gun on his ankle crossed his mind, his Irish temper ignited.

"Screw it," he announced. "We're seizing the initiative."

WEARING THE BACKPACK AND DRAGGING THE ROLLER BAG, JACK FOUND THE SOURCE of the buzzing insects when he went to the detached restroom building thirty yards down the sidewalk, which, according to an orange cone, a locked door, and a politely worded English sign, declared it closed since mid-March. A second sign directed patrons to porta-potty stalls in the parking lot.

Jack purposely caught the watcher's attention as he approached the closed building. He disregarded the cones on the cracked sidewalk, stepped over the small plastic barrier, and turned the corner toward the men's room side entrance.

He found the door locked—but only by the knob. Jack whipped out his wallet, selected a sturdy American Express card, and slid it through the doorjamb. The latch bolt sprang loose. Once inside, he shut the door, but didn't lock it.

He gasped at the terrible stench and almost fell in the darkness. The floor was so slippery with grime that he crossed it as if it were an ice rink.

Breathing through his mouth, Jack turned on the lights and surveyed three plastic stalls beside a wall with filthy urinals. One stall was missing a door, and Jack could see that its toilet was gone, exposing a putrid black hole.

The other two stalls seemed functional, but their wobbly doors created a six-inch gap above the floor. Jack examined them more closely and texted Lisanne: Plan A.

Roger, she wrote back. Headed to the Ladies'. One minute out.

With the trap nearly set, Jack rushed through his preparations, occasionally slipping on the floor. When he finished, he settled in to wait as horseflies buzzed around his face. He pondered the conditions on the other side of the wall where Lisanne took her post.

His phone vibrated. Tango headed your pos.

Rog, he texted back. Ready.

He stowed the phone, swiped his hat off his head, and breathed through the fabric. That helped—a little.

A full minute passed before he heard the doorknob click. The door opened slowly and cautiously. A shadow moved under the lights. Jack ditched the hat and listened as the footsteps struggled on the slimy floor.

A tap opened. Water hissed. Jack remained completely still, breathing through his nose as he ignored the flies. The shadow stayed motionless at the center of the room.

THWACK!

The assailant kicked in the bathroom stall door, snapping its hinges free.

A half second later, rapid pistol shots rang out. The bullets crashed into the tile wall, shattering chunks of ceramic that tinkled to the floor like broken glass.

The assailant had fallen for the decoy stall where Jack had positioned his backpack over his spare shoes. Jack jumped from the adjacent stall, where he'd been crouching on the toilet lid, his feet not visible.

He rabbit-punched the would-be killer at the base of his neck with his left hand while seizing the man's pistol barrel with his right, discovering a sizable semiautomatic. Stunned, the man whirled as Jack wrenched the barrel free from his hand.

Though disarmed, the assailant's swift leg snagged Jack's ankles. As he fell backward, Jack struck his head on the floor. Ignoring the sharp pain, he tried to reposition the pistol to slip his finger into the trigger guard.

The long barrel made it a complicated maneuver. Before Jack could aim the gun, the assaulter's knees crashed into his chest, nearly breaking Jack's ribs, pinning him in place.

Now it was Jack who struggled to keep hold of the weapon. He awkwardly gripped the pistol by the slide with his right hand, cursing the oily metal and long barrel.

"*Lis!*" he screamed.

A gunshot rang out, shattering the tile above the grappling men's heads. The assailant flinched just enough for Jack to knock the pistol from their shared grasp. It skittered across the floor before banging against the far wall near the sink pipes.

"*Freeze!*" Lisanne shouted with Jack's smoking Glock 43. She held it before her with her natural hand at the trigger and her mechanical appendage supporting the grip.

The man in the buttoned-up Nehru rolled off Jack, going for his gun.

"*Don't!*" Lisanne barked. She shot again, while Jack lunged for the assaulter's gun, intent on getting there first.

To Jack's surprise, the Indian leaped to his feet. With wild eyes and flashing teeth, he confronted Lisanne and yelled, "*Allahu Akbar!*" as he ripped open his jacket and plunged his hands to his belt.

"*S-vest!*" Lisanne roared.

She fired three times in less than a second, hitting the assassin twice in the forehead and once in the neck. The suicide bomber fell backward, arms flinging free, jacket open, a bloody mess on the wall behind him.

Jack stayed down. Lisanne took a breath.

The calm was short-lived.

It wasn't a suicide vest the man wore but rather a custom-made cotton garment with pockets for spare ammunition clips. Closer to his hips was a wide webbed belt with two dangling metal rods, each with a ring at the top. Lisanne didn't know what they were— until she saw two cylindrical hand grenades rolling on the floor. The bomber had flung them from his belt, where the pins remained attached.

"*Frag out!*" she yelled.

Jack, too, had seen the handheld bombs. They were rounded and black with Cyrillic markings, two and a half inches in diameter.

A month earlier, Ding had briefed the Campus team on Russian-exported RG-60TB thermobaric hand grenades. Ding informed the team that they were appearing all over the world, shipped into Ukraine for use by the Russian army, ending up in the hands of drug cartels, tribal warlords, and suicidal terrorists. When inserted, the grenade's pin was long, extending two to three inches from the top of the cylinder like a pineapple stem.

The grenades rolling on the dirty floor had no such pins because they were still attached to the dead Indian's belt.

"*Down!*" Jack thundered while diving for the armed grenades.

Seizing one in each hand, he lurched to the broken stall and whipped them through the floor hole where the toilet should have been.

A tenth of a second before the grenades landed in the septic sludge, they exploded in midair, priming a cloud of trapped methane gas, quadrupling the blast.

9

WHEN BRIGADIER GENERAL IMRAN KHAN LAST VISITED THE BAN'R MEADOWS, WIN-
ter still held the high-altitude bowl in its grip.

Back in late March, the alpine meadow, nine thousand feet
above sea level, appeared as a flat spot beneath overhanging snow-
drifts on steely gray cliffs. Reaching it from the village of Bheri on
the Dokhot River required a yak ride over icy trails. Twice, the
guides had to remove their hooded burnooses, start a fire, and
warm the animals' faces to melt the frost gathering around their
eyes. Khan often wondered how Mira, the resilient Tajik frontierswoman who led the clan, managed to cross the Hindu Kush passes
so early each year.

Approaching summer now, there was less wondering as the ice
veins transformed into babbling streams and the vertical granite
faces sprouted waterfalls that splashed far below. What had once
been a world of white now displayed a continuous spectrum of
color from deep black shadows to sun-soaked chartreuse and everything in between.

The brigadier stood at the edge of the sparkling meadow, his
hands in the pockets of his thick wool trousers and wearing a long

linen shirt with rolled-up sleeves. Although the thaw was in full swing, the air sweeping over the Hindu Kush felt like a blast from an open freezer. The temperature difference between shade and sunlight was nearly fifty degrees Fahrenheit.

"Aha!" Mira called from across the valley. She had ridden her brown horse while leading a second mount and three donkeys. Each animal's neck was adorned with a woven cord and cowbell.

Leaning against his battered, blue nineties-era Land Rover pickup truck—his personal vehicle—Khan waved in response. Nearby, a dozen children formed a chorus: "Mira! Mira! Mira!" The frontierswoman dismounted, shrugged off her wool shawl, and opened the lids of the woven pannier on the second donkey. She emerged with handfuls of hard candy, taffies obtained from somewhere across the mountains.

The children forgot their soccer balls and gathered to eat in small, squatting groups. The sight warmed Khan's heart for a moment, thinking of his son, Attaf. When that became painful—as it always did—he distracted himself by pulling a wad of bills from his pocket for Mira.

As was her custom, she accepted it without a word, burying the money in her multiple folds of orange, red, and brown fabric. "Will you come for a long visit?" she asked in the pidgin mix of Tajik and Russian that Khan had learned to decipher over the years.

"Three days," he replied.

"*Ochen horosho!*" she exclaimed in Russian.

She summoned a boy of fifteen to pull the bags from the rear of the Rover's pickup. While the adolescent strapped the luggage to the last donkey, Mira shook a finger at the children with the candy, warning them that the general's vehicle was not to be disturbed. She pantomimed a crude gesture that suggested anyone who did touch the truck would have a hand removed. Khan followed the young man to the caravan. The boy held the horse's reins while the brigadier dug his toe into a stirrup, swung his leg over the top, and settled in for the ride.

Khan's horse moved without command, shuffling along the rocky trail like a mining cart on tracks. The path clung to the edge of a vertical gray cliff, reflecting the harsh afternoon sun with a dazzling glare on the white peaks. Frequent stops to allow shepherds leading shaggy karakul sheep to pass reminded Khan that this route, a crossing of the original Silk Road, had been worn flat by human commerce since Alexander the Great. For the brigadier, who led Pakistan's Inter-Services Intelligence Kashmir directorate, the mountains provided an escape from his work. He came to this place because, here, no one knew what he did for a living.

The first stars glimmered over the peaks as the caravan crossed the stacked stone walls that marked the Tajiks' annual summer home. Khan lowered the hood of his burnoose and savored the aroma of roasting mutton while his horse ambled forward on autopilot. A dozen karakul sheep scampered out of the beasts' path.

"*Janerl!*" Yaqoob shouted as they passed through a gate made of rough-hewn timbers anchored to rock piles. Yaqoob always addressed the brigadier by his rank, seemingly the only Urdu word the wiry mountain man knew.

Khan returned the greeting after dismounting, placing his hand over his heart and bowing slightly. The withered, bearded Tajik held the brigadier's hand for several moments, studying Khan's face with hard dark eyes. "You are not well," he concluded in the same cross-border patois.

"No," Khan admitted. "I am not."

"It is good that you came, *Janerl*."

The nomadic mountain man whistled to Mira, who guided the horses to a corral in near darkness. Yaqoob waved his guest through a gap in the masonry wall to enter the *kat*, where mud and stone huts flickered orange in the reflection of the central bonfire, the flames leaping with mutton fat.

Yaqoob's shanty featured a circular ceiling made of inward-leaning timbers covered in a hardened plaster of mud, cloth, and shale. A tin chimney pipe jutted through the roof, hovering over a rocky circle on the ground. The dirt was smooth and compacted around the firestones, where many customers had gathered, probably for centuries, Khan thought. Beyond the cleared area, thick Persian carpets extended unevenly to the stony walls.

Khan had discovered this seasonal alpine *kat* years earlier when it had served as a way station for wild-eyed fighters from Daesh, whom the ISI had funneled into Afghanistan to fight the Americans. At the time, it was his duty with the ISI to do whatever it took to get the Americans to leave Central Asia. In those days, the fighters vied for his arms, training, and money. Now, it seemed, the tables had turned.

"*Janerl*, you rest here, okay?"

Khan settled onto the carpet and let the heat from the rocks at the edge of the glowing coals warm his limbs. That ever-present Yankee word, *okay*, forced him to think of the intelligence he'd shared with his contact at AGI, Fahim. Disconnected here in the mountains, he wasn't sure whether his star agent had been able to spur his half brother into action and pull off the Delhi hit.

"You should take that off," Yaqoob said, tugging on the brigadier's leather pistol belt. "Relax, sahib."

"I'll keep it on," Khan replied, patting the wooden grip of the semiautomatic. Since returning from formal officer training at Sandhurst, the British military academy, Khan had worn the pistol like an anatomical extension of his hip. And besides, though this *kat* was an opium bazaar, it was also a crossroads for Daesh. Only a fool would enter the village unarmed.

"*Sama daa. Sama daa.* You keep it on," Yaqoob agreed. "Chai, *Janerl*? You want tea?"

"No tea."

"*Sama daa.* No chai. Lie down, sahib."

Khan reclined on the dingy pillows, woven in shades of auburn, ocher, and brown. He wadded the borrowed burnoose into a pillow.

"We slaughtered a sheep. Should be ready now. It is better to have something in your stomach. I'll be back."

The brigadier disagreed. In his opinion, the results were better when he smoked on an empty stomach. Lying on his back, he flattened his hand on his heart and spoke to the ceiling timbers. "No food, Yaqoob. Later, maybe."

"*Sama daa, Janerl.* We will get started." The old man backed through the exit.

The brigadier closed his eyes.

Yaqoob returned with silver pots clattering in outstretched arms. Khan rose to an elbow to watch, his mind churning with anticipation.

The Tajik carefully squatted on the carpet, spread out his wares, and massaged a tar ball of *madak*, a thick, dark paste extracted and strained from the residue of boiled poppies. Although there were other ways to prepare opium, Yaqoob preferred the traditional Indian method.

Given the abundance of poppies scattered throughout the nearby fields, the inherent craftsmanship, and intercultural trade, Khan could picture the weary travelers pausing on the old road—Afghans on camels, Uzbeks on donkeys, Indians on elephants, Mongols on yaks.

Yaqoob removed a lump of smoking coal from the dented pewter urn with iron tongs. He blew on the ember until it glowed red and placed it beneath a tarnished chillum. He then leaned close to the floor, continuing to blow. Smoke danced in the firelight. The familiar scent of the melting ball and the chatter of young boys outside the rocky hut sharpened Khan's memories. He allowed himself to think of his son, Attaf, and swallowed hard.

"Not well," Yaqoob muttered with a glance at his customer.

"No."

There was a time when Khan ran the ISI's digital counterintelligence tracking unit in Islamabad. A few days before venturing to this Tajik village, the brigadier had called in a favor at the unit, asking an old friend to track down his son based on information that was two or three years old. The ISI unit was efficient. In two hours, Khan discovered that Attaf was living in Dubai, working at a property development firm that built condominiums.

Khan hadn't seen his son since the boy's mother, Murad, a beautiful Balochi, fled Pakistan for the United Kingdom because Khan beat her. Attaf had been thirteen years old when Murad took him away. Khan didn't know what Attaf was like as a man.

Although Khan had once been loyal to his British brothers in arms, proud of his association to the Commonwealth, he now viewed the United Kingdom as the ultimate betrayer, complicating his efforts to extradite his family to Islamabad.

The ball drooped on the chillum's top plate like an egg in a frying pan. Watching it melt, Khan pulled the satellite phone from his trouser pocket. He glanced at Attaf's texted response for the thirtieth time: Please do not contact me again. I do not consider you to be my father.

"It is ready," Yaqoob announced, his eyes shining under his brimless karakul cap.

The brigadier cupped his lips around the tube and inhaled the smoke. The effect was immediate. As if he had plunged into a thermal pool, a warm sensation flowed through his body, enveloping him. He took another puff and reclined on the dirty pillows, his eyelids lowering, his mind dissolving into an oozy golden glow.

"RISE," GROWLED A VOICE IN THE DARKNESS.

Bewildered, Khan tried to reply. His jaw wouldn't move.

A sinewy hand was clamped over his mouth. "Silence," the Urdu voice commanded in his ear.

The wisp of a long beard tickled Khan's cheek. He could smell the man's breath, reeking of onions. When Khan reached for his pistol, he found the holster empty. There was little he could do. He nodded exaggeratedly.

"The caliph waits."

Four strong hands seized him by the upper arms and jerked him to his feet. The fire had dimmed to a faint glow, but enough light filtered through the cracks around the chimney for Khan to discern their black turbans, long beards, and mountain boon-dockers.

They dragged the brigadier outside. Khan noticed the moon hanging low over the peaks and his breath formed clouds in the thin mountain air. Beyond the stacked stone walls, the sound of hooves scratched the ground. Khan glimpsed four dark horses, their muscles glistening in the starlight.

He was ordered into a saddle. They bound his hands to a metal ring on the pommel with rawhide. A rider flanked Khan, pulling the animal's reins as they ascended the slope.

Braced by the cold air, Khan assessed the situation, realizing what was happening. They were warriors of the Umayyad Caliph-ate, grim recruits from the mountains north of Peshawar, likely taking him to see their leader. They appeared to navigate the dark-ened trail with ease, moving swiftly and silently, their rifles slung across their backs. Of course they did, Khan thought. His own ISI men had trained them to fight in these mountains.

Along with the pistol, they had taken Khan's watch and burnoose. The low moon indicated it was around three in the morning. The brigadier began to shiver.

The lead rider, wearing a bandolier that formed an X across his back, held up a hand and turned. The others followed. They descended a harrowing, shale-strewn path, narrowing to the point that Khan's escort dropped behind him. Khan rode helplessly, sandwiched between the warriors.

After the ten-minute descent, they emerged into a grassy valley, untouched by the sheep and goats that ravaged the more traveled paths. Khan spotted at least twenty horses gorging on the grass, their saddles removed. Men lay among them, flat on their backs or sitting on their haunches around a fire. Khan heard water gurgling and noticed the moon's reflection in a babbling brook.

The lead rider dismounted and signaled to the others. A stern-faced warrior in his thirties marched out of the grass, sporting a beard that reached his eye sockets and wearing a pistol belt with a dagger. He unsheathed the dagger, cut the cords binding Khan to the saddle, and yanked the brigadier roughly to the ground, smashing his hip. The two who had woken him in Yaqoob's hut grabbed him by the shoulders and shoved him to a clearing near the brook, where they forced him to his knees.

"Face to dirt," one of them commanded.

Khan complied, shivering. He was left alone for a while, shaking, but determined not to utter a sound.

"You may look at the caliph," a gruff voice declared from behind him sometime later. "Remain on your knees. Turn around."

Khan pushed himself into a kneeling position and turned. Before him stood Rafa bin Yasin, clad in a dark cape and a black turban that shone like raven's feathers. Below the turban, white eyes glared above an arched nose. He held a polished wooden staff with an ivory medallion at the top.

"Say it," Rafa bin Yasin decreed, tilting his staff forward.

His throat dry, Khan struggled to speak. A boot slammed into his shoulder, a kick from a nearby warrior.

"You will speak the *Shahada* to the caliph!"

"*There is one true caliph. He is the king of the believers, the rightful heir of Muhammad . . .*" Khan stammered through the lengthy Islamic proclamation of faith, as modified by Rafa bin Yasin's Umayyad Caliphate.

Rafa's twitching eyes lowered from the heavens for a moment, taking Khan in. "You follow the caliph's warriors?" he accused.

"No, Caliph."

"You plot against the caliph?"

"No. I equip the caliph's warriors. I train the caliph's glorious army."

"You equip Fahim."

"Fahim, your brother—"

This time the kick landed between Khan's shoulder blades. He fell forward, his face slapping against the dirt. Less than a second later, two sets of hands propelled him upright.

"The caliph's warriors spotted you in Bheri Village. You plot. You seek."

"No, Caliph. You may ask Fahim."

Rafa looked away, as if the mention of his half brother was beneath him. "Why were you in Behir if not to report on the caliph's movements?"

"It is part of my duties."

Rafa sniffed the air like an animal while his eyes roamed over the stars. "The caliph senses a plot," he announced to the night sky. "You will atone."

Khan gasped. He'd personally known two ISI officers who'd

been beheaded by Daesh zealots accused of treachery. "No, Caliph!"

"Allah wills it."

"No! It is not true!" Khan pleaded. "I give the caliph the American names for the *qisas*, fulfilling the Prophet's vengeance."

"Treachery."

"No, Caliph! Only three days ago . . . at Fahim's request, I provided travel information on the great devil father's son, Jack Ryan. That was in offer to the caliph, better than any of the others."

Rafa's eyes returned to the heavens. "The caliph senses a plot."

"Please, Caliph! Tell me why the caliph thinks such a thing!"

"Bring sword," he commanded to one of his men.

"Caliph, no!" Khan screamed. "Why does the caliph believe I betrayed him?"

"Because the devil Ryan knew we were coming."

10

THOUGH SUMMER WAS JUST AROUND THE CORNER, JOHN CLARK HAD DONE ENOUGH airdrops to know to dress warmly.

Standing in the C-17's cargo bay as it flew at thirty thousand feet, Clark wore a pair of thin wool long johns beneath the green Nomex jacket and flight suit provided by the C-17's loadmaster, Air Force Senior Master Sergeant Irv Dupree. Before boarding the Air Force workhorse, Clark, Moore, and the Marine Raider they'd come to visit had sweated their asses off on the blazing tarmac while waiting for the plane to arrive at Camp Lejeune, North Carolina. But now, hurtling through the thin atmosphere, Clark was damn glad he'd layered up.

"Oxygen," Dupree announced, his voice crackling through the ear speakers in Clark's flight helmet. "Depressurizing now."

Clark fitted the oxygen mask in place. It was fed by tubes attached to portable O_2 canisters on his vest. The canned air felt cold and dry.

"Five minutes," Dupree added. He was the most senior loadmaster in the 437th Special Operations Squadron. They were known as the Scorpions and Dupree proudly displayed the unit's patch on his flight jacket, a depiction of the constellation Scorpius with one star highlighted in red for Mars, the Roman god of war.

"Okay, Tom," Kendrick Moore said over the intercom to the Marine. "Please explain to Mr. C. how you get in the RAVEN. Then tell him how you fly and release to free-fall."

"Sure, Master Chief," Buck replied.

Decked out in the full combat load of a Marine Force Special Operations Command (MARSOC)—also known as Raiders—commando, Buck squatted beside an oblong pod resting on the deck in the center of the aircraft's cargo bay. A black parachute rig was strapped to his shoulders; large-dial sensors were strapped to his wrists. He addressed Clark through goggles and an oxygen mask, transmitting via the Bluetooth intercom system.

Buck touched the pod's rounded, carbon-fiber roof. "Okay, Mr. Clark. This unit is the AQ-1 Rigid Air Vehicle Entry Nacelle."

"I know what RAVEN stands for," Clark said. "Skip the tech specs, Staff Sergeant Buck. Just show us how you deploy it."

"Yes, sir," Buck responded. "First, after I buckle in, Loadmaster Irv will pull these pins, freeing the RAVEN for rollback."

Dupree touched the pins and gave a thumbs-up in confirmation.

Staying low, Buck moved to the sleek pod's tapered rear. With its bulbous contours and high-tech composite material, Clark thought the RAVEN resembled the body of a Formula 1 race car. Buck's helmet had an F1 effect as well, with a clear plexiglass face shield that met his O_2 mask at the bridge of his nose.

"Back here," the Raider continued, "Loadmaster Irv will pull additional pins to arm the drag chute release. At that point, from inside the RAVEN, I wait for his green light. When I see it, I'll fire the actuator that will release the drag chute out the back of the aircraft. The drag chute will fill, and the RAVEN will kick straight out, sliding out over the ramp casters."

"Agree with everything he just said," Dupree confirmed. "It's a helluva show watching that thing eject out the back."

"What's the standard operating envelope?" Moore asked.

Buck and Dupree swapped a glance through their clear face shields. "The highest we've tested this is thirty-K. Is that right, Buck?"

"Yes," the Marine confirmed. "We've done one drop at thirty thousand feet. The others have all been closer to twenty."

"Roger that," Clark said. "Please continue. So now you're airborne."

"Right, sir. As soon as I'm over the ramp, I'll cut the drag chute's risers with an internal lever in the cockpit. I wait three seconds for the C-17 to clear. By then, I'm out of its wake turbulence."

"Pilots will initiate a climbing turn," Dupree chimed in. "We want to get the hell out of the way for when the RAVEN lights up. Damn thing will be like a missile coming at us if we don't."

Buck stood to his full height, his short barrel M27 Infantry Automatic Rifle (IAR) dangling at his side. "Exactly. The C-17 will climb as the RAVEN transitions to flight mode. At that point, from inside the cockpit, I'll straighten the folded wings and turn into a glider. Only then do I fire up the engine."

"Does it take long to power up the turbine?"

Buck touched a hatch on the RAVEN's exterior with his boot. "This door opens up and an impeller spins a generator. Air sucks into these intakes beneath the craft. Since the RAVEN is already gliding at high speed, it's a little like a ramjet, jump-started by the craft's forward motion. Takes about thirty seconds."

"Range under powered flight?" Clark asked.

"The RAVEN carries enough jet fuel for two or three hundred miles of flight at three hundred knots."

"Take Mr. C. through the separation procedure," Moore said.

"Sure. When I reach the designated drop zone, I fire the actuators that snap the RAVEN's fuselage apart. You can see the breakaway seams here, Mr. Clark. At that point, I'll be separated from the aircraft. I'll be in free fall at the target altitude. Unless I screwed the pooch."

Clark touched the pod with the toe of his combat boot. "You don't have any trouble fitting in the RAVEN with your chute and combat rig on? Where do you put your rifle?"

"You'll see, sir. It's not a problem."

"And the cockpit controls for this thing?"

"Getting to that, sir." Buck motioned to the Air Force loadmaster. "Hey, Irv, we good to go?"

The loadmaster traded a few words with the pilot and copilot over the aircraft intercom. "You're good, Marine," he announced. "Ramp can come down whenever you're ready." Dupree turned to Clark. "We kill the environmental systems before we lower the ramp to equalize pressures. Like Buck said, he'll get in, I'll lower the ramp, then pull the pins. I'll be harnessed with a tether so I don't fly out the back. But I'll need you two gentlemen to stay strapped to your seats. Pilot's orders."

"No problem," Clark said. "We're just observers."

"All right," Dupree concluded. "We're at thirty thousand feet, a hundred miles east of the Outer Banks. Everyone ready for the show?"

Thumbs up all around. Dupree relayed the "go" message to the cockpit while Buck pressed a button along the RAVEN's edge, opening the hatch. Like suicide doors on an old sedan, the two halves faced each other.

Holding a strap, Clark leaned far over the machine to inspect the RAVEN's interior. He noticed a transparent polycarbonate floor the size of a car windshield. In the front, what the Raider had referred to as the cockpit, the aircraft contained a control stick, a throttle, and two additional levers that Clark believed were related to the winged control surfaces. However, for now, Clark saw no wings. They were folded beneath the vehicle.

Buck stepped into the craft, kneeled, and lowered to his stomach. "As you can see, sir, I've got plenty of room." He tilted sideways to fix his M27 to an articulate harness along his right leg. "The rear cargo area is large enough for a second operator or additional gear that can be rigged for airdrop."

Craning his head to look down the length of the craft's interior behind Buck's boots, Clark didn't envy that second operator. He'd be squished into the pod's rear at the mercy of the pilot. The confined space reminded Clark of an underwater ingress from the torpedo tube of an old Sturgeon-class sub. He shuddered at the memory.

"We're at the center of the MOA," Dupree interrupted. MOA stood for military operations area, a swath over the Atlantic cleared of civilian traffic for military maneuvers, two hundred miles east of the North Carolina coast. Though technically international airspace, it was within the generally accepted boundary of the American air defense identification zone, ADIZ, looked after by NORAD from its bunker in Colorado.

"We ready to launch?" the loadmaster asked Clark.

"Roger that."

Clark and Moore buckled themselves to the webbed nylon seats along the C-17's bulkheads. The two halves of the RAVEN's open hatch came down, sealing Buck in.

The loadmaster and Marine communicated a checklist over the intercom. Once that was complete, Dupree requested permission from the pilot to lower the ramp. After the entire aircrew agreed, Dupree removed the pins, shot Clark a final thumbs-up, secured himself in, and operated a control panel on the bulkhead. The C-17's ramp lowered with a low, grinding groan, revealing a dark blue sky. Frigid wind whipped around the cargo bay.

"I'll see you both at the Camp Lejeune landing site," Buck said over the intercom. "Master Chief Moore, you're still comfortable with that promise you made?"

"Good as gold," Moore replied.

"What promise was that?" Clark asked.

"Tomahawk steak at Madison's if I hit the bull's-eye on the drop marker, sir," Buck responded, his voice a little different now that he was lying on his chest, sealed into a coffin-size pod.

"I'll throw in dessert," Clark added. "Go get 'em, Marine."

A light shifted from red to green inside the wind-buffeted cargo bay. A half second later, a *pop* released a stream of fabric, and the RAVEN shot over the ramp like an artillery shell.

"WELL," CLARK SAID, DROPPING HIS FORK TO HIS PLATE SIX HOURS LATER. "THAT was damn good. I'm stuffed." Beneath the table, he ran a hand over his aching gut, thinking the tall, lukewarm Guinness stout had been a mistake.

He placed the glass on the table and leaned forward. The country music was a little loud in the ceiling speakers, but then again, that made for reasonable concealment for the conversation he and Moore intended to have with their new Marine Raider friend, Tom Buck. Clark couldn't imagine spies out here at a bumpkin place like Madison's, but speaking with audible cover had become a habit.

"What's it feel like when that thing breaks apart around you?" Clark asked Buck, who wore a rodeo-style shirt with curved points on his chest. He was from Wyoming, Clark recalled from their conversation in the rental car while driving over the bridge to Sneads Ferry.

"Mostly, it feels cold and windy," he replied. "About like a HAHO free fall."

A high-altitude, high-opening jump could reach thirty-five thousand feet, but was typically much lower. Clark tried to picture how a RAVEN might operate over the Hindu Kush in Tajikistan's airspace. The aircraft would need to fly over sixteen-thousand-foot peaks for a few hundred miles before ejecting his Campus operatives into free fall.

"Does that RAVEN beat you up at all when you get out?" Moore asked, knife and fork poised over his plate, thinking along similar lines. Moore was two-thirds through the same tomahawk steak Buck had demolished in about nine minutes.

"I'll get to that, Master Chief Moore, but . . ." The Marine glanced at the menu. "Would you fellas mind if I order dessert? It's kind of a big deal at this place."

"That was part of the arrangement," Clark replied, signaling the waitress. "Tomahawk steak and all the trimmings. Dessert counts as trimmings."

The waitress arrived strangling a dishrag stuffed in her belt. When Buck asked her what was good, she told him he was getting the apple pie à la mode, no debate, no questions.

"I'm wondering the same thing," Clark continued when she left. "Do you get thrown around when you exit the RAVEN?"

"Not if you do it right," Buck answered. "When you're at the target altitude and designated coordinates, you reduce to stall speed, yank the nose up, and pull the separator cord."

"Tough maneuver?" Moore asked. "Did you have a hard time mastering the flight skills?"

"Nah. It took a little practice. The separator cord is sort of like the ejection handle in a fighter jet. As soon as you yank it, the rear hatch opens and acts like an air brake. A second later, the front portion of the hatch extends, creating a wind buffer. At that point, you do a push up, and *wham*, you're out. The craft glides away."

"What about running into it? Is that a problem?"

"It could be. Normally, I pass it in a dive, fifty or sixty feet to one side."

"And what ultimately happens to the discarded aircraft?" Clark asked.

"For training purposes, the RAVEN flies back to a designated recovery area. It doesn't have landing gear and deploys a chute for a soft landing. We try to bring her in on the baseball field across from Courthouse Bay. Every now and then, she blows into the water, and the fellas have to retrieve her with the boat. Fortunately, she floats."

"How about for a covert insertion?" Moore asked. "What if the RAVEN can't be recovered?"

Buck mopped up his plate residue with a hunk of sourdough. "If the doors have been popped, she'll explode when her pressure sensors reach two thousand feet. Of course, that's Uncle Sam destroying a two-million-dollar aircraft. So we've never done it."

"And how many RAVEN drops are under your belt?" Clark asked.

"Today makes twenty. You know, they're not at IOC yet, still considered experimental."

Clark glanced at Moore. Utilizing an entry vehicle that wasn't yet at its initial operational capability was a risky gamble. However, Clark and Moore couldn't figure out another way to covertly insert a significant armed force into Pakistan on short notice. "And I understand you're the most qualified man?"

"Actually, Mr. Clark, I'm the *only* qualified man." The Marine's eyes lowered. "You going to eat that, there, Master Chief Moore?"

"No," Moore replied. He forked over the remaining quarter of his steak and dropped it on Buck's plate.

"There was another guy," the Marine continued, a wad of meat in his mouth. "Sergeant Nico Vasquez. But, unfortunately, Nico, he uh . . ."

"We heard," Moore said. "Your CO told us Vasquez died in a RAVEN jump. That doesn't worry you?"

"It worries me—in a healthy way. The whole thing's a matter of preparation and procedure," Buck said, salting the steak. "Nico didn't wait for stall speed. He didn't listen to the training. No disrespect to him. I loved the guy."

The pie arrived with a big lump of vanilla rapidly turning to liquid on the hot, flaky crust. Tom Buck, having consumed forty-six ounces of red meat, two beers, and a russet the size of a football, slid his empty plate aside and attacked the dessert like he hadn't eaten in a week.

Moore and Clark exchanged grins.

They'd gone together to visit Buck's commanding officer that afternoon. The Marine colonel damn near genuflected when the legendary John Clark and the somewhat infamous Kendrick Moore cast their shadows over his desk.

"So, listen, Tom," Clark said. "Kendrick here and I run a little outfit that operates under the authority of the President. Trust me. You've never heard of it."

Buck looked up from the remains of his pie. "I'm sorry? Did you just say the President? As in, you know, the man in the White House?"

"Yeah," Clark replied with a modest grin. "That guy. From time to time, our unit does special missions for him. Zero-footprint ones in denied areas, where nobody's the wiser."

"Roger that, sir. I've participated in dark hits. Syria, Africa."

"I know you have. Your CO went over your record. And, well,

between us, Mr. Buck, I'll tell you that we're working on a dark hit right now. The entry's a bitch—going into a denied area in a political hot zone, if you know what I mean. We could use a pair of RAVENs, two men in each one. That also means, naturally, that we could use you."

Buck shoved a napkin around his mouth and narrowed his eyes. "I'm a little lost, Mr. Clark. I'm an active-duty Marine. Are you saying I have orders?"

"You're more than an active-duty Marine," Clark returned. "You're also a Raider, which means you live up to two mottos—*spiritus invictus*, unconquerable spirit, and *semper fi*, always faithful. And you're the only guy who flies RAVENs. Simply put, we need you."

"That's fine, sir," Buck replied. "I'm honored. Happy to help. I'm just not sure how this works. Does that mean I have orders from Raider Command?"

"Oh, better than that, Staff Sergeant Buck. You have orders from the commander in chief."

11

WHILE JOHN CLARK AND KENDRICK MOORE FINISHED THEIR EARLY DINNER, THREE time zones to the west, Gavin Biery and Mandy Cobb gulped down a late lunch at Claudia's Clarkston Café, where, according to the menu slogan, the good times never stop.

The proprietor, Claudia, bumped her ample hips against the booth's Formica table and slid the check under a glass. "Whenever you're ready, folks."

"You take cash?" Gavin asked.

That was a question Claudia had never fielded. Who didn't take cash? "As long as it's enough," she gamely replied.

She didn't expect much of a tip from these two. She'd hoped they were businesspeople with an expense account. But the cash comment worried her—especially since they seemed a bit off.

The man, a chubby, bearded ginger, seemed nice enough. But the woman, a cute blonde with an attitude, had stuck to a salad and lemon water while poring over papers in a manila file. She was big city all the way, or, at least, wished she was. Probably county workers, Claudia guessed. And, in her opinion, county workers were cheapskates.

"I've got it," Gavin announced when Claudia sauntered away. He covered the bill with two Andrew Jacksons.

"You know," Mandy replied, her blue eyes rising from her salad. "It's not like paying with your regular Hendley credit card would break cover. Not at a place like this."

They were seated near the front door, which just so happened to spring open with a ringing bell as a pair of ranchers walked through it. Gavin waited until they passed before going on.

"I don't believe in credit cards."

"No? Not at all? Even for personal use?"

"No. Not a chance."

"Not a chance?"

"No," he confirmed. "Cash is how I roll."

"Hmm," Mandy muttered, her eyebrows compressed.

It was the fourth time Gavin had noticed that verbal shrug since they met at Reagan National for the red-eye to Seattle the night before. The Campus info-tech specialist wasn't sure what to make of it. It was either an expression of genuine interest—or, perhaps, disdain.

The latter, which he increasingly considered the more likely candidate, worried him. Mandy Cobb was an attractive female, generally emblematic of the type he wished to pursue romantically. And for that reason, he'd resolved to conduct himself in a manner that would spark fewer of those *hmms*, thinking of it as practice.

Setting those dynamics aside, since this was a professional conversation with a genuine former FBI special agent, he felt compelled to explain himself to her. "Mandy, credit card numbers end up in a massive database that gets sold to criminal hackers worldwide. If this mole we're hunting has any sense, he'll purchase a large chunk of those numbers here in Clarkston to find out who's on the case. That could expose The Campus. I won't allow that to happen. So I stick to cash."

She sipped her lemon water, unblinking. "This isn't about the dark web again, is it?"

Sensing another *hmm* on the way, Gavin changed the subject. "You look like you're done."

"Yes. Iceberg lettuce, red onion, and French dressing weren't exactly what I had in mind for an entrée salad described as 'the Parisian.'"

He sucked down what was left of his Diet Coke. "Let's bounce. We can grab a snack on our way to the crime scene."

Mandy checked her watch. "Not sure we have time for that. It's twenty miles from here, country roads, middle of nowhere."

"No choice, then. Our new ride has an empty tank."

"*Hmm*," she uttered, sliding from the booth.

Gavin was still pondering that response as he struggled with the loose steering of their cover vehicle, a white 2008 Ford F-250 with black wheels, glass-pack exhausts, and thick Goodyear mudders.

"I saw a gas station near the bridge," he mentioned.

Mandy stared at the dusty shops passing by. "Third fill-up. Terrible mileage."

"It'll be quick."

The truck had sparked a controversy between the two Campus operatives during the flight. Somewhere over the farm belt, Mandy told Gavin she would requisition a vehicle from the Bureau's Seattle district office, which she intended to visit before crossing the state to Clarkston.

Gavin, a backstage participant in many undercover Campus operations, argued that an FBI sedan was a suboptimal way to operate undercover in rural, eastern Washington, and vowed to develop something better. She ignored him and went to sleep.

If for no other reason than to demonstrate his resourcefulness, he jumped on the in-flight Wi-Fi and bought a cover vehicle on the dark web's equivalent of Craigslist. To complete the transaction, he utilized a Campus crypto expense account funded by Gerry Hendley's business, which Gavin personally managed. The Ford cost a mere eight grand, a rounding error for Campus ops. He chose not to explain all that to Mandy while she slept.

When the pair left the Seattle terminal, Gavin located the vehicle in the parking lot near the ride-share-app pickup area. He slyly opened the door and found the keys under a floor mat, thinking himself pretty damned cool.

"What the hell is this?" Mandy asked. She'd been about to order an Uber for the transit to the FBI's Seattle district office.

"Our ride," Gavin answered, as if this were his standard operating procedure.

While he fired the engine and cranked the AC, Mandy rolled her eyes. He suspected there may have been another *hmm*, but the engine was too loud to hear it.

"That's Cole Hunt's property," Mandy announced with a glance at her GPS twenty miles outside of Clarkston. "Turn there, at the break in the barbed wire."

Gavin wrestled with the wheel as the truck bounced over the ruts of the long driveway. When he braked, sending up a cloud of dust, an older man in a plaid shirt, jeans, and a cowboy hat stood up from a folding chair next to a green Ram police vehicle. The lawman approached the Ford with his hand resting on his pistol, accompanied by a black Labrador retriever at his side.

"See that?" Gavin crowed as he manually cranked the pickup's window down. "He doesn't think we're from the Bureau."

The dog barked and snarled. "Please step out of the vehicle," the sheriff commanded gruffly. "Let's go. Out. Both of you."

Mandy hurriedly flashed her FBI creds with one hand, her other raised with an open palm. "It's us, Sheriff Whitcomb! The special agents from D.C. We talked to your dispatcher, Dot!"

Gavin, too nervous to move, asked the lawman if he could retrieve his wallet from his jeans to get his ID. Surveying the inside of the vehicle carefully, Whitcomb agreed. The dog continued growling.

The sheriff studied the badges and ID cards while his Lab sniffed the pickup's tires. "Sorry, folks," he said as he returned the wallets. "Your vehicle had me on high alert."

"Because it doesn't look like a standard FBI ride, right?" Gavin asked triumphantly.

"No. Because this rig belonged to Harold Wagner. He reported it stolen two years ago. Car theft rings around here send them to the other half of the state."

Mandy cracked a wide grin. "Special Agent Gavin Biery, here, is a better cop than he realizes."

12

THE AFTERNOON SUN WAS BRIGHT AND HOT, BAKING THE PARCHED YELLOW HILLS
that rose above the Asotin Creek valley.

The sheriff showed the two FBI agents the main points of the
property. Mandy shielded her eyes with her hand and studied the
ruined barn and intact farmhouse. "What's the current state of
this crime scene?" she asked.

The lawman tugged a broken biscuit from his pocket and tossed
it on the ground for his dog. "I imagine you know your FBI evidence techs have been all over the house," he addressed her. "I'm
sure you talked to the special agent in charge over in Seattle,
Kevin Zaletsky."

Mandy had done just that. A memo from Dan Murray's office
told Zaletsky to make all evidence available to the visiting agents.

"Yes," Mandy answered. "I looked through the crime scene
documents."

"Not a lot in there, was there?" the sheriff asked, absently
rubbing the dog's ears.

"No. For a rural hit on a whole family, it looks to be a surprisingly sterile scene."

"Yeah. Whoever this killer was, he didn't leave a legible footprint, tire tread, hair sample . . . nothing. Bastard knew what he was doing."

"Still," Mandy continued, snapping latex gloves over her hands. "I'd like a tour of the house."

"Follow me, ma'am."

Luna laid down on the porch as they got ready to go inside, resting her chin on her paws. "That's what she does," the lawman said. "Never goes inside the house or barn. It's like she knows something evil was here."

"Just as well," Mandy said. "We need to keep the scene sterile."

They squatted on the porch steps and put booties over their shoes before entering.

"Front door wasn't broken," Mandy noted. "And that looks like a smart lock?"

"Yes," the sheriff replied. "Smart locks on front, side, and back doors. This one was sprung."

Gavin bent to examine the glossy plastic touch pad. "Did someone dust it for prints? Maybe the killer knew the code."

"Yes, dusted," Whitcomb confirmed. "Nothing but family fingerprints. The prevailing theory is that Hunt left the door unlocked. As you can see, it's the quickest route to the driveway and barn—it probably got a lot of use."

Mandy was already looking at the upper corner of the beadboard soffit over the porch. "That security camera's aimed right at the front door."

"Yup. Five of them on the property," the sheriff noted. "They're from a company called Skylo. The cameras all use long-duration batteries."

"I saw the Skylo analysis in the Bureau's paperwork," Mandy stated. "I just didn't expect to see the camera so close to the door."

"Well, ma'am, I'm sure you also saw that the warrant for Skylo's cloud security footage didn't yield anything. Driveway . . . barn . . . house . . . nothing. Internet was out."

Gavin withdrew his phone. "There's no cell signal out here. But Wi-Fi's good. Mind if I look at the router?"

"It's over there, by the dining room."

The house was stuffy and warm from the afternoon heat. "We've kept the air-conditioning off," the sheriff explained. "For fear of disturbing fibers and whatnot. The home is exactly as it was when we found it."

"Good," Mandy said.

The kitchen was typical of a busy American household with two children. It appeared well-ordered, in line with Hunt's military background. Mandy took in the pantry and drawers. She inspected the sink and dishwasher while Gavin wandered over to a corner.

"I count eight steak knives. The big knife missing from the block is in the dishwasher."

"Correct," the sheriff said. "All the cutlery's accounted for."

"Can I see the gun safe?" she asked.

"This way."

They walked through a family room with a sectional sofa and a flat-screen, then into a back den that seemed to be Cole's study. Gavin noticed the books on cattle farming, a keyboard, and a monitor. The family's two laptop computers were already back in D.C. undergoing forensic data analysis, searching for anything that might indicate contact with a killer.

Gavin didn't much care for that arrangement, as he preferred to dig into the laptops himself. But the Bureau had beaten him to it.

The sheriff pointed out the five-foot-tall gun safe bolted to the wall. Like the smart lock on the front door, the safe had a touch keypad.

"This was dusted for prints, too," the sheriff told them, stating the obvious. "We put a call through to the company, Surelock. They gave us a break-in code." Whitcomb swung the heavy metal door open with a creak.

Mandy and Gavin examined the safe's contents—an AR-15 assault rifle, a 12-gauge, and an empty foam-core cutout for a pistol. Several boxes of shotgun shells rested on the top metal shelf.

The sheriff gestured to the cutout. "Matches a nine-millimeter SIG Sauer. The AR uses five-five-six. The spent rounds we found in the barn were seven-six-two."

"I saw that in the report," Mandy said. "The evidence techs didn't mention a search on the property for the missing pistol. Have you looked for it?"

"Not extensively," the sheriff admitted. "Your SAC ordered me to preserve the crime scene. A detailed look in the house would screw that up."

"That's fair. Let's check out the bedrooms."

They looked through the parents' master first, finding regular sheets, pillows, and a comforter. On the nightstand, another ranching book, this one on animal husbandry, lay face down. Mrs. Hunt, in contrast, had been reading a popular historical fiction novel about female British spies in World War II. Mandy had finished it three months ago.

"No sign of a struggle," she observed.

"Yeah. That's the thing that has us stumped," the sheriff said. "I didn't know Cole Hunt, but he was ex-military, owned an arsenal, and was tough enough to figure he could make it out here as a cowboy. How does a guy like that not put up a helluva fight?"

The upstairs room was deathly warm and airless. Feeling his forehead dampen with sweat, Gavin stood near the closed window, checking the Wi-Fi signal. There was a radio signal that told him the home's Wi-Fi router was still active, but it didn't connect to the internet.

"Why no internet?" he asked the sheriff.

"This area is served by the cable company for data service. The co-ax wire that runs into the house was cut just below the junction box near the home's foundation. That's why the cameras didn't work. Killers knew where to find that wire."

Mandy chimed in. "According to the Bureau's write-up, the killers likely came from behind the property, cut the wire, and entered the open door."

"The Bureau took my analysis, then," the sheriff noted. "Mighty nice of them."

Gavin studied his phone for another few seconds, then checked the home's rear approach through the window. Across the roofline, he could make out the back of the property, which led to the cottonwood trees that marked Asotin Creek. Yellow hills rose beyond the creek, where Hunt's small herd of cattle scattered.

"Let's check out the other rooms," Mandy prompted. She walked down the hall until, a moment later, she stood at the entrance to the girl's bedroom and placed her hands on her hips.

"Her name was Maddie Hunt," the sheriff said over Mandy's shoulder. "Top of her eighth-grade class at Lincoln Middle School."

Mandy surveyed the pink bedding, walls covered with Taylor Swift posters, and colorful soccer ribbons from a Coronado, California, league. She entered the room, squatted, and poked through the sheets with the back of her pen.

Gavin went to the girl's desk, which had an algebra book open and a half-scrawled homework sheet. Next to it, he saw a keyboard and monitor.

"Hey," Gavin said to the sheriff. "I saw landline phones in the kitchen and den. Are they connected?"

"They are," the lawman replied. "As you mentioned, Special Agent Biery, cell signal is nada out here. Most folks still have landlines."

"Still, everyone has a cell phone," Gavin said. "Did you check Hunt's vehicle?"

"His truck was torched in the barn. But so far, no phone. I did a little more digging and couldn't find a record of a cell phone billing account for Hunt. I thought that strange at first, but since learning a little about his background as a SEAL and all, maybe not. Could be that he worried about being found. That also explains why there were no social media accounts."

Mandy nodded. In a cooperative agreement with the Asotin County Sheriff's Office, the Bureau had briefed Mitch Whitcomb on Hunt's history as an operator, omitting details of his POSEIDON SPEAR involvement.

"Surprised he didn't try to live off the grid altogether," she added. "Or change his name."

"You have children, Special Agent Cobb?" the sheriff asked.

"No, sir."

"Well, miss, I raised three girls. And let me tell you, teenaged girls don't let you live off the grid. Maddie Hunt was fourteen."

"Fair enough. Let's go check out Robbie Hunt's room."

While Mandy and the sheriff went to the home's third bedroom, Gavin stayed planted where he was next to the girl's desk and half-finished homework.

Like Mandy, Gavin had no children. He did, however, have a sister, Amelia, who was ten years his junior and born smack in the middle of the smartphone generation. As Gavin recalled, Meely couldn't go five seconds without looking at the damned thing.

No, he corrected himself. *Three seconds.*

In Gavin's opinion, the sheriff was onto something. He couldn't imagine Maddie Hunt would let this family live *completely* off-grid. Cole Hunt might have been a tier-one operator, trained to kill. But his skills as a badass would stop short of preventing a fourteen-year-old girl from staying connected with her friends.

With that in mind, Gavin pulled his phone from his pocket and fired up a sniffer app he'd built for The Campus. The app was designed for field operatives to pick off the unique identifiers of bad guys' cell phones. Whenever John Clark's people were out on an op, they ran the sniffer and returned with radio metadata from the suspects' devices. Gavin would then run that metadata through the local wireless provider to acquire the call records, which he then fed back to the Campus operatives.

In this case, stuck out here in a valley, the Hunt residence had no wireless signal from a carrier. But Maddie Hunt went to Lincoln Middle School in Clarkston every day by bus. As Gavin saw it, there was no way that this poor girl with the Taylor Swift posters and soccer ribbons went a day without a cell phone.

If he was right, she would have stashed a prepaid phone somewhere in her room. If she were anything like his sister, Amelia, she would leave the phone's wireless radio running so it would come to life with messages when the bus neared town. The phone's Wi-Fi network would give the girl extra incentive to leave the phone powered up.

Sure enough, the sniffer app pointed to the closet. It took Gavin thirty seconds to find the prepaid Android with a hunch-backed extended battery cover tucked in the sleeve pocket of a binder on the floor.

Knowing the greedy FBI agents would yank this back to the J. Edgar Hoover Building if they found it, Gavin slid the phone into his jeans pocket.

13

AMRITSAR, INDIA

BY THE TIME JACK AND LISANNE ENTERED THE NORTHWESTERN INDIAN TOWN OF Amritsar, the moon had completed its long arc over the broad Punjab plain, disappeared on the other side of the earth, and risen yet again.

Riding in the tail end of a clanking, northbound cargo train, Jack hoisted his filthy backpack onto his shoulders. While the boxcar's steel wheels growled and moaned, he extended his hand to help Lisanne to her feet.

"Next station, Amritsar," he said in a near shout. "We just passed a lit sign."

Lisanne poked her head out the open sliding cargo door. She pointed her face into the warm, gritty night wind, her hair streaming behind her like a flag. "Damn it," she cursed.

"What?"

"The train's not going to stop."

"Say again?"

She realized she would have to yell, as Jack's ears had been ringing since the suicide bomber's blast. "I don't think it's going to stop!"

Jack closed his eyes. He felt a sneeze coming on.

Wiping his nose after a bodily paroxysm of three sneezes, he surveyed the dusty jute sacks piled at the rear of the boxcar, their textures strobing in the moonlight. For the past five hours, the burlap heaps had at least provided a cushion for his aching body, allowing him to drift off—but the airborne fibers wreaked havoc on his respiratory system. He sneezed again.

"We're going to have to jump," Lisanne hollered, her natural and mechanical hands cupped at her mouth to project her voice.

Jack nodded sadly, already missing this boxcar.

The long ride had given him time to reflect on the suicide bomber, concluding that they had only survived because of the restroom's dilapidated state. Its masonry shattered to dust when the grenades exploded beneath the floor, releasing air pressure that hurled Jack and Lisanne twenty feet backward. They landed in the surrounding shrubbery, along with a maelstrom of shattered sinks, toilets, and human waste—a literal shitstorm.

Losing Lisanne's luggage, but recovering Jack's backpack, they quickly stumbled to the other side of the tracks to hop on the first cargo train they could find.

Unfortunately, that train rattled southeast into the Punjabi interior—the opposite direction from Srini's wedding. To reverse course, the couple suffered through a half dozen rides that wasted an entire day. On the bright side, they caught up on their rest. They still had their short-barreled CIA Glock, and the confused ride had been the mother of all surveillance-avoidance routes. If the Indian police even knew to look for the two Americans, they would have no idea where they'd gone.

"That looks like a soft spot coming up," Lisanne yelled over the echoing wheels. "At least it's between the other stopped trains."

Jack nodded like a mule. "You call it! And be careful with your arm!"

She ignored his warning—because he gave so many—and counted down from three with her mechanical fingers.

When her hand closed in a polycarbonate fist, Jack tossed his rucksack onto the dirt. Ever the gentleman, he gestured for Lisanne to go first. In the pale moonlight, he watched her hit the ground like a paratrooper, roll, and snap to her feet. A hundred feet on, Jack leaped, hoping to perform the maneuver as deftly as his fiancée.

He did not.

A FEW HOURS LATER, HIS KNEE STILL SMARTING, JACK LED LISANNE TO THE TALL black gates fronting the walled compound owned by Daval Rai, Srini's father. Two handsome men in pressed short-sleeve shirts, pleated Gurkha trousers, and crimson Sikh turbans eyed the couple as if spotting Mongols from the Asian steppe come to sack their king.

"Stop right there," the first man commanded with a raised hand. His accent was somewhere between Indian and English. The sentry behind him unslung an exotic black automatic weapon that Jack recognized as a Heckler & Koch MP7 machine pistol. A flashlight beam swept over them like a searchlight on a prison wall.

Lisanne and Jack raised their arms. "We're guests," Lisanne announced.

The beam lingered on her plastic forearm and mechanical hand. "It's a prosthetic. I'm Lisanne Robertson—a patient of Srini Rai. This is my fiancé, Jack Ryan. Junior. We're here for the wedding."

The beam lowered. "I am so very sorry, madame," the guard replied, his voice lilting pleasantly. "Are you quite all right?"

"Yes. We're fine. But we're late. Can we go in?"

"We'll drive you, of course."

Despite strenuous efforts at washing, the couple stank. With military decorum befitting a palace guard, the lead Sikh breathed through his mouth without comment as he led them to the back seat of a Land Rover Defender.

The gates parted to a view of palm trees glowing in the landscape lighting. When the road curved, Jack spotted a broad building with three stacks of glowing pink arches. The walls came together at the arch apexes, much like an inverted heart, which, to Jack's mind, conjured images of the Middle East.

Lisanne had informed him that Daval Rai's residence was the former palace of Maharaja Gulab Singh, built in the mid-eighteenth century. During the Anglo-Sikh War in 1846, the Sikh king shifted his allegiance to the British, who many years later transformed the property into a social club with polo grounds, clay tennis courts, and an Olympic swimming pool.

As Jack took in the enormous pink mansion, an explosion of white glitter blossomed over the highest set of arches, followed by bursts of pink and blue. A moment later, thunderous booms pierced the air.

"Fireworks?" he asked the driver. "What's that about?"

"The *sangeet*, sir," the turbaned man said from behind the wheel. "It is just beginning."

"The what?"

A radio buried in the Rover's dash erupted in a fast-moving, singsong language. The driver responded with the word *hām* several times before angling his bearded mouth to his passengers. "We must hurry," he said with a glance in the rearview. "And— well, I don't mean to offend, you, sahib, madam—but I suggested to them that you both require a bath."

The Rover came to a stop in a gravel parking lot. Like battlefield medics, an army of servants in white uniforms hurried Jack and Lisanne into a circular marble reception hall. Matching staircases with thick balusters rose on either side. Four men guided

Jack up the staircase to the left, while a group of women ushered Lisanne in the opposite direction.

"Hey!" Jack barked as she disappeared behind a marble column. "What?"

"We need to check in with Mr. C.—let him know what happened, you know, in case there are questions."

"No time!" she cried just before disappearing behind a column. "After the *sangeet*!"

Murmuring encouragement, the four men led Jack to a marble bathroom, where he was carefully and meticulously stripped. The head usher carried the American's stiff clothing away as though ridding the building of a rotting carcass. The remaining three conducted him to a steaming pool of foamy water between two Ionian columns the size of sequoia trunks. After Jack eased himself into the hot, soapy bath, his helpers knelt on the cold white stone to scrub their visitor with long-handled brushes.

"Thank you," Jack protested. "I can do this myself."

"No time, sahib," the lead man rebutted. "We must ready you for the *sangeet*."

Jack winced at the raw bristles at work on his back. "What is the *sangeet*?"

"The reception, sahib. As a member of the honorary party, we must dress you."

"Our clothes were ruined on our way up here. We lost most of our luggage."

"No problem, sahib. Balnoor has arranged your costumes. Now please, submerge, sir. We must wash your hair."

After drying him, the attendants clad Jack in soft, golden jodhpur pants topped by a matching, heavily embroidered sherwani coat that fell just below his knees. His scrubbed bare feet were slid into embroidered blue slippers while one of the servants slicked back his hair with pomade. Finally, as though crowning him a bishop, they placed a yellow turban on his head, draped his shoulders with a maroon sash, sprayed him with cologne, and led him downstairs. He had no idea what had become of Lisanne.

Neither did the twenty gentlemen who greeted him in the courtyard, mingling on a wide field of stone pavers surrounding a gurgling fountain. Half the men wore Sikh turbans like Jack, while the other half had thick black hair greased flat. They wore the same brocaded gold sherwani as Jack, except for the groom, Sanjay, whose coat was pink with wild loops of red embroidery.

"You made it," Sanjay said with an extended hand and a smile. Educated at Yale, he spoke with an accent that was almost British. "I heard you got lost on the rails. So sorry for your troubles."

Another burst of fireworks snapped overhead, strobing them in pink.

"Yes," Jack said over the airborne explosions. "Apologies for being late. Where's Lisanne?"

"She's with the women. We were just discussing the parade later this week. What animal would you prefer, Jack?"

The fireworks boomed overhead. "I'm sorry?" he called, a little louder than necessary.

"I know you've traveled extensively. Are you more of a horse or a camel man?"

Jack cursed the ringing in his ears. "Am I what?"

Before Sanjay could repeat himself, the groom was summoned away in preparation for a ceremony. Meanwhile, Jack was sucked into a crowd of male guests in elegant Western suits. Waiters passed by with trays of food. His stomach churning, he found the buffet table and piled a plate. He slunk to a corner, avoided eye contact, and ate like a trapped animal.

He was forced to abandon his plate when the other groomsmen approached him, nineteen in all. Roughly a third introduced themselves as friends from Texas who'd flown in a day or two before. Sipping champagne, Jack talked about Texas with them, nearly relaxing, until two strong hands seized his shoulders and turned him, spilling his champagne.

"So this is the famous Jack Ryan!" boomed a thick voice. "Junior, that is!"

Jack faced a bearded man in his late sixties. He wore a bright red turban with a silver clasp where the fabric folds came together. A midnight-blue, ankle-length sherwani divided by a silky red sash completed his look.

"Daval Rai," the man announced with courtly grace. "A pleasure to meet you, my friend." Though six inches shorter, the tycoon doubled Jack's weight. He pulled the American into a strong embrace, then released him with a double clap to the shoulders.

"The pleasure is mine," Jack returned as the other groomsmen scattered to the shadows. "Your house is magnificent, Mr. Rai. I'm overwhelmed with the splendor, I must say."

Rai rolled his head around his thick neck as if noticing the flashing fireworks, tropical landscaping, three-tiered fountain, and towering mansion for the first time. "Oh, this. We don't come up here much. It's a useful compound for the wedding, I suppose. Srini insisted on it, of course, as did my wife, Reena. Otherwise, it's a rather boring place. Now. What's all this about you getting lost on my railroad yesterday?"

As Jack formed his rehearsed reply to that question, a live band strummed to life on a stage in the courtyard's corner, easing into a twangy melody of sitars and sarods.

"So what happened?" Rai asked again, louder.

Jack plodded through the cover story he and Lisanne had concocted, suggesting they'd exited the train for a shopping excursion in an unnamed town before getting lost in the streets on a rickshaw that crashed into a porta-potty.

"Horrendous," the tycoon said, his bulbous nose wrinkled.

"Well. Your first experience in India was inauspicious, but you are my honored guest now. That's the important thing. Oh! Someone here for you to meet. My chief operating officer, Fahim Bajwa."

Rai ushered Jack to the side of a smooth-shaven man in a well-tailored black suit, an open-necked silk shirt, and hair pulled into a sleek bun. He was regally tall with a long, straight nose. For all that, Jack was quickly distracted from his assessment of the man. One of the most beautiful women he'd ever seen clung to Fahim's elbow, sparkling in an elegant sequined dress, her auburn hair piled on her head, her green eyes smoldering.

"Jack," Daval Rai said, "meet our great bridge builder, Pontifex Maximus, though not the one in the Vatican. And this is . . ."

"I am Ilona," the woman offered with a Slavic accent and a smile as broad and bright as a sunrise. Jack returned the greeting, then shook hands with Fahim.

"Ilona, darling," the COO said. "Would you please carve us a niche at the front of the crowd?" He turned to Jack. "We're both great fans of the choreographed *sangeet* dance. Ilona has never seen one." Taking the cue, his European date glided off with the grace of a manta ray.

"Where did you find her?" Rai asked, transfixed by the woman's backless dress.

"Budapest."

Rai nudged Jack with an elbow. "As COO, Fahim is our great jet-setter, overseeing grand civil engineering projects from Kathmandu to Caracas. Yet somehow, every time he comes back to India, he brings a new souvenir. Oh, to be single again."

The COO laughed pleasantly. "Now, Jack," he said. "I understand you ran into some trouble. Our security men reported that you and your fiancée were rather . . . ripe."

Jack ran through his story a second time. While he spoke, Fahim Bajwa's steady unblinking eyes compelled Jack to add one detail after another. The rickshaw driver was a teenager in this version; the driver lost control of the vehicle on a hill; the porta-potties were at a construction site that blocked the road.

"Oh my," Fahim said flatly. "And what town was this?"

"I don't remember the name."

"A pity. If you recall it, let me know. I should like to have our people update the signage. And you said you stopped by your embassy. Why was that?"

"Passports," Jack replied. "We lost ours at the airport."

"Lost them? Well. You've had a rough go all around, haven't you? I am so sorry, Mr. Ryan. But now that you're settled—where are you staying, may I ask?"

"He's in Phula Mahila," Rai answered. "Reena picked it out for our honored guests. Jack, here, is engaged to Lisanne." He winked at Jack. "Phula Mahila is the most romantic guesthouse on the property. Have you set a date for your wedding yet?"

"No," Jack replied. "Working on it."

"Speaking of working on things, Daval," Fahim cut in, "I just picked up a report from the project team at the Karakoram Gorge. The bridge will be ready, they assure me."

"Excellent!" Rai boomed. Forgetting himself, he interrogated his COO on a dozen project details. Lost in the minutiae, Jack allowed his eyes to wander over the crowd. The backless beauty glanced over at him with a sultry grin that gave him a chill.

"Forgive me," Fahim said to Jack. "We shouldn't be talking business in front of you. But Sanjay mentioned you're an investor with Hendley Associates."

"Yes. That's right."

"Then you can appreciate the urgency of a major capital outlay."

"Of course I do."

"Fahim runs all of our construction projects," Rai explained. "He and I both have a special passion for bridges—though *he*, brilliant engineer that he is, has earned the nickname Pontifex Maximus."

"Stop that, Daval," Fahim intoned with a mild grin. "I'm not quite infallible."

"Perhaps you are! The Karakoram Gorge could not be crossed by anyone else!" The tycoon turned to Jack as the music rattled seductively. "Oh look, the ladies are coming in for the dance."

The twanging strings gave way to thumping tabla drums and rattling kanjira tambourines. A chorus of flutes punctuated by the sharp notes of a clarinet-like instrument fell in line with the drums.

The women sashayed and clapped in a festive march across the stone. Nineteen paraded in front of Srini, the bride, who glowed in a maroon and gold gown fit for a princess. Her bridesmaids' midriffs were bare, their hands henna-painted, their foreheads elaborately adorned with jewels. To Jack's amazement, he spotted Lisanne as the tallest among them, dancing as if she'd rehearsed for weeks, her natural arm covered in an intricate henna Mehndi.

"Your fiancée moves gracefully," Fahim said over the music, forcing Jack to wonder how the COO knew which of the women was Lisanne. But then he added, "Srini is a brilliant surgeon. Lisanne's arm is a work of art."

The women gyrated toward the groomsmen, seeking their respective partners and tugging at their wrists. Lisanne's eyes were painted into sharp dark points, beckoning Jack forward. Struggling to recall the YouTube video she had made him watch to practice the choreographed dance, he grasped her hand and took a few steps forward.

"You look amazing," he whispered close to her ear.

"Thank you," she replied, pushing him back to his position. "Dance, Jack, come on."

Painfully aware of his aching knee and distorted hearing, Jack attempted the moves in imitation of the women in front of him. He clapped when they clapped, kicked when they kicked. After two minutes, the music mercifully stopped, the women bowed, and the crowd cheered.

Srini approached them with a phalanx of bare-midriff bridesmaids.

"It's so good to see you, Jack," the bride-to-be said. "Thank you so much for coming all this way. We're very sorry for the trouble." Her painted eyes roamed over Jack with clinically trained concern. "Were you limping just now?"

Hearing his dance attempt described as *limping* stung. But it also offered him a chance to get away so he could finally check in with Mr. Clark. He flashed a glance at Lisanne. "Hurt my knee in the rickshaw accident. Aching a bit, actually."

"You should go lie down. Someone will take you to the guesthouse."

"No," Lisanne said, touching Srini's wrist and Jack's simultaneously. "He's fine."

"I believe I will lie down. And I really should check in with work," Jack responded. Lisanne's tight squint registered her silent protest.

Jack ignored it and addressed Srini. "Your father said we're staying in Phula . . . something."

"Phula Mahila," the doctor finished. "You two will love it. It's very romantic. I'll have Balnoor guide you there. Don't worry—the walk's not bad. But in case it aggravates your knee, I'll have a bottle of painkillers delivered to the cottage."

"Good idea," Lisanne agreed. "He's going to need them."

14

THE GUEST COTTAGE, PHULA MAHILA, WAS ONE OF SIX WITHIN THE WALLED COMpound of Ram Shakur, Daval Rai's summer home. Balnoor paused before the heavy carved doors and punched in a security code at a closed gate while Jack listened to throbbing Eastern dance rhythms in the distance.

"I thought this place was a Sikh palace. Why are there so many guesthouses?" Jack asked his guide.

"Ah, that," Balnoor replied. "You see, sir, the maharaja was a great warrior, a man of vigor. He felt the need to populate his kingdom with similar strength and thus required many wives—over thirty, I believe. Phula Mahila was where Rani Jind Kaur lived, considered the most beautiful. Through here, sir."

Rounding a secluded garden path within the cottage walls, Jack glimpsed a stone edifice. Like most of the other structures on the sprawling property, the cottage was marble, fronted by a packed array of pointed arches and fluted columns. To Jack, who'd grown up in the environs of Washington, D.C., it looked like a miniature Jefferson Memorial.

"And what became of the maharaja's fourth wife?" he asked, taking in the scene with his hands on his hips. "She lived here all her life?"

"I believe she was executed. This way, sir."

Inside, Jack found a modern two-bedroom home renovated to contemporary tastes. Balnoor clicked on the lights, then showed Jack around—fully stocked kitchen, master bedroom with a closet full of Indian and Western clothing, and down a rear stairwell a garage with a tan Land Rover Defender. Jack noticed the AGI logo on the Rover's doors. It matched the vehicle the gate guards had driven.

"The keys are in it, sir," Balnoor explained. "Mr. Rai insisted you have a vehicle to explore the local area. You must see the golden Sikh temple, Sachkhand Sri Harmandir Sahib Sri Darbar Sahib. And may I add, sir, I am an excellent guide."

Before he left, Balnoor briefed Jack on the home's Wi-Fi. Jack bade him good evening and saw him through the door as distant music pierced the air.

Relieved to be in secluded comfort at last, Jack ate a sandwich before retrieving his Panasonic Toughbook from his dirty backpack. It took him three minutes to launch the encrypted Campus secure communications app and virtual private network before he could send an emergency message to John Clark.

While waiting for a response, he perused a glossy annual report from Daval Rai's company, AGI, that had been left on the desk. Thinking again of Thad Vandermullen in Switzerland, he eagerly dug through the report, hoping to find an area where Hendley's investment priorities might align with AGI's. He was twenty pages into a summary of the firm's construction projects across Africa when his Toughbook chimed to life, startling him.

"Good morning, Mr. C.," he said to Clark, who, Jack noticed, took the video call from his home office in Leesburg, Virginia. "I'm sorry to disturb you."

Clark sipped coffee from a mug with the logo of his first unit, SEAL Team One. "No trouble—you sent out an op-immediate message. What's up?"

"Lisanne and I were attacked"—Jack glanced at his watch—"thirty-six hours ago. Suicide bomber, Islamic fundamentalist. We assess he picked us up as Americans when we stopped at the embassy in Delhi."

Clark gazed at Jack with narrowing eyes. "I'm sorry—did you say he followed you from a deli, as in a delicatessen?"

"No, sorry. Delhi, India. We're here now—in the northern part of the country, an old Sikh city called Amritsar."

"Hold up," Clark growled. "I'm confused. Aren't you in Texas getting Lisanne's bionic arm attached?"

"We were. Long story. I'll make it short." Jack explained the changes in their vacation plans, including the flight, the train ride, and the wedding. He noticed Clark's jaw muscles tightening the further he got into the story.

For his part, John Clark, who, along with Ding, had been working around the clock to arrange logistics for the ultra-covert hit on Rafa bin Yasin and Umayyad Caliphate fighters, kept himself in check. He had converted his den into a virtual war room, covering maps of Pakistani Kashmir with Post-it notes and inked arrows to indicate the team's likely air ingress over the Hindu Kush. Nothing had come easy. And, true to form, Jack Junior had thrown him a curveball.

The SEAL's frustration with the tactical problem seeped into his voice. "I'd still have liked to have known you were in India," he began. "You should have . . ." His voice drifted off as a new thought took hold. He swigged a long, last gulp of coffee and evaluated it.

"We lost our secure Campus phones," Jack explained, worried about the pause. "We picked up burners, but the tail stayed with us. This is the first chance I've had to get in touch." He went on to detail the tortured trip to Amritsar and the nature of their stay.

When the story was done, Clark set down the mug and vigorously rubbed his face, thinking through a long list of military dictums related to adapting, overcoming, and generally getting on with tactical pursuits regardless of the obstacle.

"Jack. After all that—do you think you got out of the fray clean? No cops? No detection?"

"Correct. We're black. We hopped onto a freight train, no trace. Now we're back on our personal agenda. The security here is tight. Daval Rai is a big deal. If cops were on us, we would know. Except that we survived a crazy suicide bomber, everything is fine."

"What's the name of the town again?"

"Amritsar."

Clark swiveled in his chair and examined one of the maps tacked to his wall. He found the city near the Pakistani border, tapped it twice, then turned back to squarely face the camera lens. "Do you have another minute? Or do you need to head back to this wedding?"

The forward posture and polite phrasing struck Jack as unusually solicitous. He was momentarily gripped by the fear that he was about to get fired from The Campus. In a flash of cold worry, Jack wondered if Gerry Hendley had considered Jack a subpar investor compared to Thad Vandermullen. He could picture Clark chiming in, saying that Jack was a handful as an operator, tough to discipline.

"I have time, Mr. C.," he said. "Lisanne's across the compound at a fancy cocktail reception. It's coming up on midnight and I was about to hit the hay. Why? What's going on?"

"You're secure?" Clark asked instead of answering Jack.

"Totally secure. This place is, literally, a fortress."

"What about access to wheels? Could you get a vehicle?"

"Yes, Mr. C. Our host is very generous. We have our own Land Rover."

Clark cracked a wrinkled smile. "Hang on, then. I need to grab Ding. He's downstairs with his bad leg."

"Why? What's up?"

"A little op we've got cooking."

Jack's pulse quickened. "Really? Can I be part of it?"

"You already are."

PART TWO

POWDER

15

KARAKORAM GORGE, PAKISTAN

BRIGADIER IMRAN KHAN PRESSED HIS FACE TO THE HELICOPTER WINDOW, ABSENTLY watching ice crystals form at its edges. The plexiglass cooled his forehead, while shafts of cloud shot by outside like ghostly arrows.

"Five kilometers to the gorge," the pilot announced over the intercom, his voice transmitted to Khan through the headphones over his ears.

"Thank you," the Pakistani government minister said from the opposite, rear-facing seat. Young and bald with thick-rimmed glasses, he looked up from a sheaf of briefing papers.

Khan avoided making eye contact with the government official. The intricate details of the ice crystals in the foreground and the looming cliffs ahead captivated his attention far more than Minister Tariq Masroof ever could.

The cliffs jutted from the high plains like island palisades from the sea. As the helicopter approached, they textured into craggy relief and the brigadier's ears popped with pressure as the helicopter climbed. The aircraft seemed unlikely to overcome the steep walls.

"Quite the challenge to build here, eh, Brigadier?" the minister remarked, an eager smile on his chubby face.

Khan allowed a slight nod, thinking through the political maneuvers that had brought Masroof to this distant, glacier-studded outpost.

Before the Pakistani president accepted the Chinese loan package, Masroof, an avowed sinophile, had held the amorphous title "minister without portfolio." Now that the taps flowed with Chinese funds, he was the head of the Ministry of Special Initiatives, MOSI, a new agency with a handful of civil servants.

"My third trip," Masroof continued airily. "Wait until you see the platform the men built for the ceremony along the tracks. You might be able to see it now if you squint."

"Seat belts, please," the pilot interrupted. "The approach to the landing zone will get rough. Wind's coming up from the river."

Tariq Masroof made another attempt to spread his enthusiasm. "How about you, Mr. Baig? How many trips here so far?"

The AGI project engineer, Sunny Baig, blinked at the minister. A clean-shaven graduate of Islamabad's National University of Sciences and Technology, he gripped the armrests on the helicopter's starboard side next to Khan. A heavy parka and hard hat rested on his knees.

"First time by helicopter," Baig confessed, eyes wide. "I prefer the road."

The canyon wall slipped from the brigadier's view. The helicopter tilted, and Khan spotted the muddy Hunza River flowing through the boulders in the shade of a steep crevasse. Above it, he caught a glimpse of a long gray vein, the famous Karakoram Highway carved into a ledge one hundred meters above the valley floor. Near the road, metallic reflections glinted where the rails emerged from a southern tunnel bored through a tree-studded hill. From there, the rails threaded a few kilometers of forest before reaching the bridge over the gorge. On the north side of the gorge, they vanished into another tunnel.

"Tell the brigadier what it took to build this," Masroof ordered Baig.

"Forty megatons of TNT, sir. Four years to bore seven tunnels and the bridge span. Three hundred workers."

Khan grunted acknowledgment. The hill through which the southern tunnel traveled would offer good elevation for a shooter. He noticed the broad platform at the bridge's southern edge, where the delegation would stand at the upcoming event, thinking through the nearby forest's concealment for supporting forces. He'd seen it all in AGI company photos, but that was a shallow comparison to looking at the site himself.

The tunnel slid from view as the Airbus H145 strained into another turn. Though maneuvering at five thousand meters— above the range of a Pakistani army helo—the executive aircraft was a pressurized, five-rotor model that gave it extra power for high-altitude work.

AGI owned the helicopter, which Fahim Bajwa, AGI's chief operating officer, had loaned to the minister at Khan's suggestion. The smooth COO was always flexible when it came to satisfying Pakistani government ministers—and Khan, so long as the ISI money taps remained open.

"There's the clearing," Baig announced nervously.

"On final," the pilot said.

Khan watched the copilot work the instrument panel. Through the windscreen beyond, it appeared as if they were descending into a well. The Airbus shuddered and shook with blinking lights on the dash. The brigadier saw nothing but flecked gray cliffs checkered with occasional patches of dirty snow flying across the glass.

In his long army career, he had flown in many helicopters in the Karakorams, and he knew how easily the winds could flip the aircraft over. With this in mind, he tugged the three-point harness tightly over his wool commando sweater, avoiding the 9-millimeter Browning on his hip. He angled his satellite phone's antenna at the window, ignoring the sickening yaw while the helo fought the crosswind. The device buzzed in Khan's hand.

The first two subject lines were encoded messages from his Islamabad staff. One was a brief bio of the Chinese security officer he expected to meet, which he'd already read. The other was an update on Indian military activity in Jammu, a few hundred miles to the southeast, India's half of Kashmir. Khan ignored it, too, as military intelligence reports tended to clog his inbox with little new information.

While the helicopter sank closer to earth, Khan touched the link for his Dropbox account and opened an encrypted file. Rather than risk messages being transmitted over data lines, the ISI officer instructed his assets to update a cloud-based text file.

He expected to hear from his highly compensated Indian asset, Fahim Bajwa, the AGI COO. Bajwa was overdue with an update on the preparation for the Karakoram op. But as often happened with this particular asset, there was no report.

The brigadier clenched his fist in his lap. He had never trusted Bajwa, Rafa's half brother. Khan was frustrated with the communication arrangement that Rafa bin Yasin required, which funneled all information through Bajwa because Rafa viewed Khan as a supporter of an illegitimate country. Although the half brothers had become the primary tools in the Karakoram operation, he detested their narcissistic symmetry: Rafa's God complex and Fahim's belief that he was a gift from God.

Khan dismissed the half brothers with a head shake. He then glanced at the phone's text message inbox, rereading the final exchange with his son, Attaf, in Dubai. I would rather not change my identity again. Please leave me be.

The Pakistani army brigadier powered down the phone. The engine's whine lowered in pitch as the overhead rotors slowed. Without waiting for the corporate pilot's approval, he unbuckled his seat belt, threw open the door lever, and stepped into the chilly wind.

Baig introduced the brigadier and the minister to a knot of AGI project engineers in hard hats, who hurried to welcome them. They stood athwart a broad, raised platform with five stairsteps on either side. They described it as the upper media platform, where cameras could gain a wide-angle view of the train emerging from the tunnel in the distance.

"But most of the media will be down there," Baig commented, pointing to a cantilevered floor jutting from the southern edge of the bridge, hazy in the distance. Khan could see workmen swarming over it. "It is not ready yet for the tour."

"But it will be?" Masroof asked.

"Oh, yes, sir. It will be. Mr. Rai himself is very involved with this project."

The minister gaped at the misty shelf by the bridge, then turned to inspect the camera platform behind him. The perch was ten meters wide, blasted, protruding from the rock face. He eyed the thick electrical cables snaking around his feet. "Unobstructed view of the sky. That will be good for the live satellite broadcasts."

"Yes, Minister. Those were our instructions."

"Good. Come. Let's have a better look at that magnificent bridge."

Khan walked to the side of the entourage, his boots crunching over shattered rocks. The air glinted with freeze-dried, floating dust. As he approached the landing zone's edge, a dank wind rose from the river valley.

According to Baig, the bridge was nearly ready for rail traffic. It couldn't take a high-speed passenger train—yet—but it was perfectly sound for the intercity express coming up from Islamabad for the grand opening, when the minister and his Chinese counterpart would make speeches from the dais about Sino-Pak cooperation and the glorious future thereby engendered.

Masroof squeezed his pugged face into a smile and swept an arm over the gorge. "The tallest suspension bridge in the world. A line that links the Red Sea to the Khunjerab Pass."

As though rehearsing his speech for the cameras that would soon be here, he swept his arms from south to north in a rousing close. "We now have a supply chain link free of Western interference, a reprise of the ancient Silk Road, linking economies from across the hemisphere. May we all celebrate the ascendency of Asia."

Khan remained mute. He admitted to himself that Pakistan and China had a new overland trade route, which, on paper, should strengthen a natural alliance that could counter the Indians and their latest imperial overlord, the Americans. But at what cost?

Still smarting from the exchange with his son, he posed the question aloud.

"So, Minister," he began over the distant clanks of earthmoving machines. "The Chinese Communist Party will now have a route to transport Persian Gulf oil without sanctions trouble from the American Navy. However—do you fear that servicing the Chinese debt payments will rob us of internal funding for our own independent governance? Might we end up a vassal state like Mongolia or Tibet?"

The workers cast their eyes downward. Masroof stared hotly at the brigadier, parting his lips in stunned reply. But a thundering roar cut him off.

Whump, whump. WHUMP, WHUMP, WHUMP.

The heavy beating thud echoed from the rocks, squelching the distant equipment's clanks and rumbles.

A People's Liberation Army Mi-24 Hind gunship soared a hundred meters above them, its stubby wings bristling with rocket pods and Gatling guns. The airborne arsenal arced into a landing next to the AGI Airbus, rudely blasting grit into their faces.

Squinting, the brigadier looked through his fingers at the red star on the craft's rounded engines and the unit markings on its tail. It belonged to Xinjiang, the mountain infantry unit that had battled the Indians in a hand-to-hand border skirmish a few years earlier.

With the rotors still spinning, an officer in a black parka jumped out and ducked. He peered through the dust, spotted Khan, and sprinted toward the Pakistani officer, adjusting a red-starred cap on his head. A Chinese civilian in a dark suit and red tie rushed behind him, running awkwardly as he ducked down.

The Hind's engines reduced to a hiss as the rotors decelerated. "I'm Colonel Chen Ming, and this is Deputy Foreign Minister Wang Zhuoran," the military officer proclaimed in halting English. "You are Brigadier General Imran Khan?"

"I am Khan. Hello."

The Chinese officer glanced at Khan's sidearm. "I thought we agreed we would come without weapons."

Khan inclined his head to the hulking gunship. Its stacked, tandem pilots remained buckled into the cockpit with their helmets on. "And what would you call that, Colonel Ming?"

The Chinese officer grimaced. "This is not the way to—"

"It's all right," Wang Zhuoran conceded with a steadying hand. "Thank you for coming, General Khan." According to ISI's internal bureau, Wang was a recent graduate of the Party's executive training academy near Shanghai, a so-called princeling as the grandson of a politburo member.

The Hind's engines fell silent, replaced by the distant bulldozers, cranes, and jackhammers along the faraway bridge. Minister Masroof hurried forward, offering his hand to the civilian, ignoring Colonel Ming as a mere military functionary. The politicians exchanged pleasantries that seemed to go on forever. Ming beckoned Khan to the far side of the helicopters, leaving the two civilians.

"How do you assess the security of this position?" Ming asked, his eyes sweeping the tops of the surrounding cliffs. A mountain gust curled his red-badged uniform lapel.

"We have sufficient interior security, Colonel. The rails are safe. An infantry brigade will man the critical choke points and switching nodes at Peshawar, to the south."

The Chinese officer shaded his brow with his hand as he inspected the vertical cliffs on the opposite side of the gorge. His gaze settled on a tilted yellow crane arm above the northern tunnel entrance, where a five-meter steel I-beam swung from a cable. "Maybe we should deploy one of our border guard battalions. This elevated cliff offers a strategic advantage. I could conceal them in the rubble over there."

"We have sufficient internal security," Khan repeated. "We will not accept foreign troops. Our position has been clear."

Ming unbuttoned the breast pocket of his parka, withdrew a pack of cigarettes, and pulled one free with short yellow teeth. After sparking a Zippo, he puffed. The smoke disappeared on the updraft.

"And . . . what of the Indian army units in these parts?" Ming asked.

"What of them?"

"You're not concerned about troop movements? Indian Para SF incursions?"

"The border is four hundred kilometers from here, Colonel."

The Chinese officer winced. "I fought them, Brigadier, in the eastern Ladakh. They came at us with ice axes."

"The eastern Ladakh is not here."

Ming studied the brigadier for a quiet moment, then replied, "I'm surprised you're not more on edge over what's happened in Kashmir."

Khan inhaled a deep lungful of thin mountain air. "Our military intelligence team watches the Indian garrisons in Kashmir. We know their orders of battle better than half the Indian commanders that rotate through them."

"Is that so? Then how do you assess the Indian position after the zero-three-hundred skirmish across the border in Jammu?"

Khan grew wary of the Chinese officer's knowing glance. "Meaning what, exactly?"

"I mean a group of Islamic terrorists attacked an Indian army outpost on the border, obviously. You must be aware of that. Surely, you're anticipating an Indian military response."

"We are always prepared for that," the brigadier replied curtly, itching to dig into his phone, thinking immediately of Rafa, the damned hothead. An unplanned military adventure could ruin all his preparations for Karakoram.

A crackling boom made both army officers flinch.

A tearing roar followed it, reverberating off the rock faces in deafening echoes. The ISI man arched his neck and searched the clear blue sky before realizing the jets were at his side, threading the gorge on a low-level flyby.

"Forgive us!" Ming shouted over the din. "We thought it best to help with reconnaissance!"

Two twin-tailed PLA Air Force J-15 fighters, their engines belching fire, raced down the valley from the north, barely three hundred meters from where the officers stood. Passing in a blink, a shock wave forced Khan forward into a steadying step, knocking the beret from his head.

"We did *not* give you permission for fixed-wing combat aircraft to enter our airspace!" he seethed over the fading exhaust while retrieving his cap.

The jets ascended vertically into the deep blue ether, two curling contrails stretching away like ribbons. The PLA colonel watched appreciatively, smirking. "They're just here for reconnaissance. And perhaps you need it. You don't have quite the grasp on military maneuvers that you thought, Brigadier Khan."

"We will not stand for a violation of our sovereign airspace!"

Ming's smirk widened. "Feel free to register a complaint with Beijing."

Khan was about to reply that he would do just that. But then Minister Masroof called to him from the helicopters. "How about that, Brigadier! Magnificent, yes?"

16

MARY PAT FOLEY HAD THE LUXURY OF HER OWN PARKING SPACE IN THE HEAVILY barricaded garage beneath the J. Edgar Hoover Building. Her Secret Service driver, Brett Johnson, eased into the spot, scanned the rearview mirror, and positioned himself at the truck's rear with his hand near his Glock 19 while she exited.

Three FBI agents emerged from a government sedan and headed to the elevator. They afforded the steely-eyed Secret Service man a wide berth.

"I think we're pretty safe here, Brett," Mary Pat muttered with a subtle smile and an elbow nudge.

Since the emergence of the POSEIDON SPEAR murders, Johnson had increased the patrol detail that monitored the DNI's suburban home. Mary Pat's husband, Ed, a former CIA director, had taken to keeping his trusty 1911 Colt .45 behind the headboard, with two extra magazines concealed under the mattress. But as Mary Pat saw it, Ed had exchanged his master spy credentials a decade ago to become a full-time historian. Even with the new intelligence coming from Indian Kashmir, she feared the Colt behind the headboard more than any crazed jihadis sent into the D.C. suburbs by Rafa bin Yasin.

Johnson led Mary Pat through three internal security stations before arriving at the director's ninth-floor office. "The attorney general will be with you in a minute," Murray's longtime assistant, Deborah Colquitt, announced while Johnson receded to a position near the window blinds.

While the FBI director was in the UK, Attorney General Murray suggested discussing the progress on the Rafa search at the FBI building. Murray's formal office was on Pennsylvania Avenue at the Robert F. Kennedy Building, commonly referred to as "Main Justice." However, with a mole somewhere in the ranks, he believed it was wiser to change venues.

"Coffee's in the conference room, Madam Director," Deborah added, opening the door.

Mary Pat declined Colquitt's offer and walked in, expecting an empty room. Instead, she found John Clark sitting at the far side of the table, blinking behind his reading glasses.

"What's up, John? I was told you'd be calling in for this."

"You were told wrong."

"You're not spending the week down at your farm?"

Clark had been scrolling through his phone while waiting for Murray in the conference room. Without looking up, he mumbled, "I was. Something came up."

She glanced at the wall's red LED clocks covering six time zones. "This early? Are Hendley and his team back in the office?"

"No. They're still in Zurich."

"Early meeting with Gerry, then? Is he making you live in the European time zone?"

"Negative."

"Some other white-side thing?"

"No. The whole white side's down for another week. Including Gerry."

Mary Pat swallowed a rising sense of frustration. Why the slow answers? She let it go when Murray slipped into the room.

"Hey, guys, sorry for the wait." The attorney general took his seat at the head of the table. Ever the lawyer, his tie was tightly knotted, his suit well cut. But the clothes couldn't disguise his wan face, pink eyes, and slumping posture. Mary Pat immediately noted the signs of exhaustion. Murray was usually a gym-before-the-office routine kind of guy.

"You need to reschedule, Dan?"

"No, no. I was on the phone with the First Lady just now. Apologies."

Mary Pat arched her eyebrows. "Oh? Something we should know about?"

The attorney general reached for the coffee carafe and filled a cup. "Cathy's attending to a surgery for my wife, Liz. The first operation's this morning, that's all. The first of four."

Clark placed his phone and glasses on the table, observing the lawyer's bloodshot eyes. "Hey, Dan—you should be with her. We can fill you in later."

"No. Liz will be out cold. No point in me standing around the waiting room making the docs nervous. And POSEIDON SPEAR victims deserve my complete attention."

"Dan," Mary Pat persisted. "Go to the hospital."

He waved at her. "The series of surgeries and adjustments will last a week. Some new-fangled Belgian procedure. It's better for me to keep busy than to think about it."

Clark slid his phone into his pocket. "Dan, Cathy Ryan wouldn't let her go under the knife if she wasn't sure. If she's attending, then you've got the best."

Murray heaved a sigh. "Couldn't agree more. Now. On to SPEAR. Mary Pat, what's up with Rafa bin Yasin? Was it his Umayyad Caliphate that hit the Indian army in Kashmir? Our legal attaché in New Delhi sent a flash message an hour ago. That was her early take."

The director of national intelligence slid her laptop from her bag, opened it, and logged in with a fingerprint and iris scan. "Your LEGAT is right. The intelligence community's consensus assessment is that this was the work of the Umayyad Caliphate, Rafa. I just received some security camera footage that the Indians sent the National Counterterrorism Center. Check it out."

She tilted the computer for Clark and Murray to see. Manipulating the mouse pad, Mary Pat scrolled through black-and-white images of a uniformed Indian soldier standing near a gatehouse with a machine gun slung over his shoulder. Digital numbers in the lower right corner indicated the attack had occurred twenty-four hours earlier, a little after midnight, India Standard Time.

"This is the Indian special operations garrison headquarters in northwestern Kashmir," she narrated, slowing the frame rate to half speed. "It's a crack outfit. They call them Para SF for Paratrooper Special Forces. Now—watch this. The raid starts right here."

The Indian Special Forces sentinel's head snapped back. Just as his helmet flew off, his face vanished in a cloud of mist. The soldier collapsed in a dark heap. A second sentry emerged from the gatehouse with a pistol, moving jerkily in the frame-by-frame footage. A bullet struck him on the side of the head, knocking him sideways into a wall, leaving a dark smear as he crumpled to the ground, dead.

"Sniper," Clark commented. "Headshots. Judging by the reactions, I'd say those were high-terminal-velocity rounds. Not exactly the usual AK-47 blasts we see from terrorists."

"There's more," Mary Pat continued. She advanced the footage to reveal a comprehensive view of the Indian military outpost. Two armored personnel carriers were parked by an L-shaped building. As she advanced the frames slowly, streaks of white sprouted across the picture. The beefy trucks shuddered as flames erupted through the armor. Behind them, the barracks building's windows blew out. Two soldiers dashed out of the building, falling one by one, their heads disintegrating as snipers found their marks.

"Jesus," Murray breathed. "How many killed?"

"The Para SF garrisoned there was platoon strength," she responded. "Thirty KIA. About half died in the building fire, half gunned down as they ran out. A few managed to get on the roof to return fire. Snipers got them, too. You can see that developing with their muzzle flashes here. There they go, just as another blast hits the building."

"Rocket-propelled grenades hitting the APCs," Clark assessed. "Based on the way the roof stove in, I'd say mortars took out the barracks building." He crossed his thick arms and shook his head. "Coordinated with sniper fire, this is no ordinary terror attack. These guys are seriously trained-up and well equipped. I'm sorry to say that I'm impressed with their execution."

"For what it's worth," Mary Pat said, "the NCTC agrees. They called it a military strike, the work of a well-organized militia."

"Do we have any hard intel to indicate it was Umayyad and Rafa?"

"As a matter of fact, yes. Watch." Four mounted riders stormed through on horseback, assault rifles pointed low over their saddles, muzzle flashes glaring. "These guys rode in and machine-gunned the wounded."

Murray drummed a pen on a legal pad. "They're sophisticated enough to coordinate snipers, RPGs, and mortars. But they finish off the job on horseback?"

"I don't recognize those rifles," Clark said. "They're certainly not garden-variety AKs."

The DNI removed her hands from the keyboard, halting the video. "Well, there are other markers here. We think the cavalry is a statement. The horses are a symbol, telling us they want to return to an era that predates Western civilization. At least three Daesh splinters think like that."

"The four horsemen of the apocalypse," Murray mumbled, assiduously taking notes on his legal pad.

"Did we get any COMINT hits out of this?" Clark probed. "For a strike this precise, they must have coordinated over radios. Possibly data links for drones."

"The NSA didn't have any over-the-air sensor tuned to that area. The Indians picked up fragments of short-range UHF. They shipped us the audio files."

"And?"

"Our NCTC experts deciphered a hodgepodge of language origins, landing on a sort of pidgin Urdu in common. The analysts think these fighters are from the tribal regions in northern Pakistan. Some Tajik, Uzbek, and Kazakh dialects."

"Like you said, could be some other Daesh splinter. Not necessarily Rafa," Clark suggested.

"It's Rafa. Keep watching." She advanced the video to a horseman who rode stiffly. The side of his saddle was adorned with what looked like silver plates, glinting in the moonlight. A long pole rose five feet over his head. It was fixed to a stirrup at the bottom and bulbous at the top. "We had our techs enhance these frames with AI. The man on the duded-up stallion is Rafa bin Yasin, in the flesh."

Murray leaned forward. "How can you be so sure?"

"We ran the images we got from the DGSE of Rafa's French ID cards through our age-enhancement program."

"I'm familiar with the tech," Murray said. "The DOJ uses it with the NCIC database."

"Yeah. Well, fortunately, the video gives us more dynamic imagery than you typically get from the National Crime Information Center. We're confident that's our boy, Rafa. The staff and decorated horse are additional indicators."

"What's that about?" the attorney general asked.

Mary Pat fidgeted with her laptop, studying a separate file. "Rafa is the son of the Emir, the original founder of the Umayyad Revolutionary Council. The Emir believed himself to be Allah's one true prophet, a direct descendent of Muhammad. Based on that self-appraisal, we believe Rafa thinks *he* is the true prophet as the next in line after the Emir. Now that we've dug further into the NSA intercepts in the Hindu Kush and Karakorams, we're hearing chatter about someone called the caliph. We think that's a reference to Rafa and that his followers believe he is God's messenger on earth."

"Oh yeah? And how did he and the Emir arrive at the conclusion that they're Muhammad's direct descendants?"

She shrugged. "You know the first part of the story. When Muhammad died around 600 AD, two guys claimed to be his successor. Abu Bakr was named the caliph. Sunni Muslims follow Bakr. Shias disagree with that. They think the rightful heir is Ali. Hence the Sunni-Shia split."

"So Iran, the Shias, aren't backing this guy," Murray said. "There's that."

"Correct," she replied flatly. "This isn't Iran."

"Are you saying Rafa follows Abu Bakr? So he's a Sunni?"

"No again. Rafa is his own brand. I'll spare you a discourse on the family tree, but the Emir, his son Rafa, and his growing band of followers believe the *true* successor to Muhammad should have been Abu Bakr's uncle, Umm Farwa. The Emir traced his lineage directly to the forefathers of the Banu Makhzum clan. To make a long story short, Rafa believes *his* family line is the true successor to Muhammad. Which is why, we think, he calls himself the caliph. He's now recruited enough followers to support his sui generis claim."

"I suppose that explains the regalia," Clark chipped in dryly, tapping the horse's silver plates on Mary Pat's laptop screen with the blunt end of his pen. "The asshole thinks he's a king."

"A king is small potatoes in Rafa-land," Mary Pat said. "We enhanced the imagery of the top of that staff he's carrying." She checked her notes. "It's a replica of the Pyxis of al-Mughira."

"What the hell is that?"

She alt-tabbed her laptop to a Google image of what looked to Clark like a decorative music box. "It's this. A hunk of ivory carved with two men picking dates on horseback, a symbol of the caliphate's legitimacy. Rafa's version is a homegrown duplicate. This real one pictured here is in the Louvre." She tabbed back to the image of Rafa.

"The guy's off his rocker," Clark grumbled.

She smiled wryly. "You think?"

Clark leaned away. "He's got a well-trained army to back his claims. With lots of fancy weapons. Where's he getting them?"

"We don't know. The NCTC is working on it. But with enough money, it's not hard to buy weapons. It's the funding source we want to find first."

"What about accomplices?" Clark followed. "Does Rafa have brothers or sisters? Old friends we can dredge up?"

"None we can find. Yet."

Murray whistled softly. "Well. This nut is clearly avenging his father, the Emir—and blames us for his demise."

"Yup."

"And based on his grandiose delusions, one might conclude these POSEIDON SPEAR murders are a mere appetizer."

"The NCTC agrees." Mary Pat sighed, before adding, "Unfortunately. Based on the coordinated attack, the chatter in the hills, and his successful recruitment, we think Rafa has bigger plans."

"Okay. Well, I'll make sure this footage gets to our FBI LEGAT in Delhi. She can work with Indian law enforcement, maybe mine something else out of this."

"Sure," she said. "I've also briefed up Suhas Chauhan, the Agency's Delhi chief of station. He can amp up local sources and try to get a fix that way."

"Will Suhas be able to deliver local resources to chase Rafa down?" Clark asked. "Would the Indians let him send a Ground Branch team in there to go kinetic before his army gets any bigger?"

She shook her head. "Indian politics are a problem for us. The current PM is playing strongman, anxious to show that India's a superpower in its own right. He keeps us at arm's length to prove he's finally thrown off the Western imperial yoke."

"What's Western imperialism got to do with this? We have a common interest here," Clark said.

"I agree. But the President doesn't want us kinetic in Kashmir, remember? He's also got the Pakistanis to consider, and Kashmir is a flat-out radioactive issue between those countries. We don't want two nuclear powers going to war. That would ruin everyone's day."

"My guess is that Rafa's hiding in Pakistan, as other fundamentalist splinters have done. What about them?" Clark asked. "When Ding and I were looking for Emir leads back in the day, we liaised with the ISI."

"I remember," Mary Pat replied. "And you're right—we've had

a good working relationship with the ISI, coordinating counterterror ops. But I'm not sure they'd be helpful with this. They're probably happy to see the Indians get smacked in Kashmir, even if they had nothing to do with it."

"What does the President know so far?" Murray asked.

"I'm headed to see him as soon as we're done. The attack synopsis and our readout on Rafa is in his PDB," she said, referring to the Presidential Daily Brief.

Clark shifted in his chair. "As long as we're summarizing things, I have an update on the mole hunt."

"Yeah? Good news?"

Clark cleared his throat. "Not yet. But out at Cole Hunt's burned-up property in Washington State, Gavin found a phone. It's here at Hoover somewhere undergoing further analysis, according to Mandy, but Gavin noticed some anomalies straight away. I'll skip his explanation—because I didn't understand it—but the net is that he believes the phone was tracked by hackers in the India-Pakistan area."

Mary Pat sat in quiet contemplation for a few seconds. "Interesting. But not actionable."

"Agreed. I'm just pointing out that the mole may be coming from India-Pak," Clark noted. "Not enough to trouble the President, yet—but I wanted you to know."

Deborah Colquitt poked her head through the conference room door. "The First Lady is on the phone for you, Attorney General."

"Thanks, Deborah." Murray gathered his things while Clark and Mary Pat uttered their well-wishes for his wife, Liz. His hand resting on the knob, the attorney general paused. "I thought we'd won the global war on terror. Here we go again."

Clark gently kicked Mary Pat's foot under the table when the door latched behind the nation's top law enforcement official.

"Hey," Clark said. "You headed over to the White House right now?"

She checked the red LED clocks. "The meeting's at nine-thirty in the tank." The tank was the Situation Room, where President Jack Ryan preferred to receive his daily briefing.

"Then you have some time to kill." Clark's eye drifted to the half-drained coffee cup in his hand. "And this Bureau coffee sucks."

"Infamously bad."

"I know a better place. And I think it's time for you and me to have a little chat."

17

CLARK'S "PLACE" WAS A GREASY SPOON DINER ON FLORIDA AVENUE, FOUR MILES north of the J. Edgar Hoover Building. The blinking sign over the door declared the ramshackle establishment THE WORLD FAMOUS FLORIDA AVENUE GRILL, SINCE 1944.

"Now, John," Mary Pat chided as they entered the door with a ringing bell. "Are you sure it's good for a couple of the President's confidants to confer at a place that's *world famous*?"

Clark declined to answer. A rotund, balding man in a streaked sailor hat, white T-shirt, and apron came from behind the counter.

"Usual table, Mr. C.?"

"Yeah, Tippy. Thanks."

The tight diner with red vinyl booths and swiveling stools was a third full. Most customers were in business attire, local D.C. government or contract workers, busily gazing at phones while devouring eggs.

"Who's your friend?" the restaurateur asked.

"Nobody you need to know, Tip."

The smile was replaced with a narrow squint at Clark. "You need discretion?"

"I do, yes. But not for the reason you're thinking. Back room, please. Like usual."

The proprietor led Clark and Mary Pat down a long corridor past the restrooms. Tippy flipped on the blinking fluorescent lights and opened the door to the room with an enormous ring of forty jangling keys.

As he worked the lock, he explained to Mary Pat that the space provided another twenty booths in a prior era. Times had changed, he added, noting that most Beltway types preferred fancier, flashier establishments. He kept this room closed except to rent it out for events, like the faculty from Cardozo High School across the street, who'd be using it that afternoon to celebrate the end of the school year.

Mary Pat took all this in with one ear while scanning the hallway and room for cameras.

"You sure this is secure?" she asked Clark after they'd settled into a booth.

"I know it is. Ding and I sweep it every few weeks."

"Come again? How's that?"

"The Campus shoots Tippy a few thousand a month to keep this place on retainer. It's a handy location to meet foreign contacts in D.C. Like the man said, nobody comes here anymore. He's fourth-generation Navy, a Vietnam vet. I consider Tip family."

She looked at the water-stained drop-ceiling roof. "Then I'll shut up."

Clark softened his tone. Aware that she was in a hurry, he felt a little guilty about dragging her five blocks south of the White House. "Look, MP, I'll get right to it. What Dan said back there—he's right. This kid, Rafa, threatens to inspire holy warriors all over the world. What happens when he starts flashing pics of our guys' dead families on the internet, claiming credit? He'll be red-hot to the crazies. That's why he needs to go, ASAP. We can't wait on the fancy-pants people at Foggy Bottom."

Tippy returned with coffee and cream. Mary Pat prepared hers while enduring a story about the time Henry Kissinger and Al Haig came in for lunch in the summer of '73, right before Nixon raised the white flag. Helluva thing, according to Tippy.

The DNI smiled silently through the story, thanked the aging sailor, and waited for him to leave before replying to Clark. "Rafa's one of the many thousands of terrorists working to hit us, John. He's just another head of the hydra. We took out his dad—and he's burning with hatred for the people that did it. Same shit, different day."

"No, it's not."

She glared at him over the top of her cup. "I'm sorry? How so?"

"Rafa has a growing legion of followers who think he's the one true heir to Muhammad. He's got a goddamned army that's conveniently out of our reach. They're well-armed, trained-up, and, somehow, they know the names and addresses of our best terrorist hunters."

"It's not like we're doing nothing. Dan authorized you to send Gavin and Mandy on the internal hunt, to keep it off the books so no mole will know there's a search. Murray will build a case when we find who's behind this, even if it's in another country. The Indians are allies—skittish, yes, but they'll extradite to us. We'll get Rafa's merry band of nutjobs a nice room at Gitmo and round up his whole network, just like we did to the Emir. Standard operating procedure."

"Just because it's standard doesn't mean it's right."

She nearly coughed as she swallowed awkwardly. "What's gotten into you?"

"Come on, MP. Do you really want to use that same tired playbook?"

She stared thoughtfully into his eyes. "Tell me what I should be doing, then."

"Okay. Here it is. This op deserves way more urgency than we're giving it."

"Who says it's not urgent?"

"The fact that we're not going kinetic. We seem to be treating this like a law enforcement issue for valid political reasons, I'll grant you. But this isn't a matter for Murray. This is another battle in a long-running war. It's a matter for warriors."

"Hold on, cowboy. We're doing what we can within limits. Kashmir is a touchy area, nukes all around, even touching China. You know that. It requires special handling."

"I also know that Ding, Jack Junior, and I nabbed Rafa's father just in time back in the day. Diplomatic niceties and congressional approvals aside, we need to move on this right now. We have to kill this kid's momentum before things get worse. There are plenty of ISIS-trained fighters anxious to join his cause, I'll bet, just looking for someone with juice. We need to nip Umayyad Caliphate in the bud. Yesterday."

The door swung open. A matronly waitress backed through it this time, carrying a tray over her head the size of a surfboard.

"What's all this?" Mary Pat asked, confused.

"I'm hungry."

"I'm not. We didn't even order."

"Tippy knows what I like."

Mary Pat soon got an education on Clark's preferences—a four-egg western omelet dripping with American cheese, a pound of home fries, and a long slab of fried gray meat she didn't recognize. When the waitress was gone, she angled her fork at the meat. "What *is* that?"

"Scrapple," Clark mumbled. "Pennsylvania Dutch thing." He threw a wad of potatoes into his mouth.

"Scrapple? Never heard of it. What's it made of?"

"Pork scraps, mush . . . cornmeal. Everything but the tail. Give it a shot."

"Not on your life."

"Fine." He reached across the table to snag her plate and slid her portion of scrapple to his own. "Kendrick Moore and I did seven miles in Rock Creek Park at five a.m. I'm starving."

"That tears it," Mary Pat said as she flattened her hands on the table. "Come clean, Clark. You're up here in D.C. at the office, training in the dark with your new SEAL buddy, when all of Hendley is on vacation, including you."

"Yeah? So?"

"So, I've seen you when you're in operational mode. Your little lecture on warriors getting into action isn't just you venting. You're readying an op, aren't you?"

Clark swallowed, sipped his coffee, and wiped his mouth with a napkin. "Maybe."

"Maybe. *Uh-huh*. You sound like Ed making excuses when he wants out of doing the dishes."

Clark took a moment to respond, continuing to eat. Mary Pat drummed her fingers on the table.

"Let's put it this way," Clark said. "A few things may cross your desk requiring authorization. Air Force logistics, stuff like that. They'll be coded for approval from the Office of the Director of National Intelligence."

The DNI primly folded her hands on the table. "The President was clear. He doesn't want anything kinetic happening in Kashmir. The place is a powder keg."

"I'm just asking you to look the other way on a few orders that may cross your desk."

"You do understand that I'm on my way to brief the President in a half hour. I'm going to tell him all about Rafa bin Yasin's terror attack in Kashmir, exactly as I told you and Dan. Then I'm going to mention that we have a covert op to find the mole that's leading to the deaths of POSEIDON SPEAR operatives, acts that we believe Rafa is orchestrating."

"That's fine. Jack should get that brief. Do it."

"Right. But then, I'm *not* going to tell Jack that I'm going to rubber-stamp military orders because The Campus has something brewing to handle Rafa with, shall we say, *extrajudicial* proceedings in the very place he told us not to operate."

"Exactly. We never tell Jack about Campus operations. That's our deal, *our* standard operating procedure."

"Yes, but our SOP is also that *I'm* supposed to be in the know."

Clark salted his scrapple and took down a quarter of the slab with a single bite. "My job is to protect this country," he said after he swallowed. "By any means necessary."

"So's mine."

"Yeah. But we're different. You're an official organ of the government of the United States. By definition, then, my job includes protecting *you*."

She chuckled from deep inside her throat. "Thank you, John. I don't need protection."

"Yeah, you do, MP. Sometimes. And so does the President."

"Meaning what, exactly?"

"Meaning this: approve any unexpected military requests that come across your desk that *might* include India-Pak. That will allow me to do my job. My budget isn't a matter for Congress. That's kind of the point of the whole white-side, black-side thing. But sometimes, I need to tap resources. I'm going to use your ODNI command for that."

Their eyes locked.

"No one will know," Clark said, breaking the standoff. "You have to trust me on this one."

She sighed huskily. "Uncle. I'll authorize whatever you put

through—have it come from Kendrick Moore's contractor command designation in Norfolk so my staff at Liberty Crossing won't ask."

"Thank you. Will do."

"But, John Clark, for God's sake—I'm the director of national intelligence. I can't be in the dark forever."

"You won't be," he answered after swallowing. "I'll give you a full download."

"When?"

"When I bring you Rafa bin Yasin's head."

18

AMRITSAR, INDIA

JACK WOKE TO THE SUN STREAMING THROUGH THE HEAVY LEADED-GLASS WINDOW on the eastern side of Phula Mahila. Carved like a gem, the window was two feet square, one of thirty in the building's elaborate fenestration. At eight o'clock, the artful, glassy geometry focused the otherwise hazy morning rays into a single white-hot beam that struck his closed eyelids with the intensity of a welder's torch.

Disoriented by the blinding light, jet lag, time zone, and foreign bed, he moved his head aside and slid his right arm to touch Lisanne's hip to see if she was awake. His wrist fell on unruffled cotton, cool to the touch.

He rose to an elbow, yawned, and studied the smooth half of the bed. The AGI annual report, which he'd fallen asleep reading, lay nearby, open on the double-spread map of the company's railroad that covered Indian and Pakistani Kashmir.

"Ah, shit," he mumbled, rubbing his chin.

The night before, Clark had told Jack he would meet Midas that afternoon and drive him to a drop-off as far north as possible for the hit on Rafa bin Yasin. Before jet lag stole him away to la-la land, Jack had been busily analyzing the map, trying to find an appropriate entry point to Pakistan. He had intended to consult Lisanne, the Campus logistics expert, but fell asleep before she was back from the latest festivity in this multiday destination-wedding extravaganza. The last time he'd seen her, she was angry with him for leaving the dance floor.

A clank in the kitchen. A cabinet closing with a hard *thwack*.

Well, Jack thought, sliding from the bed. *No sense in putting this off.* He trudged through the door like a man on his way to the gallows.

He found her settled at the breakfast table, digging into a bowl of yogurt and berries. She wore loose linen pants and a drapey blouse with a jaunty Indian print.

"Hey," he began, pouring coffee into a big mug.

"Hello."

He looked up uncertainly. "Where'd you sleep?"

"Second bedroom."

"Why?"

"I didn't want to wake you. It seemed like you'd been studying or something."

Jack frowned. "Yeah. The AGI company report. It was kind of interesting . . . Fell asleep reading it. What about you? You got in late?"

"Somewhat."

"Where are you off to?"

"The bridesmaids are having a spa day. I'm not sure what you guys are doing. I don't suppose you know, either."

He parried with a tentative chuckle. "Spa day. Nice. When are you leaving?"

"Any minute."

"I see."

"Did you speak with Mr. C.?"

"Yes," Jack said earnestly. "I'd hoped to cover that with you last night. Maybe we can do it now?"

Her eyes remained on her bowl. "Sure. What?"

He leaned forward, touching her elbow, exhausted by the rift between them and determined to cross it. "Lis—come on. Give me a break. My knee got dodgy. I felt like hell."

"You looked okay when you came down the hall just now."

He flexed his leg. "True, it feels better. The sleep probably helped . . . But . . . Whatever. We need to talk about the call I had with Clark. It's important."

"Lots of things are important."

"I mean it."

"So do I. Go ahead. I'm listening."

He put his finger to his lips, then pointed down the hall to the master, telling her that it was a covert conversation requiring audio concealment. "Let me use the bathroom. Be right back."

He pulled her to her feet and guided her down the hall to the master bath, where she perched on the edge of the tub. Jack ran the shower and sat beside her while she flexed her mechanical fingers and rotated her prosthetic wrist.

"You think our guest cottage at a wedding is *bugged*, Jack?" she whispered when he was finally settled. "Really?"

"Probably not. But this is Campus business. Countermeasures are our standard operating procedure. And let's not forget we were tailed from Delhi by a suicide bomber."

"Fine. You reported everything to Clark?"

"Yes."

"So what's up?"

"Today I have to go—"

A *thunk* reverberated from the floor.

"Did you hear that?" she asked.

"Yes."

"Kill the shower."

Jack screwed the tap shut. He could hear the hard knocks on the front door now, punctuated by a ringing bell. He shook his head in frustration. "Hell. I'll be back in a second."

After padding down the marble hall in his socks, he spied Balnoor in the door glass, standing in the portico shade in a white Nehru suit as spotless as a naval uniform. Jack wedged the door open a few inches, eager to shoo the attendant away.

"Ryan sahib! There you are. I trust you and the lady slept well?"

Hoping this was a simple courtesy call, Jack spoke softly through the narrow crack. "I did, Balnoor. Thank you. We're just having breakfast."

Balnoor ignored the remark, shoved the door open, and dashed inside. "Oh, sir. We must get you dressed. We are very, very late. Did you not see the note I slid under the door?" He angled his bald head to the floor tiles. "Ah. There it is. You didn't read it?"

"No. I missed it."

"Well, we're very late," the Indian repeated, lifting the ivory linen envelope.

"Late for what? What are we talking about?"

"Mr. Rai wishes to speak with you. Come. I've arranged appropriate clothing in your closet. We'll get you fixed up. It's no trouble—if we hurry."

Lisanne passed Jack and Balnoor in the corridor, closing a sari wrap over her shoulder. "I need to go," she announced. "We'll have to catch up later, darling, sorry."

"We will," Jack insisted, his eyes severe. "I mean it, Lis. As soon as I'm done with this meeting with Mr. Rai. Okay?"

She didn't look at him as she passed through the door.

19

BALNOOR SHEPHERDED JACK OVER THE GROUNDS TO RAM SHAKUR'S WEST WING.
Shaved and showered, dressed in brown gabardine trousers and a
short-sleeve white shirt with starchy white pleats, he arrived at the
stairs to face a long colonnade flanked by pointed arches.

"This way, Ryan sahib," Balnoor said repeatedly, maintaining a
brisk pace.

The colonnade ended with delicately carved mahogany doors
topped by the Sikh *khanda* symbol, two crossed scimitars bisected
with a dagger. Jack's pulse was high and his breathing shallow after the rapid walk. He wiped the sweat from his brow when two
well-built Indian men barred his way.

Jack had been around Secret Service, FBI, and the State Department's Diplomatic Security Service agents all his life. The two
men who blocked the door had the same look, albeit with South
Asian flair.

Balnoor introduced them as Akshay and Vinit, members of
Rai's security staff.

"I think Mr. Ryan is expected," Balnoor said nervously. Muscled
like pit bulls, Akshay and Vinit, with their arms crossed, appeared
to enjoy the steward's discomfort.

"I'm expected," Jack added with an edge.

The two men eyed him carefully. Without a word, Akshay stepped aside and opened the door.

"There you are!" Daval Rai boomed as soon as Jack crossed the threshold. The tycoon wore a Western black suit with a bright yellow tie. He'd swapped his red turban from the prior evening for a powder-blue one. His dark beard glinted as though freshly waxed. "Come! Come! We've been waiting. Balnoor, seat him at that middle chair, there."

Jack moved to the empty position between two smiling men in well-cut suits. Sanjay, the groom, stepped forward and shook Jack's hand with a pleasant grin. The only other person Jack recognized was Fahim Bajwa, Rai's chief operating officer. The handsome executive's clean-shaven face held a neutral expression.

Balnoor deposited a water bottle before Jack and gestured to a legal pad and pen. "Will you require anything else, sir?"

"Leave us, Balnoor!" Daval Rai cried. "He's not a boy, for heaven's sake. But bring us more of those scones, will you? Not the raisin! The cranberry."

The servant departed in a flurry of bows and smiles. He slipped between the two beefy security men as they shut the door.

"Let me introduce everyone," Rai continued with an outstretched, corpulent hand. "Sanjay you know, of course. My soon-to-be son-in-law."

"Good morning," the groom said warmly.

"And you remember our COO, Fahim. I believe you met at the party."

"A pleasure to see you again, Mr. Ryan."

After Fahim Bajwa's polite nod, Rai proceeded with introductions around the table. Though every executive was a middle-aged man, their geographic origins were like a UN delegation.

Jack bobbed his head in a modest introductory bow to the German chief technical officer, British chief financial officer, Polish chief of human resources, French chief construction officer, and several more foreign chiefs, most of whom Jack quickly lost track.

When it was done, Daval chuckled. "You know, Mr. Ryan, if there's one flaw in my company, it's that I have too many chiefs—and not enough Indians!"

Because he was the boss, the room erupted in laughter.

Jack clutched the arms of his leather chair as though it were an ejection seat about to fire. His mind tumbled through Lisanne's hasty exit and Clark's instruction to meet Midas that afternoon. Adding to his discomfort, he sensed from the executives' expectant faces and the title slide beaming on the screen that he was about to be subjected to an investor pitch. He'd been interested in making inroads with AGI—but that was before he spoke with Clark.

"Let's get to it," Rai continued after discarding the remnants of a pastry. "Fahim, give me the remote, will you?" The CEO stabbed buttons until landing on a PowerPoint chart deep in the middle of the deck that indicated an ascending yet jagged line representing AGI's global revenue.

"AGI is the world's fourth largest infrastructure construction firm," Rai boasted. "And this year, God willing, we will close in on number three!"

The assembled foreign chiefs murmured enthusiasm while Rai burrowed his mahogany eyes into Jack. "I trust you saw last year's performance in the report we left in Phula Mahila, Mr. Ryan? You saw our global initiatives, the capital investments, the government contracts and so forth?"

"I did," Jack replied, his mind working on an excuse that would get him back to the cottage. He drew a blank. "I'm very impressed."

"Our highest growth area is in data centers," Rai continued

while pointing to a graph with bars that ascended like stairs. "Recurring revenue, rack space as a service, power rental for artificial intelligence processing. Believe it or not, we're passing more than a zettabyte of data these days, spanning forty-six countries. We may even be on our way to yottabyte territory in another three years!"

Jack hadn't the foggiest notion of what a yottabyte was, but he smiled appreciatively.

"Our latest data project," the chairman said, clicking to reveal a construction site in what seemed to be a hilly desert. "This is Hanford, a few hundred miles east of Seattle, Jack, in the sunny part of Washington State, where we're building a data center powered by nuclear, wind, and solar energy. We've successfully negotiated power and data transmission contracts with the largest tech firms in the United States—whose names, unfortunately, I can't disclose until the contracts are finalized, which I'm sure you understand." Rai grinned widely. "I know you attend many investor presentations, Jack. I trust you, of course, not to inform any of my competitors, but nondisclosure agreements are what they are. Enough about power and data. Let's move on to the exciting parts."

Rai flipped the slides until he landed on a picture of a gleaming silver bullet train, photoshopped to reveal smiling passengers in the windows. "This, my friend, is Dieter's shining achievement. The Zephir. It will one day ride over all the bridges Fahim builds for us." After touching Fahim's wrist, Rai thrust his beefy, bearded chin toward a narrow-shouldered German man with a bald pate and thick-framed glasses. "Tell him, Dieter. Tell him about Zephir."

Dieter, the firm's German chief technical officer, explained the high-speed bullet train with an expostulation on catenary wires, electromagnetic propulsion, and drag coefficients.

"Zephir is already running cargo and passengers from Casablanca to Tangier, Budapest to Prague, Gdańsk to Berlin, and Incheon to Seoul," he concluded, pronouncing the final city as *Zole*.

"AGI has laid more than nine thousand kilometers of track," Rai cut in, unable to yield the floor. "And we aren't done—not by a long shot. I've promoted Sanjay here to business development chief. He's heading global market expansion for our transportation division. Go on, Sanjay, tell Jack what's afoot with our neighbor to the west."

Sanjay Bodas, who would marry Rai's daughter, Srini, in forty-eight hours, cleared his throat and fidgeted with his gold tie knot. "Well," he began, touching the matching pocket square at his breast. "The Pakistani government hired us to build a high-speed rail link from their port at Gwadar to the Khunjerab Pass on the Chinese border. It's been quite a construction project and, well, I take no credit. It was really Fahim's initiative. Without his engineering vision and bridge designer talent, we would never have made it through the Karakorams."

Fahim Bajwa bowed his head in acknowledgment.

"Years in the making!" Rai erupted. "A grand gamble to replicate the glorious Karakoram Silk Road with this rail service. You have to see it, Jack!" Using his remote, the CEO flipped forward to an image of a stark, rocky canyon with vertical peaks in bright sunshine under blue skies, a photo worthy of a *National Geographic* calendar. "This was how the Karakoram Gorge looked when we arrived. Two-thousand-meter drop to the river below. But, my friend, take a look at it now. Can you believe it?"

The image advanced to reveal a high bridge span that traversed the gorge by connecting two tunnels. "That bridge is the last section to be completed!" Rai boomed with a slap to the table. "Fahim and I will be on hand to mark the occasion with the Pakistani and Chinese governments in a matter of days. Isn't that right, Sanjay?"

"Yes, *Mamanar*," the groom replied, invoking the Indian address for his soon-to-be father-in-law. "The team is working furiously to prepare it for the government meeting."

"And the beauty, you see, Mr. Ryan, is that beneath every inch of our rails, we bury fiber-optic cable. We intend to string together our data centers across North Africa, Eurasia, the Nordics, and Russia. That's why I'm so lucky Srini is marrying Sanjay, *ha-ha*. This boy is a genius when it comes to international law contracts. He went to Yale, you know, after the Indian Institute of Technology Bombay. An engineer with a law degree! A rare breed! The future of this company!"

Embarrassed, Sanjay laughed nervously.

The gesture was a stark contrast, Jack thought, to Fahim Bajwa, who remained expressionless.

Rai's bright brown eyes stared at Jack with expectation. "Well—what do you think, Jack?"

Having shifted his mind to estimate driving times for his trip to meet Bartosz, Jack was caught unawares. However, as an experienced private equity investor who knew how to probe for opportunities, he quickly recovered.

"I'm curious how you can cross all these international borders," he said. "You have links across many countries that are somewhat hostile to India—including Pakistan. Don't they mind?"

"The way I think of it," Rai replied thoughtfully, rubbing his hirsute chin, "is that all these governments are like a single family stuck in a car on a long auto trip. Yes, there are fights and disagreements, but at the end of the day, we're all stuck in the same vehicle, aren't we? We have to talk to one another, move things from place to place, don't we? Assurance Global Industries is one of the only companies in the world with the scale to develop these large government-sponsored infrastructure projects. In that way, I suppose, I think of us as an agent of peace, transcending national borders, a higher calling than just infrastructure construction. Wouldn't you agree, Fahim?"

"I would absolutely agree," the COO answered. "There are no physical barriers on the sea or in the skies. Our work seeks to open land passages between nations. As a transnational contractor, we transcend the governments that hire us."

"And one of those contracts up for bid," Rai added with a wink, "is the American government's next-gen fiber-optic infrastructure program. Your Congress just approved the funding. I believe your Department of Commerce is the one evaluating proposals, one of which, of course, is ours. We are all set to lay fiber from our green-energy Hanford site out to data centers across the Western U.S., traversing federally owned land."

And then it hit Jack. They weren't pitching him because they wanted Hendley's capital. They pitched him because he was the son of the President of the United States. His pulse pounded in anger.

"Forgive me, Mr. Rai—"

"Daval, Jack."

"Daval. I very much appreciate the orientation into AGI. Your achievements are breathtaking and, as an individual investor, maybe even a Hendley one, I can see many opportunities."

"Wonderful!"

"Yes. However." He paused to weigh his words carefully. "If any of you are implying that I have influence with my father's administration or that I would entertain embarking on such a task, then I am afraid you are sadly mistaken."

The faces around the table blanched.

"We meant no offense, Mr. Ryan," Fahim Bajwa said with a sullen look. "Our apologies. We are merely trying to meet the requirements of your government."

His gaze suggested to Jack that the COO had much riding on the American expansion.

"I understand, Mr. Bajwa," Jack replied. "But I must avoid even the *appearance* of impropriety."

"I happened to be in the U.S. last week reviewing our engineering plans," the COO returned. "The passage of the infrastructure funding law was all over the news." His wrists resting on the table, Fahim turned his palms to the ceiling. "Our research indicated that Hendley Associates has invested in infrastructure projects in several countries. Didn't you purchase a shipping concern for shallow-draft oil deliveries from Venezuela?"

"Guyana," Jack corrected him. "You're right. Hendley has invested in developing country infrastructure in the past."

"You *personally*, was it not?" the engineer persisted.

"Yes. I led that investment in Guyana. Personally."

Rai clasped his hands together, holding them before his chest as if in prayer. "Then you can understand why we thought you might like a presentation of our business. Fahim and I happened to be preparing the leadership team here for our board presentation next month."

"We only wanted to give you some background," Sanjay echoed. "We thought you would like it."

"That's fine. As long as we understand each other," Jack said. "I will not have any influence on the United States government."

"We understand each other perfectly," Fahim said.

"Well," Rai offered. "Would you be willing to hear us out on the rest of this, Mr. Ryan? As a Hendley investor—not a government one?"

"I'm afraid I . . ." As Jack was about to suggest they follow up later so he could get back to his Campus priorities, inspiration struck.

He focused on the expectant faces before him. "Gentlemen. Forgive me. I may have overreacted."

"Quite all right," Rai said. "We understand. We just wanted you to see what AGI is doing in this part of the world."

"Seeing it is exactly what I'd like to do," Jack said.

Rai's eyes brightened. "You would like a tour?"

"I would, yes. I'd like to get out and see some of these high-speed rail links myself. Hendley has been evaluating data infrastructure projects. We just completed the acquisition of a low earth orbit satellite company, LodeStar. The deal will be announced in two weeks. Those satellites will need ground stations in remote areas linked by fiber. Hendley just *might* be interested in a partnership in some of those railways."

"Well, a tour of the fiber project can be arranged today!" Rai thundered, arms spreading. "Fahim can take you out to the Dera Baba Nanak roadbed right now. That's the line that will run up through the Karakoram Gorge and on to the Khunjerab Pass into China."

"Will you continue the rails and network in China, too?" Jack asked.

"Well, no. The Chinese take over at the Pass. But if it weren't for us, they wouldn't have their rail line to the Arabian Sea, part of the Chinese Belt and Road Initiative."

Through his Campus operations, Jack had studied China carefully. He was aware of China's vast BRI project and occasionally encountered it while looking at competitive private equity investments. And, were he honest with himself, he would admit that he was still miffed at being kept out of the LodeStar deal and wanted to return from this vacation with a business win.

"I'd like to see it today," Jack said, believing he could kill three birds with one stone—finding an excuse to get Midas into Pakistan, gathering intel on BRI construction plans, *and* evaluating a potential deal to contribute to LodeStar.

"Perfect!" Rai clapped with a cherubic grin. "Fahim will make the arrangements. You'll be back this afternoon in time for tonight's festivities."

"I will have someone drive you," Fahim confirmed. "It's no trouble."

"Thank you, Mr. Bajwa, but I would much prefer to travel there alone."

"Why?"

Thinking of his newfound cover, Jack replied, "As I said, I must avoid even the *appearance* of impropriety."

20

LISANNE WASN'T AT THE COTTAGE WHEN JACK RETURNED FOR THE LAND ROVER WITH a hastily laminated AGI identification lanyard around his neck.

He was eager to brief her on the mission, legitimately, because she was the Campus head of intel and logistics. He also needed to dig himself out of the hole he was in by missing one wedding event after another. He wouldn't mention the potential for an investment to rival LodeStar, which would only make things worse. He decided to leave a note.

But how should he write it? It couldn't mention anything about the Campus side of the operation. Every other made-up excuse for leaving the grounds fell flat. After pondering it, he scribbled a few lines about touring AGI infrastructure up north at Rai's suggestion, promising he'd return for the dance party that evening. He left the note on the kitchen counter, weighed down by a bowl of tangerines.

At his closet, he was delighted to see that his lavish Indian hosts had laundered the filthy Levi's, cotton Filson button-down, and underwear he'd been wearing when the disgusting restroom blew up under his feet. How they'd managed to get the garments clean, he couldn't imagine. They had even polished up his Blundstone boots, which, until then, he'd chalked up as a loss. He donned his American clothes and tossed his backpack with the Glock in the Rover. The backpack still reeked, so he stuffed it in the vehicle's rear cargo area.

Balnoor waved at Jack just as he was driving up the cottage's steep driveway and the basement electric garage door was coming down behind him.

"You are leaving, Ryan sahib?"

"Yes," Jack hurriedly replied. "As a result of the meeting with Mr. Rai. I'm headed up-country."

"I must come with you," Balnoor insisted. "Let me guide you."

"That's okay. I'm equipped." Jack flashed the paper map and credentials Daval Rai's staff had given him. "This is company business. Official. I have directions to Dera Baba Nanak to see a fiber-optic trenching operation."

Balnoor wrung his hands. "Yes, sir, but . . . Would you please let me go with you? The security situation outside the compound is not good. Roads might be closed."

"What are you talking about?"

The Indian lowered his eyes as though embarrassed. "Terrorists. Islamic fundamentalists, I'm afraid."

Reliving their trouble with the suicide bomber, Jack asked, "Where?"

"North of here, sir. In Jammu-Kashmir there are often troubles."

"What happened?"

"Terrorists attacked an Indian army outpost. The general in charge here is sending troops north to quell the violence."

Flashing back to Clark's briefing on the terrorist Rafa, Jack glanced at his map with fresh eyes. It was folded to reveal the Pakistan border area near the village of Bamiyal, where he intended to spirit Bartosz across the border to Pakistan. The rural cluster of farms was a few miles south of India's Jammu-Kashmir region. Far from being concerned about the security situation, Jack logged the uptick in activity as an opportunity for Midas to pick up a fresh scent in his search for Rafa.

"Not to worry, Balnoor," he concluded. "I'll be fine. But—what are you doing here at the cottage, anyway?"

"I have returned to Phula Mahila to gather the lady's things for her."

"What things?"

The attendant's eyes widened in surprise. "Her gauze gloves and pink salwar suit for the big event tonight. You know, sir the . . ."

When Jack showed an utter lack of comprehension, Balnoor tugged at his hands as though trying to pull them off his wrists.

"Why, Ryan sahib, the festival of dance is on the agenda I left under your door last night. You're to wear the navy-blue dhoti kurta with the rhinestones and your mauve jodhpurs with the gold topstitch."

Jack sighed. "No. I didn't see the note. What event are we talking about? What's the . . . festival of dance?"

"The wedding party is gathering to practice the grand Bollywood *filmi* dance. You're to meet for the dress rehearsal later this afternoon."

"Is that a big deal?"

"Oh yes, Ryan sahib! The dance's timing is intricate, and the clothes are highly symbolic, arranged just so. The ladies will begin their neck henna and makeup as soon as they're done with the spa. You'll be with the other groomsmen to greet them in the Lotus Pavilion as they come out to the music. It's meant as a romantic ritual, a complex dance of the sexes, if you will, heavy on symbolism from the Bhagavad Gita . . . and, if I may sir, even the Kama Sutra. The Rais are Sikhs, but the groom is a Hindu."

Jack squeezed his forehead between forefinger and thumb. "When is this thing exactly?"

"The stroke of midnight. But it will take hours to get you properly dressed. Even more so if you miss the rehearsal. I do trust you will return before sundown, sir?"

Jack glanced at his map on the seat. A search on Google from his laptop had suggested it was a two-hour trip from Daval's Amritsar fortress to Bamiyal, where Midas expected him by midafternoon. "Easily," he promised. "Please relay that to Lisanne."

The attendant leaned forward conspiratorially, speaking softly through the Rover's open driver's-side window. "I think that's a very good idea, Ryan sahib."

The tone shot a worried tremor through Jack. "Balnoor—why do you say it like that?"

"Because, sir, the spa attendants listened to the ladies talking while assembled in the group *bauli* bath. The hot springs are piped in from the Ganesha Palace. His Majesty, the maharaja, laid the piping two hundred years ago."

"Forget the plumbing, Balnoor. What exactly were the ladies talking about?"

"They were talking about *you*, Ryan sahib."

STILL WARY ABOUT THE WAY HE'D BEEN TRACKED ON THE TRAIN BY THE SUICIDE bomber, Jack left his cell phone in disassembled pieces at the cottage to reduce the risk of exposing Midas.

He used the GPS in the dash to navigate. Though it took him twenty minutes to traverse the confused, cobbled roads of Amritsar—whose city planners were fifteenth-century Sikhs—Jack found himself on a remote two-lane highway with the air-conditioning cranking, the speedometer reading a hundred kph, and the Land Rover Defender shaking over ruts.

At least, that was true in the stretches between villages. As each one approached, Jack had to brake for bicycles, mule-drawn carts and, often, a crowd of brightly dressed women carrying baskets, who shuffled down the road as if motor vehicles didn't exist.

Fortunately, the modern Defender excelled at overcoming obstacles. Its knobby tires tackled the loose dirt and fallow fields whenever Jack had to veer around traffic. Twice, he diverged from his route into the heart of a village, where the GPS adeptly guided him through narrow alleys flanked by low, ramshackle buildings.

He wouldn't have minded these detours if not for the timetable etched into his mind, which now—unhelpfully—included a countdown to a dress rehearsal for a Bollywood dance representing the Bhagavad Gita, if not the Kama Sutra. Jack kept the Rover's satellite radio tuned to an Indian pop station, trying to visualize what all that might mean.

His eyes scanned the expanded GPS view in his dash. Although he had chosen Bamiyal as a good place to cross the border when speaking with Clark the previous evening, he still wasn't exactly sure how he would get the Campus operative into Pakistan—especially since Indian border guards might be on high alert.

But such were the worries of covert logistical ops, he reminded himself. With an AGI-branded car and ID card, Jack planned to check in with the construction foreman at the fiber-laying project, ask a few questions, take a few notes, and then be on his way—a perfect method to maintain a solid cover for his trip to meet Bartosz.

And it all would have worked out were it not for his creeping suspicion that he'd once again picked up a tail.

Admittedly, he was in a conspicuous vehicle, traveling in a mostly straight line. He hadn't been zigzagging through the remote highways on an SDR. It was only out of habit that he'd been scanning the rearview mirror, where he spotted a dirty gray SUV stuck several cars behind him in traffic.

To Jack, the SUV looked a lot like an American Jeep. He'd seen several of the boxy vehicles on the road and deduced that they were four-by-fours made by the Indian manufacturer Mahindra. According to the tailgate nameplates he'd seen, the truck was called a Thar.

This Thar, which appeared at intervals in his rearview, traveled slowly, shyly careening onto side roads whenever Jack slowed down. There were long stretches in his drive where he thought he was mistaken and that his follower was just a fellow traveler headed north. But then the vehicle would reappear.

When he reached the security gate south of AGI's Dera Baba Nanak construction site, Jack waited for the guard to check his corporate credentials with one eye in the mirror. After a few minutes, the Thar passed by on the highway, too distant from the gate for Jack to make out the driver.

After they waved him to a parking spot near a construction trailer, Jack retrieved his ankle holster and snub-nosed Glock from his foul-smelling backpack, just in case.

"THE REEL HANGING FROM THE TRAILER CAR BEHIND THE LOCOMOTIVE UNSPOOLS A sixty-centimeter fiber tube," explained the AGI project engineer, his weathered face shaded by a hard hat. "Each tube contains thousands of individual glass fibers—enough to support a city of one million people at giga-speed. Please, Mr. Ryan, watch your step; we wouldn't want you to ruin our perfect safety record, as it affects our annual bonus." The engineer chuckled.

Jack lifted his boot over a railroad tie. Weighed down by the gun, he had clumsily stumbled while taking notes in a small notebook.

As the engineer droned over the bangs, buzzes, revs, and thumps of heavy equipment at work, Jack stopped and surveyed the long length of tracks. A quarter mile ahead, they curved out of sight beyond a barn. Next to the barn, Jack watched a tractor with tank tracks and a massive circular saw blade churning up the earth. The heavy-construction vehicle tailed a long tube that tossed the dirt into an open railcar with an ever-increasing mound.

Jack pointed to it. "Does that tractor have difficulty trenching at this scale?"

The engineer turned his sun-browned face to the spewing equipment in the distance. "Oh, no, Mr. Ryan, not at all. That's a tungsten circular blade spinning at two thousand RPMs. It could cut through a meter of solid concrete without even slowing."

Eager to continue the tour, the site manager continued with a long-winded, rambling explanation about the sensitivity of fiber cables, the required depth at which they must be buried, and the associated capacity of two, three, six, and nine-millimeter optical strands, all the while walking Jack farther and farther from his parked vehicle.

With relief, Jack saw his opportunity to escape when another worker in a side-by-side ATV came zooming down the tracks on a return to the construction trailer. The vehicle was roughly the size of a golf cart with a stubby open bed and an empty passenger seat.

"I very much appreciate the explanation," Jack announced, offering his hand. "But I've really got to get going. Would it be all right if I hitched a ride to my car with the guy in the ATV?"

"Oh, yes, Mr. Ryan. As you wish." The site manager grinned. "I almost forgot, sir. Mr. Bajwa mentioned that you would be performing a *filmi* dance tonight at Srini Rai's grand family dinner, yes?"

"Yes, that's right."

The Indian clutched his hands to his bony rib cage, grinning wistfully. "I still remember my daughter's dance. So much practice for her to get it right. Are you ready for it? Did you begin practicing in the States?"

"No," Jack answered. He thanked the engineer and released his hand, then slid down the railroad's slanted gravel bank and flagged down the ATV.

Five bumping minutes later, he saw a portion of the gray Thar SUV's bumper poking out from behind a mud-bricked hut along the highway. Whoever was in it hadn't anticipated that Jack would take this curving ATV trail that exposed their hiding place. It was high time to shake these guys.

To learn more about the quality of the northbound road, he spoke with the ATV driver, who turned out to be a member of the trenching team sent to the workshop to pick up a fresh saw blade.

"You're going to put one of those huge circular blades on this ATV?" Jack asked, genuinely curious.

"No, sir," the young worker replied while he moved the ATV's wheel. "This is for a side trench to feed an administrative head-end. We use a walk-behind trencher for that. Like that one over there in the equipment yard."

Jack followed the worker's finger and saw the small walk-behind trencher. Like a chain saw, it had a long bar extending from its front, ringed by a jagged-toothed metal chain.

And that was the moment Jack knew how he would lose his tail.

21

FORTY-FIVE MILES FROM WASHINGTON, D.C., TUCKED INTO A WOODY EXPANSE OF the Chesapeake coast, are fifty acres of land owned by the Ryan family trust.

Peregrine Cliff, Jack Ryan, Sr.'s residence since his days teaching at the Naval Academy, was surrounded by an eighteen-foot electrified security fence, infrared cameras, motion detectors, Secret Service agents, and an Army K9 unit with Belgian Malinois, German shepherds, and bomb-sniffing beagles. Given its coastal location, the Navy managed the acreage. A specialized contingent of Gary Montgomery's Secret Service detail patrolled the woods.

President Ryan didn't find much relaxation at Camp David because it had been so updated with communications tech that it was beginning to feel like the Situation Room itself. When it came to a respite from the burdens of his office, the chief executive and his ophthalmologist wife, Cathy, preferred their rambling shingled aerie on Peregrine Cliff with its creaking floors, wavy-glass windows, unfiltered view of the Bay, and innumerable family memories.

Growing up on the cliff, the younger Jack spent hundreds of hours exploring its sprawling, leafy forest. Along with his siblings

Sally, Katie, and Kyle, he constructed an eighteenth-century-style fort from maple trees that had fallen after a violent nor'easter.

Over the years, Jack nurtured a secret dream to improve the childish redoubt. During one savagely dull week of "staycation" in Arlington, he distracted himself with YouTube videos on log cabin construction, bought a chain saw, rented an excavator, and—with the permission, if not the endorsement, of the United States Navy—went to work.

The result was a small, crude log cabin with a woodstove pipe through a tin roof, a raised plywood floor, wobbly stone steps, and no windows in the middle of the woods. But, having built it with his own two hands and borrowed tools, Jack considered its imperfections perfect. That November, he'd dragged his girlfriend, Lisanne, to the leaning structure with two flannel sleeping bags, a candied ham, and a bottle of Cabernet Sauvignon.

Poised with her single good hand flexed outwardly on her hip and her head tilted upward, Lisanne Robertson inspected the uneven ceiling, sagging rafters, and inch-wide gaps between timbers. Arrested in this posture, she applied the deep skepticism she'd adopted as a Texas state trooper. She could think only of the Unabomber's Montana shed—but said nothing.

Following that cold night on the splintered floor, the couple had never returned.

Though not quite the outcome Jack had intended, the crude-construction experience had taught him a thing or two about chain saws, which used cutting implements like the spare trenching blades he inspected at the AGI construction site's machine shop.

And, when Jack told the young worker with the ATV that he intended to bring one of the long, barbed chains to Amritsar in his AGI Land Rover, the worker did not object.

As the laborer saw it, this interloper, whoever he was, had an Assurance ID badge and would soon attend Srini Rai's wedding, according to the site foreman. A company employee with that kind of juice could take whatever he wanted.

Two miles north of the construction site, Jack studied the rear-view mirror on his way for the meet with Midas. The gray Thar had fallen back, hiding behind a tractor-trailer.

With his windows down to gauge the landscape, he felt an uncomfortable thickening of humidity and noticed a swath of bugs splatting on the windshield. The terrain to either side was flat, dotted with patches of green wheat fields, the stalks tall, some beginning to turn gold. The air was hazy, browned by a polluted horizon. The highway, already narrow, occasionally notched to a single lane to pass over irrigation ditches. The Rover's factory GPS indicated that he had a solid twenty kilometers before he would approach the outskirts of the next village.

Jack found a route a few klicks ahead that he could use to throw off his trackers. It would lengthen his trip to see Midas, but would also measure the depth of his pursuers, and, if his plan worked as devised, give him a chance for a positive ID.

He turned right, jammed the accelerator to the floor, and raced around curves, widely spread pedestrians, and the occasional farm tractor. Estimating he'd built up a lead, he rumbled over an iron-railed cattle guard embedded in a pinch in the road and braked.

He inspected the dusty fields veined with windblown wadis.

Jack forced the Rover off-road, searching for cover. He stopped the vehicle after two hundred yards, hiding it behind a scraggly tree at a wadi edge. He killed the Rover's engine, hurried to the liftgate, and donned the leather gloves he'd taken from the machine shop while wincing at the putrid stench of his backpack. With the gloves guarding his palms, he lifted the sharp trencher chain blade and dropped it on the ground. His last act at the vehicle was to loop the strap of Lisanne's Nikon around his neck.

The chain blade was too heavy and awkward to carry, so Jack

grunted and pulled the vicious implement over the dirt like a hunter dragging a sharp-toothed carcass. His shoulder muscles aching, he tugged it up the rise to the cattle guard and disguised it among the rails.

While he worked, he heard the occasional cow lowing in the distance. Though Hindus considered the animals sacred and didn't eat beef, he'd noticed several cattle fields on his way north, crowded with dairy cows. The advantage to that, he considered, was that the cows kept to themselves. There were no farmers about. While maneuvering the jagged chain, he congratulated himself on his decision to stop here.

By the time he had the cutting chain disguised in the roadbed's cattle guard, he was panting and sweating. He surveyed the field and saw an elevated berm with a tuft of long grass that offered concealment. He jogged for it and found a sandy notch in the grass blades where he could set up for surveillance photos.

He lay prone on his stomach and rested the camera near his wrists. As a final precaution, he slid the Glock 43 from his ankle holster. Breathing hard, he pulled the slide back a half inch to press-check that a round was chambered.

He sighted the roadway. With its three-and-a-half-inch barrel, the Glock wasn't much of a weapon at this distance. What's more, Lisanne had used three rounds on the suicide bomber. Jack had his spare six-round mag in the 43 with the half-depleted one strapped to his ankle for a total of nine bullets—not much of an arsenal. Then again, he didn't expect to fire the Glock. He only wanted to stop his pursuers by slashing their tires, get an ID with the camera, and hightail it north to meet Midas.

Five minutes on, a distant engine growled over the constant bleat of cattle. Squinting through the haze, Jack spotted the gray Thar rounding a curve, the milky sun reflected in its windshield.

He'd expected the Jeep-like vehicle to be racing to catch up with him. Instead, the SUV was moving forward at about forty kilometers per hour. It seemed to Jack that they were approaching cautiously, like careful pursuers. Jack raised the DSLR, zoomed, focused, and depressed the shutter button, ripping off twenty digital shots.

His eyes laser-focused through the viewfinder, he nearly jumped out of his skin when he heard a crackling rustle in the grass a few yards behind him. He turned to see two loose-skinned, hump-backed cows lowering their horned heads and staring at him, their mouths incessantly chewing, flopping, and slobbering. It dawned on Jack that the sandy notch in the dried grass was a cattle trail.

Relax, he told himself, watching the Thar as it neared the cattle guard in the road, fifty yards across the field. *They're just cows.*

He aimed the camera lens at the Thar. The sun's reflection still obscured the occupants.

A low, grinding huff caused him to look over his shoulder.

Behind three skinny cows stood a well-fed animal with curving horns, broad shoulders, and a drooling jaw under a pink, glistening nose. The bull's breath came in steady, menacing chuffs.

The beast tossed its mighty head and groaned noisily. The bony cows scattered before the apparent master of the trail.

Thinking of Hemingway, Pamplona, and matadors, Jack studied the terrain around him, praying he might find a wadi where he could roll off the trail. His heart sank when he saw nothing but grass.

If he got up to run for another place to hide, he risked exposing his position to whoever was approaching in the Thar. If he stayed where he was, he risked getting gored. The bull's long breaths grew raspier and angrier. The animal's lips flapped ominously.

Jack glanced at the approaching vehicle with Lisanne's camera resting in his hands. It drove right over the trencher chain blade, exactly as planned.

A pop and hiss rattled over the grass as the Thar's four tires shredded. A half second later, the hiss converted to the screech of metal on asphalt. The driver pushed the Thar's engine hard, limping it forward. A shower of sparks shot from beneath the wounded vehicle as the metal rims spun like grinding wheels.

At least that worked.

Two men emerged from the Thar—Jack's best chance for a PID. He ignored the bull to focus the camera lens. He studied the men through the viewfinder and was surprised that their complexions were approximately Caucasian. Equally Western, they wore dark ball caps, khaki shirts, and tactical pants with pockets lining the sides. At this distance, Jack couldn't make out much of the faces under the hat brims other than to note that they were MAMs—military-aged males.

One of the men dropped to a crouch to survey the damage to the wheels. The other yanked the Thar's liftgate, probably going for tools to repair the damage. Jack kept his finger on the shutter button.

Behind him, the bull snorted. Jack turned to see the animal scratching a forefoot in the dirt. It suddenly galloped at Jack with shocking speed.

Jack rolled sideways with the Glock in his hand. The choice was either to get up and run blindly through the grass or turn the pistol on the beast. Either option would ruin his concealment, but if he ran for it, he would come into contact with the men pursuing him.

His Rover was parked around a bend on the other side of the charging bull. The men at the Thar were stuck. He figured they wouldn't be able to catch him before he reached the safety of his car—which meant he had to make it to the other side of the bull.

He squeezed the grip with his finger on the outside of the trigger guard. To shoot or not?

He went through his OODA loop. *Observe, Orient, Decide, Act*. The observation was that a fierce beast was about to pitchfork him with its enormous, curved horns and gore him with its half-ton body. From there, orientation, decision, and action were straightforward.

Jack lined up the two tritium dots in the Glock's ghost-ring sight, aiming for the bull's nose. He pulled the trigger.

The beast stopped in its tracks and tossed its massive head as though trying to throw a rider. It leveled its horns and sprinted forward, aiming for the man lying in the trail with the peashooter. Jack shot three more rounds at the bull's snout. One pierced the animal's eye. *Bull's-eye!* Jack would think later. But in that moment, he was too scared to appreciate it.

The bull bucked wildly, veering away, kicking in spasms like it had wandered into a nest of cobras.

Jack rolled in the other direction to check the Thar. He was shocked to see that both men held spindly AR-style long guns to their shoulders, swinging back and forth, their eyes to the scopes.

The bull gyrated, bucked, and roared, distracting them. Half blinded and dumb with rage, it was bucking toward them.

Jack saw his chance.

Still clutching the Glock and with the camera dangling from his neck, he hopped to his feet as though finishing a burpee. With the bull gnashing between himself and the men, he bolted for the Rover behind the tree, ignoring the pain in his knee, pumping his arms forcefully. He kept his back bent to stay low.

The first crack from the assault rifle sounded off when Jack was still twenty yards from his vehicle. The single, staccato round whizzed by his ear, barely missing him.

He dove to the dirt when he heard the steady rip of a rifle firing on full automatic.

22

"WE HAVE VERY GOOD NEW YORK PIZZA HERE IN CLARKSTON," DOT INFORMED Gavin.

Lolling in his conference chair, exhausted by three solid hours of crime scene analysis, the sheriff added his opinion. "Yeah. Concur. Fazzari's pizza is the best this side of Manhattan."

Gavin Biery struggled to believe that. "Have you been to New York, Sheriff?"

"Once. Molly and I did the whole deal. Broadway, Empire State, Statue of Liberty. And pizza. Fazzari's is just as good."

Gavin was ready to take this debate to the limit. A Fordham graduate who had lived for three years on the Lower East Side, he couldn't accept what he was hearing. But when he looked to Mandy for moral support as a fellow East Coaster, he was disappointed. As if she hadn't heard any of the lunch options, Mandy finished the crime scene diagram on the whiteboard and headed for the door.

"Pizza's out for me," she announced. "I'm going into town for a salad. Let's regroup in forty-five minutes."

Dot lifted the conference room phone as Mandy passed her.

"Fazzari's, then, Special Agent Biery? You ready for some *real* New York pizza?"

"I am. But I'll have to go back to New York for that."

"No you won't."

"We'll see."

Twenty minutes later, Gavin stuffed each steaming slice into his mouth with the steadiness of a tree going into a wood chipper. It was as good as the joint he used to frequent near the subway stop at Delancey and Essex.

"I told you," Dot remarked, grinning. "Didn't I?"

"It's *almost* as good," Gavin answered while chewing.

"We'll do the Red Arrow tomorrow. Good burgers because the beef comes out of these hills," she replied.

"Would Special Agent Cobb go for that?" the sheriff asked.

His mouth full, Gavin waved him away. "Special Agent Cobb doesn't eat normal food. She—" He cut himself off when Mandy reentered the conference room.

"I'm back with my abnormal food," she remarked as she settled into a chair and opened the salad's plastic lid.

"I guess we could call that a Cobb salad," Dot joked. "Maybe you'll get a reference on the menu over there at Claudia's Clarkston Café. The Special Agent Cobb salad."

"Cobb salads have cheese," Mandy replied without smiling—because she'd heard the quip a hundred times before. "I don't eat dairy." She studied the whiteboard. "Hey—what's that new stuff? You guys have something that indicates the perp is in Central Washington?"

"Yeah," the sheriff replied after wiping his mouth. "I was just about to add it to my files."

Although the Hunt case had federal interest, ultimately Cole Hunt and his family were civilians. Their murder constituted a state crime, not a federal one. While Sheriff Whitcomb was willing to keep the FBI informed, he wasn't about to relinquish his responsibility as the county's top cop and lead detective. Instead of engaging in a jurisdictional dispute with the powerful Bureau, he wisely took advantage of their resources.

"So what's up?" Mandy asked.

Whitcomb tipped his hat to a high angle on his forehead. "Agent Biery here thinks the perp is over in the Tri-Cities area, about two hours west, middle of the state. He hasn't exactly told us why yet. He made us wait for you, Agent Cobb. The pizza guy came. We ate while it was hot. Sorry. I'm usually more of a gentleman than that."

"Hang on, Sheriff," Mandy replied, fork halfway to her mouth. "What are the Tri-Cities?"

"Kennewick, Richland, and Pasco," Dot explained. "My daughter lives there. They're kind of the big town around here. Unless you go across the river to Lewiston. But then you're in Idaho."

Stunned, Mandy rotated her eyes to Gavin, who, judging by the crusts piled on his plate, had eaten five slices of pizza. "Gav, you got a lead to a city a few hours from here? Where the hell did *that* come from? I was only gone for a half hour."

Suddenly conscious of his manners and the pile of crusts, Gavin slid his plate from view. He pressed a napkin over his mouth and cleared his throat.

"Yeah. The suspect or suspects were in that area. At least he-slash-they were two weeks ago."

"Where exactly? You have an address?"

"No."

"So what do you have?"

"I analyzed another layer of data traffic from Maddie Hunt's cell phone logs. The various internet protocol hops allowed me to trace associated data traffic to a router that services the Tri-Cities area."

Mandy Cobb stared at Gavin dubiously while swallowing a wad of arugula.

The prior evening, flexing the national-security clout afforded to her by Dan Murray's credentials, she'd spun up an analytical team in D.C. at "Hoover," shorthand for the namesake building of the Bureau's first legendary—some might say infamous—director.

"You came up with a new lead on your own?" she asked.

"Yes. Why? Did Hoover find something else?"

"No," she conceded. "Not yet."

Mandy had completed a stint at Hoover, working in a unit known as CTAPU, short for the Counterterrorism Advanced Projects Unit. Young, fit, and eager to get in on the action at the time, she was part of a fly team that deployed to global hot spots at a moment's notice, usually to Iraq and Afghanistan, where her role was to assist Army ODA, Delta, or Navy SEAL units during takedowns. Afterward, FBI experts would analyze any materials the operators collected at the site.

Avoiding eye contact with Gavin, she buried her nose in her salad, unsure of herself.

Her partner pro tem was undeniably a resourceful guy when it came to shady underworld dealings involving the dark web. The Ford F-250 in the parking lot served as exhibit A. However, when it came to hardcore forensic computer analysis, she deferred to the *real* experts at Hoover. She even managed to pry Maddie Hunt's cell phone away from Gavin to overnight it to Hoover, along with the bullets the FBI's crime scene techs had extracted from the boards.

"Are you saying," Gavin asked with a smirk, "that Hoover doesn't have any additional info on Maddie's phone? Like *at all*? They still only have the India thing?"

Chagrined, confused, and mildly irritated, Mandy chewed vigorously.

The rub was that the Bureau's DMX group, short for Digital Media Exploitation, had been in possession of Maddie Hunt's phone for a dozen hours. Mandy had expected one of the team's whizbang superagents to run analytical rings around Gavin, pulling on the India thread he'd yanked earlier. In actuality, as one of them had explained on her drive back to Whitcomb's office, DMX lost the trace on the IP address in India.

"Are *we* no longer looking at India?" she asked.

"Oh, India's still relevant as the point of origination. But the terminus is in the Tri-Cities."

Sheriff Whitcomb was losing patience. He lowered his hat to its usual horizontal position. "Since you already had this India connection, it seems to me you could use this information about an IP address to keep tracing it to the source. Is that right?"

Mandy glanced at the local lawman. "The Bureau's working on that. The challenge is that we can IP-trace the source to a router in Delhi. Then it goes through another round of addressing and we lose it. That's why I'm waiting to hear how Special Agent Biery came up with a link to the Tri-Cities."

"Why do we lose the IP address?" Dot asked. "Seems crazy we can follow it to the other side of the planet and then it goes cold."

"It's complicated," Mandy replied. "According to the Bureau analysts, the IP address ends up in a switching station with fiber-optic trunk lines that serve more than a billion people across India, Pakistan, and southwestern China. At that point, it's rerouted into a VPN."

Gavin pushed himself from the table and crossed his legs. "No, that's not right."

Mandy glared at him. It was one thing for him to be glib, quite another to make her look bad in front of local law enforcement.

"Well then what, Agent Biery?" the sheriff asked. "How 'bout you dumb it down for us? Me, anyway."

Gavin waggled the foot across his knee. "If it was only a VPN, I'd be able to find that IP address again and resume the trace. I have tools for that borrowed from—" He was about to say he had borrowed the tools from the NSA, but he didn't want the sheriff to know that. "It doesn't matter about the tools," he substituted. "The real trouble is that the IP ping came in via a Tor network. And that's also what led me to Central Washington."

Sheriff Whitcomb leaned back and dropped his paper plate in a waste bin. "A what?"

"A Tor network. It's a set of volunteer routers around the world, basically, running multiple layers of encryption. Anybody can do it. But mostly, it's people who don't want to be found. Here, check it out."

Gavin angled his laptop so the sheriff could see the screen. Dot stood up and looked over his shoulder. "Why's it called a Tor?" she asked.

"Tor is short for The Onion Router, as in multiple layers. It's a free browser that allows users to maintain complete anonymity on the dark web."

"Looks like a regular old browser to me," the sheriff said, unimpressed.

"It's not the app," Gavin corrected. "It's the data path behind the app. The data travels through three waves of nodes. Each one encrypts, decrypts, and re-encrypts the path. It's more secure than a VPN."

"But you managed to track the IP address to India," Dot noted. "If it's so fancy, how could you do that?"

"I thought of a different angle to try with the data from Maddie's phone. I analyzed the advertising ID attached to her online profile. That's what led to the Tri-Cities."

When he was met with three blank stares, the info-tech specialist kept going.

"See, every time you access the internet, a bunch of smart servers somewhere munge your patterns together through an algorithm. With AI hocus-pocus, these servers know that it's you—Dot, and you, Sheriff—poking around on your phone's browser or your home computer or whatever."

Whitcomb sighed. Lying at his feet, Luna the labrador whimpered. "Come again?"

"I'm talking about an online profile that's very valuable to advertisers. It indicates where you live, what you do, how you shop. These profiles are sold to advertisers through the middlemen who run these servers. The data can be sliced and diced so that an advertiser can break potential customers into behavioral cohorts that are then used as a marketing strategy."

"Agent Biery, what in the hell does that have to do with Maddie Hunt?" the lawman asked as Luna poked her nose against his leg. The sheriff snatched Gavin's mound of pizza crusts and dropped it on the floor.

"I bought the advertising ID associated with the Hunts' zip code. It took me two seconds to find the girl's targeting info and to see who else picked up that ID in the past few weeks."

While Luna ate noisily, the Campus info-tech specialist straightened in his chair to tap a series of orange lines annotated on a bulletin board map. "This is the information the killer had to work with. You can see that Maddie Hunt basically went from school to a soccer field to home. The killer would have been able to find the school and soccer field address online. He'd then be able to deduce where the girl lived. That's how he got the Hunts' address, even though Cole Hunt went to great lengths to stay offline."

"You can just buy this information?" Dot asked.

"Yeah. It was cheap, too, about three thousand dollars. Paid with crypto. No offense to the good people of Clarkston, but there haven't been that many buyers of Clarkston zip code advertising IDs. I was able to see the pricing history in an online auction. Whoever bought the data for Clarkston came in through the Tor browser."

"Well, find the company that bought that data," the sheriff said.

"That's where the Tor network comes in. They did it with complete anonymity."

"Then how do you know the user is in the Tri-Cities?" Mandy asked, irritated that she had to indulge him, but unable to hold back.

"Ah," Gavin replied with a grin. "That would be the work of Princess."

"Did you just call her a *princess*?" Dot asked. Things were a little old-fashioned in Clarkston, but even Dot found the comment offensive.

"No," Gavin replied. "Princess is my homegrown AI engine, named after my cat. I can feed her all kinds of information—like this IP address going to India and the advertising ID to look for digital footprints. She analyzed thousands of data paths and came up with a connection."

"*She*," the sheriff replied. "You mean this . . . Princess."

"Yes," Gavin answered. "The Tor browser that bought the advertising ID had been downloaded hours before purchasing the ID from a Tor server. Princess found the server and detected the IP address as coming from that Tri-Cities area. I picked it up just now, right before you came in, Mandy."

"What does it have to do with the India router?"

"It's an overlap. I originally saw that Maddie Hunt's GPS chip had been sending information out to the India-based IP address. Now I can see that same IP address popping up on that same Tor browser. That's the connection. It's an encrypted comms interface—email."

"So you think this killer, the one who bought the advertising information, is communicating with someone, covertly, in India. Or Pakistan, Bangladesh, or China," the sheriff said.

"Yes. That's what I think."

"Well, that narrows it down."

Mandy was no longer interested in her salad. Back when she was with the Hoover fly team, she often felt she had the advantage because terrorists went to such great pains to avoid electronic communications. At that stage of internet development, the NSA was so good at sniffing out suspect data that the terrorists had to physically transport thumb drives to each other, forcing them out of hiding. Now, it seemed, they'd modernized.

"Okay," she said, standing before the whiteboard. "Let's circle back to where we are with this investigation." She marked the line items written in blue with a red check mark. "From the beginning, we couldn't figure out how the perp or perps could lure the family into the barn without a struggle. Gav—does this advertising-ID strategy the killer used help explain that?"

"It would explain that someone with data skills was feeding sophisticated information to killers about the victims."

Mandy scrawled the point on the whiteboard. "And that person is probably back in South Asia—probably India or Pakistan. Our killers are *visitors* to the U.S.—but the ones who sent them are perhaps in India-Pak."

"Yes."

"That's quite the leap," the sheriff objected. "Couldn't this just be outsourced hackers from somewhere in Asia? You don't know there's any direct conspiracy from anyone in India or Pakistan."

Mandy and Gavin traded a look. The Campus operatives hadn't shared any information about Rafa, whom they considered the root perp of the POSEIDON SPEAR murders and the customer of the mole.

"Fair enough," she said. "The tracking data would tell the killer where Maddie Hunt was. We don't have Cole Hunt's phone. If it tracked him, too, it would tell the killer that he was at a cattle board meeting until nine p.m."

"Hal Wagner confirmed that," Dot said.

The sheriff lifted a sheet of his legal pad, glancing through his notes. "How does this information contribute to the fact that the killers used military-style weapons?"

As Mandy had explained to them, the FBI's Laboratory Division in Quantico had put the ballistics analysis for the Cole Hunt murder at the top of the list. The four recovered bullets showed microscopic trace elements of blowback residue, indicating a contact shot with a suppressor.

"It tells me that this was a sophisticated hit with extensive resources," Mandy said.

The sheriff scowled at the board. "We still don't know how the murderer got Cole Hunt, a certified badass, to go willingly from his house into that barn."

"I disagree," she rebutted. "With Gavin's analysis, we now know the killer could track the Hunt family's cell phones. We also know Hunt was at a meeting with Hal Wagner. That would lead me to believe that after cutting the data lines to the home, the killer took the family hostage in the barn and waited for Cole to arrive. He went into the barn and was ambushed."

"I wouldn't want to try to get Cole Hunt in flex-cuffs by myself," the sheriff added. "Would you?"

"Hell no," Mandy said. "This was at least a two-man job."

"Okay," the sheriff finished. "So where do we go from here?"

Mandy inclined her head at Gavin. "Looks like Agent Biery here needs to get Princess into action to find us an address in the Tri-Cities."

23

BAMIYAL, INDIA

JACK WAITED AT THE LONELY INTERSECTION, BATHED IN THE DEEP RED GLOW OF THE hazy setting sun. As he glanced at the paper map spread across the Rover's steering wheel, he wondered for the twentieth time whether he was in the right place.

He and Clark had agreed on a set of coordinates that *should* indicate the intersection of two remote dirt roads a few miles east of the Pakistani border. However, after pulling the fuse on the Rover's GPS and traveling without a smartphone to avoid further surveillance, Jack wasn't entirely sure he was "on the X," as his operator friends liked to say.

Relief swept over him when he heard the grind of an engine approaching. He hadn't seen a vehicle for the last ten miles in this remote corner of the world, so he was fairly certain it must be Midas. There was one way to find out. He toggled the headlights twice, and the approaching truck responded with three answering flashes.

Parked at an angle, Jack slid out of the Rover's right-hand driver's seat and waited with his boot on the rear bumper, next to the shattered taillight and five bullet holes courtesy of the men with the assault rifles in the Thar. Thank God they'd had to turn their barrels on the bull, giving Jack just enough time for a hurried escape.

"Dr. Ryan, I presume," Midas announced with a flourish as he jumped down from the left side of the cab-over heavy-transport truck.

"Is that really you, Midas?"

"Hell yes. I'm going full muj for this op. What do you think? Decent job?"

Going full *muj*, referring to mujahideen, meant Midas donned the soft, flat Chitrali hat with rolled edges characteristic of rural peasants in Pakistan and Afghanistan. As an extra selling point, he also sported a thick, unkempt beard that flowed down his neck like ivy on a trellis. He wore a faded beige dhoti over his trousers and desert combat boots.

Another man approached from the right-hand driver's side. His beard was thinner, just a few days of growth, but his mustache was thick.

"Let me introduce you to my friend," Midas said. "This is Officer Suhas. He got me kitted up and made the drive from Delhi."

It took Jack a moment to recognize the CIA Delhi station chief, Suhas Chauhan. Jack had seen him a few days ago at the American embassy, but tonight the chief was decked out in the same muj getup as Bartosz. His dark skin and drapey clothes made him indistinguishable from the locals.

"Midas wouldn't tell me who his contact was," the CIA officer said, extending his hand and smiling. "I should have guessed it would be you."

Jack chuckled. "And I guess I should have known it would be you getting him here. Thanks for the help."

"My pleasure." The CIA man studied the AGI credential on the lanyard around Jack's neck. "I thought you were here for a wedding."

"I am." Jack inspected the luminous dial of his old Rolex Submariner. "I need to hurry up and get Midas across the border, then rush back to Amritsar. You wouldn't happen to know anything about how to do a *filmi*—one of those Bollywood dances—would you? Just a couple of moves to help me out?"

"Oh, yeah, one of those. My wife made me take a class once. I might remember a few moves."

"There's some dance that has to do with the Bhagavad Gita . . . and Kama Sutra."

Straining under the weight of a heavy box at the rear of the truck, Midas grunted. "Yo, fellas. Are we really having this conversation? How about a hand?"

"Indian weddings are elaborate," Suhas explained as they joined Midas. "You'll have to fake it. If I were you, I'd—" The CIA man was interrupted by bleating goats. He responded by spitting out guttural Urdu at the vehicle's cargo area, then turned to Jack like a mother embarrassed by her children's behavior. "Sorry. The goats are spooked."

Jack elevated himself on his toes to gain a view through the slats of the truck's bed. "Where the hell did you get a goat herd?"

"We keep them at a farm near the station. This is our standard up-country cover. Let me show you why." He opened a dusty panel that revealed a cargo area beneath a false floor. "We packed most of Midas's kit here. The embassy Marines assembled it based on the requirements specified in the ODNI tasking message."

As if to demonstrate, Midas pulled a black Pelican case free and thumped it on the dirt.

"Speaking of borrowed weapons . . ." Jack said to Suhas. He

lifted his cuff to show the Glock 43. "Thanks again for this. I'd tell you how I had to use it—but then I'd have to kill you."

"Please don't. Worse than killing me would be the cable I'd have to send to Langley to explain it."

"Well, there were some guys following me," Jack said. "I'll leave it at that."

"Not surprised. They may have been Indian army. There was a terror attack in Kashmir, just north of us. A fundamentalist militia took out an Indian infantry platoon—analysis flowing back from the NCTC suggests it was a group called the Umayyad Caliphate, a Daesh splinter. Have you heard of them?"

"No," Jack lied.

"We're pressing assets for more info on them. Anyway, be careful up here. I'd expect the Indians to be shooting first, asking questions later after the beating they took."

"That's comforting."

"Hey!" Midas shouted. "You two ladies want to help a brother out?"

Jack lowered the Rover's back seat and pitched in with stacking the heavy Pelican cases.

"If you take this road southwest," Suhas explained after five minutes of loading, "you'll reach a farming village. The reports I've seen from the NSA suggest that the Indian army patrols the main road. They're worried about chatter that a bigger terror operation is in the works. You need to be careful near the border, Jack. Copy?"

"Copy. I've got this for cover." Jack raised his company ID card. "AGI has a buried fiber line about a mile from here that crosses into Pakistan next to a railroad that goes to Lahore. I'll tell them I got lost. You know, the stupid American routine."

"Not that far from the truth," Midas added.

Suhas grinned. "You guys need anything else? The cable from ODNI just said to drop you off. My work is done here, officially."

"Yeah, we're fine," Midas replied. "Probably best if you forgot you ever saw us."

"Saw who?"

AFTER THREE MILES, MIDAS ASKED JACK TO PULL OVER. THE FORMER DELTA OPERA-tor studied his terrain map and compared it to a GPS reading on his mobile Iridium communicator. "This is the spot. We're in Pakistan. Kill the lights."

Jack did as requested.

Confident they had evaded any Indian army patrols, the former Delta man donned a Kevlar plate carrier vest with spare magazines concealed beneath his loose dhoti shirt. Now that they sat in the dark, he secured his high-cut Advanced Combat Helmet to his chin and lowered his AN/PSQ-20 enhanced night vision device, or NVD, over his eyes. They were the latest and greatest, combining infrared and ambient light for improved imagery.

"He should be here in a few minutes," Midas said, searching the scrub brush that stretched to the silver hills.

"He's not coming by road?"

"Probably not. Rustam's a Tajik. He thinks like a nomad—tends to stick to overlanding."

Jack surveyed the moonlit plain. Mountain shadows loomed in the distance. "How do you know this guy? What's his background?"

"Russians killed Rustam's wife in Tajikistan, and he ended up with like-minded fighters taking them on. We hired him when we set up our special ops base in Uzbekistan, called K-2 back then. Rustam led my kill teams against the Taliban, ISIS, and the Emir's Umayyad network."

"Mopping up the Emir's Umayyad? That sounds like POSEI-DON SPEAR."

"Because it was."

"I didn't realize you were part of that."

"I was at the NCTC then, under Mrs. Foley. I took out three Emir associates with the help of my guy Rustam. We were operating on the other side of the valley. The Pakistani tribal area."

Jack sat in silence for a minute. They faced west, away from the rising moon, the scraggly vegetation before them in varying hues of gray.

"I want to go with you," he said.

"*Uh-uh.*" Midas shook his head. "You're here with Lisanne, on vacation. I heard about the arm surgery. You need to be with her. And you're my backup exfil if anything goes sideways. Stay put. Clark's orders."

"Orders shift with the battlespace. Isn't that what you operators say?"

Midas grunted. "Sure. But you're not in the battlespace. That said . . ." He dug through the rucksack between his knees and removed a device with the rough profile of a walkie-talkie. "This is an Indian army push-to-talk satellite communicator. Suhas sourced it for us so Rustam and I could maintain deniability in case there are any foreign COMINT snoops. This is an extra. Take it. Clark gave me your number. I programmed it into the first button in my Indian comms device, just in case."

"What are you using as primary comms?"

"This Iridium," Midas said. "It's a civilian model. Blends in if caught."

"Okay."

"I'll use that Indian gear to hit you as a backup link in case I lose Iridium coverage. You never know."

Jack accepted the green SATCOM terminal. "Why did Suhas source this?"

"Because it's indig, same as the Indian army carries. The transmissions bounce off an Indian GSAT in the S, K, and CU frequency bands. The Indian birds are tuned for this area, according to Suhas."

"Roger that," Jack replied. He studied the device's keypad and earpiece. "What's your primary exfil? Who's coming out?"

"It will be me, the chief, Cary, and Jad. There's also a new guy, a Marine Raider named Tom Buck. I haven't met him, but he's been training with Master Chief Moore. Rustam will bring us back across the border, and Suhas will pick us up with Indian legends. You don't need to worry about it."

Disappointed at his exclusion, Jack replied, "Roger that. What's the latest intel on our target, Rafa?" He leaned sideways and clipped the Indian SATCOM terminal to his belt.

"We don't have much on the target area. A few fresh satellite images from the DIA—they're probably already outdated. That's why Campus needs me to get eyes-on."

"Okay. But what about Rafa? What's he doing out here?"

"The brief I got," Midas began, "is that he's bringing in fighters from the wild hills of the Hindu Kush, Karakorams, and Himalayas. Some of those guys are ex-ISIS, Daesh . . . the crazy bastards that live to overthrow civilization."

"That's all?"

"Give them credit for not thinking small. Of course, Rafa also wants to kill the people who took out his father, the Emir."

Jack gazed across the dim valley. "Huh. I was in on the hunt for the Emir, you know. Rafa's dad had big plans for mayhem in the States."

"Yeah, I know. Something about a nuclear waste dump in Nevada."

"Yup. My first Campus op. We bundled the Emir up for interrogation at Clark's farm before turning him over to Dan Murray. The chickenshit sang like a canary after a doc gave him a medically induced heart attack in custody."

"So I heard. You, Clark, and Ding stopped the father. POSEIDON SPEAR took care of the network. Now we'll get the son—pull this poisonous weed out by the root."

Jack folded his arms over his chest. "Has anyone figured out how Rafa is getting his fighters in and out of the U.S. for the SPEAR hits?"

"Mandy and Gav are working the problem."

"How is Rafa getting the SPEAR information? Mole?"

"That's the thinking, yeah. Like I said. Gavin and Mandy are working it."

"Pretty big deal to get inside our kitchen like that. Are they close?"

"I'm sure they'll unpack it before he nails the next SPEAR Bubba."

Jack glanced at him with a raised eyebrow. "What if Rafa's got more than just a kill list? What if he's trying to carry on what his father started?"

Though a lieutenant colonel, Midas was not one to ponder the deeper meaning of orders. What he'd liked about working for the Joint Special Operations Command back in his day was that he would get timely intelligence, a juicy target, and the leeway to go after it any way he wanted. Debating the higher-level strategy had never interested him much, the primary reason he left active duty before his career dead-ended in a cubicle.

"It's not going to matter," Midas answered with a dismissive hand wave. "Rafa walks around with a fancy staff like a king, acting like some great ancient caliph. I'm going to put his head on that stake and stick it in the ground. That's the language these dickheads understand. We'll finally be rid of the Umayyad Revolutionary Council . . . Or whatever the hell they want to call themselves."

"It would be nice to interrogate Rafa first, wouldn't it?" Jack persisted. "Make sure there's not some bigger op going? Suhas said the Indians have picked up chatter."

"Of course they have. There's always chatter with these nut-jobs. Look, man. A capture's not a luxury we can afford. This is a hard-target kill op. Clear, Mr. Ryan?"

"As mud."

Eyeing Jack's crestfallen chin, Midas added, "Tell you what. I'll do a complete SSE. I'll bring you plenty of intel when I—Oh wait. Hold on. I've got movement, eleven o'clock." The green glow from the NVDs lit the top of Midas's beard as he gazed forward through the windshield. "Okay. That's my guy. Flash your lights."

Jack cycled the Rover's headlights. It was answered a few seconds later by three slow blinks.

Midas grinned tightly. "Crazy bastard has the same Land Cruiser pickup he used in Afghanistan. Bought it with our money. Must be six hundred thousand miles on that thing. Hard ones."

"Before he gets here . . ." Jack said, raising his camera, still thinking of the terrorists assembling in Kashmir and the grand plans the Emir had laid many years ago. He flipped through the images in the Nikon's small digital display. "These are the guys that tailed me. Fighting-age males. Dark hair with ball caps. Suhas thought they were probably Indian army. But look—they have Caucasian skin tone. That seem weird to you?"

With the NVDs tipped up on his helmet, Midas studied the images. "I saw the bullet holes in your truck. They looked smaller-caliber, high-velocity rounds, not your standard seven-six-two AK stuff. Indian Special Forces carry some long guns with those calibers. Could have been their equivalent of an Alpha team trailing you."

"But they're white guys."

"I agree they might be Caucasian from the picture. India's a big country, plenty of different skin colors. And it could just be the lighting."

Jack placed the camera on the console between them. "If they're Indian army, why wouldn't they come at me directly? I wasn't a threat—I was in an Indian corporate vehicle."

Midas ignored the question. He plucked a red-lensed flashlight from his belt and waved it at the incoming pickup through the open window.

"Let's just kill Rafa and get out of this hellhole," he said gruffly as he opened the door. "Come on. You should meet my guy."

The battered Toyota Land Cruiser pickup skidded to a stop in a cloud of gray moondust. A hard-faced man stepped out, his dark, sooty eyes scanning the surroundings. He wore a maroon turban that wrapped around his head, extended over his shoulders and neck, and covered his face from the bridge of his nose down. His broad shoulders gave him the overall shape of a square.

The Tajik and Midas embraced like old comrades, slapping each other's backs in the moonlight. Midas introduced him as Rustam.

Rustam studied Jack with onyx eyes while lowering the cloth from the front of his face. "Nice to meet you," he said carefully— as if he'd rehearsed it during his long drive.

Jack estimated the crusty muj fighter's age as somewhere between fifty and eighty. It was difficult to tell with someone whose skin had been toughened by years of frigid, chapping wind.

Midas spoke to him in a hesitant mix of Urdu, Tajik, and Dari— the dialect in the far reaches of these mountains. Rustam covered his nose with the cloth and moved to the back of his Land Cruiser to transfer the weapons.

Jack helped lift a case into the bed of the battered vehicle. He noticed two green diesel fuel caps near the fender, stirring memories of a trip to Africa. Twelve years earlier, his mother had taken him, Katie, and Kyle on a safari vacation in Kenya. Their guide had driven the same Land Cruiser pickup, proudly showcasing its range and durability.

"Nice truck," Jack said.

Rustam didn't answer, either because he didn't understand or couldn't be bothered.

Jack and Midas shared the load of a heavy weapons case and hoisted it onto the tailgate. "I meant to ask you earlier but didn't want to tip off Suhas. What's with so much kit?"

Midas glanced at the burdened truck bed. "What do you mean?"

"You've got enough for a platoon here."

"We're in the Pakistani tribal lands, Jack. Hell comes from above, below, and sideways."

"How far in are you going?"

"Our last chunk of intel said Rafa's camp is about forty miles northwest of here."

Rustam approached, his hard eyes darting between Jack and Bartosz. He swept aside the fabric over his chest and pulled a cigar package from his breast pocket. He offered one to Midas along with a matchbook.

Midas lit it, clenched it between his teeth, and puffed until the tip glowed orange. Rustam tilted the pack toward Jack, who declined. The salty muj fighter walked away, his boots crunching on the dried grass.

While Rustam stood a dozen paces off, smoking while staring at the moon, Midas unsnapped the buckles on a case and raised the lid, exposing an M2010 Enhanced Sniper Rifle (ESR) packed in foam. "Marines did me right," he said. "This thing's a beaut."

"Custom?"

"Sort of." Midas pried the black ESR from the foam and extended the folded buttstock. The barrel was encased in a black polycarbonate chassis studded with pill-shaped vents and long grooves on either side, doubling as a monorail mounting system. The dull black barrel ended in a yellow-green self-ratcheting titanium suppressor.

Midas affixed the rifle to his shoulder and aimed at the stars, one eye to the scope. "I asked for a Horus Tremor3 scope. They delivered. Sighted it for me at five hundred yards with a minute of angle of point five. Damned good MOA. I also picked up a clip-on thermal for night work from the leathernecks. Want to see?"

Midas held the rifle out to Jack, who gripped the seventeen-pound weapon and perched it on the truck's tailgate. Jack extended the bipod, crouched, and sighted a bush on a distant hill, silver in the moonlight. "Ammo?" he asked.

"Three hundred Winchester Magnum. They add an MOA of another point five. But I'll take one-point-oh any day. The bullets are packed with Hodgdon's four-eight-three-one powder for max velocity."

Jack didn't know the ins and outs of gunpowder choices, but that sounded good to him. "WinMags. Cool," he said. "What's the max range, then?"

"Well, I'm using Sierra MatchKing hollow-point boattails. They're super-low drag. That increases terminal velocity and extends the range over the normal M24 sniper kit to about twelve hundred yards. I have six boxes, five rounds each."

Jack closed his hands around the pistol grip and dry-fired at the bush. "Damn," he remarked after a soft whistle. "Hell of a rifle."

"This one never failed me in the 'Stan. And she's not going to fail me out here." Midas folded the stock and stowed the long gun in its case. "But hey, Jack. I specked three M4s in case Rustam brought another guy. Since it's just me and him on this thing, why don't you take my extra one? Clark didn't say you couldn't defend yourself. Sounds like you've had a rough go out here."

"You sure you can spare it?"

"Consider it yours. In case those army goons, or whoever they were, follow you home." Midas opened a second case, dug out an M4 packed in foam, and handed it to Jack.

"Thanks, Midas."

"My pleasure. Sort of. You need a better pistol than that pea-shooter on your leg?"

"I never turn down a pistol," Jack said.

"Good man. Here's a Glock 17. Suppressor, too, in case some asshole gets cute." Jack set his growing arsenal aside, thinking about where he might be able to hide it at the guesthouse. He noted the rest of Midas's kit: Claymore mines, fragmentation grenades, a knife, and a stainless steel tomahawk with a sharpened pick.

"I thought you were the forward element calling in the guys from the air, not the main force."

"Well, yeah," Midas responded. "But who says I can't kill the little fucker myself?"

24

OF PAKISTANI BIRTH AND FRENCH NATIONALITY, FAHIM BAJWA KNEW HE LED A COM-
plicated life. There were days, like this one, when he genuinely
wondered whether it was worth all the trouble.

Yes, he relished the money that flowed from the brigadier's ISI
headquarters into the Zurich account to transport weapons and
recruits for his half brother, Rafa. Then there was the hefty salary
Daval Rai paid him as the AGI operations chief, along with a virtually unlimited expense account.

He had access to a company jet to zip between continents,
landing at the smaller, more exclusive airports, where customs
agents were easy to bribe. They never asked questions when they
picked up small pallets of weapons or new recruits and flew them
back to India. Such were the unusual perks of AGI's brightest and
best engineer, the man who *should* be in line to succeed Daval
Rai—if it weren't for Srini's new husband.

Fahim Bajwa's personal flight staff consisted of well-paid former
Russian air force pilots, who accepted these trips as a business mat-
ter. As far as they were concerned, Mr. Bajwa was the company's
COO, a gifted engineer and bridge builder. Erecting complex

infrastructure projects in the darker corners of the world took a knack for getting things done, as they knew from their time under Putin's Russia. Often, as in Africa, Central Asia, and the steamier portions of South America, that required men who could fight. It didn't seem the least bit strange that the company's number two man ran a gunrunning operation on the side. He was a practical man, a fixer.

On their last flight to East Africa, Fahim received a shipment of sniper weapons from a Cairo arms dealer at a desert airfield. Khan had arranged the payments to the dealer. Although Fahim would have preferred to remain uninformed for his own safety, the weapons dealer explained that the firearms were the latest Indian sniper rifles, Sabres. The Russian pilots were impressed with the brief demonstration in the middle of the desert. When Fahim delivered them to a remote AGI construction site in northern India, they asked no questions.

Colonel Khan told Fahim that the rifle had a one-and-a-half-kilometer range, proudly developed by a weapons maker in Bengaluru for use by the Indian Para Special Forces teams. They were only now filtering into the most elite Indian units. They would be ideal for the Karakoram operation—the thing that mattered most to Fahim.

There was an additional perk to flying around the world. The Egyptian weapons dealer—whose customers possessed vast bank accounts, a taste for the finer things, and a lack of morality—had connected Fahim to a madam in Budapest who dealt in the finest beauties. One of them, Ilona, was down the hall, rented for a month for a hundred thousand euros. She was laughing and speaking to a friend, as relaxed as if she'd lived in Amritsar for months.

Fahim didn't speak Hungarian, and he wasn't sure who Ilona was talking to. But he supposed it had something to do with the midnight wedding festivities that would take place over at Daval

Rai's grand palace. An event of singing and dancing at which Fahim would wear one of his elegant Italian suits and march Ilona past Srini to remind her what a fool she'd been to reject him.

He selected a charcoal Zegna from a row of nearly identical suits and hung it on a rod. Next came a purple Hermès tie and a spread-collar shirt with French cuffs. Fahim held the outfit under his face before the full-length mirror. Satisfied, he headed to the shower, thinking about his next flight to Budapest. AGI was boring a tunnel through the Carpathians, connecting Romania and Serbia, another Chinese-funded project. The madam said she would have a fresh girl waiting, provided he brought Ilona back unharmed.

When he stepped out of the shower, Ilona was still on the phone, her voice echoing on the marble floors. The Amritsar apartment Fahim rented whenever the boss decamped to his summer palace had a good view of the city. The moon was rising, and the royal enclave looked peaceful. On the horizon, Fahim glimpsed the warm yellow glow of Daval Rai's compound.

The boss had insisted that Fahim stay in one of the guesthouses on the grounds of the impressive Sikh palace. Fahim declined, feigning a pained expression. Daval knew that Fahim had courted his daughter, Srini, proposing marriage. To this day, the tycoon believed his talented engineer carried on with a heavy heart and that the wedding would be an event filled with searing pain.

The notion contained a grain of truth. Fahim had always seen Srini as the next step on his path to assume the top leadership position in Rai's vast AGI empire. Khan wanted that. Rafa wanted that. Fahim wanted that. There had been only one problem—Srini did not want *him*.

Well. She would be sorry for that miscalculation. After the Karakoram Gorge dedication, he would end up with the AGI empire anyway.

With steam still clinging to the backlit mirror, he sat naked on a padded bench and scooted it forward. He opened a small jar of La Mer skin cream and rubbed it into his forehead and eyes. On his last swing through Marseille, he'd paid nearly a thousand dollars for the moisturizer.

Touching the soft tissue below his eyes, he fretted at the network of lines. Finally, he darkened his lower eyelids with a mascara brush and slightly thickened his lashes, something he'd been doing since he was twenty and couldn't stop because everyone thought his dark rims were genetic.

After finishing with his face, he bent over his knees and let his long hair fall forward. Tending to his man bun was always the final ritual before dressing. With his eyes closed, he gathered the strands.

"May I have the makeup table?" Ilona asked in halting English. Through his curtain of dark hair, he could see her bare feet, narrow ankles, and shapely calves.

"Not yet," Fahim replied, still bent over.

Ilona took a few steps to face him directly, her crotch inches from his forehead. His eyes rose to the enticing triangle formed between her thighs. She slipped two fingers into the waistband of her silky panties and slid them down.

"Leave your hair loose," she said, forcing his face between her legs. "I like it that way."

For a blissful, fleeting interlude, Fahim forgot about Karakoram.

HOWEVER, KARAKORAM WAS MUCH ON HIS MIND WHEN HIS AGI AIRBUS H135 HELIcopter swooped into a steep turn while he studied the moonlit landscape from the rear seat. The Russian pilot announced through the intercom that he had the bonfire in sight.

"Set it down here," he instructed his pilot. "I'll cover the last fifty meters on foot. Stay in the aircraft."

Dren had converted a portion of the Thar SUV's tire jack into a rod that held a large hunk of meat roasting over the flames. The Albanian had ripped the bull apart with his Indian-made carbine on full auto. His Albanian partner, Agon, used his tactical blade to slice a two-kilo slab of flesh from the dead animal's shoulder.

"How did you miss him?" Fahim demanded in English as the three came close enough to speak while the helicopter's engines wound down. They had avoided sharing details over their cell phones. The Indian Intelligence Bureau was notorious for eavesdropping.

"He made us," Dren responded, still chewing.

"But you let him get away?"

"He strung out a spike strip. Then he fired on us," Agon answered.

Fahim struggled to keep the astonishment off his face.

Ryan was a wedding guest, out on a sojourn to tour company sites, unarmed and alone, soon to be a tragic victim of northern India's spiraling terrorist problem. Moreover, Dren and Agon had been hired away from the French Foreign Legion, which they'd both joined after service in Albania's Special Operations Regiment. They had trained on the Indian guns in the deserts of the American West, gaining proficiency for their hits on the men on the target list provided by Colonel Khan. How could they blow this?

"I don't understand. You're saying that Ryan had a weapon?"

"*Po*," Dren answered, the Albanian word for *yes*. "He had a . . ." Unable to come up with the English word, he pantomimed a pistol with his finger and thumb.

Fahim placed his hands on his hips and stared out at the dark farmland. "Where was he before he did this?"

"Dera Baba Nanak. The railroad construction place," Agon replied. His English was better than Dren's.

"What did he do there?"

"He wandered around the construction site. Spoke to workers. Where he got this." Dren gestured to the shark-toothed chain on the side of the road. Fahim studied it; from his duties running AGI's international construction projects, he recognized the string of spiked metal as part of a trencher.

"Where did he go?"

The Albanians glanced at each other. "That way."

Fahim's eyes lingered on the northern horizon, captivated by the sweep of scattered stars. Now that Rafa had a growing legion of trained psychopaths—thanks to Fahim and Khan—there was no telling how he might react to Ryan's second escape. He might even sever the relationship with the ISI, which served as Fahim's piggy bank. That wouldn't do.

The engineer glanced at the Patek Philippe on his wrist. The party was only a few hours off. Ilona should already be there, making the other men's tongues wag as she glided through the entry hall in the dress he'd bought for her in Paris.

He would need to return quickly before Daval Rai noticed his absence. Though he might attribute it to jealousy, the old baron could be surprisingly astute.

Worried the woodsmoke would infest his suit, Fahim stepped away from the fire, shaking his head, irritated by all of life's little complications, and wondering if there was some way to kill Ryan in the middle of the lion's den without implicating himself. That would make his half brother happy.

"Break the guns down and get in the helicopter," he told Agon and Dren. "You're going back to America on my jet. Tonight."

"What about the car?"

"You two have been exposed. I need you out of the country. Immediately. Torch it."

Agon and Dren unscrewed the rifles into a half dozen pieces and stowed them in padded cases. Dren opened the Thar's fuel cap and fed a chain of rags made from a torn shirt into the tank. Dren lit the end of the cloth and trudged to the waiting helicopter with his rifle case swinging from his arm. The Thar exploded behind him.

Fahim was too preoccupied with thoughts of Rafa to notice. Determined to maintain the integrity of the Karakoram Bridge dedication, he pulled his cell phone from his trouser pocket, opened the ISI app, and tapped the blue link for a heavily encrypted voice-over-IP data call. The brigadier answered after a single monotone ring.

"I'm going to need another name from the list," the AGI man said without preamble.

"No," Khan replied. "It's too soon."

"Why? There have been no aftereffects from that last hit on Hunt or the other two operatives. We can do another one if it's not too far from Hanford. My men aren't suspects and are on their way to Washington State now."

The connection hissed in Fahim's ear as he waited for the reply.

"The answer is still no. We're too close to Karakoram. We can't afford any risks. You, of all people, know that."

Fahim did know that. He also knew he needed to keep Rafa happy to finish the operation that would cement his ascendance. "You need Rafa for the Karakoram Gorge, Brigadier. You need to keep him happy."

"Don't give me orders. Rafa *owes* me the Gorge. *You* owe me the Gorge. I have everything lined up on my end. He's got the weapons and should be heading into the passes as we speak, now that the snows have melted. There's no backing out of this."

"Colonel, you know how unpredictable Rafa can be."

"*Ullu ka patha*," Khan swore in Urdu, roughly calling Fahim an SOB in a clipped tone. "How much of my cash have you wasted on your women and champagne? Control your brother." The brigadier ended the call.

Fahim stared at the blazing Thar, its flames leaping twenty feet into the night sky. As an engineer, he believed there was always a solution if one thought deeply enough.

He would find another way to kill Ryan.

That was the easiest way to keep his half brother focused on the Gorge.

25

RUSTAM DOWNSHIFTED THE LAND ROVER TRUCK AND PAUSED BEFORE THE FAST-flowing river. He lowered his window. Ten feet in front of them, sluicing water hissed and chugged like a steam locomotive.

"Rapids," Midas nearly shouted from the left-side passenger seat in the native tongue. "You sure this is the best place to . . ." He couldn't think of the right word for *ford*. He simplified it with a hand gesture.

Rustam, never one for words, answered by shifting the truck to first gear and letting out the clutch. The truck inched over smooth river rocks. When the wheels slipped at the bank, Rustam shifted to neutral, set the parking brake, and exited the vehicle.

Midas set his pistol on the dash while Rustam worked on each of the four wheels, engaging the locking differentials. After covering about thirty miles, they were well into the tribal area. The ex-Delta commando scanned the far bank with his NVDs.

The mujahideen reentered the vehicle and buckled his seat belt. Midas found that a bit humorous. Here they were, on a hunt for terrorists, about to cross a river that could sweep them away as easily as a beach ball on a wave, and Rustam was taking the trouble to fasten his seat belt.

"The snowmelt," the American remarked. "Running fast."

The mujahideen nodded grimly. His knee rose gently as he released the clutch.

There wasn't much left in the world that could frighten Midas. He'd faced craven killers, dangled from a towering oak during a botched jump exercise, and survived a firefight in Fallujah while four of his Delta buddies didn't. But this river scared him. It swirled to the bottom of the window, leaking cold water through the seals and dampening the seat of his pants. God only knew what was happening in the truck bed. The vehicle's tail end shifted like a rowboat caught in a riptide. Good thing they had tied the weapons cargo down.

"Hey," Midas said to his companion while clenching the handrail. "If this gets any deeper . . ."

Rustam's black eyes remained fixed behind his NVDs, focused on the far bank. Seated behind the right-mounted steering wheel, he was technically upstream from Midas. Water poured through the door seals, pooling inches on the floor. The vehicle crawled forward.

Midas remembered his training in the hated helo-dunker pool at the Navy base in Pensacola, where cruel instructors strapped blacked-out goggles over their eyes and pushed them into a metal cage, spinning them upside down. Only then were the Delta trainees allowed to fumble through narrow steel doors, weighed down with armor plates and ammo. Midas had almost drowned. That had frightened him—like this.

Thankfully, the hood angled up and the chassis jerked as wheels caught. Water sloshed around his boots.

Jesus, Mary, and Joseph, he thought as the truck rumbled up the other side.

An hour later, the moon had passed its peak, still bright enough to outline the jagged mountains in an eerie light. The illumination was adequate without NVDs, even with the headlights off. Rustam remained at the wheel. Now that they had ventured deeper into the ungoverned tribal area, he frequently stopped, shut off the engine, and listened. Midas didn't attempt conversation. The mujahideen had their ways.

Rustam had pushed the rugged pickup over two rocky spines that ended in narrow, boulder-strewn troughs. Midas thought they were overlanding, far from anything that might be considered a beaten path, but here on the third spine he spotted the whitish thread of a trail. Rustam broke his long silence by pointing ahead and grunting.

Midas pushed against the armrests to get a better view. Downslope, he caught sight of a curl of dark smoke and a flicker of leaping orange flames. Upon closer inspection, he saw a collection of huts with a bonfire on one side.

"That our first stop?" he asked.

"*Han,*" Rustam responded. Yes.

MIDAS LEFT HIS HELMET WITH THE NVD MOUNTS, HIS PLATE CARRIER, AND HIS SIDEarm in the truck. Feeling naked in the firelight, he laid his right palm over his heart and bowed to the village elder while the wood crackled.

"*Min sakon se aata hon.*" I come in peace. "*Shukriya.*"

The elder had a hooked nose, a grizzled beard, and a missing incisor. His dark pakol cap was pushed back on his head, softening his granite face. He wore a shirt with patterns reminiscent of a Persian rug beneath a thick, rag-wool vest. "*Salaam.*"

Rustam rummaged through his pockets and found more of his cigars. The teenagers and the elder accepted them and lit up.

Behind them, a pair of potbellied goats clacked their teeth while masticating leafless, thorny scrub into food. A young girl swathed in dark blue fabric emerged from a hut, spied Bartosz with her large brown eyes, and scurried back inside.

Midas fished through his thigh pockets and retrieved the wrapped candies he always carried for the kids and, occasionally, for himself. "A gift for her," he said, gesturing at the hut.

One of the boys grabbed the candy and vanished behind the hanging curtain that served as a door. Female voices giggled. Midas caught the scent of meat cooking, probably lamb. His mouth watered. He had learned long ago that any hellhole in the world could be made better with meat over a fire.

Beside him, caught in a gust of smoke that made his eyes water, Rustam unleashed a rapid stream of tribal language that was too fast for Midas to follow. The elder responded, waving an arm to indicate the moonlit cliffs encircling the valley. The conversation went on for five minutes, while the lightly bearded boy observed Midas as if assessing him. Then the boy dashed away.

"He has horses," Rustam announced, moving sideways out of the smoke.

The elder's mouth slanted into a strange half grin. The gap between his rotten teeth was pronounced, making him appear momentarily deranged in the deep shadows of the fire.

"Okay," Midas replied in English. "How many horses?"

"Four. Two pack. Two ride. We go from here."

The boy reemerged, leading their mounts. Midas knew a bit about the horses in the Himalayan steppe, having used them during his previous ventures into the tribal areas. The unusual thing about them in Afghanistan was their lack of fear of gunfire. But it had been a few years since the last major conflict.

"We sleep here," Rustam said. "In the morning, we load up the horses. They hide our truck for us."

"*Han,*" Midas returned. "But only three hours. We need to stay on track to find Rafa."

"Not hard. Easy."

"Why easy?"

Rustam switched to Urdu. "Because Rafa has a camp ten kilometers from here, just north. The elder hates Rafa. He says he is a false prophet."

Midas shook his head and grinned. "I'm really starting to like this guy."

26

MASTER SERGEANT CARY MARKS SHOVED HIS GREEN ACTIVE-DUTY ID CARD THROUGH the window. A Marine boot private who looked to be all of eighteen years old studied it as if it were a foreign passport.

"What's the problem?" Marks spat, irritated and impatient to get out of his Chevy Silverado. He and Jad Mustafa had driven three hours from their Operational Detachment Alpha (ODA) post at Fort Campbell after the call came in from Clark to spin up for an op. Now this skinny, pimply-faced kid in a uniform so new it practically crunched when he walked was giving Cary a hard time.

He swore under his breath as the private consulted a clipboard. Clark had told Cary to arrive at Lejeune before 1300. Despite driving like a madman, he was half an hour late.

That only added to the miserable mood the Green Beret had been in when Clark called that morning. The day before, he'd learned he had been passed over for promotion for the third time. The wound was still fresh as he sat there, getting a once-over from a boot barely out of high school.

"Come on, Private," he snapped at the Marine. "We're late."

The private had a phone receiver pressed to his ear. He nodded once.

"You gotta be shittin' me," Cary muttered to Jad.

"Easy, man. The jarhead's just doing his job."

Yeah, Cary thought. *Sounds familiar.*

He'd brooded over the missed promotion for the past hundred miles. He knew it wasn't a healthy thing to do—if his wife were in the passenger's seat instead of Jad Mustafa, she'd have taken him to task.

Nevertheless, the way Cary figured it, he'd gone the distance doing covert ops for John Clark and his merry band of Campus marauders. He'd volunteered for Campus missions in Seoul, the Philippines, Vietnam, and, most recently, an oil platform near Venezuela, where he damn near got himself killed before sniping a troop of cutthroat Wagner Group mercenaries.

He'd never imagined that while running around the world doing favors for Clark and, presumably, President Ryan—whom he'd even met once—the Army would overlook his exploits. Yet he was passed over for promotion for the third time. How in the hell was that fair?

The skipper of his ODA, a decent if straightlaced West Pointer, told him it was because Cary spent too much time away from his Green Beret unit on special TDY ops attached to the Office of the Director of National Intelligence.

Well, of course he had. The ODNI was how Clark coded the TDY orders whenever Cary went into harm's way for that crusty old SEAL. To make matters worse, when the ODA captain asked Cary why he hadn't spent more time with his unit—the famed Triple Nickel horse soldiers of Afghanistan—Cary stood there like an idiot because he was sworn to secrecy.

"Look," the captain concluded. "I'm sorry, Marks. That's how the promo board sees it. Better luck next time. *Hua!*"

Whether there would even be a next time was what Cary had been stewing on most of all. He hadn't said a word to Jad during the drive except to complain of the noxious smell in the truck cab as his brother Green Beret spewed one poisonous gaseous burst after another from his flatulent ass. Though his fellow noncom had volunteered to buy when they drove through his favorite burrito place, it was Cary who'd ended up paying the price.

Naturally. As far as he could tell on that cloudy June morning along the North Carolina coast, his life felt like one lousy deal after another. This gangly Marine private examining his ID card was just another insult to his career's unfortunate trajectory.

The Marine hung up the phone. He turned Cary's ID over and studied it. "They didn't teach us Army ranks," he said. "Am I supposed to salute you?"

"No!" Cary barked. "I'm an E-7. Same as a Navy chief or a Marine gunnery sergeant. I'm not a cake eater. I work for a living."

Jad leaned over, making himself visible. "We're both E-7s, by the way. Neither of us are cake eaters."

And there it was—the other offense that had so animated Cary that morning. Rubbing salt in the wound, Jad's promotion had gone through, elevating the two senior sergeants to the same level.

The Marine private handed the IDs back. "Thank you, sirs." He saluted crisply.

"Sergeants! And take your goddamned hand down. If you end up in the shit one day, Private, don't salute anybody. You'll get yourself killed."

"Yes, sir."

Cary sighed.

"We're supposed to get over to the Raider headquarters," Jad said. "Hangar two-four-one. You know where that is?"

"See that C-17 taxiing over there?" the private asked.

"Yeah."

"It's rolling up to the Raider hangar now."

CARY'S MOOD IMPROVED A BIT WHEN HE SAW MASTER CHIEF KENDRICK MOORE AT the hangar, signaling for the truck to enter. Although the master chief was officially retired from active duty, the SEAL knew how to navigate a Marine base, as Marines were the naval infantry extension of the American maritime service. Still, the debate over which service extended from which was a long-standing argument between jarheads and squids.

"You boys are a little late," Moore hollered over the roar of an F-35 taking off. He glanced at the enormous diver's watch on his wrist.

"Sorry, Chief," Cary shouted. "We came as fast as we could."

"Yeah, yeah. Okay. Let's head to the office, where it's quiet enough to talk like humans. Come on, follow me."

Though Moore was theoretically retired, to Cary's eyes, he looked anything but. The former SEAL wore a Crye Precision G3 combat jersey with matching camo pants and a khaki web belt. His bald head shined like a waxed bowling ball. His waist seemed half the width of his shoulders, as though he'd done nothing but PT since the last time Cary saw him.

Furthermore, Cary and Jad had changed out of their Army Combat Uniforms (ACUs) shortly after hearing from Clark. Campus missions usually required civilian attire, but seeing Moore kitted out in his SEAL combat fatigues made them wonder what was up.

"Boys, meet Staff Sergeant Tom Buck," Moore announced after closing the door to an interior hangar office. "Marine Raider. New to the team. He'll be the jump lead on this mission."

A fit Marine with a square jaw and tightly cropped blond hair offered his hand. He was dressed like Moore in an unmarked combat uniform. The cap toes of his boots shined. His eyes were blue, bright, and unlined.

Cary disliked him immediately.

To begin with, Buck had all the youthful good looks that Cary Marks had at the same age, back when he was full of energy and exuberance. However, twenty years of service in some of the world's worst hellholes had aged his skin and streaked his blond hair with gray. As if that wasn't enough, Moore mentioned that Buck would lead this mystery mission, which, given Cary's morning, seemed just about perfect.

"What's the op?" Jad asked.

"Take a seat. Lots to cover."

"Okay. What about Mr. C.?"

"Clark is driving down from Virginia to meet us, so I'll do the honors." The master chief opened a folder with eight-by-ten forensic glossies of the latest POSEIDON SPEAR murder in eastern Washington State.

Cary's personal problems vanished at the sight of the charred remains that had once been the Cole Hunt family. He knew Hunt by reputation.

"Seen enough?" Moore asked.

Solemn nods, eyes turning away. Moore closed the folder.

The SEAL crossed his arms. "This is the third murder involving guys like us linked to an operation called POSEIDON SPEAR." He detailed the operation and the DNI's suspicion that this was the handiwork of Rafa bin Yasin, son of the Emir, who was hiding out in the Pakistani tribal areas and gathering strength.

"We're going in as snipers? Hard-target kill?" Jad asked.

"Yes. Midas is already on the ground for recce. We're coming in over the top. We'll assess the target once we're on the ground. We're to hit Rafa and eliminate his force."

Cary was glad to learn that a Delta operator was part of the operation. Moore was a good man, and this new guy, Buck, seemed squared away. However, they were both from the Navy side of the house. Midas was a genuine Army D-Boy—even if he was an officer.

"So Midas is gaining intel," Cary said.

"That's right," Moore replied. "He hasn't reported in yet." The chief unrolled a terrain chart on the table between them. He held the curling edges down with four coffee cups emblazoned with Marine unit badges.

The SEAL tapped his finger on a series of tight contour lines that indicated a nearly vertical incline. "We don't have an exact pos on Rafa's base. But the dumb bastard did us a favor by hitting an Indian army unit about thirty-six hours ago, somewhere over here. The ODNI passed an intelligence report to us through the Indian military. They say Rafa is heading to the tribal areas in Pakistan. Bartosz's job is to find him. Then we strike."

"Are we working with the Indians?" Jad asked.

"Negative. This is a denied area operation. India is furious about the terrorist attack, but they can't move troops into Pakistan. That would provoke a war. Unfortunately, both countries possess nuclear weapons and have shown a willingness to destroy the planet. We need to kill this guy quietly."

"Any help from OGA?" Jad followed, using the acronym for Other Government Agency, their vernacular when referring to the CIA.

"The Delhi chief of station will help us exfil through India. He's our way home."

Cary rested his hands on his hips. "If the ODNI and OGA are on board with this, then why don't they paste him with a Hellfire from a Pred?"

"Too sensitive. A Pred would get picked up on radar. The U.S. can't officially be involved in anything in that area. Like, at all."

"Enter The Campus," Cary finished, flicking his eyes at the Marine, who stood ramrod straight.

"Precisely," Moore said. "Fully deniable black op. We'll infil with a jump. Exfil through the OGA. No one will ever know we were there."

"When do we leave?"

"Tonight."

"How?"

"We'll board a spec ops C-17 and fly to Incirlik Air Force Base, Turkey. Then we'll stand by and wait for the go order."

"Clark and Ding coming along for the ride?"

"Ding is laid up with his torn meniscus at Clark's farm. But Mr. C. will be on-site."

"He's a little long in the tooth for a jump into the Himalayas, isn't he?" Cary asked.

Moore shot him a hard stare. "If he heard you say that, he'd jam a Ka-Bar through your temple. But no, he's not jumping. He'll be in Turkey to supervise."

Jad studied the map carefully. "What else did the Indian report say about this attack? What do we know about the enemy's capabilities?"

"Clark reviewed a video. He assessed it was thirty to forty fighters with sophisticated weapons tactics coordinating mortars, snipers, and RPGs. Still, they'll be easy pickings if we can set up on the high ground for an ambush."

"Can we get Midas on the line?" Cary asked.

"Negative. Midas is operating at EMCON," he said, referring to emissions control.

Cary studied the terrain map, analyzing the battle problem. India lay due east, China north. This was a political hot potato.

It fit with the Green Berets' operational tactics: small unit, indigenous liaison, and speed of maneuver. However, there was one glaring problem that the master chief and his fair-haired boy, Buck, had failed to address—getting a plane over Pakistan undetected.

"Chief," Cary said cautiously. "You mentioned this is a black op. But if we take that C-17 out there to the drop zone, won't we be detected? I'm no Air Force pilot, but a Globemaster has a huge radar signature. Even if we execute a HALO." By HALO, he referred to a high-altitude, low-opening jump.

Moore turned to a bulletin board with an air chart of Asia tacked to it. He tapped a spot in southeastern Turkey, not far from Syria. "The ODNI set us up. Our C-17 will squawk an identifier for a FedEx plane on a normal commercial air route. We'll take off from Incirlik, then fly along an established air cargo route along this path to Bangkok. We'll jump over Tajikistan, a few hundred miles north of our target area. That way, we maintain total deniability. We'll never enter Pak airspace."

"Hold on," Jad interrupted. "It's all well and good that we jump from Gehanistan or wherever."

"Tajikistan."

"Fine. Tajikistan. But are you suggesting we cover those mountain peaks on foot? Mr. C. said we should bring our mountain winter gear . . . but Jesus, how the hell are we supposed to climb K2 and Everest before battling a terrorist army?"

Moore and Buck traded a look. "We're not covering that ground with our boots," Moore answered. "We're going to drop right into the target area. Then we'll exfil with Midas through India. We'll fly home as civilians. Easy day."

"Hold up," Cary objected. "I know it's been fifteen years since I earned my jump wings—but I don't recall being able to fly three hundred miles from an airplane to a drop zone."

Moore's face split into a wide grin. "That's the best part. Come on, Staff Sergeant Buck. Let's show 'em the RAVENs."

27

BEFORE TURNING OFF THE LIGHTS IN KHAN'S SMALL BEDROOM AT THE FORWARD operating base, he indulged in a cup of opium-infused tea.

Reminding himself that he would only allow it once or twice a month, he drank a double dose, ensuring he would surrender to exhaustion and slip into a dark, dreamless void. So close to the Karakoram operation, he couldn't risk another trip north to visit the opium den of the Tajik nomads. But his son, Attaf, had stopped responding to him altogether, making him crave opium. The tea he'd acquired in a Peshawar alley would have to suffice.

The army phone on his trestle-table nightstand had an old-fashioned bell, jerking him back to reality.

"Brigadier Khan," he mumbled, uncertain where he was for a moment.

"This is the duty officer, sir. We're moving to threat-profile Zed. Major General Wahid has requested a briefing."

Khan fumbled with the light and stared straight at the ceiling. Wahid was the two-star general who ran army units in Pakistani Kashmir.

"Sir? Are you there, sir?"

"Yes, I'm here." Khan swiveled to the edge of the bed and found his glasses. "Condition Zed, you say, Lieutenant? Why?"

"Indians are blaming us for the attack on their army unit."

"I'll be in as soon as I can." The brigadier hung up.

Although the call was surprising, its purpose would prove useful—if properly handled. Taking a deep breath, Khan pulled on his boots.

Khan joined two of his staff in the office. One was a dim-witted colonel who was a second cousin of a government minister and given his commission as a gift. The other was a sharp captain who, like Khan, had attended Britain's Sandhurst military academy.

Khan allowed the captain to lead the two-star general's briefing on the latest Indian army order of battle. As they had learned from satellite imagery and Muslim HUMINT assets distributed throughout the rural villages of Indian Kashmir, additional elements of the Indian Para SF had traveled by rail from Delhi. A squadron of Mi-8 Hip attack helicopters was forward-deployed to the Udhampur Air Force Station. A battalion from the renowned Jammu and Kashmir Light Infantry unit, known as the JAKs, had moved west, closer to the Pakistani border. Russian-built MiG-29 Fulcrums were conducting exercises out of their base in Srinagar.

"This is serious," Major General Wahid concluded to an adjutant. "The Indians are preparing for battle. We stay at condition Zed. Get me the Foreign Affairs Ministry. They'll want to respond to this."

Khan had anticipated that reaction. He concluded the briefing and returned to his office.

By ten a.m., the effects of the opium had completely faded, replaced by strong Turkish coffee. He checked his watch, closed his office door, and turned on the wall-mounted television.

If there was one rule in the Pakistani government, it was that the gentlemen of its Foreign Affairs Ministry could never keep a secret. They were like Masroof, in Khan's opinion, preening and strutting for attention, especially regarding a certain Al Jazeera reporter, a media darling named Ghida Douri.

Khan was sure one, if not two or three, Foreign Affairs boys would trip over themselves to leak the details of the Indian army movements to the reporter. In addition to her beaming smile, long legs, killer instincts, and global audience, Ghida Douri took care of her informants with favorable coverage. Her morning broadcast, *The Subcontinent*, was her flagship.

Khan watched the television expectantly. After a few commercials, there Ghida was, smiling behind her desk, a garish India-Pakistan war graphic behind her shining hair. Under her snug black blouse, a yellow chyron declared RISING TENSIONS BETWEEN NUCLEAR-ARMED INDIA AND PAKISTAN.

Khan picked up the remote from his desk and increased the volume, savoring the moment as Ghida reported on the troop movements and the Ministry of Foreign Affairs' response, a diplomatic warning démarche aimed at New Delhi. He was a few minutes into it, contemplating how best to approach this for the Karakoram operation, when the captain knocked and entered.

"Colonel Ming from the Chinese PLA on the secure line, sir. Direct from their Ministry of State Security."

Khan suppressed a rare grin. Ghida's audience really *was* global.

"Put him through." The brigadier lifted the handset.

"Brigadier Khan, this is Colonel Ming."

Ming was a colonel, Khan a general officer. As such, the brigadier noted the lack of a courteous, professional *sir*. "Good morning, Colonel," he returned.

"The Indians are massing troops."

"I'm fully aware of that. It's all over the news. That must be where you saw it," he added, a jab among intelligence professionals.

"My government has expressed concerns over the Karakoram Bridge unveiling. Do we need to reassess?"

Khan chose his words carefully. "There is no need to reassess the Karakoram Gorge security plan. The Indians are putting on a show, trying to blame us for their terror problems. My government has full confidence in the site because it's deep in our interior—as we discussed when we met."

"I see. Setting aside concerns about the Indian army, are you not concerned about the terrorists that hit them?"

When military intelligence men from separate countries—even a putative ally—asked each other for information, the answer was never straightforward.

Khan shifted in his seat and glanced at the muted television. The attractive journalist had moved on to a report about Pakistan's economy: soaring inflation, stagnant GDP growth, and high unemployment.

"We are gathering all the necessary intelligence," he said to the Chinese colonel. "We have a strong network of HUMINT assets. We believe the terrorists are Indian. If they enter Pakistan, we will stamp them out," Khan lied.

"Is that so? And what is the likelihood the Indians will pursue these Kashmiri separatists into Pakistan?"

"Low," the brigadier responded smoothly. "Our information on the Indian order of battle is up to date. They are exercising, as you have probably seen yourself. But they have not yet done anything I could call belligerent."

A garble of electronic static interrupted them, a by-product of the encryption protocol and the remote Chinese switching station at the Khunjerab Pass. Along with the new rail link between

Pakistan and China, the contractor, AGI, was responsible for laying fiber-optic cables, allowing for better, more secure data connections between the two countries.

The static cleared. "Are you there, Brigadier?"

"Yes. I'm here."

"Good. Might the Indian Para SF units have smaller, covert cells that penetrate Pakistan?"

"No. We would detect them."

"Are you sure of that?"

Khan's grip tightened on the receiver. "Why do you ask?"

"Because our signals intelligence satellites picked up a data transmission inside your border. I just sent you the precise geo-coordinates on the secure link."

"Wait one." Khan clicked his computer mouse and reviewed the colonel's message. He muttered a curse under his breath. Pakistan's SIGINT satellites were severely outdated and in desperate need of funding. Furthermore, it was evident that China felt no hesitation in spying on their new, favored ally.

"That could have been anyone," Khan retorted irritably, his good mood ruined. "Even tourists have satellite phones."

"No. You haven't read the raw data. The signal was from an Indian army SATCOM terminal operating in the KU band, hitting the Indian military's GSAT in geostationary orbit."

The head of Pakistan's military intelligence for Kashmir was at a loss. Through Fahim, he had supplied Rafa with many weapons—but not secure Indian SATCOM terminals.

"Do you understand, Brigadier? I am saying that there is an Indian Special Forces team following these terrorists into Pakistan."

Another burst of static gave Khan a moment to think. An Indian SF unit operating inside Pakistan furthered his plan—but not if it eliminated Rafa. That would ruin everything.

The static cleared on the secure line. "We will respond appropriately. The Karakoram Bridge unveiling will proceed as scheduled. You needn't worry, Colonel Ming."

"Thank you, Brigadier. Understood."

Khan killed the TV and slipped out of his office. He hurried down the windowless corridor and exited through the thick door.

The midmorning sun over the eastern peaks sharply contrasted the dim operations center. The heated desert sucked a breeze from the cool Karakorams that carried the vague tang of sagebrush. Khan inhaled the familiar scent as he fished his small burner phone from his pocket. He texted the geocoordinates to a number with a +91 prefix, the country code for India. He followed it with a call.

"Give me a second," Fahim Bajwa whispered. "I need to step out of a meeting."

Khan paced in the sunlight with the phone pressed to his ear.

"What is it?" Fahim asked thirty seconds later. "We're having a board meeting. Rai is on something of a rampage about finishing the bridge project in time for the Chinese visit."

"I don't care," the brigadier snapped. "You need to get word to Rafa quickly."

"Of what?"

"An Indian army Special Forces unit is on his ass. I just sent you their location. Get it to Rafa, Fahim—immediately. He needs to kill them. All of them."

28

AFTER SETTING UP HIS OBSERVATION POST, OR OP, MIDAS TYPED INTO THE INDIAN satellite communicator his third message since they picked up the trail. He wanted Clark to know that he and Rustam were following the intel from the village elder.

The Iridium had been ruined in the river crossing, drenched in the pickup bed. Midas had been forced to rely on the Indian satellite backup, where he manually typed Clark's number. The satellite circuit connected to the global telecommunications network, allowing him to text information directly to Clark, whose number he'd retrieved from memory.

The Delta operator lowered the device and shifted, careful not to disturb the elaborate web of twigs and grasses he'd arranged over his head and shoulders. He dragged the stubby tripod for his M151 spotting scope a few inches to get a better angle. He'd left his helmet strapped to the horse and replaced it with a floppy camouflage hat so as not to interfere with the optics.

"A group's coming out," he said quietly to his mujahideen partner, Rustam.

The wiry Tajik was snugged in beside Midas, sharing half of a crack between two boulders the size of Volkswagens. Rustam stared into the valley with long-lensed Russian binoculars, muttering. "It's them."

"Them? Who?"

"Umayyad."

"Well, shit," Midas said, looking at the distant horsemen.

According to messengers who traveled the valley, the village elder said that the terrorists used an ancient caravansary, a walled fortress that had served as a refuge for caravans crossing the steppe for the past three thousand years. Since those days, the caravansary had eroded into a dusty mound that looked like an ordinary hill from this distance.

Midas and Rustam had posted their OP to the south of the enclave to gather intel. The last thing the Delta officer expected was that he would find an armed contingent of the Umayyad Caliphate army on his first try. But if he did, he intended to follow the contingent at a distance, hoping they would lead him to his primary target, Rafa bin Yasin.

"Wait here," Midas said—or at least thought he said—in Urdu. He crawled backward on his hands and knees through the tunnel formed by the two leaning boulders. Emerging on their southern side under the bright sun, he slid down the loose shale to the scraggly tree where they had tied the horses.

He rummaged through a bundle on the third brown mare and loosened a thick backpack. He hoisted it over his shoulders and rushed to the first horse, retrieving the M2010 Enhanced Sniper Rifle. Midas unfolded the buttstock, slammed a magazine from his backpack home, and climbed up the shale. He found Rustam glued to his bulbous Russian binoculars, studying the caravansary.

Rustam spoke battle-English, which was good enough for Midas. "Any movement?" Midas asked.

"Yes. Ten men. Ten horse."

Midas aimed the ESR in their direction. He worked the bolt and squared his right eye behind the scope. As he had learned in the sniper school he'd attended God knew when, he kept his other eye open to look for threats. The tactic had become a habit as familiar as tying his shoelaces.

"I also count ten," Midas said. He could see their bodies clearly. Shimmering in the distance like a mirage, silhouetted by towering, snowcapped peaks, the fighters wore a mix of ragged street clothes, leftover combat fatigues, and ruffling keffiyehs—most of the garments were black. They rode at a leisurely pace, their rifles in scabbards.

"Umayyad," Rustam repeated. "Main force."

"Where are they going?" Midas asked.

"West. Into Pakistan."

"Then—this is their main base?"

"Yes."

What to do? Midas wondered. By Clark's order, he was here as the recon man. His job was to find the terrorist, mark the X, and send it to Moore, Buck, and the Green Berets so they could jump in to wipe out the whole army.

But spying these walking horses across a parched plain in broad daylight was simply too good. The fighters had come up from the rocky crest that hid their base. Who knew if they would expose themselves again like this before the Moore-Buck team arrived on station?

Midas peered through his Horus Tremor3 scope, placing the fine-line reticle grid over one rider after another. The optical system allowed the shooter to select the right markers to correct for wind, distance, and minute of angle. Midas was supremely confident that he could pick off any of these horsemen at this distance.

One rider stood out from the rest. His horse was draped in silver medallions the size of dinner plates. Swathed in flowing black robes, he carried a staff at his side like a cavalry guidon.

"The third one," Rustam said beside him. "I think he's Rafa."

"I think so, too," Midas agreed. The Delta commando considered rolling away to fetch the Indian communicator device. He'd sent several messages to Clark with the precise coordinates of the suspected terrorist base. Clark's last reply was an hour ago. It had been terse, but easy to understand: CR, get HVI PID. Camp OO CONUS ENR TK. Clark.

Clark was speaking in relative gibberish out of fear of intercept. It conveyed, in so many words, a command to continue the reconnaissance mission and gain a positive identification of the high-value individual. It also revealed that the Campus team was on its way to Turkey.

That all made sense to Midas, even though he couldn't know exactly where in the air his Campus brethren might be at this moment. The Air Force prohibited civilian satellite communications on its planes, and Clark probably wouldn't receive a message from Midas until he landed.

"More horses," Rustam announced.

Midas swung the scope to the caravansary. Sure enough, five more men on horseback strolled down the slope, joining the initial group of horses on the trail. He noticed that the animals were heavily burdened, much like the two horses he and Rustam had ridden from the elder's village. Midas positioned the spindly black reticle over the man he suspected was Rafa, the mission priority. The terror leader sat high in his saddle, waving an arm as if giving orders.

That's him, Midas thought with a grunt. *That's our HVI.*

A second group of horses lined up behind the first set, totaling twenty-five in all. The herd appeared to be gathering for a drive west, deeper into Pakistan. Based on the loaded horses, Midas guessed they were prepared for a lengthy trip. A strict reading of Clark's order suggested that he should wait until the horsemen were mere specks on the horizon before engaging in pursuit.

But did that order still make sense?

The HVI was literally in his sights. At roughly eight hundred yards, his ESR loaded with Winchester Magnum hollow-point boattails would have no problem taking the killer's head off. Was that not the point of all this? Did not the man in that saddle orchestrate hits on Midas's brothers in arms in the sanctity of their own homes, stateside?

Damn straight he did.

He, Bartosz Jankowski, could put an end to this right now.

Midas doubted that the terrorists would even know what hit them. He had good cover among these rocks. His ESR was equipped with a completely silent suppressor. There would be no muzzle flash. They'd probably scatter like cockroaches under a light as soon as their leader fell. Perched in this sniper hide between boulders, he and Rustam could retreat, mount up, and make a clean getaway to the south.

"He is Rafa. Third one," Rustam confirmed.

"You're sure that's him?"

"Yes."

"What is that staff he carries?"

"He believe he king, ruler of the only true caliphate. He believe he the heir of Muhammad."

"You believe him?"

Rustam laughed.

"I might shoot this bastard right now," Midas said. "Pack our gear on the horses. We may be riding out of here in another few seconds."

"Okay, Mi-dass." Rustam pushed himself rearward to attend to the animals.

Midas moved to the side to deploy his laser range finder. He aimed the red dot at a rock on the caravansary's sloped wall. The range was seven hundred sixty yards. Easy shot.

The former Delta operator punched a few numbers into his bulky Garmin sharpshooter's watch, calculating the drop of his Winchester Magnum bullets while adjusting for his minute of angle difference at seven hundred sixty yards. He also entered the wind, elevation, and humidity estimates to arrive at a final solution.

Adding to the complexity, he had to estimate Rafa's slight angle as he rode west, third in line, with the bulk of his riders trailing behind him. Midas lowered his eye behind the scope and adjusted the rifle to the appropriate section of the Horus reticle's grid. Considering the bullet's high terminal velocity, the lead was slight.

Rustam returned, crawling up the tunnel with a scrape at his elbows, his M4 resting on his forearms.

"Horses ready," he confirmed. "You shoot Rafa now?"

"Not sure. Maybe."

The procession of horses had momentarily halted. Animals wandered in front of Rafa, screwing up Midas's aim.

"Come on, asshole," the Delta man breathed, waiting for the HVI to emerge in the clear.

As Midas weighed the repercussions of shooting Rafa then and there, the terrorist suddenly flinched. With other riders flickering before him, Midas watched Rafa pull a phone from his flowing garments and press it to his ear. Two riders wandered in front of the terrorist, blocking Midas's view.

The sniper increased the pressure on the trigger, waiting, breathing slowly and evenly. Rafa's head emerged above the crowd on a rearing horse. When the animal was back on all fours, the terrorist pointed his staff directly at the hill crest where Midas had established his sniper hide. Rafa galloped east as if speeding to the caravansary's entrance while half his force rode south—straight for Midas and Rustam.

Shit, he thought. *We've been made.* No point in holding back the shot now.

The terrorist's rapid eastward pace expanded the distance, changed the shot angle, and required a greater lead. Still, Midas had encountered tougher targets. In what snipers refer to as *the space between heartbeats*, he pulled the trigger.

Two seconds later, Rafa fell from his horse.

The nearby riders closed in, forming a shield around their fallen leader. Midas waited for the dust to settle, watching through the reticle. Between the shining rumps of horses, he was shocked to see the terror leader rise, raise his arms to the sky, and tilt his head back as if in exaltation. Midas fired again, but riders closed in. The bullet thudded into a horse's shoulder.

Rustam's rattling M4 forced Midas's attention to the cloud of dust blowing on the plain. Rafa's horsemen were four hundred yards away, midway between the caravansary and Midas's position, too far away for Rustam's wild firing to do much more than waste perfectly good ammo.

"*Rustam!*" he bellowed without lifting his eye from the scope. "Get back to the horses and cover my retreat!"

A sudden gray smoke trail cut across the scope reticle. Midas looked up from the rifle in surprise. "*RPG!*" he roared.

The rocket exploded against the boulders overhead, showering him with grit. Rustam had backed most of the way through the tunnel, evading the blast. Midas resumed his position behind the ESR scope. The riders were three hundred yards away, shimmering in the distance.

He shot one in the chest, knocking him off his horse. While the brass jacket flew when he worked the bolt, Midas picked another target, slamming the onrushing fighter in the shoulder. The magazine's last bullet exploded in the chamber and rifled down the barrel, hitting a third man in the head.

As the remaining riders rushed toward him, Midas angled to the side, pulled another mag from his plate carrier vest, and slammed it home. He worked the bolt and fired once more, flinging an enemy rider backward. But at least seven more closed the distance at high speed. Worse, they had found a wadi for cover. By the time they emerged from the trench, they would be too close to the hill for Midas to hit from this perch. That was it. The only option was an armed retreat.

He rummaged through his backpack and pulled out two rectangular Claymores.

A second RPG exploded in a bright flash, showering him in a hailstorm of stone.

Midas extended the short legs of the first Claymore mine, which had extension mounts shaped like scissors. He drove their sharp tips into the dirt, then unscrewed a cover over a radio device connected to the blast cap.

A salvo of incoming rounds shattered rocks over his head, forcing him to take cover.

The Delta man wiped his eyes and returned to his work. He set the second Claymore at a modified angle, his hands flying over the controls. Rock exploded to his side, flinging a whizzing, buzzing chunk of stone into his forehead. Blood poured into his right eye.

One Claymore left. THIS SIDE TO ENEMY the front plate read in big, bold letters. But here was Midas crawling backward through the tunnel formed by the leaning boulders, the bomb inches from his face, dragging his long sniper rifle by the sling.

Finally back in daylight, he opened the Claymore legs and set it to face the boulders he'd used as shelter a moment before. He tossed the rifle to the bottom of the hill because it was getting in his way as he set the final Claymore.

Firing from the saddle, Rustam opened up behind him. Midas followed the tracers and yanked his Glock free. A fighter had flanked them, coming up the hillside. Rustam's burst wounded the assaulter. Midas finished him off with two rounds from his Glock.

Rustam adjusted his aim and fired over Midas's head, chipping the leaning boulders on full auto. Midas swung his Glock backward to confront the threat. A black keffiyeh appeared and disappeared like an apparition—gone before Midas could hit it.

A click, a zing, and a torrent of rocks zipped past his ears. As if struck by a sledgehammer, he toppled backward, sliding wildly over the sharp shale, his hand opening uncontrollably, the Glock slipping from his grip. A sharp, electric pain surged through his arm and chest.

Rustam covered him, firing his M4 on full auto until the magazine was empty. Midas's horse reared back, braying and throwing the spare M4 out of its scabbard.

Midas ignored the electric jolts screaming through his limbs and crawled to recover the Glock. Three men in black keffiyehs stood at the top of the slope, their eyes blazing vile hatred, their hands raising exotic-looking assault rifles that he didn't recognize. Two pointed their barrels at him, the third aimed at Rustam, who raced to eject his empty M4 mag and reload while struggling to stay on his panicked horse.

Midas's left hand still clutched the Claymore detonator.

He stabbed his thumb over the button.

29

"AND SO—WHAT DID YOU THINK?" DAVAL RAI ASKED THAT EVENING UNDER A PINK, rising moon.

"Of what?" Jack asked with a dainty cocktail party–size plate in his hand.

"Of the Dera Baba Nanak rail station you visited. You saw the fiber-optic-cable operation, I assume?"

Rai had donned a celebratory red turban and maroon tunic with yellow sash—his attire for the wedding ceremony that would conclude in ninety minutes. As he awaited Jack's impressions, he twirled a champagne flute between his thick fingers.

Jack shifted on his feet, wearing a red cylindrical hat like a fez, a silky orange Nehru jacket, and purple riding jodhpurs—he was not yet done with his ceremonial role.

In twenty minutes, he was scheduled to join the final *baraat* processional. Sanjay, the groom, would lead on a painted elephant. At the center of the parade, the bride and her maidens, including Lisanne, would relax on gold-leaf palanquins carried by sturdy Sikhs. Jack and his fellow groomsmen would bring up the rear on double-humped Bactrian camels.

"Well," Jack replied, searching for an appropriate answer that would satisfy business logic, conceal his nocturnal activities, and bring the conversation to a close. "It was interesting to see the speed with which you laid the fiber."

"Oh yes, that. We have it down to a science, don't we, Fahim? How fast is it?"

"Ten meters per minute," the AGI COO replied, his hand absentmindedly stroking the knot of hair at the nape of his neck.

Rai clapped his hands and leaned closer to Jack, his eyes blinking quickly. "Tell me, is that a capability that might interest Hendley? There is a lot of fiber to be laid around the world. I'm considering starting a subsidiary that focuses exclusively on data in developing countries. A perfect fit for that new satellite operation you mentioned."

Jack stood a little straighter. AGI's remote data-networking capabilities might, in fact, offer a sound opportunity to complement the LodeStar deal.

"It provides us a competitive edge," Fahim added, noticing Jack's improved posture. "We hold the easements for fiber trunks along our railways. We're in a unique position to expand networks into cities with our swift trenching operations. It's very cost-effective."

Jack placed the plate on a table. "Perhaps," he said, holding a napkin to his mouth, aware that showing too much interest might jeopardize a future negotiation. "This new subsidiary—if the numbers check out—could be an intriguing investment. If you need capital, that is."

"Wonderful!" Rai exclaimed. "Who doesn't need capital? I pay a huge dividend. Sometimes I wish I didn't. We will need a private equity backer if I structure it as an independent entity. Much of our free cash flow goes back into committed projects or is reserved for those awful dividends to our public investors, you see."

"Interesting," Jack said. "On its own, with the right financial structure, your fast trenching speed could be worth a lot, I should think."

"Of course," Fahim qualified, "the trenching speed we quoted refers to level terrain, moving along a rail track. It goes slower through mountains, where we have to tunnel or maintain a certain grade."

The bridal party walked forward amid applause and whispers of approval. Jack, Fahim, and Daval stopped their business discussion as the tycoon clapped, his eyes glistening with emotion. Srini came into view, leading a procession of women adorned with flowers, silks, and veils. Jack noticed that Lisanne was fourth in line, elegantly dressed in a sheer outfit that exposed her midriff.

Srini rushed over to her father to hug him. "Why, Jack!" she exclaimed a moment later, pulling away. "Don't you look nice!"

The parade flowed into the crowd. Jack reached out for Lisanne. She took his hand, smiled brightly, and disappeared into the throng.

"You do make a handsome groomsman, Jack," Rai said with a shine in his big brown eyes. "And I understand you're to be a groom yourself soon? Is a wedding date confirmed?"

Uncomfortable under such scrutiny, Jack ignored the question and returned the conversation to business. He faced Fahim, who had made the point about mountain operations.

"Fahim, do I understand correctly that you're laying fiber all the way through the Karakorams, the Khunjerab Pass, and into China? You can do that?"

"Yes," Fahim confirmed. "That's right. We follow the rails. Laying those is the hard part."

"The hard part, indeed." Rai laughed. "He's being modest, Jack. Fahim has engineered tunnels to take us straight *through* the mountains. We have ten boring machines around the world— massive things. They're like the sandworms in *Dune*, haha, capable of grinding through enormous swaths of earth; they even have the same horrifying teeth. Have you seen one, Jack? If not, you should."

Jack scanned the crowd to spot Lisanne among the four hundred guests gathered on the well-kept British tennis lawn. The bridal party ascended the steps of the grand white mansion. A band on the porch serenaded them with twanging sitars and tribal drums.

"We'd better get to our places," Jack said. "Looks like the bridal party is moving indoors."

"Not to worry. They're off to meet my wife, where they'll formally present Sanjay to her as a new son before the final procession. The poor boy."

Jack looked away and yawned, a fist over his mouth.

"Exhausted, huh?" Daval Rai nudged Jack playfully with his elbow. "I hope you had a big night together in Phula Mahila after Lisanne performed her dance. Is *that* what has you so tired?" The tycoon winked.

FAHIM BAJWA PRESSED TIGHTLY AGAINST HIS BOSS'S ELBOW, WAITING TO HEAR HOW Jack Ryan, Jr., would respond to Daval Rai's innocent—yet obnoxious—question.

The gate guards had reported to Fahim that Ryan arrived at the compound at two a.m. When they inquired about the bullet holes in the Rover's tailgate, the American stated that the GPS had malfunctioned and that he had become hopelessly lost. The bullet holes had appeared while he was away from the vehicle, climbing a hill to get a better view of the way ahead.

Fahim was asleep in his tenth-floor Amritsar apartment with Ilona beside him when the guards reported this hollow explanation. After dismissing Ryan's fiction, he lay awake, wondering where the American had really gone, growing angrier by the minute.

While Ilona breathed softly at his side, Fahim spent a fitful, tumultuous hour imagining his half brother's reaction upon learning that Jack Ryan, Jr., would leave India unscathed after inexplicably dodging *two attacks*.

"I apologize if I seem tired," Jack said now, stifling his second yawn. His watery eyes reflected the flickering tiki torches. "I came in a bit late after the tour. Please forgive me, Daval. I truly appreciate the insight into your business, and I'll seriously consider the investment opportunity. But most of all, I can't thank you enough for your hospitality. It's been quite a week—the best way I can imagine for Lisanne to heal from Srini's incredible surgery. How can we ever fully thank you?"

Rai downed the remnants of his champagne flute and smiled brilliantly. "It's nothing. Nothing at all. My Srini adores your Lisanne. With her beauty, talent, and bionic arm, she's become the star of the show, one could say. You should have seen her at the *filmi*. Gorgeous. You are a lucky man, Mr. Ryan. Very lucky."

"It's such a shame you missed that dance while you were . . . lost in the countryside," Fahim pressed. "What happened again?"

"I got lost. Very embarrassing for me."

"I see," Fahim said. "Daval is so right, though. Lisanne danced beautifully. A pity you missed it."

"I regret it extremely," Jack replied. "I'll make it up to her when I ride the camel, which I'd better not screw up. I should go find Balnoor for some coaching."

"You'll be fine," Rai reassured him, snagging Jack's arm to keep him from leaving. "Camels are argumentative beasts, but the drovers will spend time preparing you. Besides, Sanjay is undergoing a thorough groom's interrogation. It could take an hour, perhaps two—though I warned Reena not to press him too hard. She'll scare the dear boy off!"

"One of the things that worries me," Jack acknowledged while sipping his club soda, "is how my mother will behave at our wedding. I should go find Lisanne."

"Forget it, Jack. Lisanne is with Srini in the queen bee's chamber at the Pahila guesthouse, dressing for the *baraat*. A thousand mindless drones will shoo you off if you try to infiltrate. I'm paying for this event and even *I* can't enter the feminine apiary for fear of getting stung."

Fahim grinned, fully aware that Ryan was trying to excuse himself—and that his boorish boss wouldn't let him go.

"Then I'll find Balnoor," Jack insisted. "I don't want to blow it on our last night."

The comment gave Fahim a sudden chill, a reminder that Rafa would explode when he learned Ryan and his fiancée had returned to America unharmed. The COO wouldn't be surprised if his half brother backed out of the Karakoram op out of spite. After all, Rafa knew how desperately Fahim and Khan wanted it to happen.

However, as the gifted engineer reflected on Ryan's business interest, a light bulb glowed in his head.

"I wonder," Fahim mused, an index finger tapping his lip. "Daval, would it make sense for Jack to join us at the Karakoram Bridge dedication? Lisanne could spend more time with Srini that way, while Jack could conduct due diligence on our data operations in the mountainous terrain. All in, we could save many weeks of meetings for the potential Hendley equity investment."

Daval Rai snapped his fingers. "Yes! That's a marvelous idea. Jack, we're riding the AGI train into the mountains to a ceremony, where we will dedicate the rail bridge. Please do join us. You'll see our unique capabilities at work and witness the historic opening of China."

"I don't know if we should delay our flights home."

"Now, Jack," the CEO dismissed with a wave. "I insist that you and Lisanne join as my honored guests. It would bring such joy to my daughter, perhaps making up for me putting her new husband to work so soon. Splendid idea, Fahim, splendid. We simply *must* make it happen."

"Let me think about it," Jack replied, withdrawing. "There's Balnoor. My camel awaits. Good evening, gentlemen."

Watching the American walk away, Fahim Bajwa relaxed.

He was certain Ryan would accompany them to the Karakoram Gorge.

Daval Rai always got his way.

WHEN JACK FINALLY FOUND BALNOOR AT THE EDGE OF THE CROWD, HE LEARNED he'd blundered again.

Although Jack thought he was dressed appropriately for the *baraat*, the Indian attendant quickly corrected him, urging Jack over the leafy paths to Phula Mahila for a wardrobe change. Along the way, Balnoor explained that Srini's mother wanted all the men to wear orange Sikh turbans and bright magenta coats.

Once they entered the cottage, Jack promised to change and wearily disappeared into the master suite, locking the door behind him. He went into the bathroom to splash cold water on his face, steeling himself for this final ritual.

While leaning over the sink, a vibration shook his tunic.

He toweled off his hands and withdrew the Indian military satellite communicator from his pocket. A red light flickered at the top, indicating a weak signal. Jack stood on the toilet and aimed the antenna out a high window at the starry sky. He turned on the sink taps for concealment, inserted a wired earpiece, and cranked up the volume.

"*Hello,*" a voice said through the ear speaker, eerily clear. "*Americans. Hello.*"

"Hello," Jack replied quickly. "I read you five by five. Who is this?"

The response came after a few seconds' pause. "*I am Rustam, Tajikistan friend of . . . your friend. Mi-dass.*"

Jack recognized the careful speech of the muj fighter.

"Hello, Rustam. Why are you calling on the backup circuit? How can I help?"

"*It is not me who need help. It is Mi-dass.*"

Jack's eyes narrowed. "Tell me what's wrong. What happened?"

"*We found Rafa. There was battle. Mi-dass very injured. We retreat to village. You get him.*"

"Midas injured how?"

"*Shot. He live. But he hurt very bad.*"

"Copy," Jack replied coolly. A yellow button on the communicator in his hand was labeled POS. "I need your position, Rustam. Can you please press the yellow button?"

"*Yes. Wait.*"

The device buzzed. When Jack checked the screen, he saw a long string of geocoordinates. He rushed to his closet, took out the map he had used the day before, brought it into the bathroom, and laid it on the counter.

The lat-long Rustam sent was thirty-five miles northwest of where Jack had dropped Midas off. He still had his corporate credentials—but even if he could retain possession of his AGI Rover, no roads went anywhere near the position.

He stared at the marble counter, contemplating the mission status. Clark and the hastily assembled Campus paratroopers, led by Master Chief Moore, were en route to Turkey, where they planned to establish a forward-deployed base to launch the strike on Rafa. Midas was critically injured, and Rustam wouldn't know how to operate as the ground-based reconnaissance element for the incoming team.

Even worse, if Rafa closed in and captured Midas, all the careful planning to avoid detection in a denied area would be for naught. The Campus would be exposed, the mole would switch tactics, and Rafa would continue his reign of mayhem.

There was, however, one saving grace.

The new Pakistani AGI rail link that ascended the Karakoram Range passed within a day's hike of Midas's position.

PART THREE

BULLET

30

SWELLED BY GLACIER MELT, THE SHIGAR RIVER SPILLED OVER ITS BANKS, WIDENING to a calm, cold expanse, studded with ice.

The river lapped at the edge of an ancient highway, once flattened by caravans linking distant kingdoms. Now known as Pakistan's Highway 35, it was once called the Karakoram Silk Road. Each June during the melt, it became the hub for merchants hawking rugs from Samarkand, spices from Bombay, and wool from Kandahar.

On this June day, little evidence of the old bazaar remained except for the fruit trees stubbornly growing in the windswept loam at the foot of the mountains. Arboreal ancestors of a time long forgotten, the trees' blossoms perfumed the cold alpine breeze, pleasing Fahim Bajwa's aquiline nose, while causing him to shudder from the chill.

The AGI COO leaned on the front bumper of his corporate-leased Mercedes G-Wagon, his hands resting against his cotton trousers. He tilted his head at the sound of a calving glacier far above, where the icefall thumped like a wave crashing on a beach, crumbling and rolling in a minor avalanche.

He scrutinized the white-and-blue-studded peaks, but couldn't find the broken one. Wearing a cashmere quarter-zip sweater—a calfskin bag over his shoulder, USB drives in his pocket—Fahim checked the black-faced Patek Philippe at the end of his long arm, shuddering for a different reason. He wasn't sure how his half brother's men would locate him—he only knew they would.

After a quarter hour passed, the answer came with the sputter of an outboard motor echoing off the cliffs. Fahim raised his compact binoculars, wondering what he was in for. A wooden dhow sliced through the still water, creating a rippling wake.

As the boat approached, Fahim saw two men hunched in black. Their stubby woolen karakul hats and flying gray beards marked them as the grizzled mountain men from Rafa's handpicked personal guard, aging Emir followers who'd transferred their prophetic allegiance from father to son.

The prow touched the alkaline shore with a hiss. The mountain men commanded Fahim to board with sharp arm gestures. They wore bandoliers across their chests, carbines on their backs, and daggers on their belts.

The holy warriors remained silent as the boat puttered smoothly upriver, sloshing and thumping as stray chunks of ice bumped against the hull. The ten-horsepower Honda belched blue smoke, and the air turned frigid. Eventually, the man at the tiller steered around a bend. The water darkened in the shadows of the Himalayan peaks as he entered a side channel.

The engine went silent, and the craft skidded to a reedy bank. A younger warrior in dark green fatigues and a tattered dhoti crossed by a bandolier dragged the craft ashore. Four men in similar outfits stood nearby with snub-barreled assault rifles slung over their shoulders. Fahim recognized the weapons as Indian-made Sabres—arms he'd acquired from his Egyptian supplier.

The helmsman exchanged his tiller for his rifle. "You will see the caliph," he growled, gesturing menacingly with the barrel.

Formed up as a small troop—elders in front, Fahim in the middle, youthful soldiers trailing—they marched briskly over a rockfall, through a meadow, and into a tight growth of whispering firs.

"Wait." The forward elder disappeared into the trees with Fahim's calfskin bag in his right hand.

Chilled in the sun-starved evergreens, Fahim zipped up his sweater and briskly rubbed his hands together. The tops of the trees swayed with intermittent gusts. Fahim caught the scent of woodsmoke and heard distant voices over a crackling fire.

The gray-bearded mountain man returned and told Fahim to follow. After snaking between the tightly packed trees, they entered a small clearing split by sun and shadow.

"Down," the warrior ordered.

Fahim knelt in the shaded area of the glen, but that wasn't sufficient. The mountain man mimed a gesture and stomped his foot. Fahim read it as an order to press his nose to the ground in prayer.

He remained in this prostrate form while the breeze froze his back, wishing they had put him in the sunlight. Eventually, he heard footsteps and angled his face to observe them. The men were arranging wooden crates, forming a low plinth. On this, they unfolded a canvas chair. Before departing, they dropped Fahim's bag on the makeshift stage of crates.

Then, and only then, did Rafa bin Yasin, Fahim's half brother, emerge into the sunlight. The self-declared caliph ascended his throne.

Fahim looked up.

"Stay down," a gruff Urdu voice growled from the trees. "Do not look at the caliph."

Fahim, the talented engineer, a bridge builder who had quietly encouraged the nickname Pontifex Maximus, lay prostrate, his face pressed into Himalayan dirt.

"*Je suis prêt*," Rafa began in the native tongue they shared. I am ready.

"May I look at you, Caliph?" Fahim asked.

"*Oui*. You may gaze upon the one true caliph." Rafa knocked the hollow plinth with his staff, beating it like a drum.

A voice rasped from the clearing's edge. "Rise to your knees!"

Fahim hadn't seen Rafa for six months. He straightened his back to glimpse the self-proclaimed caliph's head and chest draped in black silk. Rafa's beard was thick, unkempt, chestnut brown. His eyes peered from sunken hollows as he held his staff like a king's scepter.

"I wait," Rafa began.

"For . . . what?" Fahim replied.

"The *Shahada*."

I should have expected that, Fahim thought.

He cleared his throat, bowed his head, and recited the old chant Mullah Fawwah had insisted on back in Marseille: "There is no God but God, and Muhammad is the messenger of God."

"And?"

"There is one true caliph," Fahim continued in a monotone. "He is the king of the believers, the rightful heir of Muhammad, the inheritor of the land stolen by the Ottomans, Allah's messenger, a direct descendant of Umm Farwa, lord of the house of Banu Makhzum, prince of the earth, commander of the believers, the one and only, the true, the caliph."

With his beard glowing red in the sunlight, Rafa closed his eyes and dipped his scepter. "Leave the caliph!" he suddenly barked at the trees, striking the staff against the wood five times.

Rafa's eyes remained on the shadowed forest, well above Fahim. "You have come quickly."

"As ordered, Caliph."

"As ordered. By your brigadier. Khan."

"He is not *my* brigadier, but, yes, Caliph. He asked me to bring you fresh intelligence. Personally."

Rafa glared at Fahim with hard, narrowed eyes. "The brigadier has failed the caliph. The brigadier is a thief."

Fahim nearly laughed at that. "The brigadier has delivered many weapons, men, and training to the caliph," he countered. "He showers the caliph with money through Mullah Fawwah—and through me."

"The brigadier is a corrupt instrument. *You* are a corrupt instrument. You have both failed the caliph."

What fresh crazy is this? Fahim wondered. Dismayed, he shook his head. "That is not true. How have I failed the caliph?"

"You know exactly how." Rafa's twitching eyes unnerved Fahim. The bridge builder looked away, thinking of the men with daggers watching at the tree line. "I did what I could, Caliph. I called to warn of the Indian ambush as soon as Khan contacted me."

"You called late."

"I had no control over timing. The Indians were responding to your attack at the border." He remembered to stroke Rafa's ego. "The caliph looks well. Lordly."

"The caliph lives in the flesh and blood of the prophet." Rafa reached into his robe as if scratching an armpit, exposing a deep, dark bruise spreading over pale, hairy skin.

The engineer raised his eyes. Khan had informed Fahim of the attempted ambush, but he hadn't mentioned a wound. "The caliph was hit?"

"Allah a protégé son prophète," Rafa answered, nodding. Allah protected his prophet.

"Inshallah."

"Oui. Inshallah."

"The caliph appears strong."

"The devil's bullet struck this."

Rafa lifted a silky black fold to expose a metal plate strung on a chain. Fahim instantly recognized it from the Mullah Fawwah's mosque.

Like the top of his staff, the plate was etched with the Pyxis of al-Mughira, two men on horseback picking dates. According to the Mullah Fawwah, the ancient metal breastplate was a treasured family heirloom, kept in Marseille until Rafa came of age.

"The caliph suffered a wound," Fahim said with all the reverence he could muster. He followed it with an apology. *"Je suis désolé."*

Rafa winced. "It was the American devils."

Genuinely confused, Fahim wasn't sure how to respond. Khan hadn't mentioned anything about Americans.

Rafa rapped his staff several times on the hollow plinth. A tall warrior bolted forward, head bowed, a rifle cradled in his arms. Rafa commanded the soldier to show the weapon to Fahim. The AGI COO inspected an American M4 painted in camouflage. After another guttural command from the caliph, the soldier displayed a handful of brass jackets.

"American weapons."

"I see, Caliph."

"The caliph has left men at the caravansary to find them. They are hiding somewhere near it. *Inshallah*, we will remove their heads and hang them on the gates."

Rafa nodded at the soldier, who retreated to the tree trunks.

Fahim's mind raced. Khan had reported to him that Indian Special Forces had chased Rafa after his attack on the Para SF garrison just across the border. But the mention of Americans was new. Khan had provided Ryan's flight information for the initial attack, but Fahim had assumed there were no other Americans involved. After Ryan eluded Fahim's men, shredding their tires . . . had he gone on to coordinate an attack?

He dismissed the notion. Ryan was a businessman like Fahim. And, as such, Fahim sensed an opportunity.

"I bring fresh intelligence on the American devils," the AGI executive announced inventively. Rafa's suspicions would strengthen the terrorist's motivation to follow through on the Karakoram Gorge hits.

Rafa stroked his beard, looking away. "*You* caused this. Allah intervened. *Inshallah*."

Fahim clenched his jaw. If it weren't for the service his half brother was going to perform at the Karakoram Bridge unveiling, he would jump up from his knees and strangle him.

"*I* caused the caliph harm?" he questioned, his pulse racing. "I do not understand."

Rafa remained staring at the trees, eyes hooded. The staff shook angrily in his hands. His voice rose. "*Oui*. You live among them. You have become them."

Aghast, fearing for his head, Fahim tried in vain to make eye contact. "I have lived among them to support the one true prophet, the commander of believers. The caliph's weapons, money, and political protection have come through me."

Rafa lifted his face to the sky, sighing, seeking worldly patience. As if speaking to the sun, he declared, "The devils who killed the caliph's father still walk the earth. Now they have come here to the center of the world. That is because of you."

"Caliph. My men have taken out three American warrior devils so far. Not long ago, we finished the devil Cole Hunt in Washington State, killing his family and desecrating them by fire, as the caliph commanded. They and their families rot in Jahannam, *inshallah*. There are pictures in the bag as evidence of our work, at your feet, my prophet. The binder."

"But you missed the devil Ryan."

"Your martyr missed the devil Ryan."

Rafa remained silent for a few seconds, then rummaged through the calfskin bag and flipped through a binder Fahim had assembled. After a brief inspection, he shook his head and scoffed. "You and the brigadier assist the devils in manipulating the caliph." He lifted his bearded chin and raised his staff, reciting a verse from the Quran. *"And when those who disbelieved plotted against you, O Muhammad, to wound you fatally, or to kill you or to drive you out; they plotted, but Allah also plotted, and Allah is the best of plotters."*

Fahim ignored the inference that *he* was the plotter. "I have asked Brigadier Khan for more POSEIDON SPEAR warrior devil names. My men are already back in America, preparing for another hit. The brigadier has given a new warrior devil's location in Oregon. He is next."

"Why does the general dole out warrior devil names so slowly when he has access to them all? It is because he plots. Like you."

"No, Caliph. The brigadier is waiting for you to finish the mission at the Karakoram Gorge. *Inshallah.* I have brought fresh intelligence for that operation. I sent messengers to your camp with it before I learned you were here. It is printed for the caliph's eyes, there, in the next section of the binder. As you will see, the devil Ryan will be at Karakoram, the devil who attacked the caliph."

Rafa leafed through Fahim's prepared pictures. "This is Daval Rai," he said, his voice suddenly commonplace in the old Marseille accent. "Who are the Hindu man and woman?"

"They are Rai's daughter, Srini, and his new son-in-law, Sanjay. They were married the day before yesterday. That is from the ceremony. If anyone plots with the devils, it is they, Caliph, not I."

Rafa grunted and flipped a page. "And this devil," he spat, resuming his remote, lordly tone. "This devil is Ryan. Dressed like a Sikh."

"Yes, Caliph."

"Who is the woman beside him with a false arm? She is Hindu? She is his wife?"

"No, Caliph. She was in the Rai wedding party. That is the devil Ryan's woman. They are not married. She is a whore."

Rafa studied the photo carefully. "The whore was with the devil Ryan when the martyr Nabeel attacked?"

"Yes, Caliph. The whore was there."

"And now the devil Ryan comes here, to the center of the world?"

"Yes, Caliph, to the Karakoram Gorge. It is a glorious stroke of fortune that he should enter the realm."

"It is as Allah commands. The caliph, the prophet, will strike the devil Ryan and his whore dead."

"You are His one true prophet. Commander of the believers. His will is done through you, Caliph. *Inshallah.*"

Rafa nodded with satisfaction. He flipped the binder forward a few pages. "And this?"

"Our energy site at Hanford, in America. From there, Caliph, my men will kill the devil warrior in Oregon. It is not far. After the Karakoram Gorge operation, the brigadier will provide all the information they need."

Rafa closed the binder with a slap. He struck the plinth with his staff, summoning an armed messenger before repeating the Quranic verse *"They plotted, but Allah also plotted, and Allah is the best of plotters."* His eyes flashed at Fahim. "Why is the Karakoram Gorge so important to the general? Because he plots."

"The general wants the Gorge operation so his country will gain an advantage over India with the Chinese."

Rafa glared harshly at his half brother. "The caliph commands the people. The caliph will liberate them in Kashmir before sweeping the infidels away like ants from a table."

Fahim didn't reply.

"The devil Ryan will die at Karakoram," Rafa stated flatly. "*In-shallah.*"

"And the Rais," Fahim added, relieved. "Daval, his whore daughter, Srini, and the whore-loving son-in-law, Sanjay."

Rafa closed his eyes, nodding.

Now that Fahim had what he wanted, he leaned forward and chanted loudly to close the proceedings. "The caliph is the one true prophet, God's hand on earth"—*la main de Dieu sur terre.*

Fahim hoped he would be permitted to leave. He wanted nothing more than to board the wooden dhow, cross the river, and prepare for the rail trip that would terminate at his glorious Karakoram Gorge bridge, where the Rais and Ryan would meet their fate.

What a pleasure it will be to watch, he thought, pressing his face into the dirt with his arms stretched out before him. In one swift move, the act would enrich his Swiss account with ISI money and grant him the chairmanship of AGI. It might even immortalize his Karakoram Gorge bridge in the history books, like the bridge at Avignon.

"May I go, Caliph?"

Rafa resumed his vacant stare at the trees. The interval grew long. Finally, he announced, "The caliph believes it is not enough to kill the devil Ryan. The devil's presence in the center of the world is a sign. *Inshallah.* The prophet commands a strike on the devil father's America, the true enemy of Umayyad."

Here we go again, Fahim thought.

He spoke in a measured tone. "As soon as the brigadier gives us more information after Karakoram, Caliph, my men will strike. We will not stop. The devils' souls will drip into the wastes of Jahannam."

Rafa was unmoved. "At-Takwir," he declared, pausing for emphasis before repeating the Quranic reference. "At-Takwir. It is time. It happens. Or the Karakoram Gorge does not. They must coincide for the world to witness God's will."

Fahim closed his eyes in frustration.

At-Takwir, the eighty-first chapter of the Quran, twenty-nine verses in all, told of the signs of the coming day of judgment. Rafa's father, the Emir, believed he was the instrument of Allah's intention to bring about that apocalypse, initiating the first of many signs when people "should run left and right in fear."

Recognizing Fahim's rare gift in engineering and his position at AGI, Rafa had skewed the words to believe Fahim's entire corrupted point on earth was to be his tool for bringing about the signs of At-Takwir, which, in his mind, would collapse international order and reestablish the Umayyad Caliphate. But the At-Takwir plan, staged from an AGI site in the American state of Washington, seemed like something so outlandish, so extreme, so far in the future, that Fahim never took it seriously.

"*Inshallah,*" the executive soothed from his prostrate position. "The caliph's Karakoram mission helps with At-Takwir. Once I am the AGI chairman, I can approve funding, import explosives, hire more believers. Have I not furnished the full plans to the caliph? They are there—in the binder."

Fahim's mind ran through the prospects for action once he was at the helm of the company. He would abandon Rafa to his crazy fate and break contact with Khan. He would emerge clean as new linen, the world's greatest bridge builder, Pontifex Maximus.

"The plans are worthless until put into action," Rafa declared as he massaged his swollen arm. "The day for At-Takwir is at hand. Because you are corrupt, the caliph himself has sent martyrs to perform it. Through Him, Allah commands it finished. Your men will meet them, supply them, help them execute the prophet's will. We will finish the Emir's work."

31

ISLAMABAD, PAKISTAN

A SUBTLE ELECTRIC VIBRATION ROSE THROUGH THE TRAIN'S STEEL CHASSIS AS IT accelerated, buzzing the soles of Lisanne's feet.

Settled into the leather seat, the former United States Marine and Texas state trooper put down the paper map she had been studying and looked out the panoramic window. A large, brown sign with Roman letters above Kufric script flashed by: ISLAMABAD.

Lisanne folded the map to focus on the X, where Jack said Midas lay wounded. She studied the terrain marks, trying to picture the Delta man's position. According to Jack, Midas was safe in a friendly indigenous village. She was imagining what that village might look like when a knock at the door startled her, ruining the image.

"How's the hand?" Srini asked cheerfully. The new bride glowed in her yellow traveling skirt suit. Her lipstick was fresh, her hair artfully braided. "All good?"

Lisanne burst into a smile. "Why, Doctor, what are you doing slumming back here? I didn't expect you newlyweds to leave the sleeping car at all."

Srini slid into a velvety bulkhead seat. "First of all, it's broad daylight. Second, my father is in the sleeping car ahead of ours, an arrangement not entirely conducive to romance."

"He seems rather preoccupied with his business. I doubt he'd even notice."

The new bride chuckled and looked away. "It's not just the layout. Sanjay is on pins and needles, worried he'll be called into a meeting any second. He's not exactly sanguine, as one might politely say."

"There are pills for that sort of thing, Doctor."

Srini glanced at Lisanne's mechanical arm, her face suddenly serious. "Speaking of medicine, it's time for your exam. Would you please remove your prosthesis?"

Lisanne felt at ease complying with the request, as the first-class passenger car was empty. She removed the silicone band and narrow electrical couplings that fused her mechanical forearm to her elbow.

Srini lifted the inert hand and scrutinized it, turning it before her eyes. "None the worse for wear," she pronounced. "Now let's see that elbow."

After Lisanne removed her outer button-down and sat in her T-shirt, Srini examined the scar tissue. The doctor tapped Lisanne's bicep and humerus to test her reflexes.

"You are a model patient," she declared.

"Thank you, Doctor."

"Let me help you get it back on."

While Lisanne reapplied the silicone mounting bands and affixed the miniature electronic plugs, Srini noticed the map folded in the seat pocket. She plucked it free and examined the folded square. "Are you curious about the geology of the Karakoram Gorge? This area of the map is a bit southeast of the bridge location."

"Yes," Lisanne answered. "I was wondering where our route would take us. What's it like that far north?"

"Ah." Srini looked through the window, directing her gaze above the blurred mud walls that surrounded the village as they sped by. "Pretty soon, those hazy Himalayan peaks will be standing right over us. The Gorge is beautiful this time of year. The rivers swell with snowmelt, and the valleys bloom with wildflowers."

"I can't wait to see it."

"Is Jack looking forward to getting into the wilds? The poor man, I feel like we've put him through hell this past week."

"He's fine. The formality of the wedding wasn't really his thing—as you know by now—but stomping around mountain peaks is right up his alley."

"He did well riding that camel. Though he looked miserable."

"I'll pass that on to him. I'll tell him he looked gallant."

"Where is he, anyway?" Srini asked.

"Lying in bed—a bucket nearby."

"Oh no."

"Oh yes. His face is Martian green."

"Should I check on him? I have some medicine available."

"It's just Delhi belly. The damage to his pride would be worse than the food poisoning."

"I feel terrible," Srini moaned, a hand rising to her mouth.

"Now, stop that. It wasn't the wedding food. It was the street fare he ate when he got lost in the country. His own damned fault—and he knows it."

"I warned him."

"We all did."

The train clacked softly over the tracks. A few low hills marked the end of dense civilization. Srini leaned toward the panoramic glass and pointed at a distant peak. "That's Mount Leepa," she said, unfolding a quarter of the map and tapping her finger on a tight set of contour lines. "See it here? Springtime in Leepa Valley is lovely."

"Beautiful," Lisanne remarked, staring at the mountains. "Will there be a stop where we can get off to experience it?"

"Yes, as a matter of fact. We arrive in Langarpura tomorrow morning, where we'll have a few hours of free time. We can stroll around the town and stretch our legs. The air is glorious."

As the train rounded a curve in a farm field, Lisanne thought through the update she would deliver to John Clark once she found a way to communicate with him. The Campus director of operations prized operational security and brevity above all else, and Lisanne intended to find a public Wi-Fi network where she could use the Campus encryption protocol.

"Who was that boarding in Islamabad?" the Campus operative asked. "I saw your father bowing and scraping before them— something I've never seen him do. Sanjay looked petrified."

"They were politicians," Srini replied. "Or customers, I should say. Most of AGI's projects are government funded."

"Pakistani politicians?"

"Yes. They're coming along for the dedication at the bridge. Also an important Chinese delegation."

"Chinese?"

"Their deputy foreign minister, I'm told. And his retinue."

"You must be rolling out the red carpet for that."

"Yes. We'll make several stops along the way: business meetings, outings, schmoozing, that sort of thing. Sanjay wants to close more Chinese-funded construction deals. I suspect my father wants more time to finish the bridge and iron out the kinks in the rail network." The newlywed grinned radiantly. "But for us, it will be a grand tourist outing. You don't mind, do you?"

"Of course not. Touring by rail is lovely. Especially on a train as nice as this—and with a friend like you."

While Lisanne outstretched her natural arm to indicate the car's luxurious environs, she mentally filed the news about the

Chinese. She intended to include a report of their presence in her update to Clark.

"I also saw Fahim in Islamabad," Lisanne added. "He came aboard with the delegation."

"Yes. He's here."

"The man is somewhat . . . Well, forgive me for saying this, but he's rather beautiful, isn't he? In a *Thousand and One Arabian Nights* kind of way."

"*Yeesh*," Srini replied, recoiling.

Lisanne laughed. "Really? You don't think he's good-looking?"

"Good-looking, perhaps. But a good man? No."

"He seems pleasant enough. Your father likes him. He's number two in the company isn't he? I would think he's close to the Rai family."

"Have I never told you about Fahim?"

"No. But you have to now, obviously."

"Oh, Ms. Robertson. The man's a complete and utter bastard."

Lisanne's eyes widened. "Wow. What is *with* you two?"

Srini cast her eyes forward and spoke in the monotone of a medical diagnosis. "Fahim travels to the U.S. frequently for business. Before Sanjay, he and I went on a few dates back in Austin. Much to my regret."

"Why?"

"On our third date, we dined at the Rooftop Cantina on Sixth—you know the one. Afterward, he drove me back to my place and came in, even though I didn't want him to. He said he left his jacket inside. When I went to get it, instead of waiting, he followed me in. After that, let's just say he became . . . *aggressive*, insisting that the third date was *the one that mattered*."

"As in . . ."

"Exactly. He thinks he's God's gift to women and doesn't know the meaning of the word no. I slapped him so hard that I thought I might have broken his zygomatics."

"What are those?"

"His cheekbones. His eyes burned with hatred. He came at me. My key ring was on the table with my pocket mace. I held it up. That scared him off."

"Good for you. And what's it like being around him since then?"

"That night, he oozed apologies, said I was overreacting, and so on. Maybe I was. Either way, we don't speak—at least I don't speak to him. But that didn't stop him from going to my father to propose an arranged marriage. Can you believe the nerve? I wish he would leave the company. He probably will, now that my father is grooming Sanjay for future leadership. Fahim has many outside opportunities. And he's ambitious. I hate the way he looks at us."

Lisanne shook her head while gazing out the window. "I can't think he'd be here on this romantic rail trip if he blazed with jealousy."

"He's all about himself and showing off. That bridge across the Karakoram Gorge is his baby. And he probably wants to impress Jack, the Chinese, everyone—before he leaves for another job. I look forward to that."

"Jack *did* say Fahim was rather insistent we attend this bridge opening. And, of course, Jack is interested in a possible investment project with AGI. Poor Sanjay, lost in the shuffle."

Srini smiled. "Well. Sanjay has an agenda of his own. He wants to prove his worth as the head of AGI's business development operations and earn my father's respect. He's promised me a real honeymoon in a month or two—after all of this. If you weren't here, I think I would be sitting alone and reading a book."

Lisanne crossed her arms. "Men," she concluded.

"Men," the doctor echoed.

After a brief, tense silence, Srini added, "By the way, when are you and Jack going to set a date for your wedding?"

"That is an excellent question."

TWENTY MINUTES LATER, LISANNE FOUND HER FIANCÉ—THE MAN WHO HAD YET TO set a date—sitting up in the sleeping compartment's narrow bed. Though designed to fit the diminutive dimensions of a train car, maroon curtains fringed in gold cascaded from the padded ceiling as though draped from a regal canopy. A dainty en suite sink, toilet, and shower gleamed at the bed's foot. Lisanne threw the door's dead bolt closed.

Jack rested against the silken headboard, his knees over his overstuffed backpack. Two torn protein bar wrappers lay at his side.

"Has anyone asked about me?" he asked.

"Srini did—just now. She wanted to check on you, medically speaking."

"Okay. What did you tell her?"

"That Delhi belly has you in its grip, that you're green, and that your head is in a bucket."

"She bought it?"

"She's my friend, Jack. She's not going to think I'm lying to her."

"Right."

The train slowed briefly, forcing Lisanne to prop her mechanical arm against a mahogany-paneled wall for balance. Her nose wrinkled at the faint whiff of oil. "Were you cleaning your rifle?"

"Yes."

"Where is it?"

"Disassembled in the backpack. It barely needed a rub. The Embassy Marines must be obsessive."

"That's how we Marines are. What about the Glock?"

Jack lifted a pillow. "Freshly oiled and wrapped in a T-shirt. I'm leaving it with you."

"With me? Why?"

Before replying, Jack leaned over a compact side table. He opened a drawer to display a device resembling a microcassette recorder with a flashing green light.

"No bugs, I take it?" Lisanne asked, half joking.

"No. But I've got it on jam mode, just in case."

"You've gone fully tactical. Should I be worried?"

"No. But I've been thinking. We still haven't found the mole giving up the POSEIDON SPEAR names—yet I've been attacked twice in this country."

"That was when you were out on your own. Getting hit on an AGI luxury train is a bit of a stretch."

"Maybe not. Remember, I was there when Clark bagged the Emir. What if I'm one of the names on the kill list? They go after families." He patted the pillow that obscured the Glock. "Which is why you're sleeping with this."

"Fair enough."

"Do you think Clark and the team have touched down in Turkey yet?"

"I think they should be to Incirlik by now, yes. They were taking a complicated route, imitating commercial flights to stay fully black."

"When will you talk to Mr. C.?"

"At the next stop."

"Good. No phones, Lis. Use encryption over public Wi-Fi only. Nothing on this train."

She flashed her eyes at him, annoyed by the patronizing tone.

"What else did Srini say?" Jack asked, missing the signal. "Did she mention anything about expectations from me at this Karakoram Bridge thing?"

"There is one thing," Lisanne replied. "A Chinese Ministry of Foreign Affairs bigwig boarded the train along with Fahim. Deputy foreign minister. And retinue."

"Do we know why?"

"To attend the bridge dedication. Srini said there will be meetings to review other projects around Pakistan. On the way to the Gorge, the train will stop frequently for tourist outings. Privately, she thinks her father is stalling to ensure the construction is sound. They also want to close additional Chinese construction deals."

"Huh," Jack replied. "I guess it makes sense that the Chinese would come along for the ride, given they fronted the money for the bridge."

"Right. I'll add that to Clark's report."

"Only over secure data comms," he reminded her.

She glared at him.

32

A PHONE RECEIVER PRESSED TO HIS EAR, JOHN CLARK PARKED A BUTT CHEEK ON THE edge of a battered Air Force desk at Incirlik Air Base, some five thousand miles west of Jack and Lisanne.

The air base lay right in the center of Adana, a city with 1.7 million residents, one of the oldest continuously inhabited settlements on the planet. With a recorded history dating back to eight-thousand-year-old stone tablets, Adana is mentioned in the Sumerian epic of Gilgamesh, Homer's *Iliad*, and the Bible. Over the millennia, it has been ruled by various kingdoms of the Neolithic, Bronze, and Iron ages, along with Alexander the Great, Roman generals, and Byzantine emperors who fought for it against the Islamic Umayyad Caliphate in 746 CE, which, as the namesake of Rafa bin Yasin's current delusions, might have been relevant to John Clark—had he given a hoot.

But Clark did not give a hoot. His only interest in Adana was its ten-thousand-foot runway maintained by the United States Air Force and its access to secure government telecommunications.

As such, he was chained to a desk anchored in a cramped room in the American base's operations center. A small, high window offered a view of the C-17 that had brought his team here. Behind him, he had tacked a map to a bulletin board beside a relatively useless high-altitude satellite image marked up with Midas's last known position. He wore khaki trousers with reinforced knees, an untucked green T-shirt, and desert combat boots, which, for him, passed as civilian attire.

"Why am I just hearing about this?" he growled through the handset of a bulky Secure Terminal Equipment, STE, pronounced *stee*, bolted to the painted cinder-block wall.

"We think we have compromised communications," Lisanne answered from a café in the village where the train had stopped.

"What's the basis of that assessment?" Clark persisted, dreading one more snafu in the growing collection that seemed to plague this op. To wit: the airlift to transport the RAVENs and his small detachment of airborne commandoes spoofed various civilian cargo aircraft, leading to unhelpful diversions and delays; Midas hadn't reported in; Gavin and Mandy were playing junior detective with nothing tangible on the mole. And now this: Jack Junior cowboying it up on a solo mission.

"I believe Jack reported our earlier brush with trouble."

"He did," Clark snapped. "A suicide bomber."

"Jack was also shot at when he went to meet Midas for the infil."

"I know. The Delhi station chief reported that to Mary Pat Foley. She passed it on to me. The CIA assessed it as an Indian army patrol chasing down suspicious drivers in Kashmir."

"That's possible," Lisanne replied. "But then there was the ambush on Midas. Jack and I both believe that the indig Indian SATCOM devices tipped off the bad guys. It's why he asked for Midas's muj guide, Rustam, to stay off the net."

Clark relented. "Fine. So where is Jack?"

"He slipped off the train last night."

"Where?"

"We passed within twenty miles of Midas's location, south of Muzaffarabad. I would guess Jack is halfway to meeting the muj contact by now."

Clark's eyes roamed over the tiny office, taking in Air Force memos, navigation charts, and boldface weather reports. His mind flashed back to the breakfast with Mary Pat Foley, where he'd promised her there would be no complications. So much for that.

Rather than execute the pinpoint black operation he'd promised, he'd created the mother of all snafus. *Situation Normal—All F'd Up.*

"Goddamnit," he groaned, his palm over his chin. "Jack can't go charging into the teeth of terrorists by himself unarmed."

"Respectfully, Mr. C., Jack isn't unarmed. He has an M4 with three mags and a pistol. He knows exactly where to go because he has Rustam's position."

"He thinks he can cover twenty miles on foot while bad guys are hunting Midas down? Jack's a good man. He's not Superman."

"It's one day's hard march, Mr. C. Jack has food and water. He took my Garmin GPS watch for navigation, and he's toting a reasonable terrain map. He's ready to act as your intelligence liaison when he gets to Midas. Our op can go forward as planned. We'll be in position to hit Rafa."

"Marine, I'll ask again. Why didn't you report in sooner?"

"You were in the air, bouncing across the globe to Turkey. And, forgive me, but aren't we still concerned about a mole? Or have Mandy and Gavin figured that out?"

Clark winced. "Yes, we're concerned about a mole. Mandy and Gavin are working the problem set with the Bureau. And yes, it took me longer to get to Incirlik than planned. You still should have found a way."

"I did find a way. This is the first chance I've had the opportunity to access a public Wi-Fi link where I can use data encryption.

That's our standard operating procedure when we're on a black op, right? Would you have preferred I risk another leak?"

Clark inhaled so fully that his lungs nearly split. He tugged at the skin under his Adam's apple and exhaled through his nose before snatching a pencil. "I hate it when you're right. Give me those coordinates again, Ms. Robertson. Slower this time."

She rattled off the numbers, accurate to the cartographic second.

"What do we know of Midas's condition?" Clark asked.

"My information is a few days old, but he was unconscious then. Sounds like he was shot near the collarbone and in the leg."

Clark swore. "Then we have to hurry this up. Do we have any tactical intel on the ambush that got him?"

"According to Rustam, Midas tried to take out the HVI with his kit. Jack reported that Midas carried a Remington M2010 sniper setup. He hit several fighters, but missed the HVI. They pulled back in an armed retreat."

Clark's pencil marks bled onto a second sticky note. "What do you mean by several fighters?"

"Unclear. I'm relaying all this as Jack heard it from the muj."

"Copy. Do your hosts on that train have any clue what Jack's doing? Any chance we could be compromised from that direction?"

"Negative. Jack slipped away last night, jumping when the train slowed. The rest of our party thinks he's still aboard. I'm covering by telling them he's ill."

"Is that working?"

"For now."

"What's the ultimate destination?"

"A bridge project that crosses the Karakoram Gorge, south of a town called Khaibar, Pakistan. By the way, Mr. C., it happens to be a Chinese Belt and Road Initiative project. There are CCP dignitaries on the train."

Thinking of Mary Pat Foley again, Clark screwed his eyes shut. "Did you just say there are Chinese Communist Party people on that train?"

"Yes, there's a deputy foreign minister from China here. He—" She cut herself off. "I have to drop. Srini, my friend, just rounded the corner. She's coming this way. I'm out."

Lisanne hung up just as Master Chief Kendrick Moore inserted his bald head through the crack in the door. Clark turned to his fellow former SEAL, who was decked out in his Crye combat shirt, camo pants with reinforced knees, and a SIG Sauer 9-millimeter on his hip. "What's the word, Master Chief Moore?"

"We're set. Our C-17 crew just got clearance to fly over Tajikistan. The plan is to spoof a FedEx flight from Istanbul to Shanghai. The crew has loaded up the squawks and filed the appropriate flight plans."

"Good. Team assembled?"

"Yup. They're in the hangar."

Clark replaced the STE receiver on its hook. " 'Kay. That was Lisanne. She had a lot to report. Midas sprung the trap early, but failed in his ambush. He's wounded. Our HVI is still on the loose and probably knows we're coming."

Moore's eyes widened. "You serious, boss? How is Midas?"

"Medical condition unknown, but alive and, according to his muj, stable. He took down some UC fighters. They're on the hunt for him. We need to get there in a hurry to pick him up and—if we still can—finish the job. The extract will be more complicated than we planned."

"Who'll act as our recon on the ground if not Midas?"

"Jack Junior. He's overlanding it to the position right now."

Moore's forehead scrunched into ten furrows. "Jack Junior? Isn't he on vacation or something?"

"Yeah," Clark replied. "Or something."

"Where's Lisanne?"

"On a train with Chinese communists, of all goddamned things." While Moore's head went sideways in confusion, Clark waved him off. "She's fine. But Master Chief, I'm worried this whole op has been burned."

"We could rely on the CIA assets to get Midas out—same way he got in."

"Negative. We're up to our elbows in shit at this point. Load up the C-17. Your team can still infil via the RAVENs. Let's hope Gav and Mandy find this mole before the mole finds us."

"Aye, aye, Mr. C. You flying with us? You could be the airborne command post."

Clark pictured Mary Pat Foley darting between Liberty Crossing, Dan Murray's pro tem digs at Hoover, and Jack Senior in the Oval Office. A botched op in this part of the world would spiral into a full-on disaster inside the Beltway, perhaps exposing The Campus.

Clark decided then and there that he'd better stay at Incirlik as the eye of this swirling shitstorm.

"You'll have tactical command for this one, Master Chief. I'll hold down the fort here and do my best to keep Washington off our backs. You good with that?"

Moore crossed his arms and recited the SEAL motto, "The only easy day . . ."

". . . was yesterday," Clark finished.

33

GAVIN AND MANDY PASSED BY THE MODEST, SINGLE-STORY HOUSE AT TEN A.M., having driven the F-250 over from Clarkston before dawn, a nearly three-hour journey.

"Keep rolling," Mandy directed from the SUV's passenger seat, her eyes glued to the house. The orange sun reflected off the picture window to the left of the front door. The yard was weedy and dry.

After days of research, Gavin had detected a physical termination point for the IP address that had tracked Maddie Hunt's phone. As suspected, it ended here in the Tri-Cities. Because the borders of the three municipalities ran together, citizens considered the Tri-Cities as one town—but, technically, the suspect's house was in Pasco, Washington.

"There's a cul-de-sac coming up," she added. "Flip around and drive by it again, but don't look at it. Let me do that."

Gavin sipped the coffee in his to-go mug from the gas station's quickie mart and kept his eyes forward. He would be the first to acknowledge that he was *not* a morning person. But he became more alert when he watched Mandy press-check her Glock, ensuring a 9-millimeter parabellum round was in the chamber.

"Park next to that shrub," she directed. "We'll stake it out from here."

He coasted to a stop and killed the pickup's engine.

"Lower your sun visor," she added.

Gavin complied. In imitation of his partner, he press-checked his Glock and left it on the center storage bin in its ballistic nylon holster. Together, they watched the house with their windows down.

Mildly uncomfortable from the rising pressure in his bladder from too much coffee, the Campus info-tech specialist tingled with excitement. He watched the sun climb over distant, windswept hills.

Though the rural scenery had been majestic, Mandy had been quiet on the drive over, studying the records Sheriff Whitcomb had emailed. The county treasurer said a person named Parvasham Chakrabarti owned the home. A quick social media search hadn't turned up anything, but they were both intrigued that it was a South Asian name.

The sheriff had suggested the local cops should be sent for a low-intensity look-see. Worried about the mole, Mandy put her foot down. All they had to go on was an IP address attached to Maddie Hunt's phone, which bounced from the India-Pakistan region and terminated here at this single-story rambler in Pasco. She wanted to lay eyes on it herself.

"We might have to start up and run the air-conditioning," Gavin suggested.

"Negative. That would be suspicious. Sit tight."

Like Clarkston, Pasco was part of eastern Washington's Columbia Basin, a semi-arid steppe. Its wide, tree-starved grassy plain froze in the winter and baked in the summer, roasting them in the truck cab as the sun climbed ever higher.

Gavin felt sweat beading on his nose. The increasingly urgent pressure in his lower abdomen made him shift positions.

"Hey, Mandy," he declared after seven squirming minutes. "I have to go."

"Negative. We're staying right here until we see who lives in that house."

"No. I mean I have to . . . you know, *go*."

Her blue eyes flared. "Damnit, Gavin. I told you that huge coffee was a bad idea."

"I know."

"It's only been forty-five minutes."

"I *know*."

"Jesus."

"I can get out and walk behind that blue house. Nobody's around."

The former FBI agent rotated her head to study the house in question. She was about to agree to Gavin's request when a Hyundai SUV approached from the far corner, facing them. Without a blinker, the car turned into the suspect home's driveway. The garage door went up, and the Hyundai vanished as it closed again.

"Okay," Mandy said. "Now we're cooking. Could you see the driver?"

"No."

"Me either. Damned sun reflected off the windshield."

After the SUV disappeared into the home's garage, Gavin resumed his plan to relieve himself behind the blue house. But his partner gripped his upper arm tightly when he unclipped his seat belt and touched the door handle.

"What are you doing?" she asked.

"You know what I'm doing."

"We just caught sight of our suspect. For all we know, they're doing countersurveillance to check the area."

"Special Agent Cobb, I'm dealing with a biological imperative. I need to—"

"*Shh!*" Mandy gripped her Glock with both hands and scrunched. "Get low. I have eyes."

Gavin slunk below the steering wheel. The crimp in his posture stabbed his bladder.

"Okay," she announced thirty seconds later. "Let's go. Safe to approach the house."

"Why do you say that?"

"Because a lady just came outside and pounded a For Rent sign in the front yard. Must be the homeowner. Or maybe a realtor. I think she's alone."

"What are we going to do?"

Mandy shoved her Glock in the shoulder holster hidden below a lightweight cotton jacket. "Act like we're boyfriend-girlfriend looking for a place to shack up. Come on."

SHE HELD GAVIN'S HAND AS THEY WALKED UP THE SIDEWALK IN THE HEAT. HAD IT not been for his physical discomfort, he would have found it a delicious thrill.

"Hello!" Mandy called when they were twenty yards from the suspect's driveway.

The woman in the yard was in her late forties, with a dark complexion and curly black hair. She was wearing capri pants, a pink button-up blouse, and gardening gloves. She walked along the driveway carrying a bucket, evidently intending to pull weeds.

"Can I help you?" she responded with a squint against the bright blue sky.

Mandy detected a faintly Indian accent that matched the woman's looks. "We're interested in renting the house."

"Oh really? How did you hear about it? I haven't even put an ad out yet."

"We were driving around and saw the sign."

"You were? I didn't see a car go by."

The former FBI agent faked a chuckle. "We're parked down there at the cul-de-sac. We pulled over to get some work done and make a few calls. We saw you putting the sign in the yard and couldn't believe our luck. Is it vacant?"

"Yes, it is. And furnished." The homeowner put her bucket on the driveway.

"Furnished? Do you rent it short term or long term?"

"Both. But there's not a lot of interest in Airbnbs. This isn't much of a vacation destination, so I tend to do longer leases."

"Are you the owner and landlord?"

"Yes. What kind of lease are you looking for?"

Mandy's eyes swept the property. She saw nothing incriminating in the open garage bay—only the woman's Hyundai. The blinds at the picture window were pulled up, zero movement inside the house.

"We're looking for a full-year lease," Mandy improvised, assuming that would be of more interest to an owner looking to rent her house. "That it's furnished is a huge bonus for us."

"Okay. What do you do for work?" The homeowner studied the couple before her.

At first, Mandy thought it an unusually penetrating question and put her guard up. She quickly reminded herself that it was reasonable for a landlord to demand proof of employment.

"We both work in software," she offered spontaneously. "He writes code. I'm in marketing. Seattle's gotten too expensive, and we can work from anywhere. We thought we'd go somewhere more rural to save money."

"Why'd you pick the Tri-Cities?"

"Because we both like the sun."

Mandy was gratified to see the woman soften. Two gainfully employed tech workers were probably a prize in the slow home-rental game in this predominantly agricultural community. With her hand outstretched, she introduced herself as Molly and Gavin as Mitch, borrowing the names from Sheriff and Mrs. Whitcomb.

"The sun is what brought me from Seattle, too—after my girls went off to college," the homeowner replied. "I'm Parvasham Chakrabarti. I maintain several rental properties in the area. I know the name's a mouthful, so just call me Parv."

"May we see inside the house?"

"Sure. The cleaning crew came through yesterday."

Gavin spoke for the first time. "If it's not too much trouble, Parv, may I use your bathroom?"

"Of course, Mitch. Come in out of the heat."

While Gavin disappeared down a narrow hall, Mandy roamed around the main sitting room that joined the kitchen and the hallway. She noted the inexpensive furniture, builder-grade carpet, and bland wall art. Two bedrooms and a single bathroom lay at the west end. Both bedrooms contained bare mattresses.

Parv Chakrabarti opened the kitchen cabinets, drawers, and pantry in the kitchen to show off the space. All were empty.

"When was the last renter here?" Mandy asked, inspecting the fridge.

"It went vacant about a week ago."

"Why? Who lived here?"

Though a blunt question, Mandy had found in her FBI career that people would give up all sorts of information in response to a direct question. A salty NYPD detective once told her that the first thing he did when arriving at a homicide was to find neighbors and simply ask, *Who did it?* About half the time, the question solved the case.

"It was two guys, foreigners," Parv answered. "I didn't know much about them. And I didn't ask. We get a lot of migrant farmworkers."

"Did they work local?"

"I assume so. They paid cash."

"I see."

"I can offer a discount if you do the same. I see no reason to invite the government into our business. Would you be comfortable with that? It's pretty common in the Tri-Cities, given the questionable . . . shall we say . . . immigration status of so many people in the short-term rental market."

Gavin was back from the bathroom with his iPhone in his hand. He spoke before Mandy could respond. "I'm not seeing Wi-Fi."

"The house has broadband," the landlord replied. "But I don't supply the equipment. If you choose to rent, you can set it up yourself."

"Do you mind if I look outside at the wiring? I need a lot of bandwidth for my job. It's important to me."

The homeowner shrugged. "Sure."

Gavin exited through a sliding glass door while Mandy continued her subtle search. The trash cans were empty, freshly lined with the cleaning crew's new bags. When the landlord showed Mandy the bathroom and turned away, Mandy hurriedly knelt by the tub and plucked hair from the drain. She stuffed the hairs in her pocket. Getting them into an evidence bag would have to come later.

"What about laundry?" she asked.

"This way."

Mandy had once dated an expert in the FBI's Evidence Recovery

Team at the Virginia field office. He told her that clothes dryers were overlooked whenever perps tried to clean up a crime scene. As Ms. Chakrabarti poked around the coat closet beyond the laundry room, Mandy opened the dryer door, removed the lint filter, and inspected it. A wadded knot of paper clung to the edge. She added it to her pocket.

"So what do you think?" the landlord asked when they were near the front door again. Gavin had returned and stayed quiet, following Mandy's lead.

"Let us think about it."

The woman shoved a business card into Mandy's hand. "That's me. How do I get ahold of you?"

"Don't worry about that. We'll call you."

Back in the Ford, Mandy dug through her backpack to retrieve the plastic bags she used for evidence. By the time she stowed the hair and paper sample, the pickup rattled down the street, passing the home. Parv Chakrabarti waved as they went by.

"Seems like quite the coincidence that she's Indian."

"I agree. Head to that Starbucks we saw and park near it so I can use the Wi-Fi. I want to summarize our findings and shoot them over to Sheriff Whitcomb. He can run a few queries with local law enforcement."

Five minutes later, Mandy powered up her laptop and connected to the Starbucks network. She typed up the substance of their contact with Chakrabarti and asked the sheriff to run down a mail-forwarding query with the local post office as an avenue to find the renters.

"Anything else to include?" she asked.

"Yeah. I installed an IP sniffer on the home's cable wiring that came in from the street. I'll be able to tap that for traffic analysis."

Mandy gaped at him. "Seriously? How'd you do that?"

"A little device I borrowed from a CIA buddy. It basically copies all the internet traffic coming in and redirects it to me via a proxy IP address."

"Will you be able to read emails and things like that?"

"No. The sniffing takes place at the packet level, not the application layer. But I'll be able to see if someone in the home was communicating and then follow that trace."

"Will you be able to see some of the historic activity?"

"Yes, a bit. As long as it's cached."

Surprised—because her FBI fly team had never used a wiretap like this one—she noted in the sheriff's report that they might be able to offer further "electronic surveillance" information to the local police department.

She hit send and closed her laptop.

"Back to Clarkston, then?" Gavin asked.

"No. Hang on."

She used a pair of tweezers to pick apart the wadded paper she'd pulled from the dryer's lint screen. Though faded, she could see that it was a cigarette sales receipt. The address listed a gas station on Highway 240, a half hour's drive northwest of Pasco.

After returning the receipt to its plastic bag, Mandy opened Google Maps on her phone. "Did that place smell to you like smokers lived there?"

"No," Gavin answered. "But when I was walking around the yard looking for the cable box, I saw a few butts that didn't look too old. The guys who lived there probably smoked out back."

"I agree. And they bought their cigarettes at a store a half hour from here. An address out on Highway 240, middle of nowhere. If they were itinerant farmworkers, maybe it's close to the fields."

Thinking she would want to return to the house to gather the butts for DNA analysis, she widened the Google Map box.

"Oh shit," she breathed, paling.

"What?"

"You know how Rafa's father, the Emir, intended to blow the Yucca Mountain nuclear waste depot in Nevada to poison the American water supply?"

"Yep. So?"

"The convenience store where these guys bought their cigarettes is five miles from the Hanford Reservation."

"Reservation? As in a Native American or wildlife preserve or something?"

"No, as in a federal reservation—for nuclear waste disposal. It sits right on the Columbia River."

34

JACK FROZE IN THE MOONLIT SHADOW OF A BROAD, SEVEN-FOOT-TALL TAMARISK shrub. He slid a shoulder free from his backpack and gently lowered it to the ground. He crouched, listened, and waited. Then he heard it again—falling rocks on a distant hillside.

Lying on his stomach, he extended his M4 ahead of him, maneuvering the barrel between the branches. A gust of wind swept down from the higher foothills and across the mesa, chilling his neck. It hissed through the tamarisk grove, scattering scents of sandalwood and juniper. He leaned over the scope and surveyed the treeless hill, placing his finger behind the trigger.

The moon was bright enough for him to distinguish shapes at a great distance. Unfiltered by moisture or dust, the stars shone brightly from east to west. The hill glowed under the white moon as if it were daytime, which Jack thought of as a double-edged sword. While he could spot the Umayyad fighters out there, they could just as easily see him. He focused his eye on the center of the scope and scanned for movement, ready to fire, aiming at the rockfall he was sure he'd heard.

He estimated it was about two hundred yards south of his position. He envisioned the rattle and echo of disturbed scree on the hillside signaling terrorist fighters creeping along the crest above him, waiting to see what he would do. The terrain in the valleys consisted of arable soil, decaying logs, and bright patches of powdery gypsum. Up the slopes, the mountains crumbled into shale.

Tactically, Jack found himself in a weaker position after giving up the high ground. However, according to the Garmin watch on his right wrist, he still had five miles to go to reach the last location the muj had sent through the Indian satellite transmitter before going dark. Midas was bleeding and alone.

Hearing nothing further, Jack slid his water bottle free of his pack and drank deeply, shaking it to test how much he had left. He judged it to be half a liter. He stayed in the prone position and watched the land through the scope.

Crickets sang and bats darted erratically, obscuring the stars. An owl hooted twice before Jack heard its wings flapping. Captivated by nature's serenade, his chin rested against the M4's cool metal barrel.

A distant, mournful cry startled him awake.

His head snapped up so quickly that a branch poked his cheek. The moon hung lower, and the land was still. Entire constellations of the enormous, dangling stars had rotated. Jack cursed himself for drifting off. The wailing animal cried out again.

He'd read a coffee-table book about Northern Pakistan on the train. Many predators lived in the Himalayan foothills—brown bears, gray wolves, leopards. Alone in his cabin, faking illness, there hadn't been much to do except read on the ride from Jammu to Jhelum to Muzaffarabad, where Jack had slipped off in the dark.

Daval Rai stopped the train at Muzaffarabad to lead his visitors on a tour of a sixteenth-century fort built by a Kashmiri emperor to ward off threats from the invading Mughals. According to Srini's comment to Lisanne, he wished to point out that while empires had come and gone, the infrastructure linking the peoples of the region remained in place.

The animal's cry peaked and warbled into a heartrending sob. The Himalayan brown bear, Jack recalled, cried like a human when wounded, warding off many a sympathetic hunter who couldn't live with the sound.

With numerous animals chattering, Jack deemed it unlikely that an Umayyad patrol was sneaking up behind him. He shook his head and checked the Garmin. Four miles to go, with dawn approaching. He scanned the valley with his scope, seeing nothing but gray rocks, black trees, and silver hills. He aimed Lisanne's Garmin watch to determine a bearing, aligning it with a distant, flat-topped acacia. With his course set, he took a few swallows of water.

He mostly jogged over the sloped terrain, his M4 clutched in front of him, and his heavy backpack thumping against his hips and shoulder blades. Following an easterly course, the bright moon cast a bulbous shadow of his pack and legs flickering over the uneven brush. Halfway to the acacia, he descended into a wadi and followed the loose sand for five hundred yards before climbing up its eastern edge.

The ascent was tough. He paused behind another scraggly tamarisk to catch his breath. He noticed the howling animal was blessedly silent, but here on this hillcrest, the night wind moaned and whistled, which was arguably worse. His breath heaving, Jack stepped to the side of the shaking bush with his rifle in hand, wishing he were making better time.

A glimmer of light startled him.

A red laser dot the size of a nickel glowed on his chest.

He dropped to the dirt immediately and rolled behind the bush. His hand fumbled over the rifle's selector switch, changing it from burst to full auto. He aimed along the path of the red laser beam that tracked him through the leaves. He was about to fire when a rough voice pierced the wind.

"*Roko!*"

The dot flashed in Jack's eyes.

He cursed, praying that the warriors of the Umayyad Caliphate wouldn't bother with such warnings. His right index finger remained poised on the trigger. He was prepared to unleash half the mag, thinking it would probably be his last act on planet earth.

"*Roko!*" the voice bellowed.

"I'm armed!" Jack hollered back, regretting that he didn't know the Urdu equivalent. He crawled sideways for better cover. The red beam was broken up in the quaking leaves. "Show yourself or I'll shoot!"

The answering pause lasted five interminable seconds.

"You have come for Mi-DASS?" the voice returned in a shout.

Jack stood tentatively, the weapon still in his hands, the dot welded to his chest.

"That you, Rustam?"

The dot vanished. Footsteps scraped over the loose ground. Jack stepped from behind the shrub, his left palm outstretched because his right clutched the M4's pistol grip.

The muj stood with his pakol cap pushed low over his brow, dark fabric wrapped around his upper chest like a poncho, and an M4 dangling in his right hand. Jack slowly placed his rifle on the ground and stepped forward, his palm aloft. The muj slung his rifle over his shoulder.

"Hello," Jack said, offering his hand. "In case you forgot—I'm Jack."

Rustam nodded, threw his cape aside, and took Jack's hand in a rough, iron grip. "*Salaam.* You Jack. You come."

"*Salaam.* Yes. Just as I said I would." Jack tapped his watch with two fingers. "You're west of our meeting site."

Rustam eyed the sophisticated, expensive watch. "I stalk you over two hills. Think you Umayyad. Almost shoot."

Jack took it as a quiet compliment that this rugged warrior thought he might be an Umayyad fighter. He resolved to share the comment with Mr. C. and Ding when he got home. "Are Umayyad nearby?"

The muj waved a thick arm as if to say, *All around us.*

"Okay. You take me to Midas now?"

A solemn nod.

"How far?"

Rustam surveyed the silver hills, judging the distance by sight. The moon was beginning to dip behind a triangular northwestern peak; the eastern horizon was purple. "Three-hour ride."

"Did you say *ride*?"

"I bring horses. We ride fast."

35

INCIRLIK AIR BASE, TURKEY

SENIOR MASTER SERGEANT IRV DUPREE HAD SEEN PLENTY OF SPECIAL OPERATORS come up the ramp of his C-17 Globemaster. As a member of the 437th Special Operations Squadron of Charleston, South Carolina, he was all too familiar with inserting men and matériel in denied areas at a moment's notice.

He'd executed orders where D-Boys jumped into war-torn Africa, SEALs leaped over the black wastes of the central Pacific, and Air Force PJ pararescuemen hurtled into the night sky over South American jungles.

It was no strange event for Irv Dupree to pick up an urgent air tasking order (ATO) from CENTCOM, INDOPACOM, SOUTH-COM, or whatever-the-COM to plan an emergency ingress into some godforsaken wasteland.

Once, he'd loaded an Abrams tank in less than thirty minutes, chained it to the deck, and rolled it out at a dusty combat outpost near Kandahar, an act that barely prevented a Ranger battalion from being overrun. That had been a hairy op. While Irv's C-17 slammed into the dirt field, an AC-130 gunship overhead dealt death by showering the area with massive 105-mike-mike rounds to keep the Rangers alive. The elite soldiers fired up the tank and won the day.

For all his experience, however, the ATO that currently flapped in Irv Dupree's hand on the taxiway near the Incirlik Air Base ops center was something he'd never encountered before.

"What's ODNI CAPCOM?" the senior Air Force NCO asked, forced to shout over the roar of a Turkish Air Force F-16 taxiing nearby.

"It's a unit of the Office of the Director of National Intelligence," Moore yelled in reply. "Special Access Program. That's all I can tell you, Irv. Sorry."

In truth, CAPCOM was a dummy command Gavin Biery had inserted into the DoD's communication structure so The Campus could request military resources. He'd shrouded it in military obfuscation by granting it presidential-level special-access program status, a revered stratum in the American national security apparatus's classification system.

Irv Dupree, a six-foot-three Black man who spent his workdays shoving heavy pallets and his off-duty hours lifting weights, wasn't intimidated by Moore, whom he took to be a CIA ground-branch operator. Nothing could undermine the Air Force man's authority as loadmaster.

"That may be all I need to know in terms of the order," he replied with a thump on the flimsy paper, "but when it comes to the physics of this airplane, I'm in charge. Understand, Moore?"

"What's the problem, Irv?"

"This directs me to launch the RAVENs at three hundred knots at forty-five thousand feet. We've never drilled that."

"The extended mission envelope is something we have to risk. Where we're going, it's imperative the aircraft maintain the characteristics of a FedEx plane over that narrow slice of Tajikistan. This is full black, like the message says. Copy?"

"Are you comfortable with that, Staff Sergeant Buck?" Irv asked the Marine Raider at Moore's side. "You're the expert."

"I'm comfortable. Gravity will do its thing."

Dupree took a few seconds to respond. "Going to be god-damned cold up there. If you exit those aircraft at that altitude, y'all are going to freeze to death."

Watching these proceedings, Cary Marks and Jad Mustafa stood ten feet behind the ramp with their thumbs hooked in their combat vests, baking in the Turkish sun while a helicopter passed overhead. Jad softly kicked Cary's boot and leaned in. "Did you know these things were untested at that altitude?"

"No," Cary replied.

"Does this Buck guy know what he's doing?"

"I trust Moore. I think."

"You think? Well, I think Irv the loadmaster is making some pretty good points."

Cary shrugged. "You want to back out?"

"Is that an option?"

"Negative."

"Awesome."

Cary and Jad lost track of whatever further points the Marine, SEAL, and Air Force crew chief ironed out. It didn't matter. The loadmaster folded the ATO into a breast pocket, and the C-17's massive engines came to life. Kendrick Moore stood on the ramp with a wide grin and a thumbs-up, facing his small team, his voice roaring over the engines.

"We're cleared hot, gentlemen! Load up!"

36

HANFORD, WASHINGTON

DREN SHALA AND AGON IVANAJ WAITED IN A WHITE TOYOTA TACOMA PICKUP WITH an AGI logo on two of its four doors. The long spiky shadows of a towering wind turbine behind them crossed the truck's hood in dark stripes.

"I'm hot," Dren announced in his native Albanian, vacantly staring at the dry plains. "Where the hell are these people?"

Agon shrugged in the passenger's seat and checked his Seiko dive watch. After leaving the Albanian Special Forces, he'd purchased it with his first French Foreign Legion paycheck. As another reminder of those halcyon days, his eyes passed over the Legion's insignia tattoo on his wrist, a seven-flame grenade resembling a fleur-de-lis.

"They said two o'clock," he noted.

"Arabs can't keep time. Ever."

Agon grunted. He surveyed the federal security guards by the gates. "You think the BLM rangers will do a special check or something?"

Dren fingered the stack of four AGI security credentials in his lap, printed and laminated in their construction trailer. "They're in the system. A special security check shouldn't matter."

The Albanian wondered at that. He was glad he'd stuffed his Legion-spec Glock 17 machine pistol under the seat, just in case.

"There they are," Dren said, inclining his head at an approaching vehicle, a duplicate of their own.

"They have a company truck," Agon said. "That was a nice touch."

"Let's hope it helps. The rangers are waving at us."

"Right. Drive."

The admittance paperwork was relatively straightforward. Someone up the AGI food chain had adequately entered the names into the system, matching them to the serialized numbers on the laminated IDs, which was all the BLM rangers needed when they did a lookup on their mobile computers.

"Keep following us," Dren told the bearded driver once they were a mile inside the gate and the BLM rangers were long gone. His security badge, which gave him an Indian name, was not a coincidence. Most of the AGI electrical engineers responsible for maintaining the wind turbines, power lines, and data center were Indian. That made sense, since AGI was an Indian company. "It's about five kilometers."

The man barely responded, staring straight ahead. A passenger in the rear seat twitched his eyes over the dusty hills dotted with wind turbines.

"Where are the explosives?" he asked.

"Do you see that jagged peak?" Dren returned, gesturing through the windshield.

The visitor nodded.

"That's a demolition site. The crew blasted away a portion of the hill that was interfering with the wind flow. They have tons of TNT set aside for earthwork."

"And the trucks?"

"There are several power-maintenance trucks that will give you access to the reservation. As post-security, Agon and I have keys."

"Are the work crews still here?"

"No. It's just us. The company declared a furlough for this site. In email, they said it was because they were awaiting government approvals. But I'm assuming it was because of you."

The driver ignored the comment and glanced south. "How far to Trench Ninety-Four?"

Martyrs, Dren thought with an inward groan.

While in the Legion, he'd killed his fair share of fanatical jihadis in the Balkans. These days, cashing checks from AGI, he was paid to hide them. Such was mercenary life. Fahim Bajwa had promised a major bonus for stashing the martyrs on the site before he and Agon headed up to Oregon for the next killing of an American soldier.

"Trench Ninety-Four is fifteen kilometers northeast of us, near the river," he replied.

The jihadi conferred with his three companions before addressing Dren again. "Our weapons?"

"At the site trailer where you'll be staying."

"You take us there now."

"Yes," Dren acknowledged, patience fading at what sounded to him like a command. "That's what we're doing."

Agon leaned forward to speak across his mercenary partner. "What's your timetable for the operation? And what's it called?"

"You are Muslims?"

Both Albanians nodded. They were Muslim by birth, but neither man practiced the religion or remembered much about it.

"At-Takwir," the driver said with a gleam in his eye.

"At-Takwir," Dren repeated.

"You know what that means?"

Dren shrugged.

The man in the driver's seat shut his eyes. His three companions followed suit. It was as if they had summoned an unexpected séance.

With head bowed, the driver chanted:

> *When the sun is down,*
> *and when the stars are dimmed,*
> *and when the mountains are blown away,*
> *and when the Hellfire blazes,*
> *and when Paradise is brought near . . .*
> *on that day each soul*
> *will know what it has brought with it.*

He opened his eyes and turned back to Dren. "You hear it? That mountain you blow away. That is the beginning of At-Takwir."

"I heard it," Dren responded. "And when do you execute At-Takwir?"

"Now that the mountain is blown away, we move when the commander of believers, the one true caliph, orders us. *Inshallah.*"

"I see," Dren acknowledged.

Martyrs, he thought.

37

TEN MILES SOUTHEAST OF AGON AND DREN, MANDY FLASHED HER FBI CREDS AT
Theodore Bolton Jackson—"T-Bolt" to his friends—a six-foot-four
former Army Ranger and current supervisory commander of the
Hanford Patrol's special response team.

T-Bolt inspected Special Agent Mandy Cobb's badge and ID
carefully. Imposing in the creased, unmarked camo uniform he'd
ironed that morning after his five-mile run, the government security specialist was not one to lie down whenever someone from
another agency showed up at his site.

"I'm sorry, ma'am, but I can't let you in," he responded, handing
back the wallet. "This is a federally protected Category One nuclear site. My team has security jurisdiction, and no visitors are
permitted without prior authorization from the Department of
Energy."

"Let's try this again," Mandy insisted. "Look me up in your access database, Mr. Jackson."

"Call me T-Bolt."

Mandy ignored him. "As soon as you log in, you'll see that
Special Agent Biery and I are with the FBI's National Security
Division. We don't need DOE permission to enter a potential Ren-
der Safe site. We're here to investigate a suspected compromise."

T-Bolt smiled at her use of the terminology.

Render Safe referred to the core of his mission—to defend this nuclear site against any attack. Working with the chief of the Hanford Reservation police, this place was wired up like the vault under Fort Knox. This FBI woman might throw around the correct mission lingo, but there was no effing way he was going to let her set foot on the property without hearing from his boss in D.C. first.

And besides, what were a couple of FBI agents and a county sheriff going to do about a Render Safe? T-Bolt's SRT unit was made up of two squads, each consisting of twelve men. All twenty-four were tier-one operator veterans from the SEAL teams or Army ODA. They were gung ho super warriors who worked for the National Nuclear Security Administration, a semiautonomous branch of the Department of Energy.

T-Bolt, who continued to serve as a Ranger company commander in the Army Reserves, did not take kindly to the idea of rolling over to some junior FBI agent with a badge and pistol. He folded his arms in a gesture that suggested he was about as likely to move as the distant hills in the panoramic window behind him.

"Listen, T-Bolt," Sheriff Mitch Whitcomb attempted, beige cowboy hat slanted on his head, good-old-boy expression softening his unkempt brows. "This is in connection to a murder investigation. We have reason to believe there are suspects on this installation. That's why we want in."

"I highly doubt that," T-Bolt replied, unmoved. "We don't let just anyone wander in here. As you can see."

"That's true. But what if the perp's someone with authorized access?"

"Every person at this site undergoes a thorough background investigation by the Defense Investigative Service."

"Yeah," the sheriff parried. "Thousands of 'em, right? That's a lot of people. And people, sadly, commit murders. Even ones who've been vetted."

T-Bolt considered that. It wasn't a bad point. "Why do you think your perp is here?"

The lawman hooked his thumbs into the belt loops of his Wranglers. "Evidence."

A heavy security door buzzed near T-Bolt. A woman behind a bulletproof window allowed a worker through after inspecting his badge.

"What evidence?" T-Bolt asked.

"Computer forensics," Whitcomb replied.

"What's that supposed to mean?"

Gavin Biery, who stood with his creds in his hand, chimed in. He had picked up additional evidence from the sniffer at Parv Chakrabarti's house that indicated data traffic passing through Hanford. "It means the murder suspects communicated through a router with an IP address indicating a Tri-Cities switching center that also handles Hanford."

"I'm familiar with our cybersecurity, Special Agent Biery. That router also manages the Pasco, Richland, and Kennewick areas. It's operated by one of the largest telecom contractors in the world and is located on protected federal land. I don't consider that evidence."

Gavin was about to present his case that this particular IP address used a subnet mask that indicated the router was tied to another one that came through a communication center that handled Hanford. He wanted to tell T-Bolt that he needed access to various communication nodes on the base to zero in on the perp's location, which would be a simple, low-touch mission. But Mandy Cobb cut Gavin short.

"Agent Jackson—"

"T-Bolt."

"*T-Bolt*," she relented. "Are you familiar with the National Security Presidential Memo thirty-six?"

"Yes, ma'am. I'm quite familiar with NSPM thirty-six. That executive order, signed by President Ryan, provides much of the funding for my team. It involves a tactical response to a nuclear terror incident. It's why I'm here."

"Exactly," Mandy replied. "But it also gives overall jurisdiction to the FBI Render Safe teams via the national asset commander."

T-Bolt rested his hand on his 9-millimeter and narrowed his eyes. "Has the National Asset Response Unit been activated?"

Sensing her hesitation, he went on. "The answer to that question, ma'am, is no. If it had, I'd be in an armored truck right now with twenty-four snake eaters about to do some serious damage. This whole area would be locked down."

"I understand. You're correct that the NARU hasn't been activated," she admitted, pronouncing the acronym as "nay-roo."

"Besides, I thought you said you're looking into a murder investigation," T-Bolt piled on, pleased with himself.

"Can you give me a minute?" Mandy asked with a charming smile.

She stepped outside the security office with her cell phone pressed to her ear. T-Bolt, Gavin, and the sheriff waited uncomfortably before the bulletproof-glass window as workers trudged through the door with their IDs held to their faces. The sheriff attempted small talk, going on about hunting bighorn sheep in the Yakima Valley, just over the hills.

A shaft of bright afternoon sunlight pierced the office as Mandy returned from outside with her phone in her hand.

"Hey, T-Bolt," she called. "I've got the secretary of the Department of Energy on the phone. He'd like a word with you."

"WELL, MS. COBB," SHERIFF WHITCOMB SAID FROM BEHIND THE WHEEL OF HIS RAM. "You proved yourself right about the FBI's jurisdiction for a NARU. But our friend T-Bolt wasn't kidding when he said they have this place covered."

"Let's just drive around and check things out," Mandy replied, punching at the computer on her lap. "Get Gavin to a good comms node so he can install another sniffer."

"I mean, come on," Whitcomb continued. "They've got motion sensors, cameras, roving patrols, armored vehicles. The only chance our perp is on this compound is if he works here. And those people get the federal investigative treatment."

Mandy paged through the Excel file on her laptop, which she had obtained from T-Bolt after the DOE secretary ordered him to provide it. The file contained over thirteen thousand names, each vetted by the Defense Investigative Service through a rigorous background check. Sub-links reported their comings and goings through the gate over the past month.

"I sent this file to Hoover," she said. "They have an analysis team going through it to see if anyone listed Pasco Parv's home as an address, which should show up in a background check—as long as the DIS is doing its job. In the meantime, I suggest we check things out for ourselves while we look for an exposed comms node for Gavin."

The sheriff slowed the Ram and stopped at an intersection. His eyes roamed over yet another camera mounted high atop a utility pole, where it would have good angles for video surveillance. The treeless landscape was unobstructed, stretching to bare, wind-swept mountains studded with churning wind turbines. His eyes skimmed over the AGI service provider logo affixed to the bulky white power transformer near the wires.

"How long will the Bureau take to get back to you?" the sheriff asked. He turned onto a fenced perimeter road that roughly followed the curves of the nearby Columbia River.

"I should have an initial report in a few hours."

"Then I think we should head back to Pasco for some real police work at the house. I can file for a warrant with the Franklin County judge."

Mandy glanced sideways at him. "Sheriff Whitcomb, why are you so pessimistic about finding the perp here?"

"Look up from your computer, Special Agent Cobb. A murderer fleeing the scene for Hanford would be like bypassing the justice system and crawling straight into a supermax prison. If your Hoover team comes up with something, all we'll need to do is call T-Bolt Jackson back there. That perp will be lucky to be alive when his shock troops are unleashed."

"Turn here, Sheriff," Mandy said, disregarding him. "Trench ninety-four is at that corner. Jackson mentioned that's the most sensitive waste storage site. Maybe there's a data node nearby. I see an acre of solar panels."

Whitcomb rotated the wheel, steering toward the trench, which reportedly contained a hundred fortified barrels of radioactive waste. He spotted another utility pole that serviced the solar panels. It, too, was topped with a security camera and a white transformer.

"This place gives me the heebie-jeebies," he drawled. "I don't like being in the same county with this crap, let alone the same street corner. I'll get a warrant for the Pasco house. If not fingerprints, then I'll find something else. Good old-fashioned police work."

"Negative, Sheriff," the former FBI agent said. "We need to run this to ground first. Between Gavin's IP trace and that cigarette receipt, Hanford is our best lead."

Whitcomb thrust his chin out. "As lead detective, this is still my murder investigation, ma'am. It's my call."

Mandy traded a look in the rearview mirror with Gavin, who sat in the back stroking Luna's head.

"Sheriff," she ventured. "Agent Biery and I have a confession to make."

"If this is about an inappropriate relationship between you two, I don't—"

"It's not that!" she snapped. "It's about the investigation. The truth is that we're not only looking for the murderer of the Cole Hunt family. We're also looking for a mole in the U.S. security apparatus with potential ties to a terrorist group. That group once targeted an American nuclear facility. It looked a lot like this one. Copy?"

Whitcomb braked to a stop along the perimeter road's shoulder. "What the hell are you talking about, Ms. Cobb? If that's true, why wouldn't you have shared that with T-Bolt? And you can't just withhold information from me. You can't just—"

"This is a highly classified, presidential-level special access program," Mandy interrupted, eyes flashing. "We couldn't tell T-Bolt or you about it. Now that we're here, I'm reading you in. That's on me. It's *my* call."

"Murder's my jurisdiction, young lady. You shouldn't have withheld evidence, even if it's circumstantial."

"Like I said, it's a matter of national security."

"Tell that to Cole Hunt and his family, God rest their souls."

Mandy closed her laptop lid and spoke rapidly. "Sheriff, Cole Hunt wasn't the first person to be killed that way. He was, in fact, the third victim. The three vics were all part of an operation called POSEIDON SPEAR that took out a jihadi terror network. Those jihadis went after a Nevada nuclear waste site, much like this one, to poison the American water supply with radioactive waste. We're worried they may be back. Okay, there you go. You're fully read into the national security program. You know everything we do. Happy?"

Whitcomb removed his hat and ran his fingers through his thin, white hair. From the start, he figured Hunt was some kind of special figure in the U.S. government, drawing the feds into his investigation. "The Columbia River . . ." he mumbled, slanting his head to the east.

"Exactly," Mandy finished for him, her eyes locked on his. "Millions of people get drinking water from reservoirs fed by the Columbia. That river also irrigates six hundred thousand acres of farmland and is a primary water source for livestock and wild animals. If terrorists blew this site to cause waste to seep into the river, then *all* of those crops would be radioactively poisoned, killing anyone who ate them. May as well drop a nuke on Portland and Seattle. Satisfied?"

Whitcomb exhaled. "Yes. Agent Biery, I'll help you find a line you can tap."

"You can't breathe a word of this to anyone, Sheriff," Mandy reiterated. "You'll have to sign papers that seal your lips for a hundred years. And that includes Dot."

"Roger that. Your secret's safe with me, ma'am. But my point still stands. The site's clean as a whistle. If there were jihadis around here, T-Bolt would know it. Has to be an inside job."

She tapped her laptop lid. "Exactly why I have the Bureau going through thirteen thousand names."

Whitcomb fixed his hat in place. "Going to be like finding one grain of sand on a beach."

"Precisely. What was it you called it? Good old-fashioned police work?"

38

NORTHERN PAKISTAN

JACK RECLINED IN HIS SADDLE AND TUGGED ON THE MARE'S REINS AS SHE DESCENDED the steep hill under the pink light of dawn. His back throbbed from eight miles of jarring over rocky ridges. Trapped in the stirrups for hours, his ankles tingled from reduced blood flow.

"Whoa!" he grunted angrily while yanking hard on the leather. "Easy!"

His horse seemed to be headed straight down, ignoring the repeated tugs on the reins. Pine and fir trees crowded the trail, forcing him to twist to avoid scraping his knees on the bark. The only advantage to this cruel foliage, he thought, was that it would break his fall when the mare finally lost her footing on this ridiculous decline.

"Whoa, damn you!"

Farther down the slope, Rustam twisted in his mount and addressed Jack with a grave head shake, reminding him that Umayyad fighters stalked nearby. Jack gritted his teeth and maintained a death grip on the reins.

After another half hour of equestrian depredations, the two-horse caravan broke into slanted sunlight. Shaded fir trees gave way to bright green grass at the bottom of the hill. Jack's mare stopped walking, lowered her head, and munched on the stalks as if there were no rider on her back.

Worried about losing Rustam, Jack yanked the reins, driving the bit harshly into the horse's mouth. The mare turned her head, flapped her lips, and bared her teeth in an attempted bite. Jack loosened the reins and thumped her ribs with his boot heels. That got the beast moving, although she tried to bite him twice more.

Farther into the valley, the aroma of roasted meat and woodsmoke made Jack's mouth water. Similarly overcome, the mare broke into a trot, galloping toward a cluster of low mud huts, nearly throwing Jack from the saddle.

A boy with a wispy adolescent beard, a fez-like hat, and a filthy dhoti hurried out of a hut to catch Jack's horse. Nearby, Rustam exchanged words in Urdu while Jack dismounted awkwardly, wobbling stiffly on his sore legs. A second younger boy grabbed the reins and led Jack's mare away. *Good riddance*, he thought.

"This way," Rustam directed, waving Jack inside a hut.

A desiccated woman and a little girl sat sewing in the dimly lit hovel. Midas was on their other side, sitting up against a splintered bench.

"Son of a bitch!" the former Delta warrior exclaimed. "You made it!"

"You didn't think I would?"

Out of long habit, Midas shrugged, the pain of which caused him to wince. "Thanks for coming."

"Of course," Jack replied, kneeling. He was shocked by his fellow Campus operative's pale complexion. Midas appeared to have lost twenty pounds since Jack last saw him. "How bad are you hit?"

Midas let the blanket fall away from his torso, revealing his bare skin covered in pale tan bandages. The old woman and girl giggled as they backed away through the door.

"They're shy," he explained. "But they're mighty fine nurses."

"Chest wound? Good Lord, Midas, it's a wonder you're alive."

"The bullet went through my trapezius muscle," he said, gently touching the bandage on his left shoulder with his right hand. "Clean exit." He leaned to his right, grimacing in pain. "Down here, another shot grazed my thigh. Same deal, though—it passed right through me."

"You're lucky that didn't hit a femoral artery."

"Tell me about it. The worst part was the headache. My own Claymore blast knocked me off the hill. I was unconscious for at least twelve hours. Probably ended up with a TBI. Please don't tell Mr. Clark about that. I like working for The Campus."

"I won't," Jack replied. A TBI, traumatic brain injury, was the bane of every operator's existence. Jack inspected Midas's bandages. He was surprised to see a used IV bag on the ground. "These muj villagers did all this?"

Midas inclined his head at the doorway. "Yeah. For better or worse, these folks have been at war since the Bronze Age. Rustam had a whole kit in his truck with IVs, antibiotics, sutures, morphine, the works. I think I may have been better off here than in an American field hospital. Oh, shit. I need to cover up. Here they come."

The woman and girl returned with bowls of a steaming meat-laden rice dish they referred to as *pilau*. Midas hovered over it and dipped his right hand, stuffing *pilau* into his mouth.

"No forks?"

Midas shook his head. "You can wait for some naan bread. I think we're out of it, though. Just eat with your right hand. Never your left."

"Why?"

"The left is reserved for . . . you know, toilet."

"Oh." Jack was too hungry to wait for the naan. Using his right hand, he scooped wads of food into his mouth. He and Midas went at the rice like children digging in a sandbox.

"Starving," Jack said between swallows. "Walked all night. Then rode a horse. Not a fan of that."

The Delta man replied with his mouth still full. "Well, don't be too rough on those combat horses. That mare you rode saved my ass."

"Is that so? She tried to kill me."

Midas gulped. "After I got hit, Rustam tossed me over that mean old horse. He lashed me down with a line that went under her ribs. I was in and out through the ride back. We forded a river thick with snowmelt. Thought I might be crossing the Styx at the time."

Jack sat on a maroon Persian rug stretched over the dirt floor, wiping his hands on his pant legs. The little girl shyly deposited a metal canteen near him, grinning as if they were playing a game.

Jack drank his fill and massaged his sore thighs. "Okay. I think I'm almost human again. Tell me, Midas. What the hell happened out there?"

Bartosz relaxed against the bench and covered his chest with a dark bear skin. "I had the SOB in my sights. Whole troop of them at their base about ten miles or so from here, kind of like an old earthen fort. Rafa was riding third in line, all decked out like a medieval knight or something. I hit him—but I didn't kill him. Maybe he really is protected by God. I thought I had the drop on him."

"You sure it was Rafa?"

"Positive. I could see his face in the scope. Just as I was squeezing the trigger, the bastard took a phone call. I swear, exactly at that instant, his guys turned to me—like looking right at me. Pretty sure we were burned. Somebody gave us up with that phone call."

"So what'd you do?"

"What do you mean? I fired. Tough shot, even with the ESR rig. Rafa took the hit, but bounced back up. He might have been wearing armor. Probably a glancing blow."

"And then?"

"And then . . . fifteen or twenty of his crazies came charging at me and Rustam. We picked 'em off as they came, thinning the herd, whatever we had to do. A handful of fighters made it up the hill to our hide. I got hit as I was backing out. At that point, I blew my Claymores."

Now that Jack had eaten and drank, he was overcome with the urge to lie flat on the surprisingly comfortable Persian carpet. "You got burned by the Indian SATCOMs," Jack said. "That's my theory."

"Mine, too. I've ditched them. Been messaging with Clark on my Iridium. It blanked out on me when we forded a river; guess it had a chance to dry out. It's working again."

"What did Mr. C. say? What's our next move?"

Midas wiped his beard. "Well, the good news is that our boys are in the air. They should be in position to jump in around four hours from now. We can still lead them in as planned. We'll assault Rafa's base and get the hell out of here."

"Okay," Jack said. "So we're back on plan."

"More or less." Midas gestured to a corner where the long M2010 Enhanced Sniper Rifle lay. "Looks like you'll be kinetic on the Rafa hit after all. Lisanne okay with you being boots on the ground with this one?"

"Better than that. Lisanne is coordinating with Clark from a train bound for northern Pakistan."

39

LISANNE HELD A COCKTAIL GLASS WITH HER MECHANICAL LEFT HAND WHILE SAMpling the lounge car's cuisine with her right.

The oversize carriage was open and airy, positioned ahead of the formal dining car. At its edges, hors d'oeuvres and glasses of fruit juice were arrayed on narrow, linen-draped tables. Well-irrigated farm fields framed by towering gray mountains whizzed by in the expansive windows. The train had begun moving north again after the layover in Muzaffarabad, where Daval Rai guided the Chinese and Pakistani government ministers through a nearly daylong tour of the ancient Red Fort.

Lisanne had opted out of that trip, choosing instead to explore the city's sprawling bazaar, where she encountered a gold merchant. She had hoped to find a deal on wedding rings, but grew more intrigued by the wide variety of pendants available for sale.

Sanjay Bodas, standing next to his bride, examined the necklace Lisanne had purchased. "That's at least eighteen karats. Intricately carved. The diamond at the top is very clear." He sipped his cocktail. "It looks marvelous on you."

"It's very lovely," Srini agreed. "A real find. With your beautiful coloring, you should always wear gold. And diamonds, of course."

"Thank you."

"It will go well with your engagement ring," Srini added. "When you get back home it will be great to see them together."

"May I ask," Sanjay inquired, "why you don't wear your ring, Lisanne?"

When Jack proposed, he gave Lisanne his grandmother's ring. Lisanne only wore it for special occasions because, as she explained to Sanjay, "When you have one natural hand, wearing a ring is tricky, hard to get on and off."

He grinned. "But thanks to my wife, that is no longer the case."

Lisanne finished her chicken satay. "Funny. I hadn't realized it until just now. As soon as I get home, I'll put it on and never take it off. Until then . . ." She touched the pendant's etched design, an ornate triangle topped with a diamond. "The merchant said this came from Zanzibar, Tanzania. It seems strange to find it all the way up here."

"Oh, not at all," Srini countered. "This train follows the Silk Road. African traders have long journeyed across the Red Sea to Gwadar. Caravans have been transporting gold and diamonds north from that port to China for ages, initially by camel, later by truck."

"And now by train," Sanjay said. "There is nothing like a drive south to the sea along the Silk Road highways. When I was a kid, before my parents moved us all to Houston, we liked to drive over to Peshawar to—"

"Sanjay, my boy!" Daval Rai bellowed from nine feet away. "There you are!"

The newlywed's head sank. His eyes darted to the corners of the car. "Damn. I thought he was napping."

"I'm sorry," Srini whispered, touching his wrist as she turned to Lisanne. "My father's a live wire with all these Chinese and Pakistani government officials around."

"In fairness," Sanjay offered quietly, "this is the selling opportunity of a lifetime for us. And it *is* a family business."

"I know, love. You're right."

Daval Rai charged through the dining car with his yellow turbaned head tilted forward like a rhino horn. He arrived at Sanjay's side with flush cheeks. "Where on earth have you been, my boy?"

"Srini and I were in the back, watching the landscape in the panorama car. We came forward—"

An imperial hand waved him to silence. "Doesn't matter. Hello, Lisanne. You look gorgeous. Thank you for joining us. Are these satays any good? My God, I'm ravenous." Rai whipped a long skewer of meat into his mouth.

"Lisanne's necklace is from the bazaar in Muzaffarabad," Srini said as her father chewed. "It came up the Silk Road from Gwadar, we think. Beautiful, isn't it?"

"It could never match the beauty of its wearer," Rai declared with automatic courtliness. He reached for a second satay. "Though I must confess, Ms. Robertson, I am somewhat hurt that neither of you ladies accompanied me to the Red Fort. You would have lent a bit of grace to our sad troupe of businessmen. We like to have women around, as you know. The fairer sex."

"Maybe you should hire more of them," Srini said.

"Of course I will. But all the bright ones leave for America. Like you, my dear. Please, Lisanne, join us next time, will you?"

"*Pita Ji*, don't blame her," Srini countered, deploying the Sikh term of affection for father. "I took Lisanne to the market. A girl deserves to do some shopping."

"And we were just talking about how the Silk Road now has a train," Sanjay added, worried the mood might turn sour.

"Were you, then? Keep doing that, lad—history warms people up. The Chinese deputy foreign minister is on his way here to discuss a new dam project in Djibouti. You have the updated numbers I emailed you on the Helmand River project?"

"I have them."

"Good, good." Rai reached for a shrimp puff. "The deputy minister is susceptible to all this talk of Silk Roads, failing empires, transnational partnerships, and so on and so forth. It's why I took him to the Red Fort. We need to be front of the line for his next BRI project award." The tycoon winked. "We're angling for that bridge proposal in Xinjiang. Fahim's job is to light him up with talk of suspension cables, spans, arches, and footings. From you, Sanjay, I want *romance*. You understand my drift, yes? Come along, my boy."

Listening to this, Lisanne imagined that a reasonably intelligent chimpanzee would understand Daval Rai's drift. The tycoon draped a heavy arm over his new son-in-law's shoulders, pulling him helplessly toward a forward lounge car that was converted into a rolling conference room.

"My father wants romance," Srini joked to Lisanne a moment later. "So he takes my new husband away."

Lisanne watched Rai and Sanjay navigate the lounge coach's crowded fray, conferring in low tones.

"Here comes Fahim," she announced with a sip of her tonic water and lime. "And I suppose that would be the Chinese foreign minister with him, learning all about bridges for the Xinjiang region, the lucky dog."

Srini turned away. "I suppose so."

The sun had set, replaced by a mauve twilight, dark enough for the train's windows to reflect the bright interior.

Lisanne eyed Fahim in the mirrored glass.

"He hasn't seen me, has he?" Srini asked.

"I think you're safe. Like your father said, he looks busy chatting up the Chinese minister."

"Good. Let him focus on his job."

"Who are the men in uniforms with him?" Lisanne asked. Familiar with Chinese military insignia, she saw that one of the uniformed men was a PLA colonel. The other was a stern, mustachioed man in the khaki, belted tunic of a Pakistani general.

"I have no idea."

"Sorry to tell you this, Srini, but Fahim's on his way."

"Good evening, ladies," Fahim Bajwa said. Lisanne inhaled a strong scent of cologne.

"Hello, Fahim," Srini answered. "How are you?"

"Well, my dear. I trust you're enjoying this business honeymoon?" He laughed softly.

"Such as it is. But we'll be going to Fiji as soon as Sanjay is done selling the Chinese. That will be the real honeymoon. You have met Lisanne, I believe?" Srini asked.

"Not formally, no."

Lisanne offered her right hand. "A pleasure," she said.

Fahim released her grip and eyed Lisanne's prosthetic. "I must say—your forearm is a marvel of craftsmanship, exquisitely engineered. Of course, you had the world's finest surgeon to install it."

"Do you know engineering, Fahim?" Lisanne asked. She received a grin from Srini, who recognized the sarcasm in the question.

Fahim smiled warmly. "As a matter of fact, I was first in my class in civil engineering at the Sorbonne. *Major de promotion,*" he tacked on in smooth French.

"Really?" Lisanne said with widened eyes, encouraging him.

"Oh yes. I thought deeply about going into mechanical engineering, working on things like your hand, there. Several professors were interested in taking me under their wings in advanced biomechanical research programs. But alas, I chose to build bridges. Now, had I known engineers would be designing things as artful as this, Lisanne, attached to such a lovely arm, I might have reconsidered."

Lisanne spread her mechanical fingers and inspected them. "Good as it is, I'd opt for the real thing."

"Perhaps not. I have seen you dance," Fahim rejoined. "You use that hand of yours with such grace."

"Thank you." Despite her intentions, Lisanne blushed.

Fahim adjusted his cuff links. "By the way—I meant to ask. I haven't seen your fiancé, Jack, on board. Is everything okay?"

"Of course. Everything's fine."

"He wasn't on the tour to the Red Fort earlier."

"No. My poor Jack is in bed. He's not been feeling well."

"Is that so? I'm so very sorry to hear that. Anything serious?"

"Delhi belly. We think he picked something up when he went to inspect the AGI infrastructure work to the north. As I believe you know, Jack got lost in the villages. Lord only knows what he ate."

"I see. I suppose I'm partly to blame for that, as I suggested he take the trip. Fortunately, we have this very fine, very beautiful doctor aboard. Have you examined him, Srini?"

The surgeon shook her head. "Lisanne will tell me if I'm needed."

Fahim shifted back to Lisanne. "And what did you do while the rest of us were at the Red Fort?"

"I took her shopping," Srini responded. "She found the lovely necklace she is wearing."

"Aha. How apropos. Do you know the meaning of the symbol you wear, Lisanne?"

"No. I don't. I just thought it looked nice."

"It is the symbol for a woman's sensuality. You must have chosen it by instinct."

Lisanne felt her skin crawl.

"I am so sorry," Fahim announced, reaching for a ringing phone in his jacket. "I am afraid I must take this call. It's a busy week for me, what with the world's highest rail bridge opening. This is probably Sunny Baig, my construction manager at the Gorge. Good evening, ladies." He retreated into the crowd.

"What a creep," Srini whispered.

Lisanne continued watching Fahim while listening to Srini complain about her father's number two. The high panoramic window glass clearly reflected Fahim's face as he ambled to a rear corner with the phone to his ear. He spoke with snappish gestures, either showing off or genuinely stressed.

She watched him close the connection and tuck his phone into a breast pocket. In nearly the same motion, he approached the lively group of Daval, Sanjay, the Chinese deputy foreign minister, and the PLA officer, who had just come from the forward business car. However, instead of joining the conversation, Fahim slipped past with a few pats on the men's backs and made his way to the serious Pakistani general in the khaki tunic standing near the bar.

A thump of changing air pressure jolted the train as it entered a dark tunnel. The reflected lights grew brighter, the clackety-clack became louder. Lisanne withdrew her cell phone from the purse draped over her shoulder. Although she had removed the SIM card to avoid tracking, the camera functioned normally.

"What was he talking about with the symbol for woman?" she asked Srini while aiming the forward-facing lens at her neck and inspecting her image on the phone's screen.

"The downward-facing triangle represents water, the Hindu symbol for a woman. That's what he meant. If you like, we can look for a matching necklace with a triangle facing the other way, representing fire, man, for Jack. When the two triangles merge, you're a couple."

Lisanne ignored this explanation as she aimed her selfie camera at the reflections in the window. She snapped pictures of the Pakistani general and Fahim Bajwa near the bar, their faces grave as they conferred in whispers.

"More shopping would be good. What's our next stop?" Lisanne asked her friend as she stowed the phone.

"We're about to arrive in a town called Bisian. Between us, Sanjay thinks we might have to wait there for a few days. He and my father are concerned that the bridge won't be ready in time. That would look bad to the Chinese. So we're putting on this royal dog and pony show as a delaying tactic."

"Any shopping in Bisian?"

"It's a small railroad village. But as I recall, there's a night market. A decent restaurant with local food, too."

"That sounds perfect," Lisanne responded, thinking of the report she would send to Clark.

40

INCIRLIK AIR BASE, TURKEY

JOHN CLARK LEANED OVER THE DESK IN THE TINY AIR OPERATIONS OFFICE, STUDYING the image on his laptop, eager to hustle to the chow hall for dinner. But Lisanne had just transmitted the photo from an internet café somewhere in northern Pakistan, and he knew he'd better act on it. He'd have to suffer through another sandwich from the Air Force vending machine.

The images in Clark's Panasonic Toughbook were too important to ignore. Lisanne's accompanying note identified the men as a Chinese deputy foreign minister, PLA colonel, and Pakistani general. Several other businesspeople were pictured, living it up with cocktails in hand in what appeared to be a fancy train car.

Clark placed his hands on his hips to study the map, tracing the rail link across Pakistan's upper, landlocked peninsula and imagining what the little town where Lisanne had stopped might be like. According to his last communication with the base ops watch officer, Clark's small hunter-killer team—Moore, Buck, Cary, and Jad—was still a few hours away from entering Tajik airspace, provided the C-17 hadn't been forced to divert again to maintain cover as a FedEx plane bound for Shanghai. He had time to investigate Lisanne's intelligence.

Clark noticed that her train would pass near Peshawar. He and Ding had been to that run-down, dusty town when they were tracking Rafa's father. Back then, they had help—a man who might still be around if Clark was lucky. He was due for some luck.

Clark opened his phone, looked up that old Peshawar contact, and stabbed the +92 number.

"Assalumu Alikum," a young voice answered.

Though it had been a while, Clark had no trouble picturing Nigel Embling's grand villa, with its cool tile floors, high Gothic arches, and attentive servants—a lifestyle he still found difficult to accept. Embling, a Dutchman, married a wealthy Pakistani woman educated at Oxford. After years of working together in MI6 at a university in Islamabad, the couple lived in splendor in the foothills of the Hindu Kush while establishing a boarding school for young women, an effort to modernize the northern region of the country they both cherished so deeply.

"I'd like to speak to Mr. Embling," Clark began. "Is he in, please?"

"He is in, sahib," the servant answered. "Stay on the line. I'll fetch him."

"Hallow," an elderly man with a fading Dutch accent replied half a minute later. "This is Nigel Embling speaking."

"Hello there, Nigel Embling. This is an old friend, John Clark."

Clark heard a sharp intake of breath on the other end of the line. "Well, fancy that. It's been ages, John, hasn't it? How are you and your young friend, Ding, holding up these days?"

"Much like the last time we saw you in Peshawar. And Ding's not so young anymore. Neither am I."

"Father Time is a cruel master, isn't he? I take it this isn't purely a social call to a retired colleague in your sister service. Are you here in Peshawar?"

"Negative. And I hope this turns into a social call after I ask you a few questions, if you don't mind," Clark replied.

"Of course I don't mind. Go ahead and ask."

"Good. This is an unsecure line, so let me speak in broad terms. Do you remember that band of miscreants we were chasing when we met?"

"I never forget chaps like them."

"Exactly why I called you. I think they may be back, making trouble again."

Embling groaned. "I suspected as much—a generational shift, as I understand it."

"You understand correctly. How'd you know about their new activities?"

"One hears things, even from the edge of the world. Peshawar is a deeply devout town. Its people are very pious. Unfortunately, that makes them easy targets for radicalization."

"I thought you were retired from His Majesty's service, Nigel."

The aging spy laughed. "Such a loaded, relative word, that . . . *retired*. By way of clarification, I *do* take calls from my old company from time to time. But I charge them by the hour these days. For you, John, I'll speak pro bono."

"I must say, with the problem set I'm working, it's a relief to hear you're still tied into the action—unofficially."

"Much like you, John, I favor the prefix *un* before the word *official*."

"Do you have access to the secure app Signal?"

"Of course. Shall I expect some information from you, then?"

"A few surveillance photos are headed your way as soon as you give me the number."

———

CLARK STUFFED A FORKFUL OF TABBOULEH INTO HIS MOUTH, OPINING TO HIMSELF that the one great benefit to waiting out an op at Incirlik was the outstanding Turkish food. It had been a long day of coffee and nerves. The tabbouleh was the best thing about it.

His cell phone buzzed in his pocket. Still chewing, he opened his Signal app. Nigel Embling, former dean of MI6 intelligence in Peshawar, wanted to talk. Fifteen minutes, Clark typed in response.

"That was quick," Clark said when Nigel answered over the app's encrypted voice function. He was back in the ops office.

"Yes, well, I do have access to a few favors at River House. The watch officer on duty just so happens to be the daughter of a long-lost flame of mine."

"Oh yeah? Wouldn't that make the watch officer a candidate to be *your* daughter, too?"

Embling laughed. "Believe me, John. This watch officer is far too good-looking to carry any trace of Embling family DNA. Too clever as well. She did a reverse-image search through our facial recognition database to come up with the names and dossiers on the men in your photos. Are you prepared to copy?"

Clark snatched a pen. "Go."

"The Chinese officer is Colonel Chen Ming. He runs the foreign intelligence attaché program for their foreign secretary now. Before becoming a spook, he deployed as an infantry officer, commanding a unit that fought the Indians in the Galwan Valley of the Karakoram mountains. You're familiar with that fair scuffle?"

Clark grunted an affirmative while scribbling down the name. He'd read about the border fight between the Chinese and Indian troops. While both sides avoided the escalation of artillery and air strikes, the commanders employed brutal, ancient hand-to-hand weapons like hammers, axes, and picks.

"And the others?" Clark asked.

"The Pakistani officer is Brigadier General Imran Khan. He's with the ISI, running the spy agency's operations in Pakistani Kashmir."

"Hell," Clark muttered, his pen stilled. "Is the ISI still running terror groups as armed agents up there above Peshawar?"

"Indeed. Though they deny it, my old section at Six believes they regularly send groups over the border to harass Indians in Kashmir. They've long wanted to take control of it, as you know. They try to stir up the Muslim populace to secede from India. It's always been their endgame."

"And this group I'm going after—the Umayyad Caliphate. Might the ISI be sending *them* across the border, specifically?"

"I don't have any corroborating intelligence for that. But I'm aware of the recent raid on an Indian Para SF outfit just over the Indian Kashmir border. It had the hallmarks of an ISI-sponsored terror raid."

"I've seen intel on that one, Nigel, video footage. It was the Umayyad Caliphate."

Embling was silent for a moment. "I suppose I'm not surprised. The Umayyads have been recruiting in Peshawar, which is already a hotbed of jihadism. They tend to prey on the mountain men to the north. The Umayyad mullahs recruit with convincing stories about Muhammad's lineage, the rightful succession of the Prophet, and so on. Those mullahs have never stopped believing in the Emir."

"Well, the old Emir is gone. Died in captivity. But it turns out he has a son."

"I hadn't heard that. What's his nom de guerre?"

"Rafa bin Yasin."

"I see. Well then, I find it highly probable that the ISI was involved with Rafa bin Yasin on that raid. Or at least his followers."

"Perhaps even this man, Khan?"

The phone hissed in Clark's ear for several seconds. "I don't believe so."

"But you said Khan runs the ISI up there."

"Indeed, but the ISI isn't all bad. And Brigadier Imran Khan is one of us. He went to the UK's Sandhurst military academy and earned a queen's commission. He fed information to our SAS teams in Afghanistan when he was a junior officer. He's built a strong reputation as one of the good ones. Given his position there with the Chinese, I suspect he is still highly regarded—not one to send *unofficial* terror groups into India."

Disregarding Imran Khan's reputation, Clark's mind quickly cataloged what he had just heard: a Chinese soldier who had fought in the war with India, a Pakistani intelligence officer whose organization—if not the man himself—instigated Islamic terror groups to assault the Indians. Both officers had been standing fewer than ten paces from Lisanne.

"Is there anyone else you can identify in that picture?" Clark asked, thinking of his airborne strike team. Were they about to launch into an ambush with intel supplied by Pakistan and China?

"In the foreground, it's hard not to miss Daval Rai next to the Chinese deputy foreign minister," Embling remarked. "Not surprising, since AGI does large construction projects around the world with Chinese money."

"Yeah, I recognize Rai. But who's the other guy talking to the Pakistani general by the bar? The guy with the pinned-up hair and the fancy suit."

"That's an AGI executive."

"Do you have a name for him?"

"According to our information, he's Fahim Bajwa."

"Got it. And what does Fahim Bajwa do?"

"He's their chief operating officer."

"That it?"

"He's the company's number two man."

"Seems like he should be sucking up to the Chinese guy, then. Why is he kibitzing with an ISI general?"

"A fair question, John. I don't know."

41

DEEP WITHIN THE CAVERNOUS RECESSES OF A FRIGID C-17, CARY MARKS RAISED HIS arms like a fledgling bird. The Green Beret was so heavily encased in cold-weather gear, a pressure suit, battle armor, and oxygen tanks that he could barely bend his elbows.

"Ten minutes," Irv Dupree announced over the intercom.

"How's our cover?" Master Chief Moore asked. "Pilots still good with it?"

Moore walked stiffly, similarly wrapped in a pressure suit. Bathed in the harsh red light of the cargo bay and tethered to the floor by a nylon "gunner's belt," Cary thought he resembled a 1920s deep-sea diver, complete with a helmet and air tube.

"The pilot in command thinks our cover's holding up," Dupree said. "We're diverting south now to get you boys as close to Pakistan as possible. That might give us trouble. But we want to minimize your trip in these damn things." He patted the nose of a black RAVEN.

Moore turned to Tom Buck, equally unrecognizable in the dim lighting. "Staff Sergeant Buck. You copy that?"

"Copy, Master Chief."

"Okay, Tom. Brief us up."

Jad waddled closer to Cary. The two Green Berets traded a wary glance in the dim light. To them, Buck was a spit-and-polish jarhead. That said, the Raider seemed to know his stuff when it came to these experimental aircraft.

He'd better, said the glance between them. They were about to soar into the abyss in what they privately called their "winged coffins."

"Okay, listen up," Buck began. "We're going out just like we briefed back at Incirlik; no change to the tactical plan. I'll pilot RAVEN ONE, and Master Chief Moore will fly RAVEN TWO. My bird, ONE, will go out first."

"Eight minutes," Dupree reminded them with outstretched fingers.

Cary studied the red LED readings on the bulkhead and shook his head. Negative seventy degrees Fahrenheit, forty-nine thousand feet.

"If you think it's cold now, just wait until the ramp comes down," Dupree said, catching him. "You're lucky that the pilot in command is fine with all this." He moved off into the darkness.

"I can't move," Jad complained.

"If we screw up and land in the Himalayan snow, you'll be mighty happy to have the poopie suit on you," Moore reminded him.

"I've been to the mountain warfare school. We didn't wear this getup."

"You didn't drop at fifty thousand feet, either."

"Check, Master Chief."

Buck resumed his briefing. "To recap. My ship, RAVEN ONE, will deploy the drag chute thirty seconds after the ramp comes down." He turned to the loadmaster. "We're still good with a thirty-second interval, Irv?"

Dupree shot him a thumbs-up.

"Thirty seconds after ONE is out the door, Master Chief Moore will deploy RAVEN TWO's drag chute. By then, I'll be powering up and flying a heading of one-eight-zero. We have to cover two hundred miles to approach our drop zone. We've got fuel for three hundred, so the distance isn't an issue. Our main problem will be managing the altitude."

"Remind me why the altitude's a problem?" Cary asked. "We've got O-2 on our backs. We should be fine once the birds open up, shouldn't we?"

"The wings won't bite worth a damn at this altitude. They might ice up, too. This whole thing's a first. Any questions?"

"So, so many," Jad replied.

Moore kicked the Green Beret's heavy snow boot. "Let's check our rigs, gentlemen."

Cary followed Tom Buck to the rear RAVEN, lashed to the deck with six hooks. The craft's flat glass canopy, nose probe, radar-absorbing black paint, narrow fuselage, and tucked wings gave it the appearance of a manned torpedo.

Buck, stiff in his extreme cold-weather suit and parachute harness, leaned over the aircraft's nose to press a button. The RAVEN's glass canopy lifted. Now that they were loading up, they unplugged their intercom cables and spoke to each other on the short-range UHF.

"*Sergeant Marks*," Buck said over the radio. "*Ready to board?*"

Cary double-clicked his mic and approached the open cockpit. He climbed into the RAVEN, lowered his knees, and flattened into a push-up position. Stuffed between the bulkheads, he inched backward to make room for his pilot, Tom Buck.

"*I'm in*," he transmitted, arms pinned to his sides. Until the unit cracked like an egg and he was ejected into the cold, thin air, he wouldn't be able to move them. Warding off claustrophobia, Cary concentrated on the one thing he liked about the evil little airplane: the six-inch square window below his face. He stared down at the C-17's shining metal cargo casters, trying to remain calm.

A few seconds later, Buck's boot soles knocked him on the top of the head.

"*Careful,*" Cary transmitted. "*You just hit me.*"

"*Sorry,*" Buck grunted. After a brief interval, the Marine transmitted to Moore, "*We're in, Master Chief. Lowering canopy.*"

Once the glass sealed over Cary's head, his world closed in. The high screech of the C-17 turbines faded to a muffle. Trapped in a sealed, oxygen-fueled helmet cavity, his breath hissed like Darth Vader's. He struggled to get his wrists and ankles into the pneumatic nylon loops that would hold him in place until the craft split apart.

"*TWO is sealed in,*" Moore announced from the forward position in the C-17 bay. "*Sergeant Mustafa and I are ready to take this thing for a little spin.*"

"*Roger, TWO,*" Buck answered. "*ONE is sealed and strapped with Marks. Green lights all around.*"

"*Same here, Tom. See you boys on the other side,*" Moore finished.

Irv Dupree rapped on the closed canopy, signaling for the final time. It would only be a few seconds now. Cary Marks tensed up like a steel bar. He felt the whine of vibrating equipment rattling through the craft's thin exterior, shaking his knees. *The C-17's ramp,* he thought nervously.

He clenched his jaw, focusing on the casters under the window, picturing his wife and kids back in Arlington—an old trick to get through adversity. For the five-hundredth time that day he wondered how in the world he'd gotten himself mixed up in this. The straps tightened around his limbs, reminding him he was trapped.

A single, piercing buzz penetrated the cockpit glass.

Staring straight down through the six-inch window, he watched the casters blur as they slid away. The nylon straps dug painfully into him as the RAVEN accelerated backward, propelled by a drag chute out the rear of the C-17.

Shot like a cannonball into the night sky, the aircraft flopped, yawed, and dipped as the drag chute fell away. Cary's helmet bumped up and down. A sudden, sickening sensation of weightlessness replaced the exhilarating speed. For all Cary knew, he was floating among the stars. His mind refused to focus on the family picture in his head. He was convinced they were plummeting toward the earth like a bomb.

"*Wings out,*" Buck announced coolly over the radio. "*RAVEN ONE, powering up.*"

The Green Beret, sealed in the rear of the tube, felt rapid thumps against his thighs. A wraith of vapor slipped by. The thumps shifted to a single, solid vibration. Cary sensed his body sliding backward. The Velcro straps tightened around his limbs as the craft accelerated under its own power.

"*Wings out,*" Master Chief Moore announced over the radio. "*RAVEN TWO, powering up.*"

Cary lifted his chin, but could only see the soles of Buck's boots. At least he could now feel faint flight motions as the Marine maneuvered the craft into a turn. The Green Beret gazed down at the top of a mountain peak.

"*Airspeed two hundred, heading one-seven-six. GPS autopilot engaged,*" Buck radioed. A half minute later, Moore confirmed the same status.

"*Roger,*" Buck answered. "*One hour to breakup.*"

Breakup, Cary thought. Here he was, barely getting comfortable with the idea of hurtling over the Himalayas in the dark, trapped in an experimental manned missile—and Buck had to go and remind him that it would soon splinter into pieces.

————

JACK HUDDLED IN THE MIDDLE OF THE BENCH SEAT, PERCHED BETWEEN RUSTAM AT the Toyota's wheel on the right and Midas on the left, studying the map with a red-lensed flashlight clenched between his teeth.

Navigating the terrain with Midas's NVDs, Rustam drove as slowly as possible over the rough, rutted track to avoid worsening the situation for the wounded man. Despite his efforts, time and again the vehicle crashed into fallen trees, crumbled rocks, and wadis filled with gypsum. If it weren't for the locking differentials on all four wheels, Jack couldn't imagine they would have made it this far north of the village.

"Jesus," Midas moaned quietly as the vehicle rocked harshly on its springs. "How much farther is it?"

Jack checked Lisanne's Garmin watch and compared it to the map coordinates. "Hang in there. Maybe three miles to the hill."

"Going to feel like thirty."

"Was it any better on the horse?"

Midas lowered his chin, closed his eyes, and gritted his teeth. "Maybe a little, yeah."

The Iridium buzzed on the seat, sandwiched between their thighs. Midas reached for it, grateful to have something to take his mind off the pain. He read the text string.

"From Clark," he said over the straining engine.

"And?" Jack asked.

"He got a download from Lisanne on that train of yours. He says there's a Pakistani ISI general on board. He's warning us to use extra OPSEC, worried we'll get burned again."

Jack pondered the message. Stuck in his cabin, faking illness, he hadn't seen the Pakistani military officer. "Make sure Clark knows we're using a sniper hide to the north of the camp this time."

Midas winced. "Roger."

The device buzzed again.

"Okay," Midas resumed. "Moore, Buck, Cary, and Jad have launched. Clark needs to relay a precise position to them over the data link where they can land. You do it. You've got the map."

"When does our team land?"

"Sixty minutes, minimum. We need to get in position to greet them. Pronto."

Jack took the device. "You seriously want to tell Rustam to drive any faster?" he said while typing with his thumbs. "It might kill you."

Midas shook his head slowly. "Rustam," he called to the muj. "Pick it up!"

A moment later, the wounded Delta operator howled in pain.

42

JACK LOOKED THROUGH THE INFRARED SCOPE MOUNTED ON THE LONG-BARRELED sniper rifle. Midas lay flat beside him, covered by his thick bear skin, adjusting a similarly equipped spotting lens.

"I've got a guy on the far right, up near that big rock. You see him?" Midas whispered. "And there's another one to the south. But I think that's all for pickets."

Jack swiveled the rifle southward, studying the camp through the scope's long-range heat sensors. He found the tiny white blob that indicated the second sentry.

Both guards were stationed at the edge of a ring of boulders that served as a barrier. Based on his earlier observation and this new perspective, Midas concluded that the camp was shaped like a C, with a hollow at its center where the terrorists had set up a bivouac. The boulders at the C's opening created a choke point.

When consulted about the rocky structure, Rustam referred to it as a caravansary, an earthen fortress that travelers had used for centuries as shelter while crossing the plateau. It had since eroded to resemble any other hill. That explained to Jack why the elevation wasn't marked on the map.

"Wish we had a drone," Midas observed quietly. "Be nice to know what's on the other side of those rocks."

"You were on the other side in your last observation post, weren't you?"

"Yeah. But the view was pretty much the same."

Staying low, Rustam crawled to their position and maneuvered beside them. He had parked the truck forty yards away in a clearing shielded by trees.

Midas offered him the spotting scope and asked for an opinion on the number of camp occupants.

"Twenty, maybe," Rustam responded. "Horse tracks. Tire marks."

"What about Rafa?" Jack asked. "You think he's there?"

The muj shrugged.

"How long until our team comes in?" Midas asked.

"Half hour," Jack said.

"Okay. I'm guessing they won't have the luxury of being that precise. Jack, get to a clearing and use your M4 to give them an IR lasso. Time to guide them in."

"Roger that."

"RAVEN ONE TO TWO," BUCK RADIOED. "WE'RE NEARING BREAK POSITION. ALTITUDE, *nineteen thousand. Decreasing speed.*"

Well, Cary thought. The master chief was right about the icy conditions in the capsule. He felt fortunate to be wearing the pressure suit.

"*Roger, ONE. Throttling back. Decreasing speed.*"

Cary mentally rehearsed the next steps, trying to remember the last briefing on the blissfully warm runway in Turkey. As he recalled, when the RAVEN reached the correct GPS waypoint, Buck, as pilot, would trigger a breakaway. The aircraft would slow to stall speed and tilt up at a thirty-degree angle. At that moment, the fuselage would snap apart, disgorging the paratroopers like toys from a plastic Easter egg. From then on, they would free-fall, performing a high-altitude, low-opening HALO jump, just like the sixty Cary had completed during his career.

"*Sergeant Marks, all good?*" Buck asked over the craft's intercom channel.

Oh yeah, Cary thought. *I'm great.*

"*Ready when you are, Buck.*"

"*RAVEN TWO, this is ONE. We're at waypoint bravo. Initiating breakup sequence. See you on the ground. Five, four, three, two . . .*"

Cary felt the pneumatic straps release his limbs. He quickly rotated his feet and hands to prepare them. He tightened his abdominal muscles in a plank and stared through the small window at the jagged lines of dark mountain peaks. His M4 barrel, secured to his back like a protruding bone, bumped against the canopy glass.

THWISH!

The craft snapped up. The black metal tube that had held Cary hostage for an hour split and hurtled away. He felt the wind beating on his arms as he fell through the sky, grateful for the oxygen mask, helmet, and four inches of nylon covering him. He was an airborne soldier again. He almost cheered with relief.

"*ONE, this is TWO. Waypoint bravo. Initiating breakup,*" he heard Moore call from somewhere above him.

Cary pushed his arms forward to soar through the free fall, watching the gauge on his wrist wind down. He snapped the contoured NVDs over his face mask, covering his eyes as if with a grade school viewfinder. The night sky glowed a pale green through the infrared sensors. He caught glimpses of light snow, dark rocks, meandering rivers, and black lakes. Buffeted by the wind, he raised his right arm to tilt his body for a view to the south. He quickly spotted a rotating infrared beacon swirling like a klieg light at a movie premiere. He flew toward it and struggled to convey the message, his voice sounding as if he were in a helicopter.

IR lasso bearing one-seven-zero true, he transmitted. *That's our target, final waypoint.*

The series of clicks in his ears indicated that Buck, Moore, and Jad had received his message. Cary knew how to maneuver his body during extended free falls like this. He adjusted his feet and bent his elbows, changing his course, a human airfoil soaring through the atmosphere. The rotating lasso approached closer.

Clark's final message to the C-17 conveyed the ground reconnaissance team's description of the terrorist base. The team characterized it as a rocky enclave shaped like a C. They reported their position as being north of the C, nestled into the hill that would serve as their overwatch.

Cary studied the ground near the IR lasso, focused on gaining reconnaissance, the first objective of their jump. Ten seconds later, he spotted the target. Inside the enclosure, he glimpsed small dark shapes—tents, he thought, possibly a vehicle. Then, just like that, the actuator on his wrist buzzed. He had reached the mean sea level target altitude—ten thousand feet, four thousand feet above the hill's elevation.

Cary yanked the thick beaded cord at the base of his back. He felt the reassuring tug at his armpits, followed by a sudden jerk and a pendulum swing. Suspended by risers, he floated beneath the parachute's compact rectangular airfoil. A tingling sense of euphoria washed over him. Whether it was due to his grateful freedom from the confining RAVEN or the fact that he was gently descending to earth on a parachute, just as he'd trained since he was twenty, he wasn't sure—but it felt wonderful, like he'd never been more alive.

"*This is four,*" Cary transmitted over the UHF. "*Chute's out. Heading to lasso.*"

"*Chute's out,*" Buck repeated. "*Heading to lasso.*"

Cary angled his NVDs forward and down. He caught sight of

Buck's chute below him. He wanted to look up to see if Moore and Jad were above him, but the chute blocked his view. A moment later, he heard the reassuring calls from each. *Chutes out. Heading to lasso.*

The hill grew larger in the NVDs. Paranoid that he was exposed over the C-shaped terror base, he steered away from it, put it behind him, and headed straight for the rotating infrared beam swirling from the hill.

"*On final,*" Buck radioed below him.

"On final," Cary repeated.

The trees were spiky pines and firs, reminiscent of his native New Hampshire—and Afghanistan. He picked a clearing that swelled quickly before his eyes, halfway up a stumpy hill. He spotted Buck, already down, sprinting along the ridge to gather his chute. Jack was there, too, standing in the bed of a pickup truck, waving the rifle in the dark while his free arm was extended in a thumbs-up gesture.

Cary pulled the guide risers into a flare. The Green Beret's boots scraped over rocky ground. Nearly automatic through years of practice, he popped the spring-loaded metal fittings at his shoulders to release his harness. The chute ballooned away, caught by a sudden gust. Buck was there to catch it. He bundled the fabric and jogged to the pickup truck.

Unstrapping his cumbersome helmet, Cary looked up at sparse, moonlit clouds. He unslung his rifle and raised it at the trees.

"*On final,*" Moore radioed. His rectangular chute appeared, with Jad floating down just above him. Buck shook Cary by the shoulder, pulling him backward, realizing that Jad might land right on top of them.

Moore struck with a mild grunt on the uneven ground, stumbling forward before regaining his balance. Buck rushed to the master chief's side, gathering his chute. Three seconds later, Jad touched down so softly that Cary enviously wondered if his Green Beret partner had even left a boot print. Releasing the billowing chute, Jad faced him with a grin like a boy on his first bike ride. Buck was already folding up the nylon.

"Wow," Jad said softly in the ethereal silence. "That was surreal."

Cary nodded. Their SOP for this insertion was to use hand signals on the ground unless they were face-to-face. The C-shaped terror base Cary had surveyed from above weighed heavily on his mind. He knew from his experience in Afghanistan that his voice could carry for a half mile. He corrected Jad with a single raised finger, the signal to stay quiet, and turned to Moore. The four of them huddled together and took off their helmets.

Moore's cheeks were streaked with black stripes. His grinning teeth shone like the moon.

"Well. Like Sergeant Buck said—I guess we just made history," he whispered.

Cary felt a resurgence of the airborne euphoria. There was something about Moore's smile that stoked the feeling. On impulse, he thrust out his hand to the Marine, Tom Buck, and whispered, "Outstanding, Sergeant Buck. That was four effing oh."

The Marine Raider with the green-painted face and serious disposition released Cary's hand. "I had a great copilot," he replied in a low voice.

"Nice truck," Moore whispered to Jack, who'd jogged over to join them.

"Thanks. Belongs to our muj."

"What's our setup?"

"We have a sniper hide at the top of the hill. Midas is up there, waiting for us."

"Excellent," Moore replied. "Thought you were on vacation, Jack."

"This *is* me on vacation."

43

NORTHERN PAKISTAN

LISANNE GAZED THROUGH THE WINDOW AT THE SILVER HILLS. THE TRAIN HAD stopped hours ago in this rural mountain village while business meetings continued in the forward cars.

She missed the constant motion and quickly grew bored with the unchanging view. Propped up on the silky twin bed, she thumbed through her purchases from that evening's trip into the night market.

Srini had taken her to a restaurant ripe with frying garlic and baking naan. After eating, the two women leafed through stalls overflowing with exotic spices, gold, and an endless array of colorful silk garments. When the shopping was done, Lisanne told Srini she needed to check in with her boss at Hendley Associates and found Wi-Fi at the train station for her latest report to Clark.

Now Lisanne folded back the bedcovers and stared at the night sky through the train window. Clark reported that Jack had reached the muj and was safe. He also updated her on the assault team's progress on the ground, specifying that the attack on Rafa's stronghold would proceed at dawn. There was little Lisanne could do but continue the ruse that Jack was aboard the train.

Nestled in her plush sleeping compartment, she caressed a small jade camel she had bought for a few dollars at the night market. She intended it as a keepsake for Jack, a reminder of the ride he endured in Sanjay's wedding procession. Despite being an athletic man, Jack had struggled with the double-humped beast—though, endearingly, he managed to put on a brave face.

Consoling herself that it would all be over soon, she clicked on the lamp and leafed through the book Jack had been reading, learning about the predators of Kashmir—until she heard a subtle knock at the door.

Crap, she thought. She closed the wildlife book and lay still, hoping whoever was there would leave. She suspected it was Srini, who'd become increasingly insistent about checking Jack's medical condition.

The knocks persisted, loud enough for Lisanne to worry they might disturb the Pakistani minister. His sleeping quarters were behind them in the same car—she couldn't allow that. Clark's report stressed that she should avoid attention, especially from the Pakistani general.

She tossed off the bedcovers and crept to the door. There was no peephole.

"Yes?" she asked tentatively.

"Lisanne, is that you?" a male voice responded. She recognized it instantly. Fahim Bajwa, God's gift to women.

"Yes, it's me."

"I've just come to check on Jack," Fahim said. "I've brought him some charcoal tablets and a tonic water. That always works for me."

"I'm sorry," Lisanne replied softly. "He's asleep. It's been a difficult day. I'll pick them up for him in the morning."

"Well then, come join me for a drink in the lounge car. We've opened up a viewing platform. The stars are magnificent."

"No, thank you, Fahim. I'm tired."

FROM THE OTHER SIDE OF THE DOOR, FAHIM BAJWA BIT HIS CHEEK, WONDERING
how far he should take this. He knew the Pakistani minister was
asleep in the aft portion of the car. It wouldn't be a good look to
force the door open on a lady.

"All right," he replied softly into the door. "Good night, then.
My best to Jack."

He went forward to the lounge car. Brigadier Khan stood near
a table of refreshments, thumbing his phone. Fahim had long considered the brigadier a sad man. But this evening, he appeared
positively morose.

The engineer swiveled his eyes over the expanse of the lounge
car to ensure they were alone. "Problem, Brigadier? You don't look
well."

The Pakistani turned his head. "Join me in the dining car.
Come on." A minute later, they sat on opposite sides of a booth in
a dimly lit corner.

Khan sipped his orange juice and stared out at the night landscape. "For God's sake, where is your brother?" the brigadier demanded in a harsh whisper. "The dedication ceremony is tomorrow
afternoon."

"He's in position by now. It's happening."

"Rafa was supposed to send a messenger. Did you see one?"

"No."

"Then how can you be certain he's in position?"

Fahim leaned in closely. "Because I spoke with my project manager at the site. He said one of our cargo trucks was stolen."

"From where?"

"From the motor pool depot south of the bridge. I left Rafa
instructions on how to steal one if his team needed it. He's surely
using it to improve his position on the hill over the tunnel."

"That was a bad idea. What if he's seen?"

"You run intelligence here, Brigadier. Have your people reported anything?"

Khan shook his head sharply. The reality was that he'd kept his troops to the south, responding to a bogus intelligence report that would keep them away from the bridge.

"These rail delays are problematic," the brigadier confided. "That Chinese colonel, Ming, keeps pressuring me to permit PLA troops to bolster my force. He thinks it's too far south. A Chinese presence would ruin everything—for both of us."

Fahim inspected his manicured hands. "I believe these delays have been beneficial, Brigadier. The caliph will be exactly where he's supposed to be; he'll have a truck to move his men into sniping positions, and, best of all, the media turnout at the unveiling will be even larger. That should make both you *and* the caliph happy."

The brigadier shuddered. "Don't call him that. Just because your brother thinks he's God's prophet doesn't mean he is. Let me remind you, he owes *me* for his exalted position."

"Or rather . . . me," Fahim replied.

44

NORTHERN PAKISTAN

CARY ANGLED THE M2010 ESR ON ITS BIPOD, ADJUSTING THE DOTS IN THE HORUS scope reticle to compensate for wind and distance.

"This is a much better position," Midas said quietly as he aimed his laser range finder. "I should have used it from the start." Their overwatch position was on a rocky outcropping at the tree line, offering a clear view of the terror base at the heart of the decayed, ancient caravansary. "Distance to target is five hundred nineteen yards."

"Five nineteen," Cary repeated. He selected a new dot in the Horus grid, centering it over the sentry's head. The target was dressed in black, standing with a slung rifle on the ramparts.

"Hey, Midas," Cary whispered. "If this hide is so much better, why didn't you use it before?"

"We were riding up from the south when we came across them. I set up over there, on that cluster of rocks. From that position, I could see them coming and going on horseback. Even if I wanted to, I couldn't have made it over here to see this entrance gap."

"Uh-huh," Cary responded, his scope following the sentry in the faint predawn light.

Midas nudged him. "Okay, hotshot. Compensating for bullet and barrel, minute of angle is one inch at five hundred yards. Copy?"

"Copy," Cary replied, factoring it into the proper dot in the Horus grid. "I got it."

"The bolt's oiled," Midas added. "It'll come back nice and smooth. You should choose three or four targets in advance, then turn to them automatically."

"Understood," Cary murmured.

By that, he meant that he understood Midas's concern. Cary hadn't been to a range with an M2010 for over a year. His preferred long-range sniper kit was the twenty-seven-inch-barrel Barrett MK 22 firing Norma Magnum .300s. He liked to tell the boys in his ODA that he could knock the sphincter out of a fly's ass at five hundred yards with his mighty Barrett. This M2010 ESR with its Winchester Magnum boattail rounds was new for him.

"This thing won't kick like your Barrett," Midas continued. "You'll be able to knock down half the gomers if they come surging out of that gap. I've got two more mags ready."

"Copy."

After another minute, Midas reported, "All right. I have eyes on Moore and Jack. Looks like they're almost in position."

"I have both sentries bored in," Cary replied.

"You should update Chief Moore."

"Wilco." Cary keyed his radio. "This is overwatch. Eyes on target."

"*Roger that,*" the master chief whispered in reply. "*Midas, how's your muj?*"

Bartosz was in no condition to hike behind the hill where Rustam waited for instructions in his truck.

"Wait one," Bartosz responded. He nudged Cary. "Go down and bring Rustam here, will you?"

"On it."

With Cary leading the way, Rustam scrambled up the hill three minutes later, the M4 dangling at his side. Midas spoke to him in Urdu.

Cary couldn't follow the conversation, but whatever the Delta man said severely impacted the muj. The withered Tajik lowered to a knee, smiled, and extended a firm, dark hand. Midas shook it, wincing at the unwelcome shoulder movement under the bear skin, his mouth slanted in a cooked grin.

"Walk with God," the Delta commando murmured in Urdu.

The muj flicked his fabric wrap from his chest and pulled out a cigar. He lit it with a Zippo, took a puff, and placed it in Midas's mouth. After responding with a quick burst of Tajik-Urdu, he turned and strolled down the steep slope, using the tightly packed trees for support.

"What did you guys say?" Cary asked.

After a puffing pause, Midas angled moist eyes to the Green Beret. He stubbed out the cigar on a rock and rubbed his nose. "I told him to go with God."

"What did he say to that?"

"He said he hoped we'd meet in the next life."

Cary glanced at the Delta man's bearded face. Midas wiped his eyes with a knuckle that came away wet. Giving him a minute, Cary rechecked the wind and range.

The Delta man rushed a breath. "Okay, let's get this thing going." He keyed his radio to report back to Master Chief Moore. "Our muj is ready and in position. He's a go."

"*Copy that, overwatch. We're on.*"

JACK GRIPPED HIS M4. BESIDE HIM, MASTER CHIEF MOORE WAITED IN A CROUCH. Dawn was two hours away, but it had grown light enough that neither man found any advantage in using NVDs.

The SEAL tapped Jack on the shoulder. "Ready, Mr. Ryan?"

"Absolutely," Jack replied, tightening his hold on the rifle. He'd been stretching his hamstrings and quads, staving off nerves and readying himself for the sprint.

"I'll do the shooting up front," Moore reminded him. "You just get to the top of the rim and take down anyone that gets past me. I'm mostly aiming left. You cover right." The SEAL grinned. "But please, Jack. Don't shoot me in the ass."

"Aye, aye, Master Chief."

Moore toggled his radio and whispered into his lip mic. "Jad and Buck. This is Moore. Report status."

Jad Mustafa and Tom Buck were in the tree line closer to the southern side of the C that formed the slanted berms of the caravansary turned terrorist camp. Their dash to the berm and up its rim would be the longest—but they were both in their twenties.

"*Tommy boy and I are a go,*" Jad answered. "*I hope you old-timers can keep up with us.*"

Moore didn't bother to respond. He stood up from his crouch and searched for the Marine Raider and the Army Green Beret hiding among the trees. He spotted the top of Jad's helmeted head, while Buck was a yard to Jad's right.

"Your position looks good," Moore confirmed on the net. "Okay. Last check. Muj Rustam?"

"*He's good to go,*" Midas reported. "*In the truck, engine running.*"

"Copy. Overwatch?"

"*Ready, Chief. Sentries sighted,*" Cary radioed in reply.

"Copy. Southern ingress?"

"*We're a go,*" Jad responded.

Moore turned to Jack. "You sure you're ready for this, Mr. Ryan?"

"Hell yes."

The master chief grinned before broadcasting: "All call signs, execute assault in five, four, three, two . . ."

45

AT THE PEAK OF MIDAFTERNOON, WITH THE SUN BAKING THE PARCHED BROWN hills, Sheriff Whitcomb found it necessary to move the AC lever to max.

"Does Luna need to get out?" he asked Gavin in the rear seat.

"Luna? She's okay. She stopped panting after that Milk-Bone."

"Well, I don't want her to overheat. Angle the rear vent at her and pour her a little more of that water," the sheriff ordered. "The sun's coming through her window. That's hard on a black dog."

"I got her, Sheriff, don't worry."

While Gavin managed the rear compartment of the truck cab, Mandy flipped through her Excel file. She was still waiting for Hoover's analysis of the document.

Using their FBI credentials, the sheriff's badge, and an authorization memo from T-Bolt Jackson, the small team had searched all over the Hanford site for an exposed data node. So far, they had come up empty. Now they were expanding their search to the land at the edge of the reservation that surrounded the site for miles.

Heading southwest on a dusty, barren road that bisected the BLM buffer land surrounding the Hanford nuclear installation, Mandy switched over to Google Maps. The browser displayed an error page, indicating that she wasn't connected to the internet.

"Do either of you have a cell signal?" she asked.

Whitcomb tapped a key on the police computer mounted to the right of his black Remington 870 pump-action shotgun. "Nope."

"Me neither," Gavin confirmed.

Mandy glanced at the dash. "I guess it doesn't matter. We'll use the truck's GPS to make sure we don't get lost."

"Maybe you didn't notice, ma'am, but the roads aren't marked out here."

"Shit. You're right. This is the BLM land, isn't it?"

The sheriff jerked a thumb at a PROPERTY OF THE U.S. GOVERN-MENT sign.

"T-Bolt's file doesn't say where this AGI site is," Mandy said. "It just indicates a patch on the far side of those mountains."

"We'll see the wind turbines soon enough," Whitcomb said. "We'll drive straight into them. The corporate office should be in there somewhere. Their data center ought to be in there, too. Let's hope it's the node you've been looking for, Mr. Biery."

"When we get to this company, will they wonder why we're not with the DOE security team?" Gavin asked.

"They shouldn't. The BLM has rangers for law enforcement, spread few and far between. But the state has jurisdiction in pursuit of a crime."

"Unless the crime is committed on federal property," Mandy corrected. "The feds can intervene then. FBI would lead."

Whitcomb conceded the point with a sigh. "Well, the good news is that we've got both kinds of badges."

Mandy studied the shadows in the rutted hills. She closed her laptop and thumbed through the binder T-Bolt had given them. "Pull over, Sheriff. We need to think this through."

"Yes, ma'am."

The pickup stopped on the dirt road, kicking up a beige cloud of swirling dust. Gavin opened the rear door, held Luna's leash, and helped the dog to the ground. "It's damn hot out here," he said. "I'll take her over there to do her business."

"Hot as hell," Mandy agreed. "I'm going to get my tactical vest out of the truck bed. Just in case these AGI security people hassle us, the big FBI letters stenciled across it will shut 'em up."

Gavin watched Mandy lower the tailgate and don her armor. He walked Luna a few paces east of the road when a vertical marker with a blue stripe caught his eye.

"Hey, girl, how about we walk over and check that out?" With the sun roasting his shoulders, he oriented himself toward it, pulling the dog through patches of sagebrush. Once they reached the marker, Gavin found it was just a few feet away from a green plastic manhole cover.

"Huh, that's strange to see all the way out here in the middle of nowhere," he said to Luna. Crouching down, he brushed off the dirt to reveal the Assurance Global Industries logo. According to T-Bolt Jackson's notes, AGI had secured a federal contract to produce wind and solar energy on BLM land. The company supplied the power to the reservation to operate backup systems whenever the nuclear power generators were offline.

"All right, Luna, you wait here while I check it out." Gavin looped Luna's leash around the thick base of a Russian olive bush, dug his fingers under the manhole cover, and pried it loose with a *thunk*. Peering down, he saw a black iron ladder bolted to the side. At the base of the ladder sat a bank of data communications equipment with blinking yellow and green lights.

Gavin rocked back on his heels. "What do you think?" he asked Luna. The black Lab gave him an encouraging wag. "I agree. I'm going down."

He descended the ladder, placing each foot carefully. At the bottom, he pulled out his phone, turned on the flashlight, and swung it around. The underground equipment room measured ten feet square with solid concrete walls. Each side was pierced by a thick blue cable running into the humming equipment racks, where the sturdy wire split into a web of multicolored strands. Gavin recognized the entire setup as a fiber-optic exchange station.

He surveyed the blinking ports and equipment designators. This, he concluded, was a major setup, serious infrastructure, all of it built by AGI.

That wasn't particularly surprising. T-Bolt's report said AGI intended to use power from its wind turbines and solar panels in the adjacent hills to run large data centers, augmented by Hanford's nuclear power. He ran his finger over the routers the way another man might run them over the hood of a classic car. Satisfied, he scrambled up the ladder and replaced the manhole cover.

"C'mon, girl, we did good!" Picking up on Gavin's excitement, Luna barked and danced around him as they hustled back to the truck. When he opened the truck's door, he found Whitcomb behind the driver's seat and Mandy in a foul mood.

"T-Bolt's site map says AGI has leased this whole area. It doesn't show where the hell the people are," she grumbled.

"Luna and I found a major fiber relay switch. I'll bet you it leads to the data center, where my patch will give us everything we need. Hey—do we have binoculars in here?"

The sheriff opened the truck's center bin. "I have binocs. Knock yourself out."

Gavin pointed the lenses at the hills. "I can see the fiber trench markers running off that way. And . . . Yup. There's a comms tower up there. My guess is that if we head to that tower, we'll find the data center. I can also do some analytical work on the network side. It might match up to the digital forensics we already have."

"Getting kind of late," the sheriff said. "Maybe we hit them in the morning."

"I disagree," said Mandy. "We're all the way out here. Let's keep going. Gavin—how sure are you that the patch will give us what we need?"

"Very. That comms tower has a fixed wireless microwave relay. My guess is it feeds the buried fiber lines. Its head end will be the data center I want."

"Why are you so focused on that data center?" the sheriff asked.

"Because—the thing is, the IP address I picked up on Maddie Hunt's phone came from the router that serves this area. But it used a subnet mask."

"Which is . . . ?"

"It's another set of numbers laid on the IP address that allows the router to use more capacity. It's kind of like if there's an address for a big apartment building, but then that apartment building has an overlay of addresses for each of the residences."

"Okay—so what do you want to do?"

"If I can access the computers running that comms tower, I bet I can pull the full list of subnet masks for the whole Hanford site. That way we can zero in on the correct physical router, even the computer that tracked Maddie Hunt."

Whitcomb glanced at Gavin in the rearview mirror. "For the sake of the Hunt family, we'll keep going."

AGON LEANED BACK IN THE CREAKY OFFICE CHAIR, HIS FEET PROPPED UP ON THE desk, as he watched the pickup truck on a closed-camera security screen. The camera feeds came from the communication tower atop the two-room construction trailer, where he and Dren spent their days waiting for more information on the American soldier in Oregon, who was Fahim Bajwa's next target.

The Albanian stood up and poked his head around the corner. Dren lounged on the sofa, playing a video game on an Xbox.

"Hey. Come here. We have a problem."

Dren gaped at the truck on the screen, his hands jammed in the seat pockets of his jeans. "Where are the jihadis?"

"In the other trailer, resting up."

"What do you mean—resting up?"

"They spent the whole night loading the construction explosives into a power-maintenance truck," Dren explained. "I think they're finished loading. Last I saw, they were laying out prayer mats and mumbling their nonsense."

"So who's in this pickup truck?"

"I don't know. Probably some rancher paying us a visit."

"Oh, shit," Dren cursed. "That's no rancher. Look at the roof—those are police lights."

46

MCLEAN, VIRGINIA

MARY PAT FOLEY REMOVED HER READING GLASSES AND SIGHED.

Perched on the top floor of the Liberty Crossing Intelligence complex—the headquarters of the Office of the Director of National Intelligence—she massaged her temples and gazed over treetops, hazy in the June heat.

She pressed a button on the black STE phone on her desk. "Do we have our appointment with the President yet?" she inquired of Kim Ngo, her chief of staff, who was on the other side of the door. Ngo, a multitalented Thai-Vietnamese-American plucked from the CIA's counterproliferation directorate, spoke four languages, ran track at Stanford, and could condense a dictionary's worth of reports into a single paragraph for her boss. In some ways, Ngo's ambition reminded Mary Pat of herself at the Agency, age twenty-eight—oh so long ago.

"Alma Winters just informed me that the President is meeting with the Israeli prime minister at the residence," Ngo said. "He left strict orders not to be disturbed. He asked for you to remain on standby."

"Okay," Mary Pat responded wearily. She could be on deck until midnight.

"Alma also said that you should be prepared to fly to Camp David with him, Madam Director," Ngo added.

"Seriously?"

"I'm afraid so, ma'am."

"Fine. Bring me the latest files on Iran, Hezbollah, and Syria. No telling where that meeting could go."

"Will do. I have your spare overnight bag. Brett Johnson is waiting downstairs with your car. We can get you to Andrews on Marine One in twenty minutes."

"Until then, I wait."

"I'm afraid so, ma'am."

Mary Pat hung up. Standing by to join a presidential meeting with a head of state was no small affair. The Israeli PM had brought the Mossad director with him. All she could do was sit here and wait while Scott Adler, the secretary of state, waded through diplomatic niceties before she could address the intelligence-sharing agreement with her Israeli counterpart.

She tapped her foot. Waiting was not how she'd made it to the top of the intelligence establishment. She lifted her encrypted, classified cell phone from her desk blotter and called the First Lady to gather RUMINT, rumor intelligence.

"Hi," Cathy Ryan answered. "Haven't heard from you for a while."

"How are you, Madam First Lady?"

"Quite good! Kind of celebrating, actually. I have a second Cabernet in my hand, a very generous pour, I might add."

"Oh yeah?" Mary Pat replied, smiling. She thought she'd detected an extra dose of mirth in the First Lady's voice. "What's the happy occasion?"

"Dan Murray's wife, Liz. My Belgian peer and I took her through her third and final procedure today. Her vision's completely restored. Better than it was when she was twenty."

Mary Pat raised a hand to her mouth. "Well, that's great news! Congratulations!"

"Thank you."

"Dan must be thrilled."

"He is. I spoke with him earlier. So did Jack—but our commander in chief and secretary of state are back to negotiating with the Israelis now. I'm left to drink alone, occupational hazard of the FLOTUS, my cri de coeur. I'm to join them after dinner with the dessert I made. I kept it easy—flan. My appearance at the table will be a quick one, God willing."

"Well, I won't disturb you any further, Madam First Lady."

"Why'd you call?"

"Frankly—to ask if Jack was really going to drag me up to Camp David tonight with Scott. Alma said he was in the residence. I thought I'd check with you."

"Oh, MP, I highly doubt that. Jack would have mentioned Camp David to me. I think he's staying put."

Mary Pat closed the cell connection in a better mood. It didn't last long.

"I have a visitor from the counterterror center here, ma'am," Ngo announced through the STE. "Navy Captain Shane Christopher."

"Send him in," she replied, worried.

"Good evening, ma'am."

Captain Shane Christopher entered in spotless dress blues. The senior naval intelligence officer had come up the stairs from the National Counterterrorism Center, also a tenant of Liberty Crossing. The NCTC was close enough to make a personal visit easy. However, Mary Pat thought, her mood darkening, Christopher wouldn't have bounded up the stairs unless he was bringing her bad news.

"In response to your RFI, ma'am," the captain began, referencing the request for intelligence she had issued after her last conversation with Clark. Christopher pulled out a folder labeled TOP SECRET NOFORN, indicating it was restricted from foreign intelligence allies.

"This is about Brigadier General Imran Khan of the ISI?" she asked.

"Yes, ma'am. It is."

She waved him to the chair before her desk. "Come on in."

Christopher crossed his legs, opened the folder, and began to read. "Brigadier General Khan has been with the ISI for nearly forty years. He attended Sandhurst in the UK and holds an honorary commission under the king." The naval officer tilted the file folder so Mary Pat could see a black-and-white printout of Khan in a cadet uniform. The face was unsmiling and severe, but the uniform was dashing.

"Following that," he continued, "Khan did a short tour with an infantry unit in Peshawar. He entered the ISI as a captain and has been there ever since. While a major, he stood up their foreign digital intelligence wing. Social media was just coming to prominence then, and the ISI used it to keep track of Indian agents, mostly."

"So he has computer forensic intelligence in his background."

"Yes, ma'am. To that end, Khan used the ISI digital tracking to aid the Brits in apprehending the 2005 London Tube bombers. Three of those bombers, you may recall, were Pakistani immigrants."

"No wonder the Brits consider him a good egg," she murmured, thinking of Clark's relayed conversation with Nigel Embling. "He went to Sandhurst, then wrapped up their worst terrorist bombing in years. So he's no Islamic sympathizer, then."

"I highly doubt that he is a jihadist, ma'am. *We* also worked with Khan."

She tapped her pen. "Did we?"

"Yes. Twice, actually. Once, a few years after nine-eleven, he was a liaison officer to us in Afghanistan. He put us in touch with mujahideen fighters loyal to Pakistan. I was with WARCOM back then. As I recall, our operators were pleased with his information."

"Okay. What was the second time?"

"He was with the ISI detachment that was part of our joint operation, POSEIDON SPEAR. That's the one where we rolled up elements of the Umayyad Revolutionary Council. As I mentioned, he's hardly a jihadi sympathizer."

Mary Pat's blood ran cold. "Shane. Are you saying he had access to information about our own operators?"

"Yes."

"And he has the wherewithal to employ the ISI to track people?"

"He does, yes. That would be his specialty."

"Good work, Captain. Please leave the folder with me. And I don't mean to be rude, but—"

"Good evening, ma'am," Christopher uttered politely, taking the hint. He rose from his chair, deposited the folder on her desk, and hurried through the door.

"HELLO, MP," JOHN CLARK SAID. THE OLD SEAL ANSWERED HIS SATELLITE PHONE ON the first ring. "You don't need to check on me. I told you—I got this."

"I'm not checking up on you. I've got new intel."

"New intel. Like what?"

"Like I think we just found our POSEIDON SPEAR mole."

"What? How?"

"I'm the DNI, that's how."

"Okay—so who's the mole?"

"It's Brigadier Imran Khan, the Pakistani ISI officer in the photo you sent. He was with the group that worked with the NCTC to get our guys into northern Pakistan, which gave him access to some of the SPEAR operators' names, including our three current victims. He was a major at the time—but he also had access to digital tracking resources. I don't know exactly how he's doing it, but based on the info Gavin gave you, I'd say Khan is behind it."

"With what motive?" Clark asked. "Why hit our guys after all these years? Sounds like he was a good ally."

"I have a theory."

"Shoot."

"The NCTC doesn't think he's a jihadist. But the ISI has helped fuel terror groups against India for years, trying to peel away Kashmir."

"What's that got to do with us?"

"Remember that attack on the Indian army garrison? We know for sure Rafa was there. We also know that the three SPEAR operators who've been killed were in on rolling up his dad's network. My guess is that Imran Khan is trading names to Rafa so the terrorist will do the ISI's dirty work."

"That's pretty low from a former friend."

"Like de Gaulle said, John: 'Nations don't have friends, only interests.' My strategic intel shop says Pakistan's interest is keeping a tight relationship with China and jamming a bar in the spokes of an India-U.S. alliance."

"If this is true, you have to give Khan credit. The son of a bitch is clever."

"Sons of bitches usually are. You said Lisanne took that photo, right?"

"Yes. They're on the same train headed to a bridge dedication. A deputy director to the Chinese foreign minister is on board.

The guy's a big fish, a member of the National Party Congress. You should look into him, too."

"I will." Mary Pat lowered her voice. "Something else bugs me about this."

"I'm listening."

"Jack Junior was with you when you took down the Emir in Nevada. What if Khan knows that? He might have already traded that info as a big prize. He and Lisanne need to get the hell off of that train. You need to call him. ASAP."

"I would call him, MP—but Jack's a little busy right now."

47

NORTHERN PAKISTAN

CARY MARKS EXHALED, WAITED FOR THE PAUSE BETWEEN HEARTBEATS, AND squeezed the M2010's trigger.

A nanosecond later, the sniper rifle's precision-machined action struck the Remington Mag cartridge's primer chamber. The primer, in turn, actuated the cartridge's gunpowder propellant, thereby exploding a one-hundred-thirty-grain lead bullet encased in a metal jacket down the rifled barrel. The aerodynamic hollow-point boattail round spun like a spiraling football through the clear, predawn mountain air, accelerating to a terminal velocity of three thousand feet per second, or a little more than two thousand miles per hour.

The jihadi sentry in black, a dedicated warrior, servant of the one true caliph at what he considered to be the center of the world, never knew what hit him. He fell backward in a cloud of red mist, tumbling over a rock with a distant *thud*. Cary nudged the silenced barrel a few degrees right. The Green Beret sniper adjusted the Horus reticle to account for the distance to sentry number two and fired again.

"Pickets down," Midas broadcast quietly beside him. "We're cleared hot. Say again, cleared hot."

With that notification, Master Chief Kendrick Moore and Jack Ryan, Jr., sprang from their hidden position like jackrabbits from a hole. They sprinted forward with their M4s raised to their shoulders, looking down the sights as they ran.

Jack's lungs heaved. Running flat out, he struggled to keep up with the athletic SEAL master chief. A sideways glance told him that Buck and Jad were already to the bottom of the rocky berm, even faster than the SEAL. Jack snapped his eyes forward, staring down the M4 barrel and concentrating on his objective at the rising berm.

Ten yards . . . five yards . . . jump!

Following Moore, Jack hurdled from rock to rock, hopping here, leaping there, until he nearly collided with the enormous SEAL at the top of the rampart, where Moore had skidded to an abrupt halt. At the center of the wide rim lay a twelve-foot gap like a moat—a chasm too wide to jump across.

"We'll have to descend and climb up," the SEAL announced between labored breaths. Without further debate, Moore vaulted into the trench between the rock walls. Jack followed, landing awkwardly enough on the rock-studded dirt to aggravate his dodgy knee.

"Hold my rifle," Moore commanded. No sooner had the SEAL slid the M4 to Jack than he scrambled up the side like a mountain lion, clawing at narrow handholds in the cracks. Once at the top, Jack lifted the rifles up to him. Moore set them aside and lowered his hands to serve as a hoist.

"Jad and Buck are in position at the top of the berm. Chief, say status."

With Moore tugging his hands, Jack kicked at the rocks and angled an elbow over the top of the berm. That gave him enough leverage to swing his aching leg up and roll to safety. The SEAL crawled forward with his M4, sweeping for targets. Jack touched his transmitter.

"This is Jack. Chief and I are at the top of the berm, in position."

Jack imitated Moore's crawl, staying prone. Nearing the rim's edge, he gained a view into the center of the C.

"Phase one complete," the master chief announced over the net, his voice husky and rushed. "Overwatch, you good?"

"*Overwatch is good,*" Cary coolly replied. "*I have eyes on all elements.*"

"Strong copy."

Jack angled his rifle down. "Anything?" he whispered to Moore.

"Negative. No movement. I think we've achieved surprise, thank God."

Jack peered into the dark interior of the terror base, distinguishing a series of crude structures resembling yurts covered in a mishmash of nylon, canvas, and animal skins. One was isolated, situated at the deepest part of the C. He assumed it was where the leader, Rafa, would bed down.

"All elements, we need rifles in flanking positions," Moore broadcast. "Jad, move down the rim forty yards and take position. Jack and I will head in the opposite direction. We'll cover 'em from behind. Overwatch, you get the squirters that come through the entrance."

"*Copy,*" Cary radioed back. "*Overwatch ready.*"

"Proceeding now," Moore transmitted. Maintaining a crouch, the SEAL and Jack trotted along the C's rim, frequently stopping to monitor movement. After two minutes of careful maneuvering, they squatted at the back side of the semicircle above the innermost yurt.

"Jad, you and Buck are on the X," Moore radioed. "Stay put. Midas, how's our muj?"

"This is Midas. As soon as I give him the signal, he's ready to go."

"Copy," Moore replied. He paused to view his and Jack's position relative to Jad and Buck's. Satisfied, the SEAL pressed his transmitter. "Roger, Midas. Send it."

The squeal of a straining diesel engine reached Jack's ears a few seconds later. Following the sound, he saw Rustam's beat-up Toyota Land Cruiser pickup bouncing over uneven terrain, aiming for the opening in the C, the once proud gate of an ancient caravansary.

Jack sighted his M4 on the yurt, waiting for the warriors of the Umayyad Caliphate to wake up, possibly even Rafa bin Yasin himself. Beside him, the master chief readied the M203 grenade launcher slung under his rifle barrel.

"Still no movement," the chief broadcast on the net.

Rustam's vehicle bounced over a fallen cedar that had half rotted to red dirt. The muj continued his drive to the C's opening. Though the engine grew ever louder, there was still no movement inside the camp.

Meep. Meeeeeeep.

Jack realized Rustam was pounding on the Toyota's horn.

That did it. Bodies erupted from the yurts.

THWUMP.

Moore launched the first M203 grenade. Rustam veered his vehicle sideways. Jack, Buck, and Jad sniped every fighter who showed his head, dropping them like bowling pins. One man ran for a technical, an old Nissan pickup with a triangular mount for a machine gun rising from its bed, his black turban streaming from his head like a pennant. Jack shot him in the neck.

Beside him, Moore lay still, his rifle silent, his eye bent behind the scope as he searched the camp. He hadn't called a ceasefire order, but he, Jack, Buck, and Jad had all stopped firing—there were no more targets.

"Breach," Moore broadcast. "On me."

He rose to his feet, aiming the M4 from a standing position, studying the scene through his scope. "Jack and I will clear the northern structures," he added on the net. "We'll work outside in. Buck and Jad, you do the same from the other side. And stay frosty—some of these guys might still be alive."

48

WHITCOMB STOPPED HIS FOREST-GREEN RAM 3500 PICKUP AT A CHAIN-LINK GATE topped with razor wire. Although the sun had hours left before it set, the windswept hills in front of him cast shade over the high desert landscape for miles. The sheriff flipped on his high beams just to be sure. They shone brightly on a sign: PROPERTY OF ASSURANCE GLOBAL INDUSTRIES. AUTHORIZED EMPLOYEES ONLY.

"They give a phone number or anything for a gate guard?" the sheriff queried Mandy, who proceeded to tab through her Excel file.

"There's a phone number. But we're out of cell range."

"Forgot."

Beyond the fence, the sheriff's headlights reflected off a construction trailer topped by a communications mast. Near it rested a collection of Caterpillar earthmoving machines, four massive utility maintenance trucks with cherry picker booms, and a pair of white Toyota Tacomas displaying the AGI corporate logo. Farther along lay another trailer and a low concrete structure that extended into the base of the hill. Wind turbines studded the hills like candles on a birthday cake.

"I'm willing to bet," Gavin remarked from the back seat, "that the concrete building there has the data comm equipment. The fiber trench markers lead to it and there's an air-conditioning unit on the roof."

"I see it," Whitcomb said.

"Get me in that building, Sheriff Whitcomb."

"Consider it done, Special Agent Biery. Let's just hope these guys don't ask for a warrant. Corporations tend to lawyer up."

The sheriff rolled down the driver's-side window. A steady, warm breeze from the Columbia Basin brushed his cheek. The citrusy scent of sage reminded him of his property back in Clarkston.

"I can see why they're building their data center here," Gavin said. "A lot of cloud companies are dropping data centers in the middle of nowhere these days, as long as they have access to re-newable energy. Google has a big one just down the Columbia at the Dalles because of the hydroelectric power. I suppose AGI is doing this here for the wind and solar."

"And access to nuclear power, maybe—for when the weather doesn't cooperate," Mandy said. She raised her eyes from her lap-top, taking in the installation. "The file indicated that AGI has owned this land for two years as part of a government lease grant for sustainable power generation, leaving no carbon footprint." She slid open the sunroof visor to get a better view of the mocha-hued hills stretching before her. "They're definitely investing a lot of money. Look at that jagged rise. They've blasted away half of that middle peak."

"Airflow," the sheriff postulated while raising his window. "Lot of that wind and solar stuff going on out here on the Palouse. It's like a new oil boom. Only, it doesn't pay as well."

Gavin stroked Luna while flipping through the vinyl-covered sheets of T-Bolt Jackson's tabbed binder stamped with classification markings. "According to this, AGI has twenty wind turbines operating in these hills." He tapped on the window glass. "You guys ever been this close to one before? That thing's *massive*."

Mandy watched the slowly rotating blades through the sunroof's glassy rectangle. "The blades look like they're about half the tower's height."

"Nailed it. Each blade is the size of a football field. The towers stand six hundred feet tall." Gavin whistled as he flipped a page. "This graphic shows that each turbine generates eight megawatts, enough to power eight thousand homes. With twenty turbines, these hills can illuminate one hundred sixty thousand houses. That's a good start to powering the Googles, Amazons, and Microsofts of the world. AGI is in a solid position, even without nuclear power. And they've secured exclusive use of it."

The sheriff took a second look at the low concrete building and trailers. "Does that thing say how many people work at this site?"

"The Excel does." Mandy clicked her keyboard. "Forty-nine workers. Most in construction or engineering. But this file is a month old. May have changed."

Whitcomb powered up the spotlight above his door mirror and rotated it over the shadowed trailer with the comms mast. "Well then, you'd think they'd divert some of their almighty power to their own damn worksite. The whole place is dark."

"Here comes a guy," Mandy said. "You lead, Sheriff."

She watched a thirtyish man work the padlock of the pedestrian gate. Out of long habit, the former FBI agent noted his physical appearance: clean-shaven, dark-haired, Caucasian, blue jeans, hiking boots, and a military-style field coat that covered his waist. The only thing that struck her as odd was the field coat because it had been a warm June day. Then again, the mountains blocked the sun, the wind was unrelenting, and night would soon settle in.

"May I help you?" he asked.

Her ears detected a mixed European accent. A lanyard around the man's neck displayed his name as Dren Shala. She promptly typed it into the search box of the Excel file.

Whitcomb flashed his badge. "Evening. I'm Sheriff Mitch Whitcomb of Asotin County. These two are federal agents."

Luna barked from the back seat. Gavin hurriedly stroked her head and gave her a treat.

"I brought along my canine unit," Whitcomb jested with a half smile. "Sorry about that."

Mandy studied the row in the spreadsheet with Dren Shala's name. His title was director of AGI site security. He was a French national on an H-1B visa who had passed security screening with the Defense Investigative Service.

She could imagine that an installation like this, with millions of dollars of construction equipment, would require a twenty-four-hour security presence. Dren Shala probably lived in the trailer near the wind turbines—the inland equivalent of a lighthouse keeper.

"May I see your identification, please?" Dren responded, his brown eyes roaming over Gavin first, then Mandy. They lingered on the bold yellow FBI letters stenciled on her black tactical vest. "No need for identification for your pup," he added with a mild grin at the lawman, keeping matters light.

Mandy and Gavin handed their wallets to Whitcomb, who then presented them to the AGI employee. Dren studied them momentarily, nodded in satisfaction, and returned them. Mandy noticed the tattoo on his hand, thinking it looked like the fleur-de-lis emblems on New Orleans Saints helmets.

"Are you the only one here?" the sheriff asked. "Place seems shut down."

"Yes, Officer. I'm it. The construction people are on corporate furlough. We're stalled until we get more funding from headquarters to add capacity to our data center. I'm told we're waiting on some big deal to close with Silicon Valley."

"But your wind turbines are operating," Mandy noted. "You can handle them by yourself?"

Dren leaned forward, his eyes scanning Mandy's laptop. "The wind turbines are straightforward. If they trigger an alarm, one of our engineers comes out. It never happens." He turned to Whitcomb. "How can I assist you, Officer?"

"This is where the fiber lines for the valley terminate, isn't it?"

The man nodded. "That's right. Our data center has a fiber head end. The nuclear site is a customer of AGI. Same with our power—for backup."

"Where is the data center exactly?"

He jerked a thumb beyond the fence. "That concrete building there."

"Not very big."

"Like I said, we're waiting on permission to add capacity. Eventually, it will take up half the hill, underground."

"I see. Well, we need to access it."

"Why?"

"It's in conjunction with a murder investigation."

Though it could be her imagination, Mandy thought she detected an involuntary twitch in one of the tendons running down Dren's tattooed forearm. The security man took one step back from the truck, said nothing, and kept his face neutral.

"Sir," Whitcomb pressed, "this is BLM land. Special Agents Cobb and Biery have jurisdictional rights for a search of federal property without a warrant. Now, I'd appreciate if you'd let us in so we can check it out and get on our way. That's not a request. It's a lawful order."

Dren shrugged. "Then I guess I'll open the gate. Come on through and park over there, near the base of wind turbine nineteen."

"Thank you."

"I'll need to make some calls back to corporate, if that's okay? Our data center hosts information for private companies. Accessing it is very sensitive."

"How long?"

"Corporate is in New Delhi, India. It's early morning there— I'll need to talk to our chief information officer. Might take . . . I don't know . . . thirty minutes? Or you can come back tomorrow. That would probably be better."

"We'll wait," Whitcomb decided. "Please make it quick."

"I'll do my best." The AGI director of site security keyed a cypher lock that unlatched the sliding gate. Mandy watched him pull it open, his field coat bright in the headlamps. The sheriff lowered the Ram's gear lever and they idled through, parking next to the white base of a towering wind turbine.

Mandy checked the security man's location in the door mirror. He was sliding the gate closed.

49

TALLER MOUNTAINS FILTERED A RISING SUN ON THE OTHER SIDE OF THE WORLD.

Jack Ryan, Jr., welcomed the slanting orange light filtering through the peaks. Since concealment was no longer required at the Umayyad Caliphate terror base, it would help with his search.

"Fifteen KIA," Tom Buck said to Moore. The Marine Raider had dragged the bodies to a flat, charred section of sandy earth where there had once been a campfire.

"I want photos of all of them," Jack ordered. "We'll get them back to the NCTC database for safekeeping." He further intended to task Gavin with building a terrorist database for The Campus's exclusive use, a rogues' gallery that wouldn't require permission from an outside agency, though he didn't say as much.

Buck tapped his phone. "Already done, Mr. Ryan."

"Good man."

"*Over here!*" Jad Mustafa called from the edge of the berm at the center of the C. "*Threat!*"

Moore pivoted on his heel, angling his M4 barrel up. "*GET BACK!*" he roared. "Cary—cover him!"

Cary Marks had been inspecting the Nissan technical, trying to find the keys. Though they'd missed Rafa, they planned to egress across the Indian border and link up with the New Delhi station chief, Suhas Chauhan, to keep the op dark. They already had the four-door Toyota Land Cruiser pickup, but the extra seating capacity in the Nissan would make more room for Midas.

Cary abandoned his search and rushed to the side of his Green Beret partner. The pair flattened themselves against a granite boulder.

"What've you got?" Cary whispered, winded from the sprint.

"I found two exhaust hoses at the top of the rocks. When I followed them down, I tripped on this wad of sage. It flew to the side and . . . look." Jad gestured at a dark crevice with the barrel of his M4. "I felt air coming up from it just now."

Cary angled his jaw. "Master Chief!" he bellowed. "We have a situation!"

"THAT'S WHERE WE'LL FIND OUR INTEL," JACK DECLARED AFTER THEY'D DISCUSSED how to handle Jad's discovery.

"Could be," Moore said. "But look around. Hoofprints everywhere—but no horses. This place is a dry hole. Based on the lightly armed crew we hit, I think we took out a UC rear guard at best. The main UC troop is somewhere else—with Rafa leading it."

"Yeah, but they might all come back here," Jack said. "This base looks semipermanent. If so, then there's going to be intel in there. Even if it's light. We need to do an SSE."

"Agree on the sensitive site exploitation," the master chief conceded. He glanced at the two Green Berets and Buck. "Which of you guys is freshest in training for CQC?"

"I did close-quarters combat training at Bragg a month ago," Marks said.

"And I completed the FBI Raider SSE course at Quantico three weeks back," Buck furthered. "For exactly this situation."

Moore massaged his chin while he stared at the opening. "Okay. Do we have any smoke, tear gas, or flash-bang grenades in our kit?"

"We only loaded frags," Buck replied. "We came to kill, not capture."

"If there's sensitive intel in that spider hole, like computers, we'll ruin it with frags. How do you two feel about going in with just your rifles?"

"I feel fine about it," Marks said.

Moore considered the two Special Forces warriors. "Okay," he decided. "Cary, you've got the lead. Buck, you support him. Jad, Jack, and I will cover rear security and come in after you. Midas and the muj will stay on perimeter."

"Roger that," Cary said. "Let's hit it, Buck."

AFTER THEY'D CRAWLED THROUGH THE ENTRANCE, THE STONY GAP ANGLED DOWN, blocking the morning sunlight. Cary rose silently to a knee with his M4, sweeping the black void before him, his NVDs tipped down over his eyes. Aside from Tom Buck's shallow breathing, the cave was as quiet as a crypt. It smelled moldy and foul. Cary wondered if bats inhabited it.

With their weapons drawn, the two intruders froze, listening intently for thirty seconds. They had crawled deep enough into the cave to be deprived of even a trace of sunlight. Cary lifted his NVDs, which required a few lumens of ambient light to function. When the blind interval felt safe, he leaned back, close to Buck's head. "Goggles are useless. I'm going to use my barrel light," he whispered. "Be ready to fire. You go high over my shoulder, and I'll go low."

Buck tapped the Green Beret twice on the back to acknowledge the order.

Cary clutched his M4 by the pistol grip with his right hand. At the center of his plate carrier vest, he rotated his Spartan Harsey dagger sheath to free the knife in a rapid down swipe. He groped with the fingers of his left hand to the rails along the upper receiver, where he found the attached light. With trigger finger poised, he was about to power the light when a muzzle flash and a tearing roar of automatic-weapons fire shocked him. The deafening buzz seemed to echo from all sides in the tight confines of the cave as if Cary had fallen into a jet engine.

He dropped to his knees immediately. With bullets chipping rocks over his head, he rotated the M4 barrel a few degrees toward the muzzle flash and returned fire in a three-round burst. His ears ringing and disoriented, he waited again.

"You good?" he said hoarsely to Buck.

"I'm good."

Cary switched on the barrel light.

The man who'd nearly killed him lay bleeding on a Persian carpet strewn over an uneven rocky floor, his exotic machine pistol still in his grasp. The bearded terrorist's legs twitched. His eyes were wide and staring.

Cary put two rounds in his skull and crept forward with his dagger in his left hand. He stepped over the corpse and swept the granite walls with the beam. The underground warren terminated here.

And, better than that, it was an intelligence treasure trove.

Beneath a black flag emblazoned with the Pyxis of al-Mughira were two laptop computers, five USB drives, a compact generator, and five red jerry cans of fuel.

Cary and Buck pulled out folded cloth sacks from their thigh pockets and looted the cramped underground office after photographing the dead man. Before crawling back into the daylight, Cary ripped down the flag and stuffed it in his plate carrier vest, just behind his dagger. The last thing he did was close the terrorist's eyes with a boot stomp.

"Bingo!" Jack called topside in the sun, pumping his fist when Cary revealed the take.

The men laid out the material on the hood of the Nissan pickup like kids with a Halloween haul. Moore opened the laptop, a MacBook Air with a decent battery charge. It was password-protected.

"I guess we won't know what's on here until we get it back home to Gavin," Moore said.

"Look again," Jack said. "The Mac has a fingerprint sensor."

Buck freed his knife. "I'll take care of that."

Eight minutes later, they used the severed right index finger of the man Cary had slain to open the Mac. The computer unlocked to an already-opened PDF file. Jack instantly recognized the AGI corporate logo and paged through the document. It contained multiple aerial photos of the bridge over the Karakoram Gorge in various stages of construction. The last page depicted an engineering graphic of a media platform to be built alongside the bridge.

"Details of the bridge dedication I was going to," Jack mumbled. "Holy hell—there are schematics of the train cars, showing who's riding where."

"What are you talking about?" Moore asked.

"This is the bridge ceremony that Lisanne and I have been invited to attend. There are more aerials here—a diagram that . . . Oh shit. This looks like they're setting up for an ambush near the bridge right after the train comes out of that tunnel."

Moore leaned in. "I agree. It's marked up with sight lines." He pointed to the diagram where the bridge widened. "To me, it looks like they would be shooting at this platform from the hill over the tunnel."

Jack's hands began to shake. "Chief—we gotta go. Now. Lisanne's on that train. I don't have a way to get in touch with her."

"Hold it! You can reach Lisanne through Clark. They have a link."

"We have to go, Chief!"

"We will. Jack—did you see there's another document open behind this? It might have something to do with the train."

Feeling numb, Jack advanced to a second open PDF: a satellite photo resembling a screenshot from Google Earth. Someone had annotated the graphic to point out wind turbines on the hills and a series of road intersections leading to a ditch labeled TRENCH 94 beside the curving Columbia River, also labeled.

"What do you suppose is At-Takwir?" Moore asked, pointing to the file name at the top of the PDF tab. "Is that a different bridge project . . . on the Columbia?"

"No," Jack said. "At-Takwir isn't a place. It's a Quranic reference."

"Meaning what?"

"Judgment day."

50

JACK HAD TO SHOUT TO BE HEARD OVER THE NISSAN'S PALTRY FOUR-CYLINDER engine as it screamed past four thousand RPMs, maxing out its speed, slamming over potholes and long stretches of broken pavement on the ancient mountain road.

"Say that again?" John Clark asked over the encrypted satellite phone's speaker.

"We hit a Rafa camp and took out fifteen guys."

"Fifteen? You say you have the HVI?"

"Negative. No jackpot. The HVI wasn't there. But we know where he's going to be. And I have to report something else we found on the SSE."

Clark was silent for a few seconds. "You're garbled. You say you hit the same camp Midas did?"

"That's right!" Moore shouted from behind the wheel, downshifting into a hairpin curve. "We have new intel on the HVI. Also info on a target in the U.S. that you need to hear, Mr. C."

Moore swerved around a cluster of fallen rocks. To Jack's eyes, the master chief resembled a Polynesian warlord, with remnants of camo paint on his large bald head and a tribal blanket draped over his shoulders to conceal his fatigues. Moore was attempting to keep up with Rustam's racing Toyota Land Cruiser pickup.

Dressed similarly, Cary, Jad, and Rustam sat in the front of the Toyota, while Midas reclined across the rear seat.

"I can't hear you guys for shit," Clark complained, his voice hollowed by distance. "I think you said it's a negative jackpot. Assume you're following in hot pursuit."

"Affirmative!" Jack shouted into the phone, frustrated by a weak satellite connection affected by the tall, leaning peaks lining the road. "Something else, Mr. C. I have important intel to share— national command authority level."

"Say again?"

"I said we have INTEL TO PASS ON!" Jack cried, the phone inches from his mouth.

"I think you asked about intel. I have some for you. It's about Lisanne."

Stunned, Jack didn't try to correct his black-side Campus boss. "Copy—go ahead."

Clark spoke slowly. "She took a photo of an ISI officer on that AGI train. I say again ISI officer. We ran his face through the traps and have assessed him as our mole. Over."

"I copy."

"We think the ISI man is working with Rafa to direct the PO-SEIDON SPEAR hits. Over."

Jack and Moore exchanged a glance in the breezy interior. They'd lowered the windows so Jack could aim the satellite antenna skyward without obstruction. Blessedly, he saw a clear patch of blue ahead.

"Pull over," he ordered Moore.

"We'll lose Rustam and divide our combat elements if we do that."

"We need to take that risk. Pull over. Now."

"Roger." Moore stopped the vehicle at the edge of the road.

"We're on our way up to the Karakoram Gorge," Jack said in a clipped tone, the phone close to his mouth. "We're moving as fast as we can, Mr. C. We think the terrorists are setting up for an ambush at a choke point just south of the bridge and north of the tunnel. Please tell me the train hasn't already—"

"Slow down, Jack. I've got you clearer now," Clark interrupted after the delay from the satellite bounce. "Train's not there yet. Lisanne said the dedication ceremony is this afternoon, Pakistan time. She said they're stopped at a village called Khaibar, twenty klicks south of the bridge. They're waiting for global media to set up on the platform to broadcast their achievement worldwide."

"Can you patch me through to Lisanne?"

"Negative. Following SOP, she's only calling in when she can get to public Wi-Fi. We agreed to talk before the train starts rolling."

"Copy," Jack replied, relieved. He had a few hours to cover the remaining eighty miles to the bridge. "Get her off that train, John."

"Of course I will. If they're planning a hit on VIPs, you're probably one of them," Clark added. "Since you were with me when we took down the Emir, Rafa would certainly like to nail you. Given the global audience, he'd hold you up like a trophy."

Jack suddenly remembered Daval Rai's insistence that he join them on this trip. Was the cheerful tycoon involved? He visualized the AGI corporate logos on the terrorist computer images and the men who had followed him while he was in the AGI vehicle. He felt like he might vomit right there in the foul-smelling Nissan.

"We'll be up there in a few hours," he managed. "I need to see Lisanne."

"Wilco. I'll coordinate a safe meet spot in Khaibar. Just get there."

"Got it. Mr. C., there's more—much more. We've received critical intel from the UC camp we hit."

"I'm listening."

"Moore and I believe it's a targeting package for a truck bomb at the Hanford nuclear site in central Washington State. There's another AGI installation there, a wind farm. I don't know how, but this ISI mole you found must be working through AGI—it's the common denominator. The targeting package was named At-Takwir."

Moore and Jack swapped a glance while waiting for Clark to respond to that terrifying tidbit.

"The Quranic day of judgment. Worldwide hellfire," Clark said.

"Correct. The same code name the Emir gave up under questioning."

"Yeah. Then . . . that could mean Rafa's trying to time a hit on the First Son of the United States with some other ungodly horror, all of it on global live television."

"Exactly."

"The bastard. Hang on, Jack. Let me check something." A moment later, Clark returned. "I've got Hanford up on my computer right now. Shit. The Columbia River is the water supply fantasy of theirs. Rafa's carrying on his daddy's work."

"Concur, Mr. C. That's how I see it."

"Jack, Master Chief—hustle up to that train and set up for a counterassault. Call me back when you're twenty mikes out. I've got a shit ton of calls to make."

51

HANFORD, WASHINGTON

SHERIFF WHITCOMB WAITED FOR THE MAN WHO'D ASKED HIM TO PARK AT THE BASE of the wind turbine. Forty long minutes had ticked by while he checked in with his headquarters people in India.

At least the view was pleasant. The angled parking space provided him with a vantage point of the entire river valley. Long shadows stretched from the taller stacks of the nuclear reactor at the Hanford site. The winding Columbia reflected the low sun, transitioning from white to yellow to orange. A steady wind rustled against the truck's rear window. Luna whimpered at the uneven, whistling breeze while Gavin fiddled with his computer, preparing it for whatever hocus-pocus he planned with the data center.

"Tell me about this guy again," the sheriff asked Mandy. A light was on in the trailer. Every now and then, Whitcomb could see the fellow moving in the window.

"He's director of site security, according to the file. Offline, that's about all I have." She closed her laptop, slid it to the floor, and unclicked her seat belt.

"Is he a direct employee of AGI?" the sheriff asked. "Or is it some other security contractor company?"

"Direct employee of AGI."

"Did your roster give a home address for him?"

"Yes," she replied. "It listed this place."

"What do you suppose his accent is?"

"He's a French national. Sounds to me like he's lived in other countries in Europe. He probably moves around a lot for the company."

"Has he passed a background check according to the file?"

"Yes."

Luna whined. Out of Milk-Bones, Gavin stroked her head while wrapping up his plan to tap the data center for IP traffic analysis. He shut his laptop and deposited it at the center of the bench seat.

The Campus director of information security gazed out the left rear window at the concrete building housing the data center's servers. Curious how the power might be supplied from the massive wind turbine just in front of the truck, he searched the hill's incline, expecting to find a power transformer somewhere. A transformer was the only way he could imagine converting the enormous wattage from the churning blades for use at the site.

To the left of the building was the trailer where the security man had gone. To the right was a second trailer with a door and two windows. Both windows reflected the glowing valley like mirrors—until a dark shadow crossed behind one of them.

"Hey—somebody's in that second trailer," Gavin announced. "Just saw movement."

"The guy said he was alone," the sheriff replied. "He said he was—"

"*Start the truck!*" Mandy urged. She'd detected movement, too—a dark shape flashing behind the reflection in the window.

The truck's headlights automatically came on when the sheriff pressed the starter button, lighting the shade at the white base of the wind turbine. Mandy detected more movement in the far trailer. A man with a gun. "Get us out of here, Sheriff. *Go!*"

Whitcomb threw the truck into reverse. "Gate's closed," he reminded her while the wheels shrieked on the pavement.

"*Ram it!*" she cried, her eyes fixed on the main trailer.

The AGI worker ran from the trailer's swinging door, his jacket open, a machine pistol rising in his hand. A second man followed him, raising a black assault rifle.

"*Down!*" Mandy yelled. "*Sheriff, go! Go! Go!*"

The truck's diesel roared as Whitcomb backed and braked to complete the three-point turn. He scrunched below the dash as low as he could, controlling the heavy-duty pickup by memory.

Glass burst into a blizzard of glinting lights. A tearing roar thundered through the cab.

His face bleeding from a dozen cuts, Whitcomb leaned sideways. He shifted the automatic transmission to the drive position and jammed his foot on the accelerator as bullets sparked on the metal doorpost.

Mandy had her pistol drawn beside Whitcomb, aiming double-fisted through the broken window overhead. Gunfire close to his ear deafened him. Whitcomb felt hot brass shell casings from the woman's Glock bouncing off his forehead amid the chaos. He slammed the accelerator down. The rear of the truck slid sideways, as if it were on snow.

"Tires are blown!" Whitcomb cried over clanging metal as bullets tore at the roof. "We're on rims!"

He raised his head far enough to glance through the windshield. The glass was white with spidery cracks and holes.

"Reverse!" Mandy shouted, swapping one magazine for another, her head low. "Give it everything! *Go!*"

Whitcomb threw the lever and floored it. Skidding on flat tires, the dying truck backed sickeningly against the concrete apron below the wind turbine where they'd been parked moments before.

The shooting paused.

"Out!" Mandy ordered as she thrust open her door, her Glock switched to her left hand. *"Follow me! This side!"*

Gavin and Luna spilled out of the back seat, covered in small chunks of glass. He clutched his Glock in his right hand while tugging Luna's leash with his left. He took cover next to Mandy and the sheriff behind the right front rim, its tire flat. Parked at an angle, its tailgate facing the wind turbine, the truck created a diagonal barrier, shielding them from the onslaught as the heavy barrage resumed, shaking the vehicle.

Mandy grabbed Gavin's arm and pulled him close to be heard over the thundering automatic gunfire. *"On three, you go for that turbine door!"* she shouted. *"I'll cover you!"*

Whitcomb had lost his cowboy hat in the melee. He held his black shotgun with both hands, crouched against the tire, knees bent, face smeared in blood.

Mandy shook the sheriff by the shoulder, repeating herself. Though she was shouting, Gavin could barely hear her over the zings, bangs, and pops blasting into the pickup truck's steel body. The sheriff wiped blood from his eyes and thrust his shotgun at Mandy. She nodded, seized it, and shoved her Glock in Whitcomb's hand. *"Seven shells!"* he yelled at her, his bloody hand cupped around his mouth.

She moved to the edge of the tire, head just below the leaning front bumper. She angled her face at the two sheltering men beside her, the bloodstained shotgun poised in her hands. *"One! Two! Three!"*

The sheriff rose. Half-blinded by the blood running down his forehead, he bolted for the door at the base of the wind turbine.

Gavin followed, staying low and dragging Luna, stepping over Mandy's exposed legs where she lay prone, firing the shotgun, one pump after another.

A lever secured the tower door like a ship's hatch. Gavin slammed his shoulder under it to force it up. Inside, he caught a quick glimpse of a cramped concrete floor, a ladder, and a locked steel cage that occupied the rest of the space. He urged the sheriff and dog inside.

"Mandy! Hurry!" Gavin yelled. Using the open hatch like a shield, he waved at her and raised his Glock, shooting over her shoulder.

Mandy leaped up and sprinted toward him, the shotgun in her hand.

Five feet away from the threshold, she pitched forward. Her head bounced off the concrete pad. Her body lay limp.

52

THEODORE BOLTON JACKSON, T-BOLT, PULLED OVER TO LOWER THE CONVERTIBLE top on his '83 Jeep CJ-7 Laredo, a half mile after exiting Hanford's main gate. When that little chore was complete, he motored over the Columbia River on the Route 24 bridge, glanced down at the wide, green water, and grinned.

Most people hated their commute—not T-Bolt.

On an evening like this, when the June sun still shone after quitting time, the Army Reserve captain didn't just like his commute—he flat-out *loved* it. He planned to enjoy every single one of the dozen miles between here and the riverside town of Desert Aire, where he was currently rehabbing a two-bedroom rambler.

That house formed the bedrock of T-Bolt's financial future. Working for the Department of Energy as a response team commander paid well, and he received an Army Reserve stipend when he drilled with his unit down in Yakima.

But thirty-one years old, full of vim and vigor, T-Bolt wanted more. Inspiration struck when he found the Desert Aire listing on Zillow six months back. In T-Bolt's view, it could be the perfect second home for an affluent Seattle tech worker seeking refuge from the big city's gloomy gray skies. All it took was a little elbow grease for a profitable flip.

His two sisters, Ashley and Gio, bought into the plan. Both women were teachers, one in Ellensburg and the other in Pullman, so they were as tight on funds as T-Bolt. Ashley was married to a carpenter, Wes, who said he would help but never did. Gio, who lived with T-Bolt at the fixer-upper, left a wake of destruction behind her every time she handled a power tool. Six months ago, it had all seemed like a brilliant idea.

Not so much now. Ashley was four months pregnant. Gio wanted her money back.

Dreading his arrival at the domestic disaster he'd created, T-Bolt drove slowly in the classic Jeep, five miles below the speed limit. His work cell phone buzzed with a call from the Hanford Patrol chief. He was relieved to have something other than the house to think about.

The chief was a seasoned veteran who had been there for years, leading the facility's police force, while T-Bolt—a direct employee of the Department of Energy—managed the site's tactical response unit.

T-Bolt pulled over to the side of the road to take the call. Partly, he deemed it a matter of gross insubordination to chat with the chief while in a noisy Jeep. It also served as another way to delay his arrival home.

"Yes, sir," the reserve Army Ranger captain answered, as was his custom.

"T-Bolt! Where are you?"

"Highway 24, halfway home. What's up?"

"Turn around. The national asset commander just called from D.C. We have a Render Safe mission."

Gasping in astonishment, T-Bolt nearly swallowed his tongue. "Holy shit. Romeo Sierra? Condition?"

"Romeo Sierra One. The NAC has activated the NARU."

T-Bolt spun the wheel, reversing course. The NARU, or National Asset Response Unit, consisted of two Boeing 757s on standby at Andrews Air Force Base stuffed with weapons and sensors to contain a nuclear incident.

"I'm on my way there. What else?"

"The NARU birds are already airborne. They have a full HRT unit aboard."

T-Bolt accelerated the Jeep to seventy on the two-lane road. He floored it to overtake a rattling open-bed truck loaded with tomatoes. If a traffic cop stopped him, he'd lead the Washington State Patrol on a chase back to the Hanford main gate. They'd be arriving soon anyway, once the chief finished his list of calls.

"The NARU will take hours to fly out here," T-Bolt said over the whipping wind. "What's the status of the Render Safe?"

"I've got protection units swarming to the Class Charlie sensitive sites. The airborne NARU command center has ordered your unit to secure the wind farm on the BLM land."

That had never been in their drills before. "That area is run by a private company," T-Bolt pointed out. "AGI, I think."

"That's right. The NAC has exposed a terrorist threat operating *through* AGI."

"Huh?"

"All I know is that the commander has ordered you to lock it down. They've designated the wind farm as a hard target."

"Hard target? They're saying there's an armed force up there in those hills?"

"Correct. They said to prepare for well-armed terrorists. I've already got watch officers assembling your team with their tactical kit. You're ordered to go now, T-Bolt. You can't wait for the HRT. Copy?"

"Copy!"

T-Bolt passed three tractor-trailers at once, damn near killing himself in the wobbly Jeep. He never imagined the FBI Hostage

Rescue Team shock troops would tell him to jump into the breach before they arrived. They were as gung ho as it got.

He rolled through logistical considerations in the blink of an eye. Four members of his team were on duty on the Hanford site. The rest would take a half hour to get in. Those were shitty odds for a hard-target assault up a hill.

"Oh hell," the chief swore through the phone. "I just got a text message from a BLM ranger near the wind farm. He reports automatic-weapons fire. The farm's already hot. Some kind of gun battle going on up there. I told BLM to set up a roadblock. They're not equipped for this."

Still cataloging mental details, a light blinked in T-Bolt's brain. "It's those FBI agents."

"Who?"

"That lead special agent woman who pulled rank on me. She showed up with another computer guy and the county sheriff. They asked for a detailed roster of the whole site, including the BLM lessees. I'll bet they uncovered this."

"Well, shit, T-Bolt. The BLM cop said it sounded like a war. You ready to fight back?"

The Army Reserve captain thought of the good-looking FBI woman, her doughy partner, and the weathered cowboy sheriff. T-Bolt was ready to fight back. He wasn't sure that motley crew was.

"Chief," he snapped, thinking more like an Army Ranger than a DOE security contractor. "Have the NARU command post scramble an Air Force Black Hawk out of Fairchild right now. My team'll meet 'em at the pad."

"Way ahead of you. The Air Force said—"

T-Bolt didn't hear the rest.

The shuddering thunder of an MH-60 Black Hawk passed twenty feet over his head.

53

GAVIN DROPPED TO HIS BELLY AND THRUST HIS ARMS OUT. HE SEIZED MANDY'S wrists and dragged her into the aluminum environmental shelter that surrounded the wind tower's core while bullets thudded into the truck.

"We can climb up," Sheriff Whitcomb called from a few feet up the ladder. Its rungs protruded from a black steel shaft. "If we stay here, we're dead meat."

Barely listening, Gavin turned Mandy over. Though she appeared unconscious, her mouth opened and closed like a landed fish. Gavin searched her head, legs, and torso to look for a wound. Nothing. Her mouth moved; her chest didn't. She was turning gray before his eyes.

"I found a fire axe!" the sheriff called, sliding down the ladder, his rubber-soled Justin Ropers nearly landing on Gavin's head. The lawman propped the axe handle in the long metal levers that worked the hatch's ship-like seals. Bullets clanged off the metal door, denting it.

"We're good in here—until they blow the door." The sheriff glanced at Mandy's pale face, closed eyes, and gaping mouth. Wiping blood from his eyes, he dropped to his knees and prepared to pump her chest with his hands. But the Kevlar vest was in the way. "She needs CPR! Blow air into her!"

Gavin pinched Mandy's nose and covered her mouth with his, inflating her lungs. Bullets rang from the door like bells.

After the fourth breath, Mandy opened her eyes. She groaned and coughed. Rosy color streamed into her cheeks as Luna licked her face. Gavin helped her sit up against the ladder.

Gasping, she surveyed the length of her arms, her eyes dancing. "I lost the shotgun," she croaked.

"We're safe in here. Door's barred. It's taking the bullets."

She focused on the heavy hatch, dimpled as a golf ball. The shooting suddenly stopped. A stew of guttural voices penetrated the metal from outside.

"They'll get in here," she warned in a rasp. "The walls are thinner than the door." She nodded at the thin aluminum walls to either side of the door.

The firing began again. This time, a few rounds penetrated the curving aluminum, ricocheting rounds in the small vestibule. The killers unleashed a furious barrage on the painted white shell.

"Ladder leads up to the top," the sheriff hollered over the clanging din. "We can climb above the worst of it!"

"We won't make it!" Gavin protested over the zips, zings, and bangs of the piercing rounds.

"We have to move," Mandy disputed through a cough.

Her voice was swallowed up by another sustained burst that dislodged hunks of metal, perforating the bulkhead like a cheese grater and spewing a howling blizzard of white aluminum jagged bits. A wide hole opened in the thin wall. The man who'd introduced himself as Agon ran from the cover of the immobilized pickup truck toward them, grinning like a jackal. Another man followed, raising his rifle. Bearded assaulters darted to either side of them.

They suddenly stopped running. The man in the lead cast his eyes skyward and backed up, seeking cover behind the pickup.

A series of low, heavy thuds shook the twisted metal at the base of the wind turbine tower. Mandy recognized the sound right away: the low *whump-whump-whump* of a military Black Hawk.

"HEY, T-BOLT," THE PILOT SAID THROUGH THE INTERCOM TO THE RESERVE RANGER captain, who stood just aft of the two Air Force officers at the controls. "You see the green truck at the base of that wind turbine?"

T-Bolt scanned the area. Six armed men dashed from the base of a white wind turbine to a green truck. One of them spotted the helicopter and pointed, directing the others to take cover behind the truck's bed.

"Yeah, I got 'em. I count six tangos," T-bolt reported, his hands running over the gear that studded his plate carrier combat vest, double-checking he had plenty of magazines.

"This is a civilian area," the Air Force major replied. "You sure they're tangos? Didn't you say there are some FBI friendlies out here?"

"I met the friendlies," T-Bolt countered. He steadied himself with a death grip on the rear of the pilot's seat as the helo turned. "Those men are *definitely* not them."

"Roger—but I can't open up on these guys unless I have proof they're hostiles. Even then . . . they're civilians. I'd rather a civilian police force round 'em up. And I can't get too close with those massive windmill blades chopping the air like—"

One of the men T-Bolt had designated as a tango stepped to the side of the green Ram pickup and fired at the incoming helo, his rifle muzzle winking with tiny yellow flashes. A round punched through the cockpit floor and buried itself in the headliner, inches from T-Bolt's helmet.

The pilot jinked the Black Hawk with his cyclic, causing the helicopter to abruptly alter course—the SOP for throwing off a small-arms ground attack.

"Belay my last," the pilot said.

He flipped a red switch with his thumb. "Buckle up, T-Bolt. We're going in hot."

54

THE SENIOR SECRET SERVICE OFFICER IN THE RESIDENCE, ANDREA PRICE-O'DAY, LED Mary Pat Foley and Dan Murray through the White House's center hall.

Before climbing the carpeted, dimly lit steps, Price-O'Day paused, placed her hand on the curved banister, and spoke into a tiny microphone hidden in her suit lapel. A few seconds later, she turned to the director of national intelligence and the attorney general.

"He's ready for you."

Mary Pat felt a little guilty about this visit. She knew Jack had spent a long day negotiating treaty proposals with the Israeli prime minister, a notoriously hard-nosed politician. But she judged that this was a rare instance where she felt her duty was to bring the President up to speed, even if that meant interrupting his private time.

Much like an usher in an art museum, Price-O'Day spoke softly to the burly agent at the door, a former Marine drill instructor who could stand at a civilian version of attention for eight hours, moving only his eyes. That wasn't the only qualification that secured him his position at this inner sanctum, but it certainly helped.

Jack welcomed them in the Yellow Oval Room, a curved room above the White House entrance. When most Americans envisioned this cherished national building, they pictured the front columns sheltering the main entrance on the first floor and the Truman Balcony on the second. The Yellow Oval Room was the elongated room situated behind the Truman Balcony.

Having just readied himself for bed, the President was dressed in pajamas and a maroon bathrobe with a Washington Commanders logo. He waved the two cabinet officers to a sofa. "Don't say anything about the robe. Lots of Ravens fans in this building."

Mary Pat smiled. "I'm good at keeping secrets."

"You'd better be."

"We're sorry to disturb you in the residence, Mr. President," Murray said. "Especially after a day with a foreign head of state."

"No problem. Today was just for show. Tomorrow, we'll tackle the serious stuff. I'm sorry I'm keeping you two from your families. Especially you, Dan, with Liz recovering from that surgery."

Like all great leaders, Jack Ryan, Sr., had the uncommon ability to couple vast personal power with genuine human warmth. "How is she?" the President asked Murray.

"Cathy did an amazing job."

"She went down early," Ryan said with a subtle toss of his head at the bedroom on the other side of the wall. "I think she collapsed from relief. And a couple of glasses of Cabernet."

"Yes, sir. Please thank her for me in the morning. Even if she has a headache."

Mary Pat worried Jack would continue in this vein for half the night if she didn't cut to the chase.

"Mr. President, there was a Render Safe incident earlier this evening," she blurted. "And to make sure I don't bury the lede, I want you to know it's been handled. Everything is fine."

"Render Safe," the President repeated, alarmed. "Where?"

"We snuffed out a plot to harm the nuclear site at Hanford, Washington State."

"I activated the National Asset Command on my authority," Murray added. "Per the protocol. The incident involved foreign terrorists, but on domestic soil."

"Who were they?"

"Umayyad Caliphate," the attorney general replied. "We believe their intent was to poison the western water supply by blowing Hanford's plutonium waste facilities, infiltrating the nearby Columbia River."

President Ryan stared at his knees. "Same thing the Emir wanted to do. Umayyad. So this was his son, Rafa, was it?"

"Yes," Mary Pat answered. "We have clear intelligence that Rafa was behind it. But he wasn't there. We secured the site before he could act. Tell him, Dan."

"The Department of Energy security unit and the Air Force worked together to neutralize the installation. The National Asset Response Unit will land at Fairchild Air Force Base in another hour. We are one hundred percent safe, Jack. The whole facility is on lockdown."

"Did we get anyone we can interrogate?"

"No," Mary Pat replied. "Six militants were killed on the BLM land near the nuclear site. We couldn't take them alive. The site team intercepted a kinetic attack on investigating law enforcement." Mrs. Foley withheld Campus involvement, seeing no obvious need to include the detail.

"Why on BLM land?"

"The terrorists infiltrated a contractor leasing the land, Assurance Global Industries. They're an Indian construction conglomerate with a lease on the land pursuant to the Renewable Energy Act you signed last year."

"I'm familiar with AGI. Where did we get the intel?"

Mary Pat paused, trading a glance with Murray.

"I'm not supposed to know?"

"It was through Clark," she replied. "A Campus thing."

The President inhaled deeply. "Okay. Where is Clark now? As in *right* now?"

"Turkey. Incirlik."

"I thought you were going to say he's in Hanford. What's he doing in Turkey?"

"I hesitate to tell you the details of a Campus op to maintain deniability, Mr. President. But this one's big."

"Forget that. What's he doing in Turkey?"

"Clark is coordinating an op to take out Rafa. He infilled a covert strike team into northern Pakistan. So far, the team has taken out a UC terror base, fifteen fighters KIA. It was there that they scooped up the intelligence that alerted us to Hanford."

"And they're still operating in Pakistan?"

"Yes. The Campus team is in hot pursuit of Rafa."

Jack shook his head slowly. "Phew. That's a lot to take in. Is the op still deniable? Zero footprint?"

Mary Pat cleared her throat. "Yes, sir. They're still black."

"And safe?"

"One man wounded. Bartosz Jankowski," Mary Pat said. "You may know him as Midas."

Ryan crossed his arms. "If the Indians or Pakistanis find out we're operating without permission, I'll have a lot of explaining to do."

"If it helps," Murray offered, "any action we take would be a direct outcome of the Hanford issue, which was obviously a clear and present danger to the United States. Mr. President, you may not have felt like you had the authority to act against Umayyad in Pakistan before—but no one would dispute your actions."

"Yes," he agreed. "And that would only matter if I gave a damn about those arguments." He blew out a lungful of air. "Thank God The Campus uncovered Hanford. How do they get the culprit, Rafa?"

Mary Pat smoothed the fabric over her legs. "That's where we may need your help, sir. We see two ways to play it. Both are sensitive—diplomatically speaking."

"MP, we just intercepted what amounts to a nuclear attack on the homeland. I think we're way past diplomacy here. What are the two options you're suggesting?"

"The first is for you to put a call through to the Pakistani president. A direct call, no bullshit through underlings or State Department productions or any of that."

"And say what to him?"

"Tell him you've uncovered a scheme by one of his ISI senior officers to collude with the Umayyad Caliphate to execute a wide-ranging terror plot, including a dirty-bomb attack here in the U.S."

"I've lectured the man on his own nuclear security problems. I can't wait to hear how he'll turn that one around."

"It's not just Hanford you're going to tell him about," Mary Pat continued. "There's another terror plot brewing that he'll care deeply about."

"Related?"

"Yes. The same intel we acquired about Hanford told us that the Umayyad Caliphate, led by Rafa bin Yasin, intends to ambush a Chinese BRI-funded train, killing everyone aboard. Its fifty-six passengers are a mix of Indian nationals, Pakistani government officials, and foreign dignitaries—including a Chinese deputy foreign minister, a member of the People's National Congress, a godson of a politburo member."

Jack's eyes narrowed. He leaned forward. "When?"

"We assess Rafa will attack early afternoon, their time, about five hours from now."

"So," Ryan concluded after a few seconds of consideration. "Option one is that we ask the Pakistanis to intercept Rafa's force to head off this ambush."

"Yes, sir. But that's not the option I'm recommending."

"And why is that?"

"I'm not confident the Pakistanis will act with the necessary dispatch. Through the ISI, knowingly or unknowingly, they've been supporting Rafa. He's their de facto agent. As you'll recall, his last raid was on an Indian Special Forces garrison in Kashmir."

"All right. I understand. So what's your second proposed option?"

Mary Pat measured her words carefully. "I spoke to Clark just before we came in. He's confident that the Campus force in Pakistan could take the fight to Rafa. If we go that route, we would want to keep the Pakistanis in the dark to avoid compromise. But with direct action, of course, we won't be able to maintain deniability."

Jack nodded solemnly. "So. Summing up—we know Rafa is about to strike this train. If we go with option one, the Pakistanis might drag their feet because it's to their advantage to blame it on the Indians. And for all we know, they might even be behind this thing because Rafa is, effectively, an agent run by their freewheeling intelligence service. Or at least a rogue element of it."

"Yes, sir."

"And with option two, we stop the ambush ourselves and probably kill Rafa in the exchange, which would be a good thing. But it would probably ruin our already tenuous relationship with Pakistan for good—and expose The Campus, which could have serious repercussions, politically. Even if I ignore the politics, the media scrutiny would take away the best tool I have at my disposal for situations exactly like this."

Mary Pat shrugged. "I agree with your summation. Regrettably, those are our two shitty options."

"No," the President countered. "I disagree. There's a third option."

Mary Pat and Murray traded a confused glance. "Care to share, Mr. President?" she asked.

Ryan reached for the phone that never left his side. He glanced at his wristwatch. "You said this attack's five hours off, right?"

"That's our best estimate, sir."

"And Clark thinks The Campus can tactically handle this? They can head off an ambush and wipe out Rafa?"

"Yes, sir. That's his view."

"All right," the President said, standing. "Mary Pat, Dan, head downstairs to the Situation Room. Get Clark on the line, too. I'll meet you there. But I need to make a sensitive diplomatic call first."

"To Pakistan's president?" Mary Pat asked.

"No. To China's."

55

FOR TEN U.S. DOLLARS, RUSTAM HAD BOUGHT A FILTHY, KNEE-LENGTH DHOTI SHIRT, a ragged gray pin-striped vest, and a flowing gray turban to cover Jack's Western attire.

"Let's take a look at you," Midas said from his spot in the Toyota when Jack returned to the vehicle. "Yeah. I think you pass muster as a local. What do you think, Rustam?"

The Tajik replied with three sentences in Urdu, emphasizing the sharpest points of his opinions with the glowing tip of a smoldering cigar.

"What was all that?" Jack asked.

"He says you should wrap the turban around your chin," Midas explained, puffing on his own cigar. "Since you have a beard like a boy. His words."

"Sure they were," Jack said, stroking his chin. He draped the fabric over his face and examined it in the pickup's side mirror. "How's that?"

"Good!" the muj barked in English. "We go."

Jack gazed down the backstreet behind the bazaar where they'd parked.

"I wish you were coming along with us to translate," he told Midas.

"Rustam will take care of you. He's got some English. Just don't say anything fancy."

Fifteen minutes later, Jack and the mujahideen strolled through the town, dodging stray dogs, women beating carpets, and the occasional potbellied pygmy goat. In his element, the muj confidently strutted while Jack hurried alongside him, constantly adjusting the turban over his face.

It took three turns through the maze to find the main boulevard. Jack was met with a wide dirt road choked with traffic. A policeman in a khaki uniform stood at the median, directing cars left or right and frequently pointing to the hastily erected detour sign. The AGI train that bisected the town caused the reroute.

While Rustam trudged along as if he had lived in this town his whole life, Jack paused to examine the gleaming train, which had paused here before gliding north for the grand bridge opening. The train's panoramic windows were mirrored, obscuring the elite passengers inside. A wide stripe adorned the midsection of each car, displaying a chain of blue AGI logos. The shining cars stood out against the village's mud walls in stark relief, as if tourists from the future had slipped through a portal to visit a bygone era.

A harsh tug at Jack's elbow broke the trance. "This way," Rustam urged.

Jack and the Tajik walked two blocks on a bright, dusty street lined with slow-moving cars paralleling the tracks. While trying not to be obvious, Jack gazed northward at the rise of the majestic mountains, brown at the bottom, gray in the middle, and white at the peaks, thinking of the Gorge.

"There," the muj grunted, inclining his swathed head.

Jack had suspected they were approaching the café. A heady

combination of baking bread and frying meat had sent his saliva glands into overdrive.

Lisanne sat inside at a corner table draped in an embroidered blue chador that concealed all but her eyes. On the wobbly table before her were a phone, an empty Coke bottle with a straw, and a smeared plate. While a cricket announcer excitedly narrated a match on a heavy, corner-mounted television, Jack pulled up two chairs. He and Rustam sat down.

"This must be Rustam," she said, lowering the fabric to reveal a smile.

The muj fumbled through his vest to produce a cigar and awkwardly offered her one. She shook her head and thanked him.

"You're all chadored up," Jack remarked.

"Srini said this is a very devout town. Mullahs come out of the hills and try to punish women who are indiscreet."

"Looks good on you."

"It doesn't. But thanks anyway."

"Did you get the passes?" Jack asked.

Lisanne nodded. "I hope they work. There's only one color copier in this town, and it's not that great." She withdrew an envelope from the folds of fabric and slid it to Jack. "These are media passes. They'll allow access to the last three cars," she explained. "The team can store gear on the luggage car that's at the back."

"Where's Srini?" Jack asked. He passed the envelope to Rustam.

"She's been roped into another event on the train. The Rais are entertaining the Chinese and Pakistani politicians, trying to close a deal for a highway construction project God only knows where."

Jack leaned close to her. "Did you get the whole download from Clark?"

"Yes."

"So what do you think? Could Daval Rai be in on this?"

"Not a chance," she replied. "At this point, I know that family. They have no idea they've been used."

"That's a relief."

"What about the Chinese?" she asked. "Has that been handled?"

"Yes," Jack said. "Clark said we've got a green light. The Chinese know to remain with the Rais up front. You still have your Glock?"

"On me." She lifted a paper bag from the dirty tile floor. "And I brought this for you."

He opened it to find a pink bottle of Pepto-Bismol. "Good idea, Lis."

"You'll change clothes?"

"Yes. I have jeans and a button-up on under this. I'll ditch the rags and meet you at the station."

"We're expected at the reception being held this last leg of the trip in the forward lounge car."

"I'll get fully cleaned up in our cabin."

"Good. Because, Jack, honey. You stink."

"I AM SO GLAD TO SEE YOU UP AND ABOUT!" DAVAL RAI CRIED, HIS SMILE BROAD, his eyes compressed to slits. The tycoon pulled Jack into a back-slapping half hug.

"Thank you," Jack answered, freeing himself. After showering and shaving, he'd donned a chalk-gray suit with an open-necked white dress shirt. Ironically, though he and Lisanne had faked the illness, it was the freshest he'd felt since landing in Delhi.

Srini, dressed for business in a dark pantsuit, inspected Jack's complexion. "You look pretty good for a man who's been throwing up this whole trip."

"Well—thinner, perhaps," he replied with a modest smile.

Fahim Bajwa scrutinized Jack carefully. "We were worried we wouldn't see you at the bridge."

"I wouldn't miss that for the world, Fahim. I've been on the phone with Gerry Hendley in Virginia. I've told him all about AGI's work. He's become interested in developing an international fund for large civil projects like this."

Rai clapped his hands together. "That is excellent news! Perhaps I could meet with him after you return to the States?"

"Of course. I'll coordinate the details with Sanjay."

"Wonderful. Jack, we've been rude. Let me introduce you to Deputy Foreign Minister Zhuoran and Pakistan's minister of the interior, Tariq Masroof. Our guests of honor, much to my delight."

After Jack shook hands with the dignitaries, Fahim added, "And this is Jack's fiancée, Lisanne. With both Srini and Lisanne on the podium this afternoon, I'm afraid they'll steal the show."

PLEASED WITH HIS CHARMING REMARK, FAHIM RETREATED TO THE BACK CORNER OF the lounge car. Brigadier Imran Khan and Colonel Chen Ming of the People's Liberation Army were standing by the bar, speaking in hushed tones. They paused when Fahim came closer.

"Are we feeling confident about the security situation, gentlemen?" Fahim asked.

"We were just discussing it," Khan replied. "We've had no reports of Indian incursions. We both feel the security at the Gorge is well under control, don't we, Colonel?"

The Chinese officer nodded grimly. "Yes, Brigadier."

"What a day," Fahim exulted, rubbing his hands together. "We have finally opened up the ancient Silk Road from the Red Sea to the Middle Kingdom. Have you seen my bridge, Colonel?"

"It is quite an achievement," the PLA man acknowledged. "Forgive me, gentlemen. I feel I must stay close to the deputy foreign minister. I will see you both on the podium."

When the Chinese officer moved out of earshot, Fahim leaned in toward the colonel. "I hope the little shit *is* near his foreign minister on the podium."

Khan checked his watch and nodded. "The media will be assembled on the bridge by now. I'd like to see the Al Jazeera coverage."

"I wouldn't miss that for the world," Fahim agreed. "Come, I'll take you to my club car to watch it."

As they exited through the lounge car's aft door, Lisanne watched them in the window reflection. She subtly nudged Jack with her elbow.

56

FAHIM'S CLUB CAR WAS SEVENTH IN LINE BEHIND THE BUSINESS COACH, LOUNGE car, dining carriage, and the suites occupied by Daval Rai, his daughter and son-in-law, and the Chinese deputy foreign minister. From the narrow side corridor, he slid the door open, offered Khan a chair, dropped into his own, and handled the remote.

"Right on time," Khan remarked.

The brigadier's favorite female Al Jazeera reporter, Ghida Douri, stood on the platform with half a dozen other journalists. Beyond her, the tall bridge spans extended out of the frame as she praised the engineering achievements of the Karakoram Gorge Bridge. After a few introductory remarks, the video transitioned to a B-roll accompanied by prerecorded narration.

Fahim leaned forward, his hands on his knees, savoring his achievement. He felt slighted when the video shifted back to the live shot. The recorded footage mentioned only AGI and Daval Rai—not a word about Fahim Bajwa, the talented bridge builder, Pontifex Maximus.

"And so," Khan said. "Here we come."

The camera panned to the dark tunnel from which the train would soon emerge. A banner atop the stony arch read CHINA—

PAKISTAN—A NEW ERA OF PARTNERSHIP in Mandarin, Urdu, and English.

The train jerked under Fahim's feet. He looked out the tinted window and across the low mud houses of Khaibar, grateful to be leaving the squalid town, but annoyed with Daval Rai for domineering the various receptions and speeches on the long journey. The B-roll video lauding Rai as a visionary builder was the last straw. It would all end today.

NINE CARS BACK, KENDRICK MOORE, JAD MUSTAFA, AND TOM BUCK CROUCHED IN the press coach. The media credentials that Lisanne had forged enabled them to pass through the station. Moments after they settled in, a man from the Pakistani government offered van rides to the reporters, which would take them over a hill to the media platform on the far side of the tunnel. All the journalists had departed, leaving the Campus operators alone.

"The train's rolling," Jad said. Like the others, he wore blue jeans and an untucked shirt—the civilian clothes the operatives had packed into their kit for the planned exfiltration through India.

"Let's give it a few seconds," Moore replied, reaching for his sat phone.

"How long is the tunnel?" Buck asked.

"Two miles, straight through the hill." Moore punched a programmed button on his phone and aimed the antenna at the sky. "Overwatch, how do you read?"

"*We're five by five,*" Midas answered. He sat on a hill over the tunnel, abutting the road the media people had taken to the platform. Rustam had driven him there, borrowing Jack's disguise. "*Got a clear view of the tracks. Cary's behind the ESR. Rustam's spotting. I'm comms.*"

"Roger that," Moore answered. "You see anything in the trees? Rafa and his boys gotta be in there somewhere."

"Negative, Chief. Nothing so far."

Moore puzzled at that. The intelligence he had reviewed at the caravansary bivouac had been clear on the UC ambush position.

"We're entering the tunnel," he said. "I'm about to lose you on comms. Remember—we'll be on the train roof. We'll take tangos the train blocks from your sight line."

"Copy. See you on the other side, Master Chief," Midas answered. *"By then Rafa will be missing a head."*

After hanging up, the SEAL unzipped a heavy ballistic nylon bag and withdrew his plate carrier vest, helmet, and NVDs. "Overwatch is ready," he told his two partners. "Time to go topside, gentlemen. Jock up."

"I SUPPOSE WE SHOULD JOIN THE OTHERS," FAHIM SAID. "THE SATELLITE BROADCAST is blocked in the tunnel anyway."

"Aren't we going quite slow?" Brigadier Khan asked.

"About fifty KPH. It can take ten kilometers for a train at that speed to come to a full stop. We intend for it to halt as soon as it emerges on the other side for the grand reveal. Come, Brigadier. It's showtime."

Khan stood and aligned the buttons of his dress uniform. Using the plush car's full-length mirror, he checked that the holster flap was unlatched over his Browning pistol.

They entered the lounge car to find a festive atmosphere. The well-dressed riders spoke loudly, talking over one another. Jack Ryan, Jr., and his fiancée were in the small circle of the Rai family, the men from China, and the Pakistani minister. Fahim snagged sparkling water from the bar and wandered up. The dark tunnel outside the windows made the lights seem brighter.

"You'll stand at the center," Sanjay Rai explained to his father-in-law. "Minister Zhuoran, Minister Masroof, you'll be beside him. Hello, Fahim. I trust you heard that. You'll be next in line. Srini, myself, Jack, and Lisanne will be at the edge of the dais, out of the camera shot."

Or not out of the shot, Fahim laughed inwardly, visualizing his half brother and his band of snipers perched in the tree line, waiting until the cameras rolled before unleashing their fusillade.

"That all sounds fine," Rai boomed. "Except that—"

A hideous screech cut the tycoon off. Yellow sparks flew past the windows. Every person standing in the VIP reception car hurtled forward, landing in a tangled mess of bodies. When Jack struggled upright, pulling Lisanne along with him, he was shocked to see a black-clad holy warrior spring through the opening at the lounge car's rear, wielding an assault rifle, screaming in Urdu.

CRAWLING ALONG THE TRAIN'S SLICK ROOF, THE SUDDEN STOP CAUSED MOORE TO slide forward. The shower of sparks flying from the train's wheels blotted out the view through his NVDs. He flipped them up. The cold air rushing past his face moments before was suddenly as still as a dank cellar.

"What's up?" Jad shot as he regained his position on the roof's centerline. "Why'd it stop?"

"Maybe something wrong with the bridge," Buck suggested.

Moore didn't bother to respond. Now that the sparks had ceased, he readjusted his prone position and flipped the NVDs over his eyes. Ten riderless horses trotted along the side of the tracks in the dark, brushing against the rock walls. Far ahead, across the fourteen train cars, he spotted a dump truck parked sideways on the track, blocking the train's path. He crawled to the edge of the car and lifted the NVDs, opting to look through his IR scope.

A warrior with a flashlight spun it toward him and shot. Moore unleashed a burst. The man with the flashlight fell. "Contact right!" he roared, choosing another target.

Jad and Buck lay at an angle beside him, choosing targets, shooting at will, the suppressors at the end of their barrels muffling the shots into metallic clicks. Moore shot until he saw nothing moving except horses.

"We have to get to the VIP section!" he shouted, sprinting over the stopped train cars, his head bent.

A bullet whizzed by his ear. "Contact left!" he shouted, returning fire and flattening himself on the roof.

THREE BLACK-CLAD WARRIORS ENTERED THE LOUNGE CAR FROM THE REAR, CLIMB-ing up the coupling. Wielding an exotic black assault rifle, the leading terrorist aimed it at Daval Rai's head.

Barely recovered from the fall, the tycoon shuffled to the front of the group. "You will leave this train immediately!" he shouted, his turban askew.

A warrior in black seized his shoulders and propelled him to the floor. "Stop that!" Srini cried, jumping to her father's defense.

The warrior grabbed her by the throat and hurled her over her father, knocking her down. He aimed his rifle at the top of her head. Rai immediately shuffled his bulk to cover her. "If it's me you want, take me!" he yelled.

"*Marne ki tyari karo!*" the terrorist screamed in reply. Prepare to die!

Another holy warrior darted between them and grabbed Rai by his lapels, pulling the overweight Sikh to the center. A third seized the pistol at Imran Khan's side, while another aimed a rifle at his chest. The terrorist gestured for all the passengers—the Chinese foreign minister, PLA colonel, Jack, Lisanne, and the rest—to move against the right bulkhead. The warriors waved their weapons back and forth, their balaclavas obscuring their faces except for their eyes, which glimmered white with hate.

A black-clad warrior wearing an elaborate, silky turban entered, strode to the center of the car, and stood with his legs apart. At his side, he held a long staff topped with carved ivory.

Rafa, Jack thought.

With a distant look in his eyes, Rafa barked at his three soldiers—one guarding Rai, and the other two aiming weapons at the passengers huddled against the bulkhead. The terrorist in front reached out and struck Jack on the shoulder, a rude gesture indicating he should get on his knees. Jack complied and lowered himself beside Rai and Srini.

Rafa approached.

"The devil Ryan," he said in French-accented English, his face twisted in abhorrence. He shifted his gaze to Daval Rai. "And the Sikh who would usurp the caliphate."

Rai's breath came in deep gasps. "No, my friend," he began, his palms raised. The holy warrior looming over him slammed the rifle butt into his temple, knocking him flat. Srini screamed.

"The commander of believers, the caliph chooses the devil Ryan to die first."

Jack looked at Lisanne. She stood with the others, her arms casually positioned behind her. He ripped his attention away from her, locking eyes with the man who would kill him.

"Can I pray to the caliph?" Jack asked, remembering Clark's summary of the Emir's interrogation at the Leesburg farm. "Can I offer the *Shahada* to the commander of believers today, this holy event of At-Takwir?"

Rafa heard the request as though it were completely expected.

He tilted his staff and raised his other hand. "Devil Ryan. You recite the *Shahada* to the caliph with your face to the floor."

Jack bowed his head, lowering to the floor to say his final prayers. In doing so, he slid his hands along his shins. When his right fingers reached the cuff of his trouser leg, he moved his hand subtly to touch the top of the Glock 43's grip.

"Say it to the caliph!" Rafa screamed.

Jack whipped the 43 up and looked him in the eye. "No," he said while pulling the trigger. Rafa's forehead snapped back. The terrorist fell.

Jack instantly rotated the pistol to the guard just over his head, catching the Umayyad warrior in the chin. To his right, he heard a loud report from the Glock 17 Lisanne had tucked into her belt below her jacket. Aiming expertly, her natural hand supported by her artificial one. She fired four times, killing the remaining guards.

Fahim Bajwa, his mouth gaping wide, stared at the Pakistani brigadier in the immaculate dress uniform. "Well, do something, for God's sake!" he shrieked.

As though slapped, Khan stepped forward and took the machine gun from the fallen man. "It's an Indian weapon!" he cried, eyes twitching, raising the carbine with both hands for all to see. "These terrorists are Indian!"

"Khan! Drop your weapon!" Jack shouted, shifting his Glock's aim to the general. "Drop it now!"

A dozen thoughts collided in Khan's head as he stood with the carbine in his hands, an Indian Sabre. Ryan and Daval Rai were just ten feet in front of him, the American wielding a pistol. Ryan's girlfriend held him under her sights, too.

With a single burst of the Indian weapon in his hands, he could shred the lot of them to ribbons.

"Kill them!" Fahim Bajwa roared.

His co-conspirator's plea came to Khan's ears as though from a great distance.

Khan wondered: *What if I did kill them? All of them.*

Shattered bodies, scattering terrorists, a disabled train . . . the evidence would suggest that the Indian-armed fighter had perpetrated the massacre. Pakistan could rightfully send troops to quell the terror brewing in Kashmir—this time with China as a supporter. Daval Rai would be gone. Khan's agent, Fahim, would accede to the head of the corporation as planned, giving him new inroads to China. Fahim would have every incentive to support Khan's story. Then again, Khan had always hated Fahim.

"*You bloody fool!*" Fahim screamed, dashing at him as if to seize the weapon himself. "*Do it!*"

And then, because he had nothing to lose, the brigadier pulled the trigger. A diagonal line of crimson dots crossed Fahim's immaculate white shirt, flinging him backward. The Pakistani swung his weapon to take out Ryan—but while the barrel rotated, Daval Rai roared and lunged like a grizzly. The tycoon's three-hundred-pound bulk knocked Jack sideways and sent his Glock skittering across the floor.

While Khan had lost the angle on Ryan, he'd gained it on the Chinese foreign minister and his colonel. "Drop it, Khan!" the Chinese officer screamed. "We know you planned this! It's over!"

The quick movement of Lisanne's shifting pistol caused Khan to duck instinctively.

Her shot nicked his skull, a glancing blow three inches above his ear that tore his beret off. It didn't matter. Enraged, he increased the pressure on the trigger to kill her first, before swinging the iron sights over Ryan, Rai, and the Chinese. No one would be left alive.

But just as he was about to pull the trigger, his body jerked and shuddered in a blizzard of flying glass.

Master Chief Moore, Jad Mustafa, and Tom Buck pierced the brigadier's skull with a dozen white-hot rounds of M4 5.56, flying through the splintering windows at a speed of three thousand feet per second, two thousand miles per hour, terminal velocity.

EPILOGUE

"THAD VANDERMULLEN, COME ON UP HERE!" GERRY HENDLEY ROARED.

The retired senator, head of the private equity firm Hendley Associates, clapped boisterously. "Come on, folks! Give the man a hand!"

Thad Vandermullen stepped from the crowd of Hendley Associates employees assembled at the all-hands meeting. The tall former Wall Street banker, with curling chestnut hair and a long jaw, returned handshakes and backslaps on his way to the front of the meeting room.

"I'll have you know," Gerry went on with Vandermullen towering over him, "that this fellow here closed the biggest deal we've ever done when we were back in Zurich. And to add to that, he's just signed the papers on a tentative distribution deal for LodeStar Communications' satellites to carry data transmissions all over the world for LuftDraht, the German wireless company. Two years' worth of revenue is almost as much as we paid for the company! And that's just the start! Come on, Thad, when will that revenue start flowing?"

"Can you give me until tomorrow?" Vandermullen gamely replied to a chorus of cheers.

The all-hands meetings were one of the few times when Hendley's black-side, white-side, and hybrid employees stood shoulder to shoulder. Gerry felt this get-together was necessary following the extended vacation all his employees had enjoyed. Now that they were back in the office, he wanted a genuine rah-rah session to energize the team for the second half of the year.

As a member of the executive staff, John Clark stood with Gerry and the chief investment officer, Howard Brennan. The three men had taken a few steps back to make room for Vandermullen.

"Seriously, Thad," Gerry went on, "tell us the size of the return we think we can expect on LodeStar next year if we sell it based on those new revenue projections."

Vandermullen accepted the wireless microphone and put it to his lips. His green eyes blazed over the crowd as he took a dramatic pause before announcing the grand figure.

"Six hundred percent return," he estimated to wild, cheering applause.

And so the rest of the all-hands meeting continued as Howard took the mic to introduce five new hires who'd come aboard to assist with the LodeStar work, reporting to Vandermullen. Howard predicted profit sharing, a triple bonus, and improved expense accounts. He implored them all to thank Thad Vandermullen personally when they got a chance.

John Clark peered through the gap between Gerry, Howard, and Thad to observe his small black-side team. Jack wore a blank expression. Lisanne seemed deep in thought, as if she were solving math problems in her head. Nearby, Mandy fidgeted restlessly beside Gavin, who appeared bored. At the very back, Moore, Midas, Cary, Jad, and Buck stood in a slightly relaxed version of parade rest. Steven "Chilly" Edwards was attending virtually on the speakerphone, still on leave with his wife's family in Oaxaca, Mexico.

As the white-side employees cheered, Clark's leadership instincts fired into gear, making him fidget.

The applause faded and Vandermullen slipped back into the crowd of admirers. Clark asked Gerry for the microphone. As the director of Hendley Security, such things were his prerogative.

"My team," he announced tersely into the mic. "Meeting, downstairs, fifteen minutes." He handed the mic back to Gerry. While leaning in close, he added softly, "I need to see you in your office. Now." Hendley nodded and drew the meeting to a close.

A quarter hour later, Clark entered the basement black-side conference room. Ding sat with his leg in a foam cast with Velcro straps, propped on a chair, his crutches leaning against a wall. The rest of the team waited for Clark around the conference table, swiveling in their chairs and speaking in low tones.

Clark perched on the credenza at the front of the room, one eyebrow lowered, fingering his reading glasses.

"Well," he began, "I guess we have our funding for another year. Thanks to Thad Vandermullen."

Lisanne, Gavin, and Moore laughed out loud. Jack, who should have savored the sarcasm, stared straight ahead.

"In all seriousness," Clark continued. "I asked you folks to come in today for an all-hands meeting of our own. We black-siders only seem to do them when the shit's hit the fan. I thought it was high time we got together for a different reason."

Clark surveyed his team from beneath uneven brows—Midas, with freshly shaved cheeks; Lisanne, her mechanical arm brightened by white plates to match her blouse; Buck, Cary, and Jad in their civilian suits; Moore, leaning back, grinning; Mandy and Gavin sitting solemnly; and, finally, Jack, looking at the wall. The

Polycom speakerphone at the center of the table indicated Chilly's remote presence.

"First, let me deal with the active-duty folks," Clark began. "Cary, Jad, Tom, come on up here. That's an order."

The three active-duty military members moved forward to stand by the black-side boss. As they walked, Ding leafed through his canvas messenger bag, producing a thick envelope that he handed to Clark.

Clark donned his reading glasses. He made a show of tearing the yellow legal-size envelope flap and removing an official memo with a colorful seal in the top margin.

"For conspicuous gallantry in the face of enemy fire, Staff Sergeant Buck, USMC, and First Sergeants Marks and Mustafa, U.S. Army, are each hereby awarded the Bronze Star—with Vs for Valor." Clark flashed the paper at them. "Your citations, gentlemen, are rather short on descriptions, given the classified nature. But who cares? They're each signed by the President of the United States, dated yesterday. That's the important part."

Ding fetched three rectangular cases with the medals and passed them out.

Lisanne raised her phone and took pictures as the proud soldiers accepted the boxes to the team's hooting applause. When they were about to return to their seats, Clark added, "Hang on, First Sergeant Marks, you're out of uniform."

"On your orders, Mr. C.," Marks replied while hitching his suit pants, earning a chuckle from most at the table.

"Yeah, well, let me see your ID card, then."

Marks fished his green active-duty armed forces ID card from his wallet.

Clark inspected it like a traffic cop. "It says here you're a first sergeant."

"I am."

"Not anymore." Ding slid the promotion order across to Clark, who handed it to Cary. "Your promotion order was also signed by the President yesterday. And might I add, Master Sergeant Marks, that he thought it was long overdue."

"Hear hear!" Kendrick Moore shouted as the others drummed the table and whooped in celebration. His face turning pink, Cary grinned sheepishly and returned to his seat next to Jad as the drumming from all the black-siders thundered.

Clark hooked his thumbs in his belt loops, waiting for silence. When it came, he said, "This op was a bitch, folks. Not going to lie to you. We took out a clear and present danger to the United States of America—and that fact isn't lost on our national leadership team. Well, those who know about it, anyway.

"I just had a quick chat with Gerry, upstairs. It's not lost on him that *this* half of his organization makes the other half possible—by protecting the freedom in which it operates."

Twirling his reading glasses in his hand, Clark allowed a grin. "I know you all had your leave time cut short. Probably not a surprise to you that our boss, Gerry, has a few vacation properties around the world. One of them is just thirty miles from here at St. George Island. A half mile of beach, twelve bedrooms, tennis courts, three offshore fishing boats, and a full-time staff of attendants. I'm pleased to tell you that Gerry has generously offered his St. George Chesapeake Bay property to all members of The Campus and their plus-ones for the entire month of July. Go for a day trip, stay for a week, or the whole month. It's up to you. Gav, can you set up an online sign-up sheet so we can work out schedules?"

"On it, Mr. C."

While the Campus operatives murmured their general approval—along with a few jabs at each other about how they were all going soft—Clark turned to Jack and Lisanne. "Jack, you grew up on the Chesapeake out at Peregrine Cliff, across the water from St. George Island. So maybe this is a busman's holiday for you. But there's more. Mrs. Clark and I would like to fire up a barbecue down at our Leesburg farm next week for the whole team. We're going to show you all what real hospitality—and gratitude—looks like. Ain't that right, Ding?"

"Hell yes, Mr. C."

"Even for you, Staff Sergeant Buck. Though your appetite might bankrupt me."

"Ooh-rah," Buck answered with a laugh.

Clark shifted to Jack. "No horse riding down there. I promise."

Jack nodded at the good-natured barbs about his now well-known struggles with Midas's mare in Pakistan. "You should've seen him on a camel," Lisanne added.

When the banter died away—and perhaps to change the subject—Jack said, "This is all very generous of you and Gerry, Mr. C. Thank you. But while we're all here, could we get an update on the Umayyad Caliphate and the network we took down?"

"I was about to get to that," Clark replied. He waited for the room to quiet and cleared his throat. "I caught up with Mrs. Foley last night," he said seriously. "The NCTC, working through the intelligence you folks gathered, have rolled up three dormant UC cells here in the U.S. The NCTC has also figured out that Fahim Bajwa wasn't just a co-conspirator. He was Rafa's half brother, a French mother in common. Our good friend ISI Brigadier General Khan had been running Fahim as an agent for years. The plan was to install him at the top of the construction company to help with future terror and espionage operations, to be carried out by Rafa."

"And Hanford?" Mandy asked.

"That was the crown jewel of their operation. If they'd had another week, it would have happened. The FBI's crime scene techs reported that the power-maintenance trucks were loaded to the gills with construction explosives. The DOE and FBI national security team think the martyrs were planning to blow a trench of plutonium waste roughly timed to coincide with the attack on the train."

"And the Chinese?" Lisanne asked.

Clark grinned. "I saved the best for last. Ding, get that other envelope out for me, will you?"

"Bit more than an envelope," Ding said. He handed over a stiff red folder neatly wrapped in a yellow ribbon.

Clark removed the ribbon, opened the folder, and read, "'For the brave American service men and women who protected our official delegation in Pakistan, the People's Republic of China offers its eternal gratitude. Sincerely, Huang Xihuan, ambassador to the United States of America.'" Clark looked over his reading glasses with a sly smile. "The Chinese ambassador sent it over back-channel to Mrs. Foley's office."

"That's a new one," Master Chief Moore said.

Clark replaced the ribbon. "Ties a bow on the whole thing, I believe. And mind you, this letter will be on file at the DNI's office—in case we ever need a return favor."

GAVIN PLODDED UP THE STAIRWELL TO HENDLEY'S MAIN FLOOR, EXPECTING TO GET back behind his desk and plow through hours of paperwork that the new banker, Vandermullen, had created for him. Clark had said his piece, they'd all been recognized, and now all Gavin wanted was to finish his job and hustle home to his apartment to watch a few episodes of *Survivor*. Princess, his cat, had missed him.

"Hey!" a voice echoed up the stairs.

Gavin waited while Mandy climbed rapidly up to him. "Who are you going to bring for a plus-one out to Gerry's house?"

Her blue eyes glittering, her complexion tanned by the eastern Washington sunshine—Gavin thought she'd never looked prettier.

"I don't know," he said, looking away. "Maybe Sheriff Whitcomb. He said he might come to D.C. He and I could make a day of it. He said he likes to fish."

"Well, yeah. But the sheriff said he'd come to D.C. with his wife," Mandy countered. "Besides, Dan Murray asked the sheriff to deliver a lecture at the Academy on the best way for the FBI and local law enforcement to interact. He's going to be busy."

"True," Gavin replied, turning to resume his climb. "Guess I'll think about it."

"Hold on." She held his elbow. "Think about this. Or rather, her."

Mandy thrust her phone in front of Gavin. He found himself looking at an attractive brunette's Facebook page. "Who's Julia?" he asked.

"My Quantico roommate when I was at the Academy. She's a government hacker at the CIA now. Works in a group that defends against exploits. I told her all about you. She can't wait to meet you."

Gavin snatched the phone and thumbed through three pictures. "*This* woman wants to go out with me?"

"I told her how you cracked our case—and saved my life." The former FBI special agent retrieved her phone. "Anyway, I thought we could go on a double date—dinner and dancing or something. If it works, you could invite her out to Gerry's place for a day trip."

"A double? I thought you broke up with your DEA guy."

"I did."

"So . . . who are you bringing?"

Her cheeks reddened. She smiled bashfully.

"Who?" Gavin persisted. He'd never seen Special Agent Mandy Cobb blush.

"Well . . . while I was recovering at the hospital at Fairchild, I sort of started seeing that head of security guy from the DOE. You know, Captain T-Bolt."

———

JACK AND LISANNE WERE ON THE MAIN FLOOR IN A CORNER CONFERENCE ROOM BE-
cause Jack's office had a glass wall—and he needed to vent.

"Thad. Vandermullen," he said, as though each syllable bruised
his mouth. "Gerry just can't get enough of Thad. Vandermullen."

"Come on, Jack," Lisanne protested. "Give the guy a break. He
got a deal done. Everyone's happy. You've completed a ton of deals
here. How many at this point?"

"I don't know."

"Yes, you do. You did the Vietnam GeoTech minerals deal. You
got the Guyana oil shipping thing done. So this guy, Vanderwhat-
ever, has one deal under his belt. So what? We just got access to a
multimillion-dollar beachfront home for a month."

"I swear, Lis. I'm never taking a vacation again. If I'd been
around, I'd have gotten that LodeStar deal." Too late, Jack realized, he'd walked into quicksand. "I mean, it was good to have
time off so we could take care of your hand," he recovered rapidly.

"Sure. Glad you think so."

"And seeing Srini and Sanjay was great. How are they?"

"Finally on a real honeymoon. As I think you already know,
since Sanjay intends to follow up with you on that investment in
their fiber operation."

Jack nodded ponderously, staying mute.

"You need to stop thinking about this," she said. "It's not good
for you."

"Lis, I'm just saying. I don't like taking time off. Whenever I'm
on a business deal, I miss out on a black-side thing. If I'm on an op,
I miss out on a white-side thing. This time, I almost missed out on
both. If Midas hadn't gotten hit and if Rustam hadn't contacted
me over the Indian SATCOM, then . . . what? Count me out of a
week of downtime at Gerry's villa."

Lisanne quietly stood. "You're saying you're never going to take vacation again?"

"I mean. Not literally. I'm just saying. I think they're a mistake. Sometimes."

"A mistake. What about for *our* wedding and honeymoon, Jack? Would a vacation for that be a mistake?"

"Of course not."

"So when are we going to do that, Jack? What's *our* date?"

With his fiancée standing over him, hands on her hips, Jack hesitated. He had thought about many different dates for their wedding. In truth, being the President's son, it was a matter of avoidance because he hated the fuss of it all. If there was one thing he'd learned at the wedding of Srini and Sanjay in India, it was that he was *right* to hate it all. He didn't enjoy the spectacle—and he'd been sincere when he said he never wanted to miss out on white- or black-side action for personal reasons again.

Three answers occurred to him that he thought might work.

But none of them came out of his mouth fast enough.

"Well," Lisanne said. "Remember how I didn't wear my ring because it was hard to take on and off by myself?" She extended her natural hand, displaying the diamond solitaire that had once belonged to Jack's maternal grandmother.

"Yes," he replied weakly.

"Check this out." Lisanne raised her prosthetic hand and deftly slid the ring free of her finger and placed it on the table.

"Lis . . ." Jack stammered, paling. "What are you . . ."

She leaned close to him and gently held his cheeks between her two hands. She tilted his face, gazed directly into his eyes, and kissed him on the lips.

"You're a good man, Jack Ryan," she said, pulling away. "But you're not the marrying type."

She left the ring on the table and closed the door behind her.

READ THE PREVIOUS, PULSE-RACING JACK RYAN, JR. THRILLER

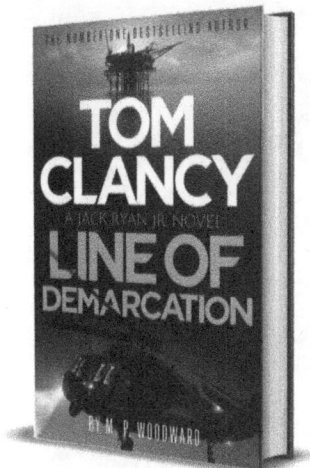

**The discovery of an oil field off the coast of Guyana plunges
Jack Ryan, Jr. into a cauldron of lies in the latest entry in
this internationally bestselling series.**

It starts with the destruction of a US Coast Guard cutter and the
loss of her entire crew. But the USCG Claiborne was on an innocuous
mission to open a sea lane between an oil field off the coast of Guyana
and the refineries of southern Louisiana. The destruction of the ship,
tragic as it is, won't stop that mission from continuing.

So who would sacrifice twenty-two men and women just to slow down
the plan? That's the question plaguing Jack Ryan Jr. He's in Guyana to
work a deal to get his company, Hendley Associates, in on the ground
floor of this new discovery, but the destruction of the Claiborne and
the kidnapping of the Guyanese Interior Minister make it clear that
there's a malignant force working to destroy Guyana's oil industry.

It's up to Jack to identify the killers before they draw a bead
on him, but how can he do that when the line of demarcation
between friend and foe is constantly shifting?

OUT NOW

JACK RYAN RETURNS

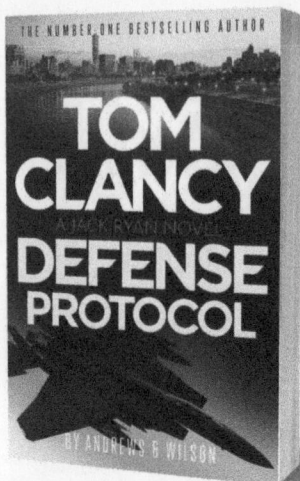

THE NUMBER ONE BESTSELLING AUTHOR

TOM CLANCY

A JACK RYAN NOVEL

DEFENSE PROTOCOL

BY ANDREWS & WILSON

For decades, Taiwan has been a thorn in the side of the Chinese government. Previous governments have tried to conquer the island, but new Chinese President Li Jian Jun is done fooling around. He's devised a secret military operation to take the island. Only one man knows how to stop Li's bloody plan for reunification and that's Minister of Defense Qin Haiyu. Fearing for his life, Qin covertly contacts the CIA in Beijing and signals his desire to defect to the West.

To get Qin out, John Clark creates an international task force reminiscent of Rainbow Six and goes undercover in mainland China. Meanwhile, Lt. Commander Katie Ryan is deployed to the tip of the spear on the destroyer USS Jason Dunham to defend Taiwan. Threatened by an encircling Chinese armada, she's under pressure to find a flaw in the invaders' plan.

President Jack Ryan may have the power of the entire US military at his disposal, but what he really needs are Li's secret plans from Defense Minister Qin so he can stave off a war. Because America's Defense Protocol could lead to a game of mutual destruction that will cost the lives of thousands of young soldiers, sailors, special operators . . . and his daughter.

OUT NOW

HAVE YOU READ THE UNMISSABLE JACK RYAN, JR. THRILLER?

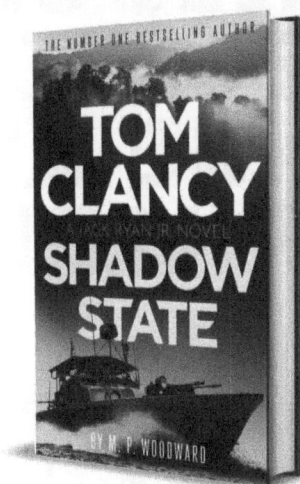

Surviving a helicopter crash in the Vietnamese Highlands is only the start of the challenges facing Jack Ryan, Jr.

The vibrant economy of the new Vietnam is a shiny lure for Western capital. Companies are racing to uncover ideal opportunities. Not wanting to be left behind, Hendley Associates has sent their best analyst, Jack Ryan, Jr., to mine for investment gold. And he may have found some in a rare earth mining company, GeoTech.

But a trip with a Hendley colleague to observe the company's operations takes a treacherous turn when their helicopter is shot down. Some things haven't changed, and Vietnam is still the plaything of powerful neighbours. The Chinese are determined to keep Jack from finding the truth about what exactly is being processed at the isolated factory.

Now Jack is in a race for his life. He's got to stay one step ahead of a pack of killers while supporting his wounded friend. And he'll get no help from the government, because in the jungle, it's the shadow state that rules.

OUT NOW